THE VANISHING WITCH

Karen Maitland travelled and worked in many parts of the United Kingdom before settling for many years in the beautiful medieval city of Lincoln, an inspiration for her writing. She is the author of *The White Room*, *Company of Liars*, *The Owl Killers*, *The Gallows Curse* and *The Falcons of Fire and Ice*. She has recently relocated to a life of rural bliss in Devon.

THE VANISHING WITCH

KAREN MAITLAND

headline
review

The right of Karen Maitland to be identified as the Author of
the Work has been asserted by her in accordance with the
Copyright, Designs and Patents Act 1988.

First published in Great Britain in 2014
by HEADLINE REVIEW
An imprint of HEADLINE PUBLISHING GROUP

1

Cataloguing in Publication Data is available from the British Library

ISBN 978 1 4722 1500 0 (Hardback)
ISBN 978 1 4722 1501 7 (Trade paperback)

Typeset in Garamond by Palimpsest Book Production Ltd, Falkirk, Stirlingshire

Printed and bound in Great Britain by Clays Ltd, St Ives plc

Headline's policy is to use papers that are natural, renewable and recyclable products
and made from wood grown in sustainable forests. The logging and manufacturing processes are
expected to conform to the environmental regulations of the country of origin.

HEADLINE PUBLISHING GROUP
An Hachette UK Company
338 Euston Road
London NW1 3BH

www.headline.co.uk
www.hachette.co.uk

'The children born of thee are sword and fire,
Red ruin, and the breaking up of laws.'

The Idylls of the King, Alfred Lord Tennyson (1809–92)

'So hideous was the noise, a benedicite!
Certes he, Jack Straw and all his meinie,
Ne made never shouts so shrill
When that they would any Fleming kill.'

A reference to the Peasants' Revolt in *The Canterbury Tales*
Geoffrey Chaucer (c.1340–1400)

The scrupulous and the just, the noble, humane, and devoted natures;
the unselfish and the intelligent may begin a movement – but it passes
away from them. They are not the leaders of a revolution. They are
its victims.

Under Western Eyes, Joseph Conrad (1857–1924)

Cast of Characters

Lincoln

Robert of Bassingham – wool merchant and landowner in Lincoln
Jan – Robert's eldest son and steward
Adam – Robert's twelve-year-old son
Edith – Robert's wife
Maud – Edith's cousin
Beata – Edith's maid
Tenney – Robert's manservant

Catlin – a wealthy widow
Leonia – Catlin's thirteen-year-old daughter
Edward – Catlin's adult son
Diot – Catlin's maid
Warrick – Widow Catlin's late husband

Hugo Bayus – elderly physician
Father Remigius – Robert's parish priest
Fulk – overseer at Robert's warehouse
Tom – Robert's rent-collector
Hugh de Garwell – member of the Common Council of Lincoln
    and former Member of the Parliament
Thomas Thimbleby of Poolham – Sheriff of Lincoln
Matthew Johan – Florentine merchant in Lincoln
Master Warner – Adam's schoolmaster
Henry de Sutton – a boy at Adam's school

Sister Ursula – nun at the Infirmary of St Mary Magdalene
Godwin – a seafarer

Greetwell (a village on the outskirts of Lincoln)

Gunter – a river boatman
Nonie – Gunter's wife
Royse – Gunter and Nonie's fourteen-year-old daughter
Hankin – Gunter and Nonie's twelve-year-old son
Col – Gunter and Nonie's four-year-old son
Martin – rival boatman
Alys – Martin's wife
Simon – Martin's son

London

Thomas Farringdon – leader of the Essex men
Giles – rebel from Essex

Proem

Legend tells that seven hundred years before our story
begins . . .

. . . in the days of the Saxons, in the kingdom of Lindsey, there was
Ealdorman who had a beautiful daughter, Æthelind. She was famed
throughout all her tribe not only for her knowledge of herbs and
healing, but for her ability to tame animals. There was no bucking
horse that would not grow calm when she fearlessly laid her hand
upon its flank, or a savage dog that would not roll over like a puppy
when she approached.

One day when she was out in the forest gathering herbs, the men
were hunting a wild boar that had killed several villagers and trampled
their crops. As their hounds trailed after it, they saw to their horror
that it had changed course and was charging straight towards Æthelind.
When she grasped its lethal tusks, it laid its great head meekly in her
lap, and there remained until the huntsmen came to slay it. In
gratitude for her bravery, her people gave her an amulet for her cloak
in the form of a golden boar's head studded with red garnets.

Æthelind's reputation spread far and wide and many noble Saxons
came to ask for her hand in marriage. Her father finally agreed to
give his daughter to the son of the king himself, a match that would
bring great honour to his hall, peace and prosperity to the tribe.

But the day before the wedding, Æthelind fell asleep in a grove of
oak trees and a snake crawled into her mouth, slid down her throat
and coiled itself inside her. When she returned to her father's mead
hall, her belly was swollen as if she was great with child. The king's
son, who was being entertained in the hall, was seized with rage that
his intended bride should have shamed him by taking a lesser man
to her bed.

Before all the company he drew his sword and struck off her
head, but as her body fell to the ground, the snake slithered out
from between her legs, like a newborn babe, and transformed into

1

a beautiful human child, who cursed the prince. At once, the ground that was stained with Æthelind's blood fell away and the prince plunged through the dark earth into a pit of vipers. As the earth closed over him the serpents stung him to death, then instantly revived him that he might be tormented to death again. And thus he will suffer night and day throughout the ages until the great wolf Fenris breaks the chain that binds it, heralding the end of the world.

Meanwhile, Æthelind's kin sorrowfully gathered up her head and body and burned them on a great funeral pyre. They placed her ashes in an urn with the golden boar's head they had given her. The urn was inscribed with the ouroboros, the snake that devours its tail, a symbol of the eternal cycle of death and rebirth. That night, when the moon rose, they carried the urn in a torchlight procession to the top of a cliff, close to the walls of a ruined city the Romans had called Lindum. There they laid it in a cave with the burial urns of her elders.

And they say that when lightning flashes from the sky and thunder roars, Æthelind rides out over the cliff, her hair streaming in the wind, leading the wild hunt. But woe betide any man who witnesses that fearful sight, for she will hunt him down until he can run no more and his body lies broken at her feet.

Prologue

A killing ointment made of arsenic, vitriol, baby's fat, bat's blood and hemlock may be spread on the latches, gates and doorposts of houses in the dark of night. Thus can death run swiftly through a town.

River Witham, Lincolnshire

'Help me! I beg you, help me!'

The cry was muffled in the dense, freezing mist that swirled over the black river. As his punt edged upstream, Gunter caught the distant wail and dug his pole into the river bottom, trying to hold his boat steady against the swift current. The shout seemed to have come from the bank somewhere ahead, but Gunter could barely see the flame of his lantern in the bow, much less who might be calling.

The cry came again. 'In your mercy, for the sake of Jesus Christ, help me!'

The mist distorted the sound so Gunter couldn't be sure if it was coming from right or left. He struggled to hold the punt in the centre of the river and cursed himself. He should have hauled up somewhere for the night long before this, but it had taken four days to move the cargo downriver to Boston and return this far. He was desperate to reach home and reassure himself that his wife and children were safe.

Yesterday he'd seen the body of a boatman fished out of the river. The poor bastard had been beaten bloody, robbed and stabbed. Whoever had murdered him had not even left him the dignity of his breeches. And he wasn't the first boatman in past weeks to be found floating face down with stab wounds in his back.

'Is anyone there?' the man called again, uncertainly this time, as if he feared he might be speaking to a ghost or water sprite.

Such a thought had also crossed Gunter's mind. Two children had drowned not far from here and it was said their ghosts prowled the bank luring others to their deaths in the icy river.

'What are you?' Gunter yelled back. 'Name yourself.'

'A humble Friar of the Sack, a Brother of Penitence.' The voice was deep and rasping, as if it had rusted over the years from lack of use. 'The mist . . . I stumbled into the bog and almost drowned in the mud. I'm afraid to move, in case I sink into the mire or fall into the river.'

Now Gunter could make out dark shapes through the billows of mist, but the glimpses were so fleeting he couldn't tell if they were men or trees. Every instinct told him to ignore the stranger and push on up the river. This was exactly the kind of trick the river-rats used to lure craft to the bank so that they could rob the boatmen. The man they'd found in the water had been a strapping lad, with two sound legs. Gunter had only one. His left leg had been severed at the knee and replaced by a wooden stump with a foot in the form of an upturned mushroom, not unlike the end of one of his own punt poles. Although he could walk as fast as any man, if it came to a fight, he could easily be knocked off balance.

But the stranger on the bank would not give up. 'I beg you, in God's mercy, help me. I'm wet and starving. I fear dawn will see me a frozen corpse if I stay out here all night.'

The rasping tone of the man's voice made it sound more like a threat than a plea, but Gunter had been cold and hungry often enough in his life to know the misery those twin demons could inflict and the night was turning bitter. There'd be a hard frost come morning. He knew he'd never forgive himself if he left a man out here to die.

'Call again, and keep calling till I can see you,' he instructed.

He listened to the voice and propelled his punt towards the left bank, eventually drawing close enough to make out the shape of a hooded figure in a long robe standing close by the water's edge. Gunter tightened his hold on the quant: with its metal foot, the long pole could be turned into a useful weapon if the man tried to seize the boat.

The friar's breath hung white in the chill air, mingling with the icy vapour of the river. As soon as the prow of the punt came close, he bent as if he meant to grab it. But Gunter was ready for that. He whisked the quant over to the other side of the punt and pushed away from the bank, calculating that the man would not risk jumping in that robe.

'By the blood of Christ, I swear I mean you no harm.' But the man's voice sounded even more menacing now that Gunter was close. The friar stretched out his right arm into the pool of light cast by the lantern. The folds of his sleeve hung down, thick and heavy with mud. Slowly, with the other hand, he peeled back the sodden sleeve to reveal an arm that ended at the wrist. 'I am hardly a threat to any man.'

Gunter felt an instant flush of shame. He resented any man's pity for his own missing limb and was offering none to the friar, but he despised himself for his distrust and cowardice. It couldn't have been easy for the friar to pull himself free of the mire that had swallowed many an unwary traveller.

Gunter had always believed that priests and friars were weaklings who'd chosen the Church to avoid blistering their hands in honest toil and sweat. But this man was no minnow and he was plainly determined not to meet his Creator yet, for all that he was in Holy Orders.

Gunter brought the punt close to the bank, and held it steady in the current for the friar to climb in and settle himself on one of the cross planks. His coarse, shapeless robe clung wetly to his body, plastered with mud and slime. He sat shivering, his hood pulled so low over his head that Gunter could see nothing of his face.

'I'll take you as far as High Bridge in Lincoln,' Gunter said. 'There are several priories just outside the city, south of the river. You'll find a bed and a warm meal in one, especially with you being in Holy Orders.'

'It's close then, the city?' the friar rasped. 'I've been walking for days to reach it.'

'If it weren't for this fret, you'd be able to see the torches blazing on the city walls and even the candles in the windows of the cathedral.'

Gunter pushed the punt steadily upstream, trying to peer through the mist at the water in front. He knew every twist and turn of the river as well as he knew the face of his own beloved wife. He didn't expect other craft to be abroad at this late hour, but there was always the danger of branches or barrels being swept downstream and crashing into his craft.

'So what brings you to Lincoln?' he asked, without taking his gaze from the water. 'You'll not find any of your order here. I heard tell there was once a house belonging to Friars of the Sack in Lincoln, but that was before the Great Pestilence. House is still there, but none of your brothers has lived in it for years.'

'It is not my brethren I seek,' the friar said.

They were passing between the miserable hovels that lined the banks on the far outskirts of the city and the mist was less dense. Gunter was anxious to drop off his passenger as soon as he could: he was impatient to get home, but there was something in the man's voice that unnerved him. There was a bitter edge to it that made everything he said sound like a challenge, however innocuous the words. Still, that was friars for you, whatever order they came from. When they weren't shrieking about the torments of Hell, they were demanding alms and threatening you with eternal damnation if you didn't pay up.

'So,' Gunter said, 'why have you come? I warn you, Lincoln's going through hard times. You'll not find many with money to spare for beggars, even holy ones. You'd have done better to make for Boston. That's where all the money's gone since we lost the wool staple to it.'

The friar gave a low, mirthless laugh. 'Do you think I walked all these miles for a handful of pennies? Do you see this?'

Using his teeth and left hand, he unlaced the neck of his robe and pulled it down. Then he lifted the lantern from the prow of the punt, letting the light from the candle shine full upon his chest. What Gunter saw caused him to jerk so violently that he missed his stroke and almost fell into the river. He could only stare in horror, until the man dragged his robe into place again.

'You ask what I seek, my friend,' the friar growled. 'I seek justice. I seek retribution. I seek vengeance.'

September 1380

September pray blow soft, till fruit be in the loft.

Chapter 1

To guard against witches, draw the guts and organs from a dove while it still lives and hang them over the door of your house. Then neither witch nor spell can enter.

Lincoln

While I lived I was never one of those who could see ghosts. I thought those who claimed they did were either moon-touched or liars. But when you're dead, my darlings, you find yourself amazed at what you didn't see when you were alive. I exist now in a strange half-light. I see the trees and cottages, byres and windmills, but not as they once were to me. They're pale, with only hints of colour, like unripe fruit. They're new to this world. But I see other cottages too, those that had crumbled to dust long before I was born. They're still there, crowded into the villages, snuggled tight between the hills, old and ripe, rich with hues of yellow and brown, red clay and white limewash. They're brighter, but less solid than the new ones, like reflections in the still waters of a lake, seeming so vibrant, yet the first breeze will riffle them into nothing.

And so it is with people. The living are there, not yet ripe enough to fall from the bough of life into death. But they are not the only ones who pass along the streets and alleys or roam the forests and moors. There are others, like me, who have left life, but cannot enter death. Some stay where they lived, repeating a walk or a task, believing that if only they could complete it they might depart. They never will. Others wander the highways looking for a cave, a track or a door that will lead from this world to the one beyond, full of such wonders as they have only dreamed of.

Many, the saddest of all, try to rejoin the living. Sweethearts run in vain after their lovers, begging them to turn and look at them. Children scrabble nightly at the doors of cottages, crying for a mother, any mother, to take them in and love them. Babies lurk down wells or lie

9

under sods, waiting their chance to creep inside a living woman's womb and be born again as her child.

And me? I cannot depart, not yet. I was wrenched out of life before my time, hurled into death without warning, so I must tarry until I have seen my tale to its proper conclusion for there is someone I watch and someone I watch over. I will not leave them until I've brought their stories to an end.

Robert of Bassingham gazed at the eleven other members of the Common Council, slouching in their chairs, and sighed. It had been a long afternoon. The old guildhall chamber was built across the main thoroughfare of Lincoln city, and the bellows of pedlars, the rumble of carts and ox wagons, the chatter of people clacking over the stones in wooden pattens meant that the small windows of the chamber had to be kept shut, if the aged members were to hear the man next to them.

As a consequence, the air was stale with the sour breath of old men and the lingering odour of the mutton olives, goat chops and pork meatballs on which the councillors had been grazing. It being a warm day, they'd been compelled to wash down these morsels with flagons of costly hippocras, a spiced wine, which had already worked its soporific magic on several. Three of the sleepers had carefully positioned a hand over their eyes so that they could pretend to be concentrating, while a fourth was lolling with his mouth open, snoring and farting almost as loudly as the hound at his feet.

Robert was inordinately fond of hippocras but had deliberately refrained from imbibing, knowing he, too, would doze off. He was painfully conscious of the heavy responsibilities he had now assumed as the newly elected master of the Guild of Merchants, the most powerful guild in Lincolnshire and still the wealthiest, even though it was not as prosperous as once it had been.

Robert was a cloth merchant of the city of Lincoln, well respected – at least, by those who measure a man's worth by the size of his purse and influence. He made a good living selling wool and the red and green cloth for which Lincoln was justly famed. Having only recently been appointed to serve on the Common Council he was one of its younger members, still in his early fifties.

He had acquired his wealth painstakingly over the years, for though he was a numbskull in matters of love, he was shrewd in business. He'd bought a stretch of the land on the bank of the river Witham from a widow after her husband's death, having persuaded her it was worth little, which you could argue was the truth: the ground was too marshy even for sheep to thrive on it. But a Lincoln merchant must have boats to send his goods to the great port at Boston and boatmen must have somewhere to live close to the river: Robert had built a few cottages on the wasteland and earned a good sum renting them to those who carried his cargoes. If 'earn' is the right word for money that a man demands from others but never collects in person. And, believe me, there were many men in England that year who had cause to resent all such landlords . . .

Robert banged his pewter beaker of small ale on the long table. The slumbering members jerked upright, glowering at him. Had not the newcomer the common courtesy to let a man sleep in peace?

'I say again,' Robert announced, 'we must petition King Richard to give us leave to raise an additional tax in Lincoln to rebuild the guildhall.' He gestured to the ominous cracks in the stone wall, which were almost wide enough to insert a finger in. 'If another wagon should crash into the pillar below, it will bring us all tumbling down into the street.'

'But the townspeople will never stand for it,' Hugh de Garwell protested. 'Thanks to John of Gaunt whispering in the young King's ear, the commonality have already been bled dry to raise money for these pointless wars in France and Scotland.'

Several council members glanced uneasily at one another. It was hard to determine how far you could criticise the boy-king in public without being accused of treason, and while King Richard might yet forgive much, his uncle, John of Gaunt, had spies everywhere and was known to deal ruthlessly with any man who so much as muttered a complaint in his sleep. And since Gaunt was constable of Lincoln Castle, no one in that chamber could be certain that one of his fellow council members was not in that devil's pay.

Robert regarded Hugh sourly. They were, for the most part, good friends, but it irritated him that Hugh seemed convinced a city could be run on pennies and pig-swill. He heaved himself from the chair and paced to the small window, trying to ease the cramp in his legs, as he stared down at the crowds milling below.

'See there! Three carts trying to barge through the arch at the same time and none of them willing to give way to another. The people may not want to pay, but if this building collapses on top of them, dozens will be crushed in the rubble. Then they'll be demanding to know why we didn't do something sooner.'

'So tax the guilds to pay for it, not the poor alewives and labourers,' Hugh said. 'The Guild of Merchants alone is wealthy enough to build a dozen new halls, if they were to sell some of the gold and silver they have locked away. They've grown as fat as maggots on the carcass of this city, so they . . .'

But Robert wasn't listening. His attention had been caught by a woman standing quite still among the bustle of the crowd, staring up at the window. She was clad in a dark blue gown, over which she wore a sleeveless surcoat of scarlet, embroidered with silver threads. Even at that distance, Robert could tell from the way the cloth hung, accentuating her slender figure, and from the vivid, even quality of the dye that it was of the best. His thumb and fingers twitched as if they itched to feel the weave.

Ever the merchant, Robert always took more notice of the cloth a woman wore than her face and he probably wouldn't have taken another glance at her, except that she was gazing up at him intently. He stared back. He couldn't distinguish her features clearly enough to determine her age, though the gleaming black hair beneath her silver fret suggested youth.

She seemed to make up her mind about something and, with a nod towards him, she threaded her way through the jostling pedlars to the door that led up to the council chamber and disappeared.

A merchant who prides himself on his calm and calculated reasoning is not a man to act on impulse but, to his surprise, Robert found himself striding rapidly to the door and out onto the staircase, leaving Hugh staring after him open-mouthed.

Robert, descending the steep spiral stairs with care, fully expected to encounter the woman on her way up, but he reached the bottom without passing anyone and found only the watchman squatting in the doorway, picking his teeth with the tip of his knife blade. On sensing Robert behind him, he hauled himself upwards against the wall, and made a clumsy half-bow.

Robert eyed him with disgust. His tunic was open and covered with the stains of ancient meals and his hairy belly was so large that it hung over his breeches. Robert was portly, but a wealthy man was expected to look sleek and well-fed. A watchman, on the other hand, was supposed to be as fit as a battle-hardened soldier, ready to defend his betters against danger. This blubber-arse looked as if he'd collapse if he was obliged even to lift his pike, never mind fight with it.

'Did a woman come to the door a few moments ago?' Robert demanded.

'A woman, you say?' The watchman scratched his navel, gazing absently at the passing crowd. 'Aye, there was a woman. Matter of fact, she were asking for you, Master Robert. But I told her, I says, Master Robert's an important man. He's in council, and he'll not thank you for disturbing him and the other gentlemen.'

Robert frowned. It was not unheard of for women to buy or sell in the cloth trade, especially if their husbands were absent, but why should she come to the guildhall, rather than his place of business? Robert's son, Jan, who was also his steward, would still be hard at work in the warehouse at this hour, which was why Robert could afford to waste an afternoon on the city's affairs.

'Did this woman leave a message, her name? Where am I to find her?'

He had asked the man three questions at once, which was like throwing three sticks for a dog: it wouldn't know which to chase first. The watchman pondered for an age, then admitted he couldn't answer any.

'You should have asked her business,' Robert snapped.

The watchman gave Robert a resentful look. 'They pay me to keep people out as shouldn't be in there, not to ask their business, which is their own affair.'

Frustrated, Robert lumbered back up the stairs, steeling himself to re-enter the stuffy chamber.

The debate had not moved on by a jot or tittle since he'd left. He wondered, not for the first time, whether the Common Council ever managed to reach agreement about anything. He pictured them still sitting round that table in a hundred years, their beards grown to the floor, cobwebs hanging from their ears, wagging their gnarled fingers and repeating for the thousandth time what someone else had said not five minutes before.

Robert had never been accustomed to consulting others. Once he had made up his mind to do something, he began it at once. He'd no more patience for these endless discussions than he would have to stitch a tapestry. Perhaps that was why he found his thoughts constantly wandering to the still figure who'd stared up at him so intently. He couldn't drive her image from his head.

13

Chapter 2

If you fear that you are in the presence of a witch, clench both your hands into fists with the thumbs tucked under your fingers. Then she cannot enchant your mind.

Mistress Catlin

I did not intend to fall in love. In truth, I had not set eyes on Master Robert before that hour when I stood outside the guildhall. I didn't know then that he was the man looking down from the window. But on that sultry September afternoon, Robert of Bassingham and I were about to find ourselves both pieces and players in a game of romance, both slayer and sacrifice. But of all the players who were to be drawn with us into that dangerous game, none could have guessed who would finally call checkmate.

Although I did not know Master Robert, I knew well his reputation and had come to the guildhall that day for the sole purpose of speaking with him. My children and I were newly arrived in Lincoln and I had no kin in the city to whom I could turn. Many men, and women too, delight in seeking out the vulnerable to gain their trust, only to rob them of all they have. I was determined not to become their prey.

But if I had believed the gossip of my neighbours, as they waited for the butcher to slice a piece of cow's tongue or the fishmonger to knock a live carp on the head, I would have concluded there was not a single man of sound character left within the city walls. A woman called Maud, who lived in the same street as I, was the worst of the tale-bearers, with a tongue as sharp and malicious as the devil's pitchfork. Before long I knew which men drank, who beat their wives and who had a string of whores. I learned the name of every feckless husband who'd lost his money in wagers on the fighting cocks, and all the miserly fathers who made their children wear splintered barrel-staves on their feet to save on shoe-leather.

14

But I knew how to sift the words of others and so it was that, in spite of what the witch, Maud, had said about him and his little weaknesses, or perhaps *because* of what she had said, I came to believe that of all the men in Lincoln the one I should seek out was Robert of Bassingham.

I thought carefully about how I should approach him. A merchant like Master Robert would be pestered by all manner of people begging for his precious time and I feared I might be brushed aside. But if you want to capture the attention of a thief you flash a gold coin, if a scholar a rare book, so I had taken care to dress in a gown that would gladden the heart of any cloth merchant.

I'd meant to wait patiently outside until the meeting of the Common Council ended and ask someone to conduct me to him, so we might speak in the privacy of the empty chamber, but as I waited a man came to the window and stared down at me so fixedly that I was ashamed to be seen loitering and approached the watchman to ask if Robert was within. I was dismissed as though I were a stew-house whore.

A weaker woman might have given up. Not I. I'd already discovered that Robert of Bassingham had a warehouse on the Braytheforde harbour so I made my way there, hoping he might return.

The banks of the Braytheforde were crowded with warehouses and taverns, chandlers and boatyards. The screams of the gulls mingled with the shouts of the workers, the hammering and sawing of the boat builders. Men strode past, carrying long planks on their shoulders, and women hurried by, with panniers of fish on their backs. Everyone was scurrying about, so it was hard to find anyone who would stop long enough to point out Robert's warehouse. Finally a boatman gestured towards the largest and busiest building on the quayside, a great wooden structure facing the jetty where little boats were moored.

A man with red-gold hair was standing with his back to me in the doorway, directing the men who were offloading bales from a nearby boat and hefting them into the warehouse. He turned as I approached and his mouth stretched into an easy smile, as if he was always ready to call any stranger 'friend'. I realised he was far too young to be the man I sought.

'Forgive me for disturbing your work,' I said. 'I'm looking for Master Robert of Bassingham. Is he within?'

'My father? No, mistress. He's one of the Common Council and they're sitting this afternoon, but he'll probably call here before returning home. He usually does, to be sure I haven't burned the place down or struck some ruinous deal.' The young man grimaced. 'I may be his son and his steward, but he watches me closely.'

I couldn't help smiling. 'I'm sure he trusts you, but a good merchant keeps his eye on every detail. No doubt that was how he became successful.'

The young man laughed, showing fine white teeth. 'You know my father well, mistress. That is exactly what he says.'

'I know him not at all, but that was what my own late husband used to tell me.' I hesitated. 'Do you think your father would spare me a few words on his return? I seek his advice in matter of some investments. I'm told there is none better, unless, of course, you can assist me.' I touched his sleeve. 'I'm sure you must know as much as your father.'

He flushed with pleasure. I had no intention of taking counsel from such a callow youth, but men are always flattered to be trusted. Compliment them on their handsome appearance – as I might have done now without a word of a lie – and they grow suspicious. Ask a man for his advice and he purrs and preens like a tom-cat.

Robert's son gave a modest shrug. 'I've worked with him since I was a boy and have run his business for some time now. And I do know—'

'And what is it you know, Jan?' a voice boomed.

Jan's chin jerked up and a flicker of annoyance crossed his face.

I turned to look at the man standing behind me and saw the expression of surprise on his face that was undoubtedly on my own, for he was the man who had stared down at me from the guildhall window.

There was no mistaking that he was Jan's father. Master Robert's hair, though greying, showed the same red-gold threads as his son's. Both were tall and broad-shouldered, but while Jan had the trimness of youth, his father's waist had thickened. Maturity enhances the features of some men's faces, though, and it had done so for Master Robert. He carried himself with the confidence of a man who knows he has achieved more than most in his life.

He inspected me as if I were a bale of cloth or a fleece to be graded and priced. 'Mistress, I believe you came earlier to the Common Council and were refused admission.'

16

'Please forgive me,' I said, 'I'd no wish to interrupt. I merely hoped to speak to you once your discussions were ended, but your loyal watchman—'

'An idle cod-wit and an oaf. He'll not be watchman by tomorrow. That I can promise you.'

Several of the men carrying loads quickened their pace as if they feared the same fate.

I clutched at his arm. 'I would not have any man lose his post because of me. It's his duty to see the council is not interrupted. You've many important matters to discuss.'

Robert gazed down at my hand. I withdrew it at once, but not before I saw a movement of his own hand towards mine as if he had meant to touch it.

Jan must have noticed it, too, and frowned. 'Mistress . . . I don't believe I know your name.'

'Catlin. Widow Catlin.'

Jan nodded. 'You mentioned your late husband.' He turned back to his father. 'Widow Catlin came seeking advice on investments. I was telling her I can certainly advise—'

'Mistress Catlin was seeking me,' Robert said firmly. 'Where investments are concerned, it's the mature, sober mind that's needed, not the hot head of youth. You've a lot to learn yet, my boy, before you may advise others, except on where to buy the best ale or find the prettiest girls. That's what you're expert in, lad.' He gave his son a playful thump on the back and winked at me.

Jan clearly didn't appreciate the joke and seemed on the verge of snapping at his father, when his gaze was arrested by something behind me. 'Fulk!' he called.

A short, stocky man scuttled across, his legs as bowed as if they were straddling a barrel. He pulled his cap from his greasy hair and bobbed obsequiously several times to me and to Robert.

Jan clapped a hand on his shoulder and turned him to face the side of the warehouse. A man in a long robe was waiting, motionless, in the shadows. 'How long has that friar been standing there? We don't want him preaching and distracting the men, or begging alms from them. Tell him to try his luck with the rest of the beggars in the markets.'

'He's not been begging, Master Jan, leastways not since I noticed him. I'd have sent him off with a boot up his backside if he had. He's staring at you, Master Robert. I thought you must know him.'

17

'What business would I have with a friar?' Robert said indignantly. 'If you saw him loitering here, why didn't you send him packing straight away? He might be a spy for one of the robber gangs on the river, watching for likely cargoes to steal. God's blood, must I do your job, man, as well as my own? Here, you!' he shouted, taking a pace towards the friar.

Then he stopped, confused: the place where the friar had been standing was empty, leaving only the long, dark shadows cast by the sinking sun. We all scanned the bustling crowd, but there was no sign of the man anywhere.

Robert drew a deep breath. 'Too late. We'll not get hold of him now. If either of you see him here again, tell the men to seize him and ask him what he's doing. Shake it out of him, if you must. And the watch is to be doubled on the warehouse tonight. See to it, Jan, a man within and two to patrol outside.'

Jan nodded, but I could see he was irritated. Clearly, he had not exaggerated when he said his father didn't trust him.

Robert, seeming oblivious to his son's scowls, looked down at me, his expression softening. 'Now, Mistress Catlin, these matters you wish to discuss with me. Shall we go somewhere we can speak in private?'

'It's growing late, Father,' Jan protested. 'I can help Widow Catlin. Mother's expecting you early tonight. Sheriff Thomas is coming to dine.'

'I'm not in my dotage yet, Jan!' Robert snapped. 'Instead of telling me things I know perfectly well, you'd be better occupied making sure that thieves don't empty the warehouse while you stand around picking your nose.'

So saying, he offered me his arm and led me past the warehouse, but as I glanced round, I was certain I saw someone moving in the shadows and had the uneasy feeling that Master Robert was still being watched.

18

Chapter 3

A child's fingernails should never be cut in the first year. The mother must bite them off or he'll become a thief. But when they are first cut at a year old, they must be buried under an ash tree so that witches can't take them and cause the child harm.

Lincoln

Mavet, my ferret, is not in the best of moods. A dog that was stabbed to death defending his mistress's honour has taken to chasing rabbits in the warren where Mavet has his sport. The rabbits are alive, of course – when did you ever hear of a ghost rabbit? – but all the more fun for that, as far as a dead ferret is concerned. If you've ever seen a rabbit shoot out of a burrow when a living ferret is put down it, you should see the panic that ensues when a ghost one chases them: he can be behind them at one moment, then pop up in front of them at the next.

The ghost of the dog seems to regard the warren as its territory and refuses to be intimidated by Mavet's snarls. But at least the wretched hound keeps the villagers awake by howling all night, and terrifies travellers by springing right through them, which affords me some amusement, even if it annoys Mavet.

But give me the choice between a ferret in a bad mood and a woman in an ill humour and I would choose the ferret every time. A ferret's bite is nothing to that of a woman when the supper's been spoiled, as Master Robert of Bassingham was about to discover.

He had talked with Mistress Catlin far longer than even he intended. She had money, a good deal, and was naturally fearful: first, of leaving gold in the house, but also of investing with unscrupulous, scheming rogues. There is nothing like knowing a woman has complete trust in him to make a man glow with confidence. Robert had intended to suggest a few safe investments and recommend a broker he used, but instead he found himself leaning back in the chair expanding at length about his own business.

19

He had even mentioned the ship, *St Jude*, that would shortly set sail from the Low Countries, with exotic new fabrics and spices. It had been jointly leased by several of Lincoln's leading merchants including the former Member of the King's Parliament, Hugh de Garwell. At some point during their conversation, though he couldn't now remember how or why, he had agreed to invest some of Mistress Catlin's money in the ship, and had arranged to call upon her the following day to collect it.

He had had no idea how long they had been talking until the ringing of the church bell shocked him into realising how many hours had passed. But, though he remembered guiltily that Edith would be waiting for him, he had insisted on seeing Mistress Catlin safely to her door. She had protested that she didn't want to put him to the trouble but he knew he had been right to do so. Several times he'd thought he heard footsteps behind him, keeping pace with their own, and had turned, glimpsing just a flicker of movement, then nothing but the shadows cast by the guttering torches on the walls.

Now that he was walking back alone, he had the same uneasy sense that he was being followed. He was annoyed with himself for feeling nervous as he walked in his familiar city but, nevertheless, he was relieved when he reached his street.

Robert's house, a fine stone building, stood within the stout walls of the city. He was satisfied that it reflected well upon his status and justly proud that he had been able to provide such a comfortable home for his family, a considerable improvement on the timber house in which he had been raised. The fear of fire spreading through the city had been a constant anxiety for his parents.

The hall of Robert's house was nothing like as large as that of a manor. The long table that occupied most of its length would seat no more than a dozen people, five on either side and one at head and foot, but Robert still referred to the modest chamber as the *great* hall, for indeed it was as great as any merchant's in the city.

The finest English oak panels lined the walls, painted a fashionable green with a red trim that reminded visitors of the colours of the cloth that had paid for them. The sumptuary laws that prevented merchants, though they might be wealthier than many noblemen, from wearing sable, velvet, damask or satin had not stopped Robert employing generous quantities of these luxurious fabrics to adorn his chairs, cushions and casement seats.

His pride and joy hung on the wall directly opposite the main entrance, where all those of sufficiently high rank to be admitted through that door could not fail to see it. It was a tapestry woven in Flanders, where the best in Europe were made, depicting huntsmen on the edge of a forest of dark and twisted trees. In the heart of the forest a giant savage boar, with a golden band about its neck, meekly laid its great head in the lap of the Saxon virgin, Æthelind.

Every night, when Robert returned home from his warehouse, he would pause in the doorway, looking up at the tapestry. If he returned late, as now, when the candles were already lit, his pleasure increased as the light caught the gold threads in the boar's collar and in the coronet that adorned the girl's flowing hair.

That evening, Robert was denied this pleasure, for his manservant Tenney had scarcely closed the door behind him when his wife pounced.

'Where have you been, husband? A fine host you are. Thomas has been waiting this past hour.'

'I've had business to attend to, my dear, the new cargo from Boston. I couldn't get away sooner.'

Robert wasn't sure why he hadn't told Edith the truth. There was nothing to be ashamed of in giving financial advice to a widow. It was a respectable and worthy thing to do, yet the lie had sprung from his mouth.

Edith snorted. 'I dare say Thomas also has business to attend to and a great deal more than you, seeing he is sheriff of this city, but he still manages to arrive in time for supper. It will be quite ruined. The beef will be as dry as kindling.'

For the first time in many years Robert looked at his wife and saw that she was no longer a shy, slender little bride of fifteen, but a stout matron in her fifties. Her greying hair hung in looped braids on either side of her face and was dyed a fashionable saffron yellow, which served only to emphasise the sallowness of her skin.

And what had he been thinking, having that gown made for her? It was the latest fashion, of course, but it didn't flatter a woman of her age or girth. The low-cut top revealed a neck and bosom that were puckering with age, and the narrowness of her white surcoat, which hung like a tabard over her scarlet gown, drew attention to the thickened waist and hips that bulged out on either side beneath it. Edith was not given to over-indulgence in food or any other pleasures of the flesh, but having given birth to six boys – and lost all but two – she no longer possessed the proportions of a maiden.

Thomas rose from a chair set next to the blazing hearth, a sheepish grin on his florid face.

'Don't scold him, Edith. As we all know, when Robert is at his ledgers a week may pass and he thinks it an hour. You should be used to that after all these years.' He winked at Robert. 'You should have married me, Edith. I merely send out the men-at-arms to see to my business, then retire to my dinner without another care.'

Robert's irritation mounted. 'Well, you should care, Thomas. Those men-at-arms need sharpening up. The streets are full of vagabonds and beggars and no one moves them on. They should be rounded up, the pack of them, and whipped out of the city at the cart's tail. Word would soon get round that this is not a city for easy pickings.'

Thomas frowned. 'Has there been trouble?'

Robert hesitated. He could hardly call it *trouble*. 'It's nothing . . . Coming home this evening, I thought I was followed by someone who'd been at the warehouse earlier.'

Edith gave a little cry. 'How many times have I begged you to hire one of the linkmen to light your way home? It isn't safe to walk the streets at night without an armed man. But, of course, if you came home at a decent hour . . .'

Robert ignored the last little dagger thrust. 'I'll not waste money hiring men to keep me safe in my own city. I'm already paying a king's ransom in taxes for the watch to patrol the streets.'

'It's money well spent if it keeps you from robbery or worse,' Thomas said. 'Edith's right. You shouldn't be walking abroad alone, especially in clothes that tell every cutpurse and thief in the shire you're a wealthy man. My men can't be everywhere at once. Most of their time is taken up with the taverns and cockpits. I've not the money to put a watchman on every street corner. As one of the Common Council, you should know that better than most.'

'What I know—' Robert began, but was interrupted by a clatter of footsteps on the stairs at the back of the hall and the crash of a door being flung open. A boy raced into the room.

'I've told you a hundred times not to run in the house, Adam,' Robert snapped.

The boy's face fell and he edged nervously towards his mother, who placed a protective arm about him.

Thomas beamed at him. 'Finished your Latin copy, have you, my boy? Nothing like Jan, is he? As I recall even if you'd nailed his backside to a bench, he wouldn't study. Jan takes after you, Robert. The only kind of books you'll tolerate are ledgers. But Adam here,' he ruffled the boy's curly head, 'I hear he's quite the scholar. Edith tells me he's hoping to study at university.'

Edith gazed fondly at her son, who smiled shyly up at her. Robert gave a noncommittal grunt. He was gratified that the boy attended to his lessons – but as long as he could read, write and had mastered figures, what more education did any man need? Unless he was entering the Church, and Robert didn't intend his son to waste his life as a priest, scraping a pittance from tithes and alms. But if Edith didn't stop coddling the boy, it would be all he was fit for.

Adam was Edith's baby. Jan had arrived after two stillborn boys. The two others who came after him had died in infancy and Edith had despaired that she would ever have another child. So when Adam mewled his way into the world, he was to her an Isaac, born to Sarah in old age and destined for great things. Edith had refused to allow any but herself to nurse him, day or night, certain that only constant vigilance would keep him safe.

Robert supposed it was only natural that his wife should cosset the lad. Not that his own mother had ever fussed over him, quite the contrary. He'd been raised on a diet of indifference, thrashing and hard work, and had convinced himself he was glad of it: at least he had been able to stand up for himself when he was sent to work as an apprentice. As soon as Adam turned twelve in a few months, Robert was determined that his son should learn a trade too, however much Edith protested. His own business was naturally entailed to Jan as the eldest and Adam would have to make his own way in the world.

But if the boy didn't toughen up, a miserable time he would have of it. Apprentices and journeymen could spot a weakling the moment he walked through the door and would make him the butt of every cruel jest that young lads can devise. Barely a month went by without some young apprentice hanging himself in his master's workshop to escape the torment. And for all that Robert did not dote on the boy, he would never want to see his son unhappy.

Tenney flung open the door at the back of the hall, which led to the courtyard and the kitchen, and bore in a great dish of beef stew. A rich steam, heavy with vinegar, cinnamon, cloves, mace, ginger, sage and onion, wafted through the room. Beata, the maid, followed with a basket of fresh bread. She gave Robert a reproachful look, as vexed as her mistress by his late arrival, but Robert knew it was more because he'd put Edith in a bad humour than for any fear that the stew would spoil. Beata took far too much pride in her cooking ever to allow that to happen.

The arrival of supper was a welcome diversion and the piquant steam sharpened their already keen appetites. They had barely swallowed a mouthful when the door from the courtyard was flung open and Jan strolled in. Adam scrambled from his chair and, heedless of his father's earlier warning, ran across to him, jigging expectantly from foot to foot. 'Did you get it, Jan? Did you?'

His brother grinned and, with a flourish, produced a small wooden model of a trebuchet, used to hurl stones at castles under siege. He held the toy high in the air, making Adam leap for it. Adam's eyes shone as he whispered his thanks.

Robert's elder son had lodgings near the warehouse on the Braytheforde harbour. It was an arrangement he and his father had come to by mutual consent. It was easier for Jan, as Robert's steward, to keep a close eye on the business, but it also meant that if the lad came home drunk after a night with his friends at the cockpits or with some girl hanging on his arm, Robert, and more importantly Edith, wouldn't know of it – at least, not immediately. Nothing happened in Lincoln that was not round the city by the following day. Even so, Jan usually called in each day to see his mother and reassure her that he was not lying dead in a ditch and had not contracted some fever in the night, which Edith would imagine, if a day passed without her seeing him.

With a friendly nod towards Thomas, he crossed to his mother, planting a kiss on her cheek as she lifted her face to him. She patted his shoulder. 'Even later than your father,' she murmured. 'He works you much too hard.'

'The last of the cargo arrived late from Boston and I wanted to check that the tallies were correct,' Jan said, helping himself to a large measure of wine. 'And don't worry, Father, I doubled the watch on the warehouse.'

Edith's head snapped round. 'But I thought you said you were checking the cargo, Robert.'

Jan glanced sharply at his father. 'He was, but I knew you'd want him home, so I said I'd finish.'

He slid into the chair next to his mother, who patted his hand affectionately. 'You're a good son to your father, Jan.'

'Yes, I rather think I am, aren't I, Father?' Jan said, staring pointedly at Robert.

Robert avoided meeting his son's questioning gaze and concentrated on the stew. He felt irritation mounting again. He had done nothing for which to reproach himself but he was annoyed to be caught out in a lie by Jan. The boy had always looked up to him, and he was proud of the way his son was shaping up to follow in his footsteps. Not that he would tell Jan so, for Robert did not believe in indulging his sons.

'I trust the loads all tallied?' he asked sternly.

Jan hesitated.

Robert lowered a sop of gravy-soaked bread that was halfway to his mouth. 'Out with it, lad.'

'One of the boatmen lost a bale overboard on the way back from Boston. He said he'd been rammed by another punt. It's the third accident of this sort in as many weeks. But I got talking to a man in the inn last night. He'd just returned from Horncastle market. He swore he'd seen a bale of our cloth being hawked by one of the pedlars. The seal had been cut away, but he knew it for our shade of dye and reckoned it had never been near a drop of water.'

Robert's face turned puce. 'One of our own boatmen stealing from us? What have you done about it?'

Thomas looked equally furious. 'Have you sent for the bailiff, Jan, had him arrested? I can assure you, Robert, if this is proved, he'll be dangling by the neck from the castle walls after the next assizes.'

Jan refilled his goblet and drained it before he seemed sufficiently braced to answer. 'It's not just one boatman. These accidents are happening to different men, different boats. We can't arrest them all – we'd have no men left to work the river. Besides, proving that any of them stole the bales rather than lost them will not be easy.' Seeing the fury building on Robert's face, he added quickly, 'I reckon someone's behind it, paying them to do it. That's the man we've got to find. But I will find him, Father, and when I do, I'll hand him trussed and bound to Sheriff Thomas. That I swear.'

Thomas nodded approvingly. 'The lad's right, Robert. They must be selling them on to someone, and once we have him in the castle dungeons, I'll soon make him talk. Show him the gallows and he'll be eager to turn king's approver and name all those involved. We'll winkle them out, Robert, don't you fear. I'll have my informers keep their ears flapping in the taverns and marketplaces. They're bound to hear something sooner or later.'

'It's the talk of *later* that concerns me,' Robert said. 'I can't afford to keep losing goods while your spies loll at alewives' doors, drinking the city's savings in the hope of hearing something. Between these thefts and the King's taxes, money is running out of my coffers like sand through an hour-glass, and with the weavers in Flanders in rebellion, there is precious little going back in to refill them.'

He slammed his goblet onto the table. 'At least this evening has resolved one thing. The rents on my properties must be raised. And this time I'll not let you talk me out of it, Jan. This is your future as well as mine and your mother's. I'll not stand by and see my family ruined.'

'But I've told you before, Father, they're struggling already. I inspect our tenants' cottages each year and I can see things are getting worse for a good many of them.'

'Since the boatmen who are stealing from me are my tenants, they may think themselves well served,' Robert said. 'Thieves deserve no less.'

'But it won't fill your coffers if they can't pay,' Jan protested. 'You can't get water from a river that's run dry.'

'They can pay. When they're stealing the cargoes I'm giving them money to deliver, they're earning twice over. You're too easily gulled, lad – isn't that right, Thomas? They know you're coming and spirit half their stock and belongings away to make themselves seem poor, then fetch it back when you've gone. It's a game they've been playing for years.'

The same mulish expression darkened the faces of father and son. If only they were not so alike, they would lock horns less often. Robert would win, he always did, but Jan was right: it was the cottagers who would suffer.

October

If the October moon appears with the points of her crescent up, the month will be dry, if down, wet.

Chapter 4

A woman was carrying a little boy who was eating an apple.
They met a neighbour on the road, who took a bite from the
apple and returned it to the child. Until that hour, the boy had
been strong and healthy. From that moment he began to waste
away, and shortly after, he died.

Greetwell

Master Robert thinks he has troubles and so he has, for when you own much, you fear much too. And no man who's spent a lifetime building his wealth fleece by fleece, bale by bale relishes the prospect of having it all snatched away before he can pass it to his sons. But such fears are not confined to the wealthy. The poor also dread losing what little they have and some have troubles enough to fill the nine lives of a cat, but without so much as a whisker of a cat's good luck.

Gunter was one such man, who scratched out a living in Lincoln, or rather in a piss-poor village nearby, known as Greetwell, though Gunter, who'd never known better, counted the place home.

The sun hung low in the sky, as he hefted the heavy peats from his punt. He pushed them up onto the riverbank so that his daughter, Royse, and her brother, Hankin, could carry them to the lean-to shelter beside the cottage and stack them ready to burn through the long winter months. As usual, Royse was trying to outdo her brother, and they were piling them under the reed thatch with such haste that Gunter warned them to take more care. 'Get a good steddle laid first, else the whole stack'll tumble down.'

But he might as well have been talking to the wind. Royse, just coming up to fourteen, was a headstrong, wiry little lass. The first signs of womanhood were pushing out the front of her kirtle, but she still behaved more like a boy than a woman, never walking when she could run, never sitting still if she could climb. Hankin, a good year or so younger, was already taller than his sister, shooting up like

29

a sapling and just as skinny. Ever since he'd managed to pull himself to his little feet and toddle after her, he'd been determined to prove himself tougher than her, but she'd never made it easy for him.

Gunter blew on his numbed hands to warm them. It was a raw day, the wind sharp and wet, the ground sodden after all the rain. He'd be glad when the frosts came. The damp ate deep into the bones. Great pools still covered the fields where the river had flooded. It had at last receded, but it would take longer to drain from the land. They'd waded through stinking river water inside the cottage for nigh on a week before it had gone, but they were used to that. It happened most years, and Gunter could read the river like the back of his hand. He knew when to shift kegs and barrels up to the hay loft, so little was lost.

With the last of the peats safe on the bank, he hauled himself out of the punt and picked his way down the muddy track, eager for something warm to fill his belly.

He was a short, stocky man, and the muscles of his arms and legs were thick and corded from years of punting. Despite the cold he wore only a sleeveless tunic of stained brown homespun, which reached to his thighs, and breeches so faded and grimy that it was hard to tell if they'd ever owned a colour.

He walked with a strange gait, heaving his left leg out in an arc until he could place it flat directly beneath him. On the water, his element, he appeared no different from other men, but on land the stranger's gaze was immediately drawn to his leg. He had tried many different shapes of wooden leg over the years, spending the long winter evenings whittling whenever he had a fresh idea and could find a good piece of wood. But finally he had settled on this as being best for balancing on the punt as his body twisted, and for spreading his weight as he limped across the boggy ground around his home.

His cottage huddled close to the riverbank on one of the few firm patches of ground between the river and the Edge, a ridge of cliff that ran behind the fields and marshlands. The main village of Greetwell sat high on the Edge, safe from floods and the midges that swarmed over the bogs and mires below in summer, but a boatman couldn't live up there: he'd lose hours each day traipsing to and from his punt, precious hours when he should be earning. Besides, Gunter had lived by the river all his life and couldn't sleep without the sound of water rushing through his dreams.

He pressed down on the latch and pushed against the door, swollen and warped after the flood. The stench of damp and river mud rolled out. The bunches of dried herbs and onions hanging from the rafters rocked in the sudden draught as he stepped inside. He closed the door hastily behind him as a billow of smoke swirled up from the fire. The single-roomed cottage was a tight squeeze for five people, but Gunter had never known bigger. Two beds occupied the space against the walls on either side, with shelves above to store boxes and clay jars. The rest of the room was pretty much taken up with a table and stools, but they needed little else.

Nonie glanced up briefly as her husband entered and straightway spooned pottage into a wooden bowl from the pot hanging over the fire. She didn't need to be told that her husband was hungry. There were no cargoes to fetch on a Sunday, but that meant work of a different sort, fetching fuel for the winter and fodder for the two goats.

In the fifteen years since they had hand-fasted, Gunter had never once returned home without feeling thankful to find Nonie there. As a child, he'd watched his mother stirring a pot over a fire, turning to smile at him, as Nonie did now. It had never occurred to him that his mother would not always be standing there when he returned from play. Even as the Great Pestilence swept through the land, he had not believed it could reach his cottage, until the day he had come home from gathering kindling to find his mother dead and his father dying. Ever since, it had been Gunter's nightmare that one day he might return to find the fire cold and his family once again ripped from him.

Gunter glanced down at the beaten-earth floor where four-year-old Col, his youngest child, was sitting. The tip of his pink tongue stuck out in concentration as he tried to knot pieces of old cord together.

'What you up to, Bor?'

When the boy didn't answer, he looked at Nonie.

She shook her head in exasperation. 'He's making himself a net, says he going fishing. This is your doing, it is, telling him what you used to catch as a lad. A fish with a gold piece in its belly, indeed.'

Gunter chuckled, holding up his hands. 'It's true, I swear it. Didn't you ever hear tell of St Egwin? He fettered his ankles with an iron chain, threw the key into the river, then walked all the way to Rome to see the pope. The pope ordered a fish for dinner and when he opened it, the key to the saint's fetters was inside.'

31

Nonie snorted. 'Well, you're no saint and neither is your son. I don't want you encouraging him. If he slips and falls into the river he'll be swept away, like those poor children who drowned.' She crossed herself hastily to prevent some passing demon turning her words into a prophecy.

Col glanced up anxiously at his father, but grinned when Gunter winked at him. They knew it was a mother's job to cosset and fret over her sons, and a boy's job to alarm his mother a dozen times a day.

The door groaned again as Royse heaved it open, sending the smoke swirling around the small room. She was not alone. A woman followed her, slipping quickly inside with a fearful glance behind her. Alys was the wife of a rival boatman, Martin, who lived further along the river towards Lincoln. She was no older than Nonie – they'd been childhood friends – but she seemed ancient enough to be Nonie's mother, a rag worn threadbare and grey. That afternoon she looked worse than usual: her cheek was black and her eye purple and swollen.

Anger boiled in Gunter. Martin had hit her again, or that great lump of a son of hers, Simon, who used his fists on her just as his father did. Gunter knew that some men beat their wives, but the thought sickened him, especially when it was a great bull like Martin, against whom most men would have had a hard time defending themselves. Why would any man so ill-use his wife? Didn't he realise how precious your family was, how easily it could be lost to you for ever?

Nonie hastened forward and put her arms round her friend, drawing her to a stool close by the fire. She shot a glance at Gunter, warning him to say nothing. It would only shame Alys to speak of the bruises and, besides, what could anyone do about it? She was Martin's wife. Over the years he'd crushed her till she was old long before her time and now he lusted after any younger woman. There was scarcely a girl along the river on whom he hadn't tried to force himself, and his poor wife knew it.

'Will you have a bite, Alys?' Nonie asked, reaching for a wooden bowl.

She shook her head. 'Martin and the lad'll be back soon, wanting their supper. They had some business . . .' She faltered, darting a nervous glance at Gunter.

Whatever business a river-man conducted on a Sunday was hardly likely to be lawful. It wasn't the first time Gunter had had cause to wonder what Martin was involved in. Several cargoes recently had been delivered short. Accidents were blamed, which happened, of course, but of late there had seemed to be far more. Still, it was none of Gunter's affair. He prided himself on delivering his cargoes safely. Surely the overseers would have the sense to stop hiring the careless men and employ those who could be relied upon to do a good job.

Alys stared into the flames of the small fire, her brow furrowed with anxiety. It was plain she had come with something on her mind, but was finding it hard to confide. Nonie looked at Gunter and jerked her head towards the door. Alys had some woman's problem she wanted to discuss and was embarrassed to mention in front of him. But Nonie had to repeat the gesture several times before her husband understood.

'Goats want feeding,' he said, making for the door.

'Wait. There's . . . summat I need to ask you,' Alys said. 'It's my faayther.'

'Is he sick?' Nonie asked.

Alys shrugged. 'Ailing, but no worse than afore. But thing is, the steward says he still owes money for last quarter's rent. He reckoned Faayther's not been taking care of his cottage. Threatened to throw him out. Martin says I'm not to give the old man so much as a farthing. I've managed to scrape together a little here and there. I've sold a few bits, but they didn't fetch much – I could only sell what Martin wouldn't notice had gone missing. I've enough to pay the rent Faayther still owes for last quarter, but I can't pay someone to repair the cottage, like the steward says we must. Roof's in a bad state and some of the daub's fallen away. You can see straight through the wall near the door. It'll only get worse, come the frosts. Faayther can't manage it himself any more. I don't know what to do.'

Tears slid down her cheeks, and she wept silently. Gunter guessed she had long since learned to cry without making a sound.

The animosity between Alys's husband and her father was legendary in Greetwell. No one could recall exactly how it had begun, but each passing year had seen more wood heaped on the fire of their enmity. It was unheard of in the village for infirm parents not to live with their children, if they were fortunate enough to have family: who could afford to pay the rent on a cottage for themselves and another for the old folk? But Martin swore he would see the miserable old bastard begging in the streets before he'd offer him so much as a mouldy crust. And Alys's father told any who would listen he'd sooner drown himself in the Witham than set foot across Martin's threshold. Poor Alys was trapped between them.

The old man got by helping neighbours to move livestock, collecting kindling and scaring birds, jobs normally given to boys. In truth, what little food or few coins he received in exchange were given to him out of pity: he was so doddery that he was more of a hindrance than a help, but they knew he would not accept charity. When pride was the only thing a man had left, who would be so cruel as to take it from him?

Nonie gave Alys a rag to wipe her tears. 'Don't you fret, Alys. Gunter'll see to his cottage, won't you?' She glanced at her husband, but there was no question in her eyes. She knew he would.

Alys stared down at Gunter's wooden leg. He guessed what she was thinking: how would he clamber about on a roof?

'I'm no thatcher, but I've patched this 'un up often enough. If the damage is not too bad, I reckon we can fix it. You should see Hankin on a ladder – like a squirrel up a tree, he is. I'd ten times sooner have that lad at my side than my leg grow back.'

The boy grinned proudly up at his father.

'But the reeds for the thatch, I've no money to pay for them.'

'Aye, well, there's others'll pitch in,' Nonie said. 'I'll talk to the neighbours. We'll find a way.'

Alys gave her a frail, anxious smile. 'Martin'll not be best pleased if he learns you're helping Faayther.'

Nonie put her hands on her hips. She was wearing the stubborn expression that her children and her husband knew meant she would brook no argument. 'Martin,' she said, 'had better not raise an eyebrow, never mind his fist, or he'll have me to reckon with.'

Chapter 5

If a witch tries to bewitch you, spit at her so that the spittle lands between her eyes. That will break the spell.

Mistress Catlin

The door banged in the wind as my son Edward lurched into the hall. He sank into a chair and slumped across the table, almost toppling the jug of small ale. I didn't need to ask if he'd been drinking. His clothes were stained and dishevelled, his eyes bloodshot. Little Leonia, still finishing her breakfast, looked up at her brother with amusement, but lowered her gaze demurely when she saw me watching her.

'Where did you spend the night?' I asked, trying to keep the anger from my voice. 'I was concerned for you. We all were.'

'Cockpit . . . tavern . . . Lots of taverns, as I recall.'

'I suppose that means you lost heavily.'

He raised his head, licking his lips with a white-furred tongue. 'As a matter of fact, sweet Maman, I won . . . then lost . . . at dice.' He giggled, then winced, clutching his head. He pulled himself upright, came round the table and kissed me. His breath stank.

'At least you know I wasn't with a woman. You're the only woman in my life, little Maman.'

I pushed him upright as old Diot waddled in, a platter of fat bacon clutched against her great belly. 'Thought I heard you come in, Master Edward.' She laid the platter on the table, and pushed a greasy lock of grey hair back under her cap. She folded her arms firmly across her massive breasts in the way she always did when she was vexed. 'Mistress was right upset when you didn't come back last night. Leaving two helpless women alone all night – anything could happen. Any man could've climbed in that casement and had his wicked way with us.'

'Or you'd lean out of the casement and drag him in, kicking and screaming, you naughty old woman. Don't think I haven't seen you making cow eyes at the butcher.'

Edward lumbered over, caught Diot round her bulging waist, kissed her plump cheek and spun her round, while she roared with laughter. Edward could always charm his way round anyone, as I knew too well.

Flushed and still smiling, Diot pushed Edward into the chair and dragged the bacon in front of him. 'You get that down you, Master Edward. It'll sop up all that wine. When I worked at the inn I always used to serve that to my customers, come morning, after they'd had a hard night drinking. Plate of that inside them and they could ride all day.'

Edward, looking decidedly queasy, stared at the glistening white fat and tried to push the platter away. But Diot pushed it back.

'I think you might regard that as penance, Edward,' I said.

He glowered at me, but dutifully picked up a small piece and manfully chewed it. Diot waited until she was satisfied he was eating, then waddled back out of the hall towards her kitchen.

Even though his face was puffy from lack of sleep, Edward was still a handsome man, with eyes the colour of blue gentians, framed by long, thick lashes, and a streak of pure white in his dark hair – it looked as if he had thrust a jaunty feather into it. Women of all ages turned their heads to look at him whenever we went out together, giggling like tavern maids when he bestowed a smile on them. It made me uneasy. He could so easily fall prey to the wrong woman.

He took a swig of small ale, gagging as he tried to wash down the mouthful of fat.

'Did you have any visitors last night?' he asked, as if the answer was a matter of indifference to him. But I knew it was not.

'Master Robert came, didn't he, Mother?' Leonia's large brown eyes were wide and guileless. 'He stayed for ages.'

'We had much business to discuss,' I said.

'Of course you did,' Edward said, with a smirk. 'How is that business going? I trust the investment is paying off because I'm growing tired of living here. It's too small and cramped.' He waved the point of his knife about the narrow hall. 'And you know how easily I get bored, little Maman.'

I glanced at Leonia who was watching us intently. Sometimes my daughter unnerved me, always watching, always listening, her expression revealing nothing of her thoughts. Like Edward, she could charm the fish from the sea when she chose. I thought of her as a child, but she was already twelve and I wondered how much she really understood.

'Investments of this particular nature take time to mature, as you well know, Edward. I cannot—'

I broke off as a shriek echoed through the house. Edward leaped to his feet and bounded to the door. He only just avoided colliding with Diot as she came hurrying the other way, panting and sweating.

I held her arm to steady her – the old woman looked as if she was about to collapse. I dragged a stool close to her and steadied her as she sank onto it, fanning herself with her sacking apron.

'Whatever's happened, Diot?'

She was still too breathless to speak, but grunted, gesturing wildly out through the door. 'Horrible . . . Who would do such a thing?'

Edward disappeared outside, and Leonia darted after him.

'Stay here, Leonia!' I shouted. But she ignored me.

Moments later Edward reappeared, looking as if he was about to vomit and firmly gripping Leonia's arm.

'Sack left hanging on the kitchen door,' Edward said grimly. 'Neighbour's brats playing a trick, I should think.'

'Thought it was the meat from the butcher,' Diot wailed. 'He sometimes sends a tasty portion, if . . . I opened it and nearly climbed out of my own skin.'

'What was in the sack?' I asked.

'A fox,' Leonia said matter-of-factly. 'It was a fox with his head cut off.'

'Disgusting little monster wanted to take it out and look at it,' Edward said.

'It was interesting!' Leonia protested.

'It was crawling with maggots,' Edward retorted, giving her arm a savage pinch.

She flinched, but did not cry out or draw away. She grew more like me every day. We had both learned never to let others see they have wounded you, or they will know your weakness and attack even more ruthlessly.

'That wasn't all,' Diot said, shivering. 'There was a knot of periwinkle tied about the beast's muzzle. It's what felons wear when they're dragged off to be hanged. Marks 'em for death. Evil, that's what it is. The fox is the devil's sign.'

'Guilty conscience, you old witch?' Edward said. He bent low to

37

murmur into her ear. 'The devil always comes for his own and you sold your soul long ago. I reckon it won't be long before he comes to carry you off on his black horse.'

Diot squealed in fear and pushed him away. 'I never kissed the devil's arse, not once—' She broke off, clapping her hands to her mouth, her frightened gaze darting to me, as I glared her into silence. With another terrified glance in my direction, she heaved herself up, tottering from the room. She knew the rule. Her past was not to be spoken of, not even between ourselves. Diot knew what the consequences would be if she broke it, and it amused Edward to try to trick the old woman into saying something she shouldn't.

'Stop tormenting her, Edward.' I took his arm and drew him across to the small window. 'I told you Robert was being followed. The dead fox is a warning to me to stay away from him. I know it.'

Edward shook his head, wincing: the movement was still too painful. 'Why would anyone want to frighten you off? It's just a typical boy's trick. A gang of them probably came across a dead fox when they were out roaming the countryside and thought they'd put it to good use to annoy someone.'

'But I saw someone on the day I met Robert, hanging round the warehouse. He and his son saw the man too and Robert was unnerved, I could tell.'

'So he has enemies,' Edward said. 'What man in his position doesn't? I should think half the cut-purses in the city follow him daily, waiting their chance. If I was a thief he'd be the first man I'd mark. He doesn't disguise his wealth. You can't wonder at the man being nervous at having his head staved in every time he sets foot outdoors. But thieves don't waste their time with rotting carcasses, and if someone is threatening Robert, why leave it on our doorstep, not his? Don't start jumping at shadows, little Maman. You need all your wits about you now.'

Edward could never see danger. He sauntered through life as if nothing could touch him, expecting all he wanted to fall in his lap when he snapped his fingers. And I gave him everything he demanded. I knew that if he didn't get it I'd lose him. I smiled and pretended to be reassured, but I knew that whoever had left that curse at my door had not intended it as a joke. It was a warning: a warning of death. I had seen such signs before and they were not to be ignored.

But whoever Robert's enemies were, they would not frighten me away. Like pain, you can use threats to make you stronger. If they hide a serpent in your bed, you must catch it and make it bite the hand of him who left it.

November

When November takes up the flail, let the ship no more sail.

Chapter 6

On St Catherine's Day, men and women jump over the two-foot-high Cattern Candle to ensure good fortune, but if, when you jump, the flame is extinguished or you catch fire, this is a bad omen.

Lincoln

There is no doubt that there are a few disadvantages to being dead. For one thing we lack the lips to enjoy a roasted piglet basted in honey or the thighs to take pleasure in the welcoming bed of a lover or the throat down which to pour a flagon of sweet wine. Those pleasures I miss dearly. Make the most of those delights while you still can, my darlings. But there are compensations for a lack of corporeality: the favourite pastime of the dead is watching the living squirm and suffer. And there can be few pleasures more entertaining than that.

Haven't you ever felt a little quiver of gleeful anticipation watching a man blithely walk towards a hole he doesn't know is there? While you still live you may feel shame or guilt about letting him walk into danger, but when you depart from life you slough off guilt with your body, never again to experience a twinge of remorse about another man's suffering.

And on that particular night Master Robert of Bassingham was about to suffer – at least, he was if his dear wife had her way and, believe me, she'd had more practice in making his life hell than any imp of the underworld.

The silence in the hall was growing ever more chilling and oppressive as Edith's needle stabbed viciously into the long, narrow strip of embroidery. On the other side of the table Beata was also stitching: the far more mundane task of mending linen. For the hundredth time that evening Edith glowered at the great door as if it remained shut deliberately to provoke her. Beata knew her mistress was working herself up into a fury: her silver scissors snipped at the threads with the force of an executioner severing a head.

Beata glanced anxiously across at her. 'Will you not take your supper now, mistress?' Her own stomach was protesting so she knew Edith must be famished.

'I've already told you, no,' she snapped. 'If you can't control your appetite you may go to the kitchen and eat.'

Beata lowered her eyes to her mending, trying to stitch while pressing her elbows into her belly to stop it rumbling in the echoing hall. She'd tried to ward off the storm she knew was brewing, suggesting that her mistress might sew in the small solar above, which was much less draughty than the hall. If she had been able to coax Edith upstairs and persuade her to take some wine laced with soothing herbs, she might have fallen asleep and not discovered how late her husband had returned. But Edith had insisted on waiting in the hall and had refused to eat until her husband dined with her.

Beata had worked for Edith since her mistress had come to the house as a shy, slender bride of fifteen. Robert's parents had arranged the marriage when he was twenty. Edith's father had sheep, plenty of them, and Robert's was in the cloth trade. It was, everyone agreed, a perfect match. Beata had seen no more than fourteen summers then. She had gazed on Edith with envy – a husband, a house and in time, if God granted, children. It was not a future Beata dreamed of for herself. The pox that had taken her parents had spared her life, but not her skin. Her face was as pitted as pumice stone, her eyebrows and lashes gone for ever and her eyelids, thick with scars, drooped so that she seemed always half asleep. No one had ever kissed her or, she supposed, would ever be tempted to. In those childhood days she'd wept for her face but had soon learned that tears were too precious to waste on might-have-beens.

There was a rapping at the door. Beata sighed with relief. After all these years, she knew her master's knock. 'There he is at last, mistress.'

Dropping her sewing on the table, she hastened to open the door. Robert strode in, pulling off his damp cloak, his face flushed and wet from the rain. He wiped his brow and shook out the skirts of his ankle-length robe, which was thick with mud nearly up to his calves.

Edith impaled her embroidery savagely with the needle and rose, gesturing impatiently to Beata. 'Fetch our supper quickly. I'm sure your poor master must be hungry after working so late. I know I certainly am.'

Robert was not deceived by the sweetly reasonable tone of his wife's voice. Her eyes glittered in the candlelight, like sharpened flint, and even a stranger would have sensed she was furious, but still he tried to deflect her mood with an air of innocent cheer, which was no mummery for he was indeed remarkably happy. 'Have you not yet had your supper, my dear? You should have eaten. You didn't need to wait for me.'

'A good wife should always wait for her husband to return before she dines. A man shouldn't eat alone, or so my poor mother taught me.' Edith crossed herself, as she always did whenever she reminded Robert of something her late mother used to say.

But Robert did not need reminding. The querulous old besom had lived with them for ten years before she relinquished her grasp on life. Suppressing his irritation, Robert attempted a fond smile. 'Excellent advice for a mother to give a young bride, but after all these years . . .' He trailed off: it would hardly pacify Edith to remember that the evenings of shy, romantic suppers were long over.

He wheeled to face Beata, who was already lifting the latch on the little door that led outside to the kitchen on the farside of the stable-yard. 'Why didn't you serve your mistress hours ago? You know hunger brings on her headaches. Hurry, woman, and fetch meats for her at once. I've already eaten, but you may bring me some wine.'

'Don't trouble to fetch food for me, Beata,' Edith snapped. 'If my husband does not wish to eat, then neither do I.'

'Come, my dear. You must have something,' Robert coaxed. 'You know you'll feel better for it. Beata shall bring you a hot posset. That'll soon have you warm and cheerful.' He crossed to his wife and tried to kiss her well-plucked forehead, but she turned away and he found himself kissing empty space.

Beata pounced on this last suggestion. 'I'll fetch a posset at once, Master Robert,' she called back, although she had no intention of fetching Edith any weapon as dangerous as hot liquid when she was in such a mood.

Robert strode to the fire and stood with his back to it, lifting the skirts of his houppelande to warm his backside. It was a habit Edith thought vulgar, but mostly, as now, he did it without thinking.

45

'Where's young Adam? No greeting for his father tonight?' He frowned. 'The boy's not sick, is he?'

'He is well, though he certainly would not remain so if I kept him up half the night to wait for his father. I sent him to his bed hours ago.'

Robert felt his own temper rising. She cosseted the boy as if he was still an infant. Another few months and he'd be out learning a trade, as many boys of his age already were.

Edith resumed her seat with dignity and took up her embroidery again. 'Did business go well today?'

'Fair, fair,' Robert said, raking his grizzled hair. 'We got a good price for the Lincoln Green from the Florentines, but I'm told the river-men have started demanding a penny extra per cargo. Some of the merchants have already given in to them, devil take them. We have to stand firm on this. If any one of us gives in to these thieving knaves, it is that much harder for the rest.'

'Is that why you had to work so late? You were meeting with the other merchants?' Edith's eyes slid upwards, watching her husband carefully.

Robert hesitated only for a moment. 'You know how it is, my dear. You start talking of shearing costs and transport charges, and the way England is facing ruin, and before you know it you've strayed into the latest gossip from the King's court.'

'Do tell me,' Edith said, with an exaggerated tone of interest, 'what is known of the King?'

'They say the lad will go to Parliament at Northampton to call for another tax to fight France, not to mention the Scots. Mark my words, John of Gaunt's behind this. It's his lands the Scots are raiding. He's up there now, negotiating with them to save his own wealth not England's. But young King Richard swore he'd demand no more money for eighteen months, and it's been less than a year since he required funds for these wretched wars. The Commons'll not take kindly to that and neither will the rest of us, if we've to pay it. What the King should be doing—'

'And what about gossip from nearer home?' Edith broke in. 'Did you discuss that with your guild brothers too?'

Robert was annoyed to be interrupted when she had asked him for news.

'Gossip concerning a certain Widow Catlin,' Edith said. 'Are you sure it was the merchants' table you dined at tonight and not hers? You were seen twice in her street last week.'

'I'm a merchant in this city, I walk twenty streets a day to do business. I dare say I've been seen in some streets a dozen times this week.'

Edith had abandoned all pretence at her stitching. 'You were seen entering her house.'

'By your cousin Maud, no doubt, who should be tending her own husband and children instead of squinting through her shutters all day. That nose of hers grows so long from poking into other people's business, it's a wonder some bird hasn't pecked it off. Damn it, Edith, first it was your mother, now it's your cousin whispering the devil in your ear. Have you recruited every female in your family to spy on me?'

'It's a good thing Maud does take an interest in our family. But for her I wouldn't know whose bed my husband was sleeping in, though I dare say half of Lincoln knows and is laughing at me behind their hands.'

Robert, flushing scarlet, rounded on her in a fury. 'How often do I have to tell you? I am sleeping in no one's bed but my own. I have merely called on Mistress Catlin to offer her advice in certain business dealings and investments. She cannot be expected to understand contracts or deeds.'

'There is a plague of lawyers in Lincoln. Can she not employ one to deal with these so-called *contracts*?' Edith spat the word as if it were a tainted oyster.

'It's the lawyers she needs protecting from,' Robert said. 'Once they fasten onto a man they'll not be content till they've shorn him of every penny he owns, then taken his house as fee for doing it.'

'And you're the one who has to protect this innocent from the slavering wolves, are you? Who appointed you her guardian?'

'You seem to forget, Edith, that I'm master of the Guild of Merchants,' Robert barked. 'Naturally she came to me for advice. Isn't Father Remigius always reminding us to seek justice for orphans and widows? In all charity I could hardly turn her away.'

'I'm sure you could not, husband. Though I find it curious that there are dozens of poor widows in this city but I haven't heard of you calling at their houses to help them. But Maud tells me Widow Catlin is the kind of woman men find attractive. Tell me, Robert, if she was a withered old crone, would you be so quick to leap to her rescue?'

Words sting most when they strike a guilty conscience, and Robert was feeling their smart, but the barb didn't subdue him.

'What right have you to question me as if I was one of your servants? I'm master in this house. Many of my guild-brothers rent houses for their mistresses and visit them openly. They even father brats by them and their wives offer not a word of reproach. Hugh de Garwell was a Member of Parliament and he has a different whore every night in the stews, but his wife greets him with a smile and a good supper when he returns. I've never been other than a faithful husband to you, and this is the thanks I get – wild, spiteful accusations flung at me. Perhaps I should accompany Hugh to the stews tomorrow and then you would have cause to feel hard done by.'

Edith sprang to her feet. 'Faithful! Faithful!' she shrieked.

She whirled round as the door behind her creaked open and the tousled head of her young son peeped fearfully into the hall. 'Mother? Are you hurt? I heard you shouting.'

Edith bustled over to him, pulling him tightly against her and turning to face Robert, holding the boy in front of her as if he were a shield.

'Nothing is amiss, precious. Poor little Adam, you've been worrying about your dear father being out so late, haven't you?'

She forced her narrow lips into a smile, though her eyes were as cold and hard as if they were painted glass. She kissed the top of her son's head several times.

'There, your father's home safe. All is well,' she crooned. 'Come, sleepyhead, I'll take you back to your bed.'

Still holding her son tightly she propelled him from the room, slamming the door behind her.

Robert stood dumbfounded, gaping like a herring. It was typical of Edith that, no matter what her mood, the moment the boy appeared she pretended all was well, as if he was an infant who must be shielded from any unpleasantness. He slammed his fist on to the table. She had set his blood boiling with her accusations, then simply walked away, leaving him without anyone to vent his spleen upon. He strode to the door and flung it wide. 'Beata, damn you, I know you've been standing there listening. Where's my wine? What's taking you so long, woman? Are you treading the grapes?'

Beata bustled into the hall, her cheeks flushed and her eyes lowered. Her lips were pressed tightly together as if she were trying to hold back a torrent of angry words. She crossed to the table without looking at him and set down a flagon next to the goblets, which stood there ready to be filled. She poured some and handed it to him, then strode back to the door.

'Wait, Beata.' Robert gulped half of the wine in his goblet without drawing breath, then held it out for her to refill. 'It wasn't your fault that Edith didn't eat. She can be . . .'

There was no need to supply the word. Beata, of all people, knew how stubborn and difficult her mistress could be.

Edith was no longer the shy, pretty creature Robert's parents had presented to him as his bride. Back then she'd habitually kept her head lowered, glancing up, when she was addressed, from under her pale lashes, which he'd found both charming and disarming. Now the gesture only accentuated her sagging skin.

Her mother had schooled her in a few meaningless pleasantries, which had had the effect of turning Robert into a tongue-tied ploughboy, though he'd had no trouble in exchanging banter and a good deal more with the fishmonger's daughter. He'd wondered how on earth they would pass the time together when they were alone. But his father had taken him aside before the wedding, telling him sternly that his first duty was to sire sons, and once they were safely begotten, Robert might amuse himself as he pleased. With a lap full of babies to occupy her, Edith, like most women, would be glad to have her husband out of the house. As long as she was kept content with trinkets and new dresses, a sweet, biddable girl like her would hardly raise any objections. But Edith had not proved as biddable as his father had imagined.

Those first few years after Jan was born had been a time of growing affection between them. Edith had been eager to please him, asking his advice and opinion on everything from clothes to friends. Although her attention would wander if he spoke of business or politics, that was only to be expected in a woman. Robert had taken immense pleasure in seeing her delight at the gifts he'd brought her and found himself eagerly anticipating her smile when he came home. If he'd considered the matter at all, Robert would have declared that Edith loved him, and would even have admitted that he was fond of her, not that he ever told her as much.

But as the years passed, Edith's grief at losing her children had encased her, like a rough, painful callous growing over a sore. She began to push him away from her body and out of her head, blaming him for the babies that had fled this life. Love, if such had ever existed between them, had slowly rusted into familiarity, custom, routine. Sometimes he thought he saw contempt in her hard eyes.

But they were resigned to their lot, surrendering the hope that there could ever be anything more between them, save the kind of affection you might feel for a house you had always lived in. After all, it had been a marriage of convenience, and convenience was still being served, as it was for countless other couples, who rubbed along with each other day after day, as they shuffled inexorably towards their twin graves.

Robert was suddenly aware that Beata was still hovering awkwardly by the door.

'I did try to get the mistress to eat,' she said. 'And I've left some cold pigeon pie in the ambry in the solar in case she should change her mind.'

'Then stay. Drink with me.' Robert waved his hand at the other goblets on the table.

Beata glanced anxiously at the door. 'Mistress Edith will be wanting me to help her undress.'

'She'll still be fussing with the boy. Sit for a while.'

Beata poured herself a small amount of wine and resumed the seat she had occupied earlier in the evening. She didn't much care for wine, but she understood it was Robert's way of apologising.

Robert settled himself in a chair drawn up beside the hearth and gulped another mouthful from his goblet. He stared glumly into the crackling flames. 'Why must she be so unreasonable?'

'She worries, Master Robert. There's been so many attacked and robbed lately. Why, the fishmonger was telling me only yesterday that a man was seized just paces from his own house. They near broke his skull, they did, and took three silver ingots he had hidden under his shirt. I reckon they must have known he was carrying them . . .' Beata trailed off, realising that her master wasn't listening.

'Edith's always suspicious and entirely without cause. I've been as faithful as any man in my position could reasonably be expected to be.'

Beata sipped her wine and said nothing. It was strange how 'faithful' had one meaning for men and another for women. She remembered the quarrels between her master and mistress over a young serving wench in one of the quayside taverns. Then there had been the cook in his own household, though Robert hadn't had time to taste any of her wares before Edith's cousin Maud had come sniffing around and persuaded Edith to dismiss her. But those petty dalliances were as nothing compared to what most men got up to.

If Robert had ever suspected his wife of taking a lover his fury would have been a hundred times greater than hers, as is always the way with men. Not that Edith had ever given her husband a moment's cause to doubt her. Beata sighed. Men demanded all women be virgins and used them as whores.

Robert scowled into the fire. 'I don't want to lie to Edith, but she forces me to, then blames me for deceiving her.'

Beata threw him a shrewd glance. 'So you did dine with Widow Catlin this evening.'

'Yes . . . yes,' Robert said. 'But I've done nothing that even the Bishop of Lincoln would need to confess. Mistress Catlin is the most chaste and virtuous of women. But she is the most enchanting company and her young daughter, Leonia, is as delightful as her mother. I would have stayed longer, but Mistress Catlin herself urged me to return home. She knew that Edith would be anxious. She's a saint – always putting another woman's concerns above her own.' He grunted. 'I was in such a good humour when I left her, but now even this wine tastes sour.'

He drained his goblet and lumbered across to the table to refill it. 'If Edith could only meet Mistress Catlin . . .' A thought struck him and he brightened. 'I could ask her to invite her and her daughter to dine here one evening. Leonia is just thirteen and already a young lady. It would do young Adam good to spend some time in her company. Might make the boy let go of his mother's skirts for once and start behaving like a man.'

Beata snorted with laughter. 'I reckon Widow Catlin wouldn't be best pleased to have any young lad acting like a *man* around her thirteen-year-old daughter.'

Robert still wasn't listening. He slumped into his chair. 'I'm sure if Edith came to know Catlin, they'd become great friends. They've so much in common. They're both mothers, after all.'

Beata shook her head in disbelief at the sheer stupidity of men, and husbands in particular. 'A falcon and a partridge both have chicks, but that doesn't make them friends.'

But Robert was not to be dissuaded. 'Why don't you speak to her, Beata? Edith would take the suggestion more easily from—'

He was interrupted by a hammering at the door. Both leaped up, staring at each other. It was not the hour for neighbours to come calling. Robert strode across the hall and snatched up the staff that stood near the door. 'Quickly, woman, fetch Tenney.'

But before Beata could find the manservant, the knocking came again and this time a voice called, 'Tenney? Beata? For pity's sake, let me in. I'm drowning.'

Beata grinned. 'That's Jan.'

'What the devil is he doing here so late?'

Robert felt a surge of apprehension. Jan called at the house most days, but never so late. He had scarcely unlocked the door when his son barged through and stood dripping on the stone flags. He pulled off his cloak and threw it over the table. The short skirts of his vivid scarlet and yellow doublet were clinging to his sodden green hose. Beneath his cap his close-cropped red-gold hair was plastered to his head. Shivering he hurried to the great fire and crouched to warm himself.

Beata scurried to fetch him wine, which he acknowledged with a curt nod. Beata was used to that. The bull and bull-calf soon learn to bellow alike, as she often said to Tenney.

Robert couldn't contain his impatience. 'Is there trouble at the warehouse – a fire?'

Jan threw the contents of the goblet down his throat and wiped his mouth with the back of his hand, his fair cheeks already flushing in the heat of the room.

'The ship, St Jude, has been taken. French pirates.'

'God's teeth! I thought the King's fleet was to stop this. All that money they raised in taxes last year and we might as well have thrown it into the sea for all the good it's done. Do you realise what we've lost?'

'Not nearly as much as Hugh de Garwell and some of the others. A score of bales, but it might have been worse.'

'Might it indeed?' Robert snarled. 'Perhaps you'll take the losses more seriously when it's your money the pirates have stolen.' Another thought struck him and set him pacing in agitation up and down the hall. 'Mistress Catlin had money invested in cargoes aboard that ship! How am I going to tell her?'

Jan, who was warming his hands at the fire, whipped round. 'That widow? What cod-wit persuaded her it was a safe investment? I know as merchants we have little choice – how else are we to bring goods in? – but it's always a risk, even without the pirates. If the ship founders or . . .' He stopped, catching sight of his father's face. 'Please tell me you didn't, Father. What on earth possessed you?'

Now that Jan had asked the question, Robert found he couldn't remember. He'd certainly talked to Mistress Catlin about the ship and her cargoes at their first meeting, but they had spoken of many things. She'd been so fascinated by his business, asking such intelligent questions, which no woman had ever done before. Had he suggested investing in *St Jude*? He'd have told any man in Lincoln that it was utterly irresponsible to persuade a widow to put money into a venture so uncertain. And he couldn't think what on earth had made him do it. Now her money was gone. The woman had come to him because she trusted him and he had betrayed that trust, like some petty swindler. If she told others – and why wouldn't she? – his reputation would be in tatters. How was he ever going to face her?

Angrily, Jan snatched up his sodden cloak. 'You're making a fool of yourself with this woman, Father. Mother says you've been seen going to her house after dark on several occasions and staying there for hours. You know how gossip spreads in the city. I won't stand by and see my mother hurt.' He strode across the room, and turned with his hand on the latch. 'At least there's one good thing that's come from *St Jude* being captured. Widow Catlin has lost her money and I'm glad of that, for at least now she'll want nothing more to do with the man who was stupid enough to tell her to invest in it!'

Chapter 7

If a woman does not desire you, and you would arouse her and make her lust after you, take the genitals of a wolf with the hair on its cheeks and eyebrows and burn them together. Give the ashes to the woman to drink in such a manner that she does not suspect. Then she will desire you and no other man.

Lincoln

Mavet, my ferret, gives an irritated squeak and scratches behind his ear, then nibbles the fur on his paw, peering at me reproachfully. I tell him often there is nothing I can do to rid him of his fleas. Since he is dead, of course, he could roll in a swarm of living fleas with impunity. But, alas, the fleas that perished so suddenly with him when he was killed are ghosts themselves now and will continue to irritate him in death as they did in life for as long as we two remain trapped on this earth. Pay heed, my darlings, and always take the greatest care over the company you keep in life: if death strikes without warning, you may be stuck with them till the moon turns to blood and wouldn't that be a torment? But, as I remind Mavet, look on the bright side: though the fleas cannot be killed a second time, at least they cannot multiply.

Unlike Mavet, I am enjoying myself and no more so than when I enter at will the house of one of the most charming women in Lincoln. I certainly couldn't do so when I was alive, unlike Master Robert. But then, as you will have begun to realise, in spite of his recent losses, Master Robert was still more fortunate than many men in that fair city.

It had been grey and gloomy all day and twilight had flowed early into the alleys. With the coming of night, a bitter wind had sprung up from the river, rattling the shutters along the narrow street. Robert pulled his heavy woollen cloak tighter about him, glancing up the

54

street to the house where Edith's cousin lived. No doubt the witch Maud had her eye to the crack in the casement, but surely not even she could recognise him in darkness.

Robert rapped on the door and waited. His supper, though it had been nothing more than a bite or two of rabbit in sharp sauce, now lay as heavy in his stomach as a slab of whale meat. He was dreading breaking the news to Mistress Catlin. But he had always prided himself on owning up to his mistakes, and better he told her than she hear it gossiped in the marketplace. News had not yet spread abroad, but it was only a matter of time. He'd spent most of the day consulting with the other merchants, but the ship and her cargo were lost. There was nothing more he could do but confess as much to poor Catlin.

The door opened and a stout old woman, without her front teeth, stood framed in the lamplight from the chamber behind. She beamed at him. 'Master Robert. Calling again so soon?' She chuckled, and her bloated belly jiggled, as if she had a live squirrel concealed beneath her stained gown.

Robert brushed past her, catching the smell of cooking fat and stale urine that followed Diot everywhere she went.

The house he had entered was nowhere near as fine as his own. There was no oak-panelled wainscoting in the small chamber that served as the hall. Instead the walls were limewashed and the room simply furnished with a long table, chairs and two brass-banded chests. A fire burned brightly in the hearth, but the light came from an oil lamp in the form of a star suspended from the ceiling on a long chain. Five small flames burned at the tips of the star's five arms.

'Master Robert, how wonderful! I didn't expect to see you this night.'

Mistress Catlin stood framed in the archway on the opposite side of the chamber. Robert's heart gave a little jolt as it always did when he heard the welcome in her tone. She was dressed in a green gown, which hugged her small breasts and slender waist. Over it she wore a sleeveless russet surcoat. A necklace of silver set with large, dark-green bloodstones encircled her neck and her hair was caught up in a silver fret.

Robert had seen her in daylight and he knew that she was neither young nor stunningly beautiful, although there was not a single thread of grey in that dark hair. Most men would have described her as

55

handsome, with her fine high cheekbones. In truth, though, her upper lip was too thin, her eyes too pale, and a spider's web of lines was starting to creep round her mouth and lids. But just then, seen in the soft yellow lamplight, she looked twenty years younger, and when she smiled Robert neither saw her imperfections nor cared about them.

But he had barely a chance to return the smile, before a girl uncoiled herself from a low stool near the fire and rushed eagerly towards him.

'You've come to see us again!' Catlin's daughter curtsied, her narrow back held perfectly straight as she bent the knee. 'Will you take some supper, Master Robert?' she said gravely, as if she were already the mistress of the house, but the hand she extended towards a half-eaten dish of mortrews on the table was still that of a child.

Robert and Catlin exchanged amused glances at the child's attempt to imitate her elders.

'Thank you, but no, Leonia, my dear, I've already dined,' Robert said, indulging her with a formal bow. 'But please eat. I would not keep you from your meal.'

Look at the mother, they say, to see what the daughter will become, but you may equally look at the daughter to see what the mother has lost. Leonia was an enchanting girl, balanced on the cusp between child and woman. Her hair hung loose in a luxuriant tangle of soft black curls, but it was her huge eyes that never failed to captivate, tawny-brown, with curious gold flecks, fringed by long dark lashes. She glowed with the radiance of promise that makes even jaded old men believe that, however ill the world, there must be some good in it to have cradled such innocence.

Leonia glanced towards Diot's ample backside as the old woman disappeared out of the door to the kitchen, then lowered her voice, grinning mischievously, to say, 'It's just as well you're not hungry, Master Robert. There are so many breadcrumbs in that mortrews, you can't even taste the meat.'

'Leonia!' her mother said sharply. 'You shouldn't exaggerate. Upstairs with you. It's time you were asleep.'

Unlike most girls of her age. Leonia didn't sulk or pout, but made another graceful little curtsy, then bade them a cheerful goodnight.

As soon as she had left the chamber, Robert turned to Catlin, feeling even guiltier than before. 'My dear, I can't bear to think of you or that sweet child going hungry . . .'

56

Catlin laughed. 'Diot is far thriftier than she needs to be. She was once a cook in a busy pilgrims' inn, before the work got too much for her. It's her habit to stretch meat with cheaper ingredients. The innkeeper insisted on it and I cannot seem to break her of it. But we manage very well and, with the excellent investments you have made for me, I have no anxiety about our future.'

Robert felt the sour liquid from his stomach rise into his throat and swallowed hard.

'It is about one of those investments that I have come to speak to you. I'm afraid I have grave news.'

He sensed, rather than saw, Catlin sit down, for he couldn't bring himself to look at her, and see the trust and respect die in her eyes to be replaced with – anger? He feared she would despise him and he couldn't bear that. He cleared his throat and addressed himself to the flames in the hearth. 'I've received grave news,' he repeated, needing to recite the words exactly as he had rehearsed in his head. '*St Jude*, the ship that was carrying the cargoes for the Lincoln merchants, has been seized by French pirates.'

There was a gasp from Catlin, but Robert rushed on, anxious to deliver every scrap of painful news, like a surgeon trying to amputate a limb as quickly as possible to spare the patient prolonged agony. 'We've sent word to the King to demand that the pirates be hunted down, but they usually run for shelter into the French ports. Unless the King's ships were able to catch *St Jude* in the open sea there is no chance they would have been able to retake her. I fear her cargo had already been landed and dispersed long before word reached us.

'We've demanded recompense for our losses from King Richard for his ships are supposed to patrol the seas, defending us from such attacks – and, by God's bones, we pay enough taxes to keep them afloat. And I dare say the King will in turn demand restitution from the French, though they will naturally deny it was a French vessel. We shall press the matter, but I fear that with these skirmishes against France and Scotland eating through England's treasury, like a plague of mice, we'll be lucky if we see a penny. You have my humblest apologies, Mistress Catlin.'

'I'm so sorry for you, Master Robert. I hope your losses are not great.'

Robert had anticipated any number of reactions from Catlin – rage, tears, recriminations. Women, in his limited experience, were apt to explode into fury or collapse weeping over something as trifling as a smashed pot. But her tone was calm. He realised that she hadn't understood the implications. 'My dear, I'm afraid I haven't made myself clear. Some of the money you invested on my advice, which I now bitterly regret, was placed in the cargoes on that ship. It, too, is lost.'

For the first time since he'd started speaking, he glanced at her to see if she had finally understood, expecting to see shock or anger in her face, but he saw only a gentle sorrow.

'I understand, Master Robert. I won't pretend that this hasn't come as a terrible blow. But when a friend has also suffered a loss, naturally one is more concerned for them than for oneself. Did you lose a great deal?' she repeated.

'I can stand to lose the money.' This wasn't quite true, and he would never have said as much to Jan. 'But I am far more grieved that I involved you in this venture. You put your trust in my experience and I've betrayed it. The whole of Lincoln will brand me a swindler. But I swear by all the saints that I am not.'

Catlin rose and gently touched his arm in reassurance, gazing up into his face. 'The very fact that you, too, had invested money in the ship is proof enough for me that you acted in good faith, believing that you were doing your best for me. I've told no one that you invested money for me, nor shall they ever learn it from my lips.'

She turned away, fingering the bloodstone necklace at her throat. 'We shall just have to find a way to manage.'

He thought he heard her give a little sob and saw those slender shoulders heave as she struggled to regain her composure. He would a thousand times rather she'd shouted and raged at him, as Edith would, if she ever came to learn of his losses, though Robert had no intention of telling her. But Catlin's quiet, brave resignation made him feel guiltier than any angry words she could have uttered.

He reached into the leather scrip that hung from his belt. 'It's only a little of what you lost . . .' He held out the purse to her. 'Take it, Mistress Catlin, for Leonia. I would not have her suffer for my folly.'

But he could tell at once that he'd offended her.

Catlin's head jerked up. 'You owe me nothing and I will not accept money from a man who is neither my father nor my husband.'

'It's not from me,' Robert said hastily, realising at once the insult he'd offered her. 'From the Merchants' Guild. They have a fund for widows and orphans.'

'For the dependants of former guild members,' Catlin said firmly. 'My husband was not from Lincoln or a member of your guild.'

But her outrage melted as swiftly as it had arisen and her mouth curved into a smile. 'You are an honourable and generous man, Master Robert, and I'm truly grateful that you should care about my daughter, especially when we are no kin to you.'

'I wish that you were,' he murmured, unaware that he had uttered the words aloud.

Her smile deepened. 'I would not take so much as a farthing from you, Robert, for that would be taking money that belongs to your own dear wife and sons, especially when you yourself have suffered losses. Your advice and protection are gifts beyond price to me and, as a widow and stranger in the city, I'll be for ever in your debt for your friendship.'

Robert found himself so entranced by the movement of her lips that he was barely listening to her words. She was standing close now, gazing up at him. He could smell the perfume of rosewater and bergamot in her hair. Before he even knew what he was doing he found himself bending forward and grasping her shoulders. Then he pressed his lips to her soft, warm mouth.

Catlin sprang away from him, alarm flashing in her eyes. 'No, Master Robert!'

He turned away to hide the flush of embarrassment. He was afraid to look at her again. But when finally he glanced at her, to his surprise, her expression was one of pleasure.

'My daughter is a better mistress of the house than I am,' she said, 'for I haven't even offered you any refreshment and on such a cold night too.'

Mention of the innocent child lying asleep above him, fell like a sharp reprimand on Robert, though he knew Catlin hadn't intended it as such. He watched her, covertly, as she crossed to the table and poured spiced wine into a beaker. She crouched in front of the hearth. He couldn't tear his gaze from the round curve of her buttocks as the fabric pulled tight against them. The sudden hiss when she thrust a red-hot poker into the wine made him jerk violently. A cloud of white steam gushed from the beaker. She rose and handed it to him. He clasped it gratefully.

'Please be seated, Master Robert, and tell me of your dear wife and sons.'

Her tone suggested that nothing whatever had passed between them, and for a moment he wondered if he had imagined what he'd done. But he knew he had kissed her. He could still feel the tingle of her mouth on his lips.

He felt a surge of overwhelming gratitude to her for her forgiveness – for the foolish investment and the fumbled kiss. Though it shamed him to admit it, a good measure of his apprehension in facing her had lain in the fear that she would take revenge by letting everyone know that he had been responsible for losing a widow's money. And it wasn't merely the damage to his reputation he feared. If Maud heard a whisper of such a rumour she would go straight to Edith, and there was no news so dark that woman couldn't paint blacker. He had not a shred of doubt that Catlin would keep her word and no one would be any the wiser.

They sat in the high-backed chairs with the fire blazing between them. Catlin, as always, encouraged him to talk, though even he was not aware of how skilfully she prompted him with questions that allowed him to hold forth at length on his favourite topics of business, politics, taxes and wool. But, for once, Robert did not look for excuses to prolong the evening. Catlin might pretend there was nothing between them except friendship, but Robert could not. Even when he was talking, he found his thoughts straying back to that fleeting touch of his lips on hers. He knew that if he stayed longer, he might not be able to stop himself repeating his clumsy advance.

He pushed himself out of the chair. 'Edith . . . I should return. She frets about me being attacked by footpads after dark.'

He felt no shame at stealing the excuse Beata had offered him the night before. Like most men of wealth, he assumed he owned all that came his way or, at any rate, had the right to take it.

Catlin rose too. 'Of course you must go home at once. I would not have another woman distressed. I know only too well the pain . . .'

For a moment her eyes clouded and she stared at the floor. She'd briefly confided to him before how wretchedly her late husband had treated her, flaunting his many whores, mocking her before his friends and taking a malicious delight in her public humiliation. Catlin had said little about her past and Robert had not pressed for more because it was clear that she would never want others to pity her.

He took a step towards her to comfort her, but she looked up at him, her composure restored, and he knew he would offend her if he tried to touch her again.

'You must take the greatest of care, Master Robert. These robbers grow bolder and more reckless by the day. They seem to care not one jot for the law. Diot tells me they even break into houses while the owners are sleeping in their beds. The poor old woman starts up at every noise in the night.'

'Then I'll speak at once to the night-watch. See that they patrol this street more regularly.' He was glad he could do something to make amends. 'Sheriff Thomas is a good friend of mine, he—'

But Catlin was shaking her head. 'And give what reason for your interest? A widow's reputation, once lost, cannot be restored. I have my daughter's future marriage to think of. I would not have her disgraced. Besides, you've no cause to worry about us.' She laughed. 'Anyone who glances through the door can see we have nothing worth stealing.'

But fears, once they have formed, are as hard to banish as ghosts and when Robert walked out into the cold night, he was suddenly conscious of how empty and dark the narrow street appeared, how flimsy the shutters, how easily they might be forced.

Mistress Catlin did not seem to understand that certain men might find more worth stealing in her house than any jewels, gold or silver. If ever a woman needed his protection it was her. He resolved that in the morning he would buy a dog and have it sent round to her. Little Leonia would love a pet, he was sure, and at least it would deter anyone from breaking in. Catlin could not refuse to accept it, if it was sent as a gift for her daughter.

He turned on the corner to take one last look at the house, and saw that, where the street had been empty a few moments before, someone was standing now opposite Catlin's house, silhouetted against the flickering orange flames of the blazing torch on the wall at the other end of the street. The man's face was covered with a deep cowl and his tattered robes billowed in the breeze. He turned slowly, as if reluctant to drag his gaze from the thin blade of light that glittered beneath the wooden shutters. He lifted his arm and extended it towards Robert, but the end of the sleeve was empty, as if there was no body beneath the robe, only a terrible void of blackness. For one horrifying moment, Robert thought that Death itself was beckoning to him.

He groped for the hilt of the sword hanging from the belt at his hip, but his foot slipped in some foul mess on the path. He struggled to regain his balance, fearful of crashing to the stones. Breathing hard, he looked up again towards the figure, but saw only a cat sniffing at some scrap. The street was empty once more.

Chapter 8

Rocking stones or logan are the meeting places of witches, who ride there on stems of ragwort. If a woman is desirous of becoming a witch she should go secretly to a logan at night and touch it nine times. When a child's legitimacy is in doubt, he is placed on a logan. If he is a bastard the stone will not rock.

Mistress Catlin

I peered out through the finger hole in the shutters, catching just the wisp of movement, as something or someone passed in front of the house. But I could hear no footsteps, only the distant barking of a dog and the yelling of the husband and wife further down the street. I told myself I was being foolish. No one was out there.

But even if no stranger was watching the house, that sour cat, Maud, was certain to be. Would she report Robert's visit to his wife? She would if she'd seen him.

I jerked round as I heard footsteps in the courtyard, grabbing the poker from the fire, but breathed again as Edward sauntered in.

'I thought he'd never leave. I've been lurking outside for hours, freezing.'

'In the street?' I asked, relieved it was his shadow I'd glimpsed.

'Of course not! I was in the courtyard, or he'd have run right into me.'

A cold chill trickled down my back. Then it hadn't been Edward I'd seen outside.

'So, did he tell you?' Edward demanded.

'About the ship? Naturally. He's an honourable man. He looked wretched at having to confess it, but I let him think I knew nothing of it, until he broke the news.'

'You made him feel horribly guilty, I trust,' Edward said. 'The question is, my sweet Maman, how guilty can he be made to feel? Did you ask for money?'

'I asked for nothing. I told him I didn't blame him.'

Edward's grin vanished. 'You weren't stupid enough to tell him I'd already forced the captain to give me the money back before the ship sailed?'

'I am not stupid at all, Edward!' I reminded him sharply. 'I'd hardly confess that my own son had appropriated the money he had so kindly tried to invest for me. As far as Robert knows, my money is gone with the ship.'

The smile returned to Edward's face.

'So you'll ask old Hog-belly for the money, won't you, little Maman? How soon do you reckon he can get it? I am tired of living like this.'

'I told you,' I said firmly. 'I will not ask him for anything.'

My son scowled petulantly. 'But he owes us, or thinks he does. He won't refuse you, even if it's to stop you spreading gossip in the city. The longer you leave it, the less guilty he'll feel. You must strike now.'

I brushed back his white streak of hair that had flopped across his face. 'You already have the money, *my* money. You kept every penny you took back from the captain.'

He had the grace to blush a little. 'We'd have it twice over if only you'd make Robert pay. And you could easily,' he mumbled, pouting, like a spoiled child.

'I've always taken care of you, haven't I? Always given you everything you wanted. And I will again.'

He grinned, but I knew I would not be able to appease him for long. He had the patience of a wayward infant. I would have to act soon.

'My angel, see that the courtyard is secure, there's a good boy. I thought I saw someone watching the house again. Are you sure you owe no money? Dicing? Wagers on the cocks?'

A slightly guilty spasm passed across Edward's face. But he shook his head. 'If the men at the cockpits set their hounds on you, they don't follow you around for weeks, believe me. It takes them just minutes to grab a man in the dark, break a few bones and, if he doesn't agree to pay up, break a few more. What did this person look like anyway?'

I tried to think, but to conjure his image was like plaiting a rope of smoke. 'It was more as if I saw their shadow, not the man.'

Yet even as I said it, I knew that that shadow had exuded a malevolence that was more tangible than the man himself.

Edward snatched up the stave that stood always by the street door and went out to the courtyard. I crouched beside the fire to make the signs that would keep us safe for the night. And tonight that seemed suddenly more important than ever. Of all the work in a house that might be entrusted to a servant, this was the one task the mistress of the house must always perform herself. I wouldn't let Diot do it, though she knew it better than I, as well she might, given what her mother had taught her.

I used the fire irons to rake the glowing embers into a round disc, like the sun. I divided the circle into three equal parts and laid a dried peat in the centre of each segment before covering it with powdery grey ash, banking it down to seal in the heat. Finally I traced a circle in the ash and drew a cross through it so that the arms projected to north, south, east and west.

I rose and crossed to the five-flamed oil lamp. Standing beneath it, I unclasped the silver necklace set with the polished green stones, flecked with madder and cold as a toad to the touch. I ran my fingers around the setting of one stone until I found the little groove and pushed on it with my thumbnail. A shallow oval tray slid out from beneath it. A lock of hair lay inside, tied with thread. I looked at it for a long time in the flickering lights. I stroked it softly with my finger. It was as baby-fine and silky as the day I had placed it there. My first. It's always special, isn't it? You can't help feeling a bond of affection with the first, can you? It brings a delight that none who come after may ever quite match.

I pressed the strand of hair to my lips, holding it there for a while before replacing it in the little tray and sliding it back into position beneath the bloodstone. Then, one by one, I extinguished the flames in the little lamp, until only the red veins of fire beneath the ash in the hearth pulsed in the darkness.

December

If it freeze on St Thomas's Day, the price of corn will fall. If it be mild the price will rise.

Chapter 9

*On St Thomas's Day, the witches gather at the church in
Dorrington, Lincolnshire, to gossip, sing and amuse themselves. If
the moon is shining brightly, and you look through the keyhole,
you will see Satan himself playing marbles.*

Greetwell

Royse pushed her head round the door. 'Mam, bailiff's here. Just seen
him walking up the track.'

Nonie and Gunter exchanged anxious glances. If the village bailiff
paid a visit it always meant trouble somewhere, a killing or a robbery.
Gunter sighed. They'd be rounding the men up to make a search for
the felon – just when he was about to tuck into his supper too.

'Fetch him in, lass . . . quickly,' Nonie said, wiping her hands on
a sacking apron.

She pulled out a stool, gesturing towards it as a large man filled
the doorway. He ducked in, nodding solemnly to Nonie and Gunter,
then heaved his great hams onto the too-narrow seat.

With another worried glance at Gunter, Nonie poured their visitor
some small ale, and set it on the table in front of him. The bailiff
took a swig from the beaker and wiped the beads of liquid clinging
to his beard.

'Has the hue and cry been raised?' Nonie demanded, too anxious
to wait for the man to come to the point in his own time.

The bailiff shook his head. 'It's news from the King as brings me
here.'

Nonie's hand flew to her mouth. 'Have the French invaded?'

The bailiff shook his head impatiently. 'Hold hard, will you? You
women are all alike, never let a man get his words out afore you're
asking questions.'

'Yes, let the man speak,' Gunter said, knowing quite well he'd never
have got away with saying that to Nonie if they were alone.

She glowered at him.

The bailiff took a second gulp of ale. 'There's to be another poll tax. I've to record all the families and register them that has to pay in every cottage.'

Gunter groaned. 'How much this time?'

'Twelve pennies. We've to pay eight by January and the rest by June.'

'But last time it was only four pennies all told,' Nonie said indignantly. 'And it was hard enough scraping that together.'

'You can't have heard right,' Gunter said. 'It'll take weeks to earn enough, that's if I can get the cargoes, and there'll not be many of those afore the new shearing in spring.' He looked round the small cottage despairingly. 'And if I pay it all over to the King, where am I to find food to put in the pot or money for rent? Rushes and candles too. The King expects us to sit in the dark, does he?'

The bailiff grunted. 'King doesn't give a pig's fart where you sit, so long as you pay up. And it's more than the twelve pennies you'll have to be finding. I've orders to register every soul in the house over fifteen years.'

'The lass isn't fifteen yet,' Nonie said hastily. 'So that only leaves me and Gunter to divide the tax between us same as last time.' She gave her husband a frightened smile. 'At least you'll not have to raise more for Royse.'

The bailiff lifted the beaker and drained it. 'It's not like last time. It was only one sum between husband and wife then. This time it's twelve pennies for each and every man and woman that draws breath, no exceptions.'

Nonie gaped at him, as if she couldn't make sense of what he was saying.

Gunter smashed his fist on the table. 'They can't expect us to pay that. It's chicken scraps for the likes of Master Robert, with his great warehouse and all his properties, but my Nonie earns nothing save for what food she grows for the pot, and that's not enough to feed us, never mind have any spare to sell. And what about the likes of Alys's faayther? Is he to pay 'n' all? He can't even find his rent and Martin won't pay for him. You've got to tell them – tell them none of us can pay.'

The bailiff clambered to his feet. 'It's no good you ranting at me. If you've a complaint about the poll tax take it up with the Parliament and the King. I've to pay for my wife and she earns nothing either. I've two girls and the wife's mother living with us as well. I'll have to find the tax for all them, if they get recorded. I'm sorely tempted to take the old woman out one dark night and dump her in a bog pool. At least that way I'd not have to pay for her or put up with her mithering night and day. Your wife's right. You'll not be as hard hit as some. Be thankful for that much.'

He paused with his hand on the latch. 'If I were you, Gunter, I'd take one of your goats to the beast market in Lincoln. It's a waste feeding two over winter anyway, when they're not in milk. But you'll have to find the tax somehow, or they'll come and take the worth of it from the cottage. And trust me, Gunter, it's better to pay up, even if you have to sell your bairns to do it, than have them smashing your home.'

Chapter 10

If a maid desires to see the man she shall marry, let her go at midnight to the graveyard and throw hemp seed over her left shoulder and recite, 'Hemp seed I sow. Hemp seed I grow. He that is to marry me, come after me and mow.' If a man appears behind with a scythe, it is him she shall wed. If no man appear, she shall remain a maid, and if a coffin lies behind her, she shall die before her wedding day.

Lincoln

The problem with life is that you can never tell where those insignificant decisions are going to lead, not while you're alive, that is. Once you're dead, you can see the living setting off blithely down a path that will take them straight into the jaws of a wolf. There are ghosts who try to warn the living, but the living pay no heed, so why try? If you ask me, my darlings, the dead should sit back and enjoy the entertainment the living provide for them, especially when they're cheering for the wolves.

Robert hurried towards his warehouse through the stream of paggers staggering under the weight of kegs, bales and baskets as they hefted them to and from the waterfront. Horses and oxen stood between the shafts of wagons and carts, flicking their ears and waiting patiently for cargoes to be loaded or unloaded. Merchants and tally clerks bustled between them, each believing himself a person of importance to whom others should give way. But men are as stubborn as bulls in refusing to step aside and collisions were so frequent it was a wonder the Braytheforde wasn't bobbing with bodies.

To a visitor, the city's frenetic activity along the waterside would have given the impression that trade was flourishing, but it was not. Ever since Lincoln had lost its wool staple to its rival Boston two decades before, the city had been in decline. Wool, the very cornerstone of England, was no longer compelled to pass through Lincoln, and as the foreign merchants had moved on, so had Lincoln's prosperity. There were, Master Robert reflected bitterly, only half the boats in the Braytheforde today that there had been when he had started in the business.

His mood was not lightened when he climbed the stairs outside his warehouse and entered the tally room, an open loft suspended high above the ground, from which those who did not have to sweat for their supper could look down on those who laboured for them.

Jan was already seated at the small table, moving jetons around on the counting board, as he checked the sums against a sheaf of parchments. He glanced up, cursing as the gust of freezing wind from the open door threatened to sweep everything from the table. He made a grab for the slips, shoving them under weights and measuring sticks to secure them, before turning his attention back to his father.

'What brings you here? It's not Mother, is it? Has she got worse?'

Robert picked up one stack of parchments and flicked through them, oblivious of his son's furious glare. 'Your mother's no worse, but she's no better either. I've sent for the physician. No doubt he'll charge a barrel of gold for telling her to keep abed and drink a posset to soothe her, but Beata kept pressing me to fetch him. Seems to think Edith should have recovered before now.'

Edith had fallen ill four days ago. Robert was sure it was nothing more serious than bad gripes of the belly, caused by something she had eaten. True, none of the rest of the household had become sick, but a fragment of spoiled meat had been known to affect one person while others were left untouched, and gentlewomen were known to be more delicate of stomach than menfolk or servants.

Jan wrenched the parchments, now in the wrong order, out of Robert's hand. 'You didn't have to come today, Father. You could have stayed with Mother. I told you I could manage.'

Robert grunted. 'She sent me. She said I disturbed her, pacing about. Besides, I want a word with Tom. He must make plain to the cottagers that the rents will be rising next quarter, no exceptions.'

'I've told him that already,' Jan snapped. 'You want me to be firmer with the men, but how can you expect them to take any notice of me, if you keep—' He broke off as they heard two pairs of feet ascending the stairs outside.

There was a timid knock at the door, and Robert, assuming it was one of the men, strode over and wrenched it open, prepared to bark at whoever was standing there. But, to his delight, he saw Catlin and behind her the diminutive figure of Leonia. Beaming, he stepped aside, ushering them in. Leonia went to the edge of the platform to peer down into the warehouse with undisguised fascination at finding herself so high up.

'Do take care, my dear. It's a long way down,' Robert warned.

She smiled up at him and obediently stepped back. 'Is this all yours, Master Robert?'

He nodded, gratified to see the awe and delight in her eyes. 'All mine, and one day, it will all be Jan's, won't it, my boy? Mistress Catlin, I believe you know my eldest son, Jan?'

She bestowed one of her enchanting smiles on the lad, and Robert saw a red flush creep across Jan's face.

'Mistress Catlin's late husband was a member of the Guild.'

Robert didn't know what had possessed him to say that, except that it seemed to justify his continuing acquaintance with her. Not that he should need to explain his actions to his son, or anyone for that matter, he told himself. But guilt always makes a man feel he has to say more than is wise.

Catlin smiled. 'Your father is such a shrewd businessman, Jan. I don't know what I would have done without his guidance.'

'Is that so, Widow Catlin?' Jan said, darting a sharp look at Robert. 'But if you will excuse us, we have work to do. My mother's sick. My father's anxious to return home to her as soon as he can.'

Catlin nodded earnestly. 'Of course. I won't detain you either, Master Jan. I understand how busy you must be. Your father has told me how hard you work and how much he relies on you. But it was because I heard your poor mother is sick that I came. A neighbour of your wife's cousin mentioned it and I thought perhaps a jar of sweet oil might comfort her. It will help her sleep if she rubs a little on her temples. I always find it soothes me to have such oils to perfume my chamber.'

She bent and pulled something from her basket. It was a small clay jar, sealed with wax. Even though the seal had not been broken, a heavy fragrance hung about it of lavender and other herbs that, though vaguely familiar to Robert, he had never troubled to identify. She set the jar on the table.

Jan muttered something that might have been his thanks, while

Robert beamed at her. It would never have occurred to either of them to buy such a thing for Edith. Only a woman would think of it. Robert decided it might be prudent not to tell Edith who had sent her the gift. Better to pretend he had bought it himself.

'And how is that little dog of yours, Leonia? I trust he is behaving himself.'

'I'm afraid he's rather naughty,' Catlin said, with a tiny laugh. 'He seized Leonia's favourite gown when it was drying and tore it, then nipped her when she tried to stop him. But as I told her, he's only a puppy and will learn.'

Robert was about to say that he'd buy the child a new gown but, catching sight of his son's face, he thought better of it. He'd have one made up and sent to her. There was no reason for Jan to know.

Leonia was once more edging close to the edge of the platform and Robert could see that she was fascinated by the hooks and pulleys, as the men swung them to lift great barrels and bales onto the stacks below.

'My dear, do be careful!' he warned again. 'Jan, why don't you take the child and show her the warehouse before she tumbles into it?'

'Father, I have these bills of sale to check. Besides, a warehouse is no place for a little girl – she may easily be crushed.'

'All the more reason for you to go with her. After Mistress Catlin has come all this way to bring a gift for your mother, the least you can do is show her a little courtesy.'

'Please will you take me?' Leonia beamed eagerly up at Jan. 'I'm sure you know everything about how it works and I've never been inside a warehouse before.'

Jan, it appeared, could no more resist her large brown eyes than his father could, and his expression softened as he held out his hand to her. 'I can spare only a few minutes.'

Robert waited until he heard their footsteps reach the bottom of the stairs outside, then positioned himself on the stool behind the table close to Catlin. They were seated right at the back of the loft, where he knew they couldn't be seen from the floor of the warehouse.

'You're tired, Robert,' Catlin said. 'You've been exhausting yourself worrying about poor Edith and the business. You must rest else you'll fall sick too.'

Beata, Edith or even his physician might have said exactly the same thing to him for there was nothing intimate about the words. But a look of wondrous tenderness shone in her eyes as she said it, as if she were deeply concerned for him.

He caught again the sweet, heady perfume from the jar of oil, as she leaned closer and whispered, 'I couldn't bear it if anything happened to you, Robert.'

He edged his hand towards hers beneath the table, reaching out until he touched her delicate little fingers. For the first time since he had known her, she did not pull away. He felt her thumb stroking the back of his hand, like the caress of a feather. Neither spoke. They had no need for words as they gazed entranced at one another. It was as if they were fifteen again and this was their first and only love.

Chapter 11

If a person is possessed of the evil eye against their will and does not wish to do harm, let their first glance in the morning, which is always the most deadly, fall upon some tree or bush. In this way the tree will wither and die instead of a man or beast.

Greetwell

Snow was whirling in the darkness as Jan stepped out of the last cottage in Greetwell. After the warm, smoky fug of the tiny room, the biting wind seemed unnaturally cruel. He shivered, drawing the long point of his hood across his mouth and nose. The snow was not falling in soft flakes, but as frozen powder that stung the skin and eyes, like blown sand.

He cursed himself for having left it so late to start for home. It was still early evening, but he'd forgotten how quickly a winter's night closed in on the bleak marshes where no burning torches lit the streets or warm candlelight spilled from the houses. He was relieved, though, to have finished the unpleasant task. He'd dreaded telling the tenants their rents were going to rise, but it had had to be done.

Tom was his father's rent-collector, but Jan could hardly send the man to deliver such unwelcome news. Such tidings must come from Master Robert's steward, the sooner the better to give the cottagers a chance to earn the extra coins. The news had not been welcomed, of course, and Jan had been obliged to listen to the shouts and wails, the pleas and arguments in every cottage he visited.

We can't find the money, not with the poll-tax too. Our bairns'll starve.

Jan pitied them, but all he could do was listen to their angry protests. He was not a man to give them false hope by promising he would try to change Robert's mind. His father would not be moved, he knew, and deep down, he understood Robert's reasons. Their own business had suffered badly this past year, with the weavers' revolt in Flanders and the loss of *St Jude*. If their business failed, the very men who were shouting at him now would be put out of work and out of their cottages too. Yet it made Jan cringe to see the fear in the eyes of the women and know he had caused it.

He stumbled over to where his horse was tethered. She had turned her head from the driving wind, pulling the leather rein tight against the tree branch. His numb fingers could scarcely undo the knot and the old mare was stubbornly refusing to give him any slack, not that he blamed her with the snow stinging her face. He tried to position his own body between her and the wind to shield her eyes as he fumbled to loosen the tether.

As he struggled, he half glimpsed a movement behind him. He spun round, peering intently through the swirling white. Had one of the cottagers come out to argue with him again, or even attack him?

'Who's there?' he demanded.

He thought he heard an answering shout, but the wind was shrieking through the dried marsh-reeds with such force that a herd of bulls might have been thundering towards him and he wouldn't have heard them. Unnerved, Jan hauled himself up into the saddle and turned his horse towards the distant torch-lights of Lincoln Castle and the cathedral high on the hill. But even those lights, which could usually be seen for miles in the dark, kept vanishing behind the swirling snow.

His face already felt as numb and stiff as a block of wood and he hadn't even reached the outskirts of the city yet. The horse was old and standing out in the bitter cold had made her joints stiff. Buffeted by the wind, she was pushed sideways on the path. She rolled her eyes nervously as the long, thin branches of the willows snaked out towards her. Jan kept a good grip on the reins, holding himself alert. This was a treacherous stretch of track, squeezed between the icy black river and the oozing marshes. He didn't relish falling into either, especially not in the dark. Several times he twisted in the saddle and peered behind him, still convinced he had seen someone. But now he forced himself to face straight ahead, knowing that if he tugged on the reins or unbalanced his horse they could both plunge to their death.

Jan's mood was as dark as the bog pools. If only he'd come to Greetwell earlier in the day, as he'd planned, he'd be safely back at his lodgings by now or, better still, in a tavern, enjoying a stewed hare and a jug of wine before a roaring fire. It was all his father's fault, entertaining Mistress Catlin at the warehouse and insisting that

Jan act as nursemaid to her brat. He didn't dislike the child, but she was a strange creature, asking questions about how this pulley worked and what that tool was used for, matters he had thought no girl would be interested in. She had a disarming way of looking up at him with those great tawny eyes, as if every word he uttered was enthralling. But there was something about her that disturbed him, as if a woman was looking at him through the child's eyes and mocking him.

As for Mistress Catlin, Jan could see only too plainly why his father was drawn to her. She was handsome, charming and graceful, all the things his mother was not. Much as he loved Edith, he had to admit she didn't help her own cause, nagging her husband continually, like a beggar picking at a sore. Though Jan had never admitted as much to his parents, it had been a relief to move out of their home to have some peace from her constant fretting and ill humour. But even so, it embarrassed him to see his father behaving like a lovelorn minstrel around Mistress Catlin.

Jan's horse gave a whinny of distress and stumbled. Jan steadied her, and felt her trembling. Had she cast a shoe or lamed herself? Clicking soothingly to her, he swung his leg over her back and dismounted. Between the darkness, the falling snow and eye-watering wind, he could barely distinguish the shape of the horse's leg, never mind what might be amiss with it. He ran his hand down over her knee and fetlock, then lifted her hoof. But he could feel nothing wrong and the shoe was still in place. Maybe something had been driven into the hoof, but whatever it was he didn't want to go digging around blindly with his knife, risking more damage.

He contemplated returning to one of the cottages to borrow a lantern, but knew none of his tenants would do him any favours tonight. They'd probably dump a pail of water over his head and hope he froze to death. Better to keep heading towards the safety of the city. Sighing and muttering a stream of oaths that would have made his mother swoon, he pulled his cloak tighter and trudged on down the track, leading the horse behind him.

'Jan! Jan!'

This time there was no mistake. Someone was calling to him. The voice, though muffled by the wind, was as harsh as the grinding of a stone millwheel. Was it an angry tenant who had followed him, or one of the thieving bands of river-rats luring him into a trap?

Jan turned, shielding his face with an arm and blinking in an effort to clear his blurred vision as the frozen shards of snow rasped his eyeballs.

He thought he saw a dark shape forming on the track behind him, the outline ragged and flapping in the wind, like the wings of a giant raven. Again Jan heard his name drifting out of the darkness towards him, taunting him.

Grasping the hilt of his sword in numb fingers he struggled to draw it from its sheath as his cloak billowed around him. His horse, unnerved by the wind, was shying and pulling at the reins. If it came to a fight, Jan knew he couldn't wield the sword and hold the beast still with his other hand. There was no time to find a tree to tether her, so he let her go.

Even in the darkness, the creature on the track must have glimpsed the steel blade for it halted some distance from him.

'. . . father . . . revenge . . .'

Jan could only distinguish odd words as the stranger shouted through the wind. But he caught 'revenge' clearly enough. There was no telling if the man was carrying weapons, or indeed how many might be concealed in the tall reeds that fringed the track.

'Stay back,' Jan yelled defiantly. 'I'm armed and know how to defend myself.'

But the figure was advancing towards him. Against even the brawniest of the boatmen, Jan would have stood his ground. But the creature moving silently towards him did not even look human. It resembled a monstrous black bird. Only the white snow clinging to its hood and shoulders gave it any shape or form. Where the face should have been there was a black hollow, as if there was nothing inside the robe but darkness.

Jan found himself stumbling backwards, beads of sweat breaking out on his face in spite of the cold. But the snow had made the track slippery and his foot slid from under him. He crashed to the ground, twisting his knee and losing his grip on the sword, which spun away across the stones. He lunged for it, flinging himself full length to slam his hand on the blade before it could slide down the bank and into the rushing water. He tried to pull it towards him, while twisting round to protect himself from the man who, he was sure, must now be almost upon him. But his pursuer had halted and was standing motionless a few yards away.

Grasping the hilt of the sword, Jan tried to scramble to his feet, but his knee was throbbing painfully and he couldn't get purchase on the ground to heave himself upright. He half crawled, half dragged himself across the path until he could grasp the branch of a tree growing low on the bank. Gritting his teeth he hauled himself up, and stood, for a moment, letting the pain in his leg subside.

From this angle, he could see the part of the bank that had been hidden by bushes, and now he saw what had captured his pursuer's attention. A child crouched at the edge of the water, staring into the river, a little girl. She must belong to a cottager, he supposed, and had wandered out to relieve herself. In spite of the bitter night she was clad only in a thin shift. He could see her mouth moving as if she was calling, but the wind was rattling the rushes so violently he couldn't hear her. She leaned forward, reaching so far out over the water that Jan was certain she would fall in. He yelled a warning, but though the robed man on the far side of her jerked round to face him, the child did not seem to have heard him.

In spite of his fear of the stranger, Jan let go of the tree and began limping towards the girl. He had taken no more than a couple of paces when she straightened and jumped into the surging river. She was borne away instantly. Jan staggered to the bank and, gripping a tree to stop himself slipping, stared through the falling snow into the dark water. There was no sign of the child. Jan could swim a little, but not against a current like that, and he knew he'd never catch up with her as the river swept her along. Unless she was tossed against the bank and managed to haul herself out, she would drown in the icy water. She had probably done so already. A wave of nausea swept over him.

He heard a shriek of fear and turned. His pursuer was backing away down the track, an arm thrown up as if trying to ward off an attack by some vicious beast. But there was no dog or other animal, only two children ambling towards him as if it were a summer's day. One was a small boy, perhaps three years old, his hand thrust into that of an older girl. Though he could only see her back, he was sure it was the little girl he had seen moments before jump into the swollen river. Water ran from the clothes and hair of both children. It went on running, black and shining against the white snow. Jan shook his head, trying to clear his vision. It couldn't be water, just a trick of the wind.

The robed figure ran back towards Greetwell, vanishing round the curve of the track, as the two children walked slowly towards him. Then swirling snow obliterated them too. Jan stared after them. He had to have been mistaken about what he'd seen. The girl couldn't have jumped. She must have moved out of sight behind the willow scrub, no doubt looking for her brother.

Jan realised he'd been holding his breath and let it out, almost choking. At least the children had frightened off his pursuer, which meant he was either a madman or a would-be murderer who didn't want witnesses to his crime. There was no comfort in either thought, and Jan certainly wasn't going to wait around for the man's return. The pain in his knee was gradually easing. It had been a wrench, nothing more serious. He offered a silent prayer of thanks for that.

Jan limped down the path towards the distant lights of Lincoln, calling for his horse as he went. Only much later, once he had reached his lodgings and was shaking the snow from his cloak and hood, did it strike him that he'd seen no snow on the girl's hair, and her shift had not stirred in the wind.

January

In Janiveer if the sun appear, March and April pay full dear.

Chapter 12

If you fear there is a sorcerer or witch living nearby, you should hold a bean in your mouth, whenever you go out, ready to spit at them, should you encounter them on the street, before they can curse you.

Mistress Catlin

'It's no use looking at the door every other moment,' Edward snapped. 'That won't bring him. It's been three days since he last called. Three days, little Maman! You've lost him.'

My son crouched by the fire, warming his hands against the winter chill. The room suddenly turned cold. His body blocked out the heat from the fire as if he had sucked it all into himself. He'd been in an evil temper since he had returned and I guessed he'd lost heavily on some wager. He was itching to lash out at someone.

I rose abruptly and crossed to the table, pouring myself a glass of wine to conceal the hurt his words had inflicted. 'According to our neighbours,' I told him, 'Maud has visited Edith and says she's getting worse by the day. Apparently she's described her cousin's illness to anyone who'll listen, and revels in every horrible detail. But if Edith's only half as sick as Maud claims, I dare say Robert feels he must stay at her bedside.'

'And what about your bed?' Edward muttered sullenly. 'If he wanted to be with you, he'd find some excuse easily enough.'

Edward knew how to wound me. But even I was becoming anxious. I'd been trying to convince myself that Robert's concern for Edith's health was the only reason for his absence, but I confess I felt a hollow ache of disappointment that another evening would pass without him. I needed him. I wanted him.

The night Robert had kissed me, I'd convinced myself he had discovered feelings for me that went beyond friendship. But a kiss means nothing to a man. He revels in the excitement of stealing one whenever he may – it matters not from whom – just as a boy enjoys the thrill of stealing an apple whether he intends to eat it or not. I, above all women, should have known that.

I turned away, angrier with myself than I was with Edward. Leonia had been playing with knuckle bones in a corner of the room, but now she was watching me, the bones grasped in her hand. Her eyes were wide and a mocking smile played at the corners of her mouth, as if she, too, were taunting me. 'What are you doing, Leonia?' I snapped. 'You're far too old to be playing with toys. A girl of your age should be occupied with useful pursuits, like sewing. How do you expect to find a husband if you can't even sew a straight seam?'

'Is that how you caught my father, with your sewing?'

Edward brayed with laughter, which ceased abruptly as he grabbed Leonia's arm. 'Watch your tongue, brat. Maman's right. It's high time you learned how to be a dutiful wife. And you can start by getting rid of those. Throw them onto the fire!'

Leonia gripped the bones more tightly. Edward dragged her towards the hearth and forced the hand that grasped the bones over the fire, gripping her arm at the elbow, so that she couldn't move her hand away.

They glared at each other. Leonia was clenching her jaw against the burning heat, but she would not give in easily. Finally, pain forced her to open her fingers. The bones tumbled into the flames and Edward released her. She ran from the chamber and I heard her feet clattering up the stairs. Edward's eyes flashed, defying me to reprove him.

But before I could say anything there was a familiar rapping at the door. As I hurried past my son to open it, he gave me a swift kiss and grinned. 'It seems your charms still work, little Maman.'

Robert was standing in the darkened street, hunched against the cold. He glanced anxiously towards Maud's house, before ducking swiftly inside and closing the door quickly behind him. He stood, panting a little and rubbing his arms vigorously. His smile froze as he caught sight of Edward standing by the fire. He nodded curtly.

'I apologise for the lateness of the hour, Mistress Catlin. My son was coming to sit with his mother, but he's only just arrived. He was detained on business.'

I knew Jan called to see his mother most days for he was devoted to her, though from odd remarks Robert had made, I had the impression she favoured the younger boy. But I think even Jan found his mother wearing when she was ill. Sickness makes saints of some, but Edith, alas, was one of those women who became more querulous when she was unwell. One moment she was demanding Robert leave her in peace, for his fidgeting disturbed her, the next she was shrieking at him for leaving her alone so long, accusing him of neglect, when nothing could have been further from the truth.

'I trust I find you in good health, Master Edward.' Robert broke the awkward silence. 'Have you been fortunate enough to secure employment yet?' He remained stiffly beside the door, as if he couldn't bring himself to sit while Edward was in the room.

Edward shrugged. 'I haven't found anything to suit my talents.'

Robert frowned. 'And what are your talents, Master Edward?'

'Gambling, drinking and wenching. Now, if I could find someone to pay me to do that,' he said, grinning and winking.

But Robert didn't share the joke and his jaw tightened. 'You should be out looking for any honest work you can find. It's your duty as elder son to provide for your widowed mother and your sister. I'll make enquiries among my fellow guild members. With men defying the law and leaving their masters, one of my guild brothers may need to hire a willing man. That is,' he added, staring pointedly at my son, 'if you will work for the old wages instead of the outrageous sums some of these men are demanding.'

Edward's eyes narrowed. 'You needn't trouble yourself, Master Robert. I can find many interesting ways of earning a living.'

'Now, Edward, Master Robert was merely trying . . .' I began, but I let the words fall, fearing they might provoke him. I'd no wish to see the two men quarrel.

Edward snatched up his cloak and strode out into the street, slamming the door behind him.

'You must forgive my son, Robert. He didn't have an easy life growing up. His father was a cruel man, and I'm perhaps more indulgent with him than I should be to make up for that.'

'All the more reason for him to be taking care of you and the child now,' Robert said sternly. He sank into the chair that Edward had recently occupied and gazed at me earnestly. 'I cannot understand any man being cruel to a woman like you, Mistress Catlin. It is unthinkable. It must have been a relief to you when your husband died.'

I shuddered. 'Not a relief, no. Grief is more painful than any physical wound, especially when you've loved a man as I once did . . . Indeed, it was that very love that made my husband's wickedness harder to bear. If I'd not loved him so much, his vile acts would have seemed less cruel. But, in the end, it was another woman he wronged who brought him to judgement.'

Robert's brow furrowed. 'I don't follow you, my dear. Was your husband convicted of some crime? I thought he had left you money, and if he was hanged that was surely not possible because all is forfeit to the Crown.'

I gnawed my lip, staring at my fingers in the firelight. 'We came to Lincoln to escape the idle tongues. I fear what people might think of me, if my story were known . . . what *you* would think of me Master Robert, for I couldn't bear to lose you as a friend.'

He reached for my hand and pressed it to his lips. 'I'd never blame a woman for the sins of her husband, or spread the story abroad. I know only too well the importance of a good name. That's why I'll be for ever in your debt that you didn't let it be known I had persuaded you to such a risky investment. I would . . .' He hesitated, flushing. 'My dear, will you not trust me?'

Now that his curiosity was aroused I knew he would not let it go. A man likes to be trusted, becoming hurt and enraged if he is not. Was this the right moment to tell the story? I crossed to the table to pour wine for us both. When I handed him the goblet, his fingers closed around mine and it was several moments before he let me go.

'We've talked for many hours about my business,' Robert said. 'You know more about me than even my own wife. But I know so little of your life before we met. I dare say that is my fault for I always talk too much in company. Edith often reproaches me for it. But I've thought of you a great deal these past few days, when I've been sitting with Edith, and I realised I know nothing of your life before you came here. How your husband died. I don't even know his name. It seems to me, my dear, that you are keeping something from me, and it troubles me.'

I sank into the chair and, without looking at him, finally began to tell the dreadful truth I'd hidden for so long. A tale not even my children knew in its entirety.

'My husband . . . was Warrick de Fenton. I was barely fifteen when we met. I'd accompanied my parents to the wedding of a neighbour's daughter. I was in the bridal party, helping her to dress, then holding the candles as we led her to the church door to say her vows. Warrick was in the groom's party. As you know, there is much teasing and horseplay between the bride's attendants and the groom's on the wedding day, with the groom's men trying to steal the bride from the maids before she reaches the church. I was wearing a garland of flowers in my hair and it was knocked to the ground. Warrick saved it from being crushed, but demanded a kiss before he would return it. Naturally I refused, but such is the licence on such a day that in no time my friends and his had surrounded us, insisting I kiss him, so at last I gave in.

'The feasting and dancing lasted several days, for the bride's parents were wealthy landowners. Warrick and I had many opportunities to dance and walk together, and before the guests dispersed, he had persuaded his father to seek my parents' permission for us to marry.

'They were reluctant to grant it at first, for they knew little of his family, who lived many miles away, but I entreated them on my knees, for I was hopelessly in love with Warrick. He seemed to me then the most charming man who had ever walked the earth. He swore to my parents he would provide for me and do all in his power to make every hour of my life one of happiness and joy. At last, my parents gave their consent and the second wedding followed swiftly upon the first, far too swiftly as it transpired.

'At first all was as he had promised. His father granted him one of his houses and he would inherit his father's entire estate on his death. We were scarcely out of each other's company, in those early days, but I began to notice a cruel side to his nature even then. He would mock and humiliate the servants to amuse his friends, and once he snatched a cat from a cottager's child and drowned it in front of her. The cat had caused his horse to shy when it ran across his path to escape being mauled by his hounds. Warrick's greatest passion was hunting. He was never happier than when he was in the saddle with a hawk on his arm and his dogs streaming out behind him.

'I tried to ignore these flaws in his nature for I refused to see any wrong in the man I loved. I confess I was weak and naïve. I would have done anything to make Warrick love me as I loved him. My day was pure heaven if he smiled at me and hell if he did not.

'All seemed well between us until my belly swelled with child. Then I became the object of his mockery. "My wife is a great sow," he said, in front of the servants. "You should feed her swill with the other pigs. We should set her running and throw spears at her, see who can bring the hog down." They laughed, fearing his anger would turn on them if they didn't.

'All the while I was carrying his son, Warrick wouldn't touch me or have me in his bed because I disgusted him. He didn't bother to disguise how often he went to the village and had his sport with the women there. I kept silent, praying and hoping that when the child was born all would be again as it had once been between us.

'But it never was. I had been spoiled in his eyes, and though he came occasionally to my bed, when he could find no other woman to satisfy his lusts, his lovemaking was savage, as if he were punishing me. For all that he didn't want me, he was insanely jealous when I showed affection to my son. He found any excuse to ridicule and hurt the boy.

'In spite of his infrequent visits, I fell with child again. This time he accused me of being unfaithful, saying that the child could not be of his getting. I swear on Leonia's life I'd never had an unfaithful thought, much less committed an unfaithful act, in all the years we were wed. And I feared for my unborn child, for by then I knew what he was capable of. But what could I do? Warrick was my husband and, as the priest reminded me, I had vowed before God to stay with him until death, no matter how ill he used me. My soul would be damned if I broke that vow.

'But not all the women Warrick slept with did so willingly. He forced himself on many a helpless maid and there was one he raped who found herself carrying his child. Her mother brought her to the house demanding restitution, but as soon as Warrick saw her swollen belly he mocked and taunted her, as he had me. That very night the girl, humiliated beyond endurance, hanged herself in the forest.

'But the girl's mother was a witch. All the village knew it, but Warrick refused to believe in such things. The woman took her daughter's body in her arms and swore by the spirits of her daughter and her unborn grandchild that she would hound Warrick to the very gates of Hell.

'Word spread quickly, and many cautioned Warrick to find some means to appease the woman before she carried out her threat, but he laughed. "What can the miserable hag do to me?" he demanded.

'It seemed he was proved right, and the woman was powerless to harm him, for he continued as he had before and suffered no ill-luck or sickness. Then on St Stephen's Day he decided to take our guests hunting. He had his favourite mare saddled and away he rode, the hounds barking excitedly in the winter sunshine. I did not go with them for I was heavy with child and not far off my time.

'The ground was frozen and every tree sparkling with frost. Some of the children ran behind the hounds to hunt the wren, as is the custom on that day. But Warrick led the chase with the men after bigger game. It seems they'd not been riding long, when the hounds put up a fine stag. It sped away, the hounds streaming after it and the men on horseback galloping behind them. They had thought to bring the beast down quickly, but it darted into the woods and the riders had to slow because of the low branches and the tangle of old undergrowth.

'Not so Warrick. His blood was on fire from the chase and he led the way, spurring his horse and recklessly jumping it over fallen trees. Then, just as the stag, exhausted, turned to face the dogs, a great hare sprang out of a tangle of brambles and shot right across Warrick's path. His horse reared and threw Warrick against a tree. His head hit the trunk and he crashed to the ground.

'When the rest of the party caught up, they found him still alive but with a great wound in his skull where the stump of a branch had driven into it. With his dying breath, he pointed towards where the hare had run, begging his friends to track it down and throw it to the hounds to avenge him.

'Some of the party went off at once with the hounds, in the direction he had pointed. The dogs quartered the ground and quickly picked up the scent. Baying, they ran after the hare and the men followed. But when they came to a clearing they were forced to stop. The hounds were milling around the glade in chaos, trying in vain to pick up the scent of the hare, but they seemed baffled and kept returning to a tree stump on which a woman sat, panting, as if she had been running hard.

'"Dead is he, Master Warrick?" she asked the men.

'They gaped at her for the clearing was some distance from where the accident had taken place. But they told her he was.

'"Then my daughter and grandchild are avenged," she said, and walked through the huntsmen back towards the village.

'I knew as soon as I saw them returning that something was amiss, for the party was silent, riding with their heads bowed, and a horse was dragging something behind it on two long poles, covered with Warrick's cloak. I ran down to the courtyard. Before they could stop me, I uncovered the bundle and saw the bloodied face of my husband. The shock was so great that the labour pains came upon me at once. Before the midnight hour on the day her father had died, my sweet Leonia was born. Two spirits passing each other as they made their journeys. But I fear my husband's journey was to Hell for that was where the witch had cursed him to and I know the devil will have claimed his own.'

As I finished my tale, I buried my face in my hands and sobbed. I felt a strong arm slip around my shoulders. Robert's touch was hesitant at first, as if he were afraid I would rebuff him, but as I burrowed into his chest, he drew me tightly against him, pressing his face to the top of my head. At that moment, I knew that if Edith had ever possessed his heart I had taken it from her.

Chapter 13

A witch may calm a storm she has called up by saying, 'I adjure you, Hailstorm and Winds, by the Five Wounds of Christ, by the three nails that pierced his hands and feet, and by the four Evangelists, Matthew, Mark, Luke and John, to dissolve into water and fall down.'

Lincoln

Gunter sat hunched in the corner of the Mermaid Inn. He was in no mood for company, and had no money to spend on ale or food. He'd only entered in the vain hope of catching a whiff of any work that might be going. Most of the men from the quayside drank in the Mermaid, leastways those that had money to spend. If they had money, they had work.

A widow ran the inn. She'd taken over after her husband had been killed trying to break up a fight among his customers. She couldn't afford to be soft, not when she'd a tavern full of river-men and sailors. She'd not allow any man to drink unless he had the money to pay for it in his hand, but neither would she throw out a man who wasn't drinking. She knew well what hard times were.

Gunter had spent the morning trailing from warehouse to warehouse, trying to find a load. In winter few ships put into the port of Boston and the cargoes that were sent downstream to the villages or monasteries had already been assigned to others. When he was a lad, before his parents had died of the Great Pestilence, cargoes were taken by punt up the Foss Dyke to Torksey and York. But that had become impassable long ago, even in winter, to all but tiny craft, and in summer the landowners, including the Bishop of Lincoln, who were supposed to keep it free of silt and weed, had allowed it to become so choked they had even taken to driving their cattle over it. Now all loads heading for York had to go by wagon.

Gunter couldn't face returning home to Nonie just yet. She never uttered a word of reproach, but she searched his face as he came in, and when she saw from it that he'd nothing to give her, her gaze would dart towards the low door in the wall that led directly into the byre. He knew what she was thinking. As soon as the bailiff had left that night, she'd set her hands on her hips and told him she wouldn't sell either of her precious goats.

'Without the goats, come spring there'll be no kids to take to market, no milk or cheese to fill the bairns' bellies. "Sell your gown afore your beasts," my mam always said. The goats stay!'

But Nonie's spare gown wasn't worth twopence, even if they could have found a buyer.

Gunter was aware of voices growing louder at the table in the centre of the inn. He took little notice. Men always became rowdy when ale was flowing. His ears fastened only on the words 'poll tax'. They had been buzzing like trapped wasps in his head these last few weeks.

He glanced up, groaning as he recognised Martin and his oaf of a son, Simon, among the four men at the table. He'd never liked them and not just because of the way they treated poor Alys. He usually found himself in competition with Martin for cargoes, and of late Martin had always seemed to win. Gunter had his suspicions that Fulk, the overseer at the warehouse, was deliberately favouring Martin over the other river-men, though God alone knew why: every boatman on the river reckoned him lazy and careless. His son was a nasty piece of work too. Simple Simon, Hankin called him, but he was always careful to do it well out of earshot, for what the lad lacked in wits he made up for in brawn.

Gunter debated whether to slip out, but thought he'd draw less attention to himself if he remained quietly in the dark corner.

'What's the King going to spend it on? That's what I want to know,' a man demanded. 'Fighting in France. Fighting the bloody Scots. It'll not keep us safe. The French sail here any time they please, set fire to our towns, rape our women, then sail off again with our gold, without any of the King's soldiers lifting a finger to stop them.'

'The King's nowt but a boy of thirteen, scarce out of clouts,' another growled. 'It's his uncle, John of Gaunt. It'll be him behind this, you mark my words. Owns half the country as it is, and he won't rest until he's got his hands on the rest. All of the gold he's got, I reckon he could pay the tax for every Jack and Jill in the land, and he'd still not see the bottom of just one of his chests.'

'Boats'll be sailing on dry land before he'd part with a penny to help any man but himself,' Martin said. 'I reckon we've got to look closer to home if we want justice.' He tapped the side of his crooked nose. 'If the rich take it from us, then we take it back.'

The others grinned. 'Seems fair to me,' the first man said. 'How—'

He broke off as the door of the inn opened and a fresh-faced young girl came in, balancing a tray of pastries on her head. She gazed around uncertainly, evidently searching for the woman who owned the tavern, then wove her way between the benches towards the back.

Martin winked at the man beside him. As the girl drew level with him, he reached out and grabbed her gown, tugging her towards him.

'Here's the trouble, see, lads. Her poor faayther is going to have to pay the King money for her. It doesn't seem right, does it? Tell you what, lass, why don't I pay for you instead? Reckon your faayther would thank me for that.'

Martin's hand slid around her waist, while the other fumbled to drag up the hem of her skirts. The men around him grinned broadly.

'Shall we go out back to that nice little hayloft and have a tumble? And if you're a good girl, you can have my Simon here afterwards too. See he's dribbling already and, believe me, it's not for your pastries.'

The girl, who looked no older than Gunter's own daughter, was close to tears and struggling to push Martin away with her free hand, while still trying to balance the tray of pastries and stop them crashing to the ground. But even a full-grown woman would have been unable to fight off a man the size and strength of Martin. She raised her head, pleading silently with the other customers to help, but they were studying their beakers of ale. No one wanted to take on Martin and his son.

If Gunter had stopped to think, he would have realised he was no match for four strapping men. But all he could see when he looked at the girl's frightened face was his own little Royse. It took him three limping strides to get there, but he could move as fast as any man when his blood was up. He grabbed the back of Martin's jerkin near the neck, pulling it tight against his throat, half throttling him. 'Leave the lass alone!'

Coughing and choking, Martin tried to prise himself free. The girl collided with the bench behind her, spun round and barged to the back of the inn, but Gunter barely had time to register where she'd gone before Martin twisted sideways and slammed a great fist into his belly. He crashed to the floor, doubled up in pain and gasping for breath.

Martin was on his feet and had landed a vicious kick into Gunter's thigh, and was drawing back his boot to strike again when a wolf-hound bounded across the bench and leaped straight for him, snarling and baring its teeth. He stumbled backwards.

'Down, Fury!' a woman's voice commanded.

The dog sank to his haunches, growling its resentment.

The innkeeper's widow stood in the back doorway, grasping a stout, knobbly stave, tipped with a thick band of iron. Not a man in that inn moved a muscle.

'You've a choice, Martin. Take your rabble and get out or I feed your miserable carcass to Fury here. Be warned, he's not had his dinner. What's it to be?'

A long string of drool fell from the hound's mouth and he gave an excited bark.

Martin hesitated. Then, his face contorted with anger, he turned to go. Gunter, still too winded to rise, braced himself, expecting another kick as Martin passed – he would have got it, had Fury not moved between them, baring his teeth again at Martin.

Martin backed away, the others following.

He turned at the door. 'This isn't finished, Gunter. Not by a long way! You won't always have a woman's skirt to hide behind. You'll be sorry you crossed me.'

February

If in February the midges dance on the dunghill, lock up your food in the chest.

Chapter 14

Whenever you eat an egg, you must be sure to crush the shell, or a witch can sail to sea in it and sing up a storm that will cause a ship to founder and all those aboard to drown. For the same reason, you must never utter the word 'egg' on board a ship.

Lincoln

Lincoln has many ghosts like me: Roman soldiers, who march for ever into the treacherous fens from which, in life, they never returned; the Jews, slaughtered on the road as they were driven out of England; the nun, walled up alive for breaking her vow of chastity, who stretches her pale hand out through the solid stone into the street to drag the unwary passer-by into her vertical tomb. Only the night-watch and the beggars sleeping in church porches or huddled in archways see these phantasms. The drunks do too, of course, but they cannot tell a whore's scream from the cry of a vixen, much less the living from the dead. I've even known some of the old tosspots to wave at me and ask me to join them in a flagon of ale, as if we were old friends.

Of course, some men wouldn't notice if a ghost galloped headless and naked through their own bedchamber, banging pots and hurling chairs. And Robert was one of them, but on that particular day he might have been forgiven it, for he had much to occupy his mind. He was pacing his hall impatiently, every so often looking upwards at the ceiling as if he could see through the wood into the bedchamber above. He heard the sound of something being scraped along the boards – the brazier, perhaps, or a table. Was the physician bleeding Edith again?

His wife's health was worsening by the day in spite of all the potions and remedies the physician had prescribed, at no little expense – purging syrups of succory, dandelion, maidenhair and rhubarb; mint water to strengthen the stomach, wormwood to kill any worms of the gut, and dried grasshoppers to ease the colic. During the first week after Hugo Bayus had begun treating her, the pains had seemed to lessen. But now they had returned, and nothing the physician could prescribe or the apothecary prepare eased them.

Robert glanced again at the ceiling. What was taking so long? A messenger had arrived before breakfast saying his son needed him at the warehouse. Infuriatingly Jan had not explained why to the dolt who had been sent to find him. Robert's gullet burned as if he'd drunk too much cheap wine. Had there been some new disaster?

Only last night he'd heard that a shipload of Lombards had arrived in Lincolnshire and were trying to strike bargains with the farmers and the monasteries to buy their fleeces before a single sheep had been shorn. The broggers were up in arms, for as middle men they were being cut right out of the deal and, come spring, they would have no fleeces to sell to the Lincolnshire merchants. If the Lombards succeeded, it could spell ruin for many of the Lincoln men.

Robert stared at the ceiling with mounting irritation. Didn't the man realise he had business to attend to? When he finally heard the physician's heavy tread on the stairs, he strode across the hall, wrenched open the door to the stairs and all but dragged the poor man into the hall in his impatience to hear the verdict.

Hugo Bayus was a small-boned man, with a disproportionately large, spherical head, which seemed all the rounder because he was completely bald. His grey eyes were magnified to the size of hen's eggs behind thick spectacles, which he held up on a long handle, as he peered about the room. He was well respected in his profession, having tended the victims of the Great Pestilence without falling prey to it. Any physician who can cure himself was thought to be worth his weight in gold, and many said, only half in jest, that that was exactly what he charged.

'My wife,' Robert asked, 'how does she fare?'

The old man slowly shook his head. 'Not well, not well at all.'

Robert could not contain himself. 'I'd not have sent for you if I thought she *was* well.'

He knew all physicians liked to present their patients as more gravely ill than they were, not only to increase their fees but also their reputation should the patient be cured, or to excuse failure if they died. Robert was prepared to pay a king's ransom to help his wife, but he disliked being taken for a fool when it came to money.

'Have the goodness to tell me plainly what ails her and what must be done to cure her. I'll pay for whatever physic she needs so long as the price is fair and it brings her to health again.'

'She has a weakness of the stomach,' Hugo said, 'which I fear may have caused the liver to overheat.'

'What can be done for her?'

'I will treat it with rupture-wort, brimstone and dried liver of hare. But . . .' He spread his hands, as if to say that he did not hold out much hope for any of these working.

Robert raked his grey hair. 'Edith's in so much pain, moaning and tossing all night. I've been reduced to sleeping down here with the servants. Is there nothing you can do to calm her?'

'I'll have the apothecary make up a draught of my own devising.' The physician tapped his nose. 'You must instruct your maid to put three drops of it in spirits of wine and give it to her mistress each night. It will soothe the pain and put her into a deep sleep. No more than three drops, for it contains henbane and too much will bring about a sleep from which she will never wake.'

Beata's head appeared around the door. 'The mistress is asking for you, Master Robert.'

The physician tugged his cloak from the chair where he had discarded it and swung it over his shoulders. 'Go to her, Master Robert. Your attention will do as much to soothe her as any of my physic. And, Beata, remember what I said. Your mistress is to be fed tripe, lean beef broth with no fat in it, and a little mashed sheep's brains for strength. On no account is she to have milk, cheese, honey or any sweet thing.'

He turned back to Robert. 'It's known that fretting weakens the stomach. Do all you can to keep her calm and put her mind at ease. Now I must be off, Master Robert. Have your servant call upon the apothecary this afternoon after the None bell. The draught should be ready by then.'

Beata opened the great door for the physician and he scurried out, pausing only to make a little bow to Robert. Gathering up his own cloak, Robert strode to the door, his mind still tormented by what might be amiss at the warehouse.

'Sir, the mistress wants to see you,' Beata reminded him.

Robert sighed heavily, thrust his cloak into her hands and made for the door at the opposite end of the hall, which led to the solar and the bedchamber.

He jerked back in surprise to find Adam standing at the foot of the stairs, staring up to the room where his mother lay.

Robert frowned. 'I thought you'd left for school. You'd better hurry. You don't want a birching for being late.'

Adam swallowed. 'But Mother . . . will she get better?'

Robert pursed his lips. 'Hugo Bayus is the finest physician in Lincoln. We have to trust in his skills . . . and in God, of course,' he added hastily, feeling it his duty as the boy's father to remind him, not that he himself had any great faith. 'You pray for your mother, don't you?'

'Every day and night,' Adam said. 'As hard as I can.'

'That's all you can do. Off to school with you, boy. You don't want to add to your mother's burdens by making her think she has a dunce and a wastrel for a son.'

He had meant it kindly – better that the boy concentrate on his studies and not worry about his mother – but he could see from the way Adam stiffened that he had said the wrong thing. His son was frightened for his mother. She tried to hide her pain whenever he was with her, but too soon she had to send him out of the room.

He knew he should spend more time with the lad, but Adam was always ill at ease and tongue-tied with him. The boy prattled on freely enough with Beata and Tenney, but whenever he summoned his son, Adam stood awkwardly, like a servant waiting for instructions, plainly anxious to get away. It annoyed and hurt Robert when he thought about it, which wasn't often: too many other concerns jostled for attention in his head.

Robert watched his son retreat out of the door, then climbed the wooden stairs. He paused outside the heavy door, steeling himself for what lay beyond. He took a deep breath and stepped inside.

The stench hit him as soon as he entered. The windows were closed tightly against the cold and pastilles of incense and thyme burned on the small brass brazier, but that did little to mask the odour of Edith's breath, which filled the room like rotting fish guts. His wife lay in the four-poster bed, propped up on bolsters and pillows, a linen cap tied beneath her chin. Each time he saw her Robert was appalled at how thin and drawn she had become in such a short time. Her pallid skin was dry and withered, like that of a woman twice her age. Her eyes were dull with pain and lack of sleep.

'Robert?' She patted the cover beside her, inviting him to sit on the bed.

102

He took a few paces into the room and forced a smile, but he did not sit down. 'How are you feeling, my dear? You look brighter today.' It was a lie, but he meant well.

She smiled weakly. 'I'm a little stronger. I think I shall be well enough to get up this afternoon.'

'You must stay in bed. Hugo said you were to rest and Beata said you hardly slept last night.'

Edith coughed in the smoke from the brazier, wincing and clutching her belly. It was several moments before she could speak again. 'I was worried about you, Robert . . . Beata said you were sleeping in the hall, but you didn't come to see me . . . say goodnight . . . I know Beata sometimes keeps it from me when you're late coming home. She thinks I fret.'

'I didn't want to disturb you.'

Edith jerked as a wave of pain rolled through her. Then she lay back, panting. 'Tell me the truth, Robert. You're not still visiting *her*, are you?'

Robert rounded on her: 'Stop this, Edith! Why are you tormenting yourself? I swear constantly gnawing on your suspicions is making you ill. Hugo practically said as much. I've told you a hundred times, my business with Mistress Catlin was concluded long ago. These fancies are in your head, and the sooner you banish them, the sooner you'll be well. And now, if there's nothing you need, I must go. I'm wanted urgently at the warehouse.'

'You are wanted here too, Robert,' Edith said softly, as he turned to the door. 'Won't you kiss me, husband?'

Angry with her for delaying him and her insane jealousy, it was all Robert could do to stop himself striding from the room and slamming the door behind him. But he turned and forced himself to take the few paces to her bed. He bent and brushed his lips to her forehead with distaste. Her skin smelt sour. As he straightened, he saw something lying on the creamy linen pillow. It was a lock of dyed yellow hair, white at the root. Only then did he notice other strands caught on the bolster and covers. Edith's hair was falling out in handfuls. Swallowing hard, and blinking back tears, he kissed her again, with a tenderness he had not shown her for a long time.

Robert spotted his son standing near a wagon by the doorway to the warehouse. Even from a distance he could see he was in a dark humour.

He was bellowing at a clerk, who repeatedly held up his tally sticks in an attempt to ward off the other man's wrath.

Robert leaped forward to avoid being brained by a man carrying several long planks on his shoulder, and approached the pair. 'Trouble, Jan?'

His son frowned. 'Two bales short, but this cod-wit keeps telling me it was a full load.'

'It was,' the man protested. 'You can see for yourself. The notches match. There is nothing missing.'

'Except that they *are* missing!' Jan retorted.

Robert elbowed him aside. 'I think you would be well advised, Master Clerk, to count them again or perhaps you'd like my steward to count them for you with his staff across your back. Would that teach you your numbers?'

The clerk scooted off like a frightened rabbit.

Jan spun round to face his father. 'I don't need to be told how to handle my men. I was dealing with it.'

'*My* men,' Robert corrected. 'You've many things to learn yet, boy, before they become *yours* and one is to make men so terrified of your very shadow that they dare not slacken even when your back is turned. If you did that, we wouldn't have stock going missing!' He scowled at one of the paggers to emphasise the point. 'Now, you sent word for me to come. Is something amiss besides those bales?'

Jan's cheeks flushed a dull red and his eyes were blazing as fiercely as his father's. 'I sent word over an hour ago.'

'I was detained speaking to Hugo Bayus about your mother.'

Guilt and anxiety instantly replaced the anger in Jan's face. 'What did he say? Is she any better?'

Robert tried to push away the pitiful vision of the bright yellow hair lying on the pillow.

'He says he knows what ails her now. An overheated liver. He's treating her with a new remedy. She'll be well again soon.' Robert was by no means as confident of that as he sounded, but it wouldn't help business to have Jan distracted from his work. 'The boy you sent didn't say why you wanted to see me, and you still haven't told me.'

'I didn't tell him,' Jan said quietly. 'I thought it best that as few people as possible hear, in case it gives the others ideas.'

He led his father to the side of the warehouse, glancing around warily to make sure they were not overheard. 'Tom, our rent collector, didn't return home the night before last. His wife was concerned, but the neighbours told her he was probably holed up in some tavern somewhere.'

Robert frowned. 'Tom's not a man for the drink. I'd have never given him the job if I thought he was. Too much temptation having a scrip full of coins. Hugh de Garwell employed a rent collector who was over-fond of wine—'

Jan interrupted: 'Yesterday afternoon when Tom still hadn't come back the neighbours agreed to help her search and took a couple of dogs with them. But they couldn't find hide nor hair, though they searched as long as the light held. They were on their way home when one of the dogs started barking at something floating in one of the marsh-pools. They thought it was an old sack at first, then realised it was a body. It would have sunk right to the bottom except that the clothes had snagged on a dead tree half submerged in the water. It was Tom, all right. They think whoever dumped him in there had done it in the dark and couldn't see properly where they were pitching him. There was a fair bit of mist on the marshes, the night he went missing.'

'Then isn't it likely he blundered into the bog himself?' Robert said.

'He was found too far from solid ground. If he'd been floundering in there, he'd have been able to grab a hold of the tree. Besides, a man doesn't get marks like that on his body from falling into a bog. He'd been beaten, and I don't just mean a black eye. He was covered with bruises from head to toe. They say if he wasn't dead when he was thrown in, he was as close to it as pork is to pig's meat.'

Robert shook his head. 'This is a bad business. You think he was set upon by footpads and robbed? They're becoming more daring by the day. Remember that friar who was hanging round the warehouse? I swear I've seen him lurking in the street where Mistress . . .'

Jan's chin jerked up and he eyed his father with suspicion.

'. . . lurking in the streets,' Robert finished lamely. 'He could have followed Tom, if he'd been watching men's movements, waiting for a chance to steal.'

Jan nodded. 'I was followed, too, one evening, coming back from Greetwell. I reckon it could well have been the man we saw at the warehouse. But as for him attacking Tom . . .' Jan frowned. 'Bailiff's certainly convinced it was thieves and that's what the men who found

105

Tom are saying too, but I'm not so sure. His purse had been cut from the straps, but if it was a band of robbers, they usually rip a man's tunic off, see if he's any ingots or valuables strapped to his chest. His shirt was still in place and his belt. He'd not been searched. And if a robber wanted to kill a man he thought might identify him, he'd stab him or slit his throat. A beating takes too long and it's noisy. Anyone might chance upon them while it's happening.'

'A tavern brawl that went too far?' Robert said dubiously.

'You said yourself, Father, that Tom wasn't a man for taverns or drinking. No, I think it's more serious than that. His wife said he'd gone to the cottages along the river at Greetwell. Three of them didn't pay their rent for the second quarter in a row. He was following your orders, Father. Went to give them warning they'd be out if they didn't pay up next quarter and Tom wasn't a man to butter his words. From what I've heard there'd been mutterings against him before.'

'You think the cottagers beat him to death?' Robert was shocked. In the past month a number of the landowners had reported dung being thrown at their rent-collectors' houses, their children tormented, even the odd hen killed or vegetables spoiled, especially if they were thought to favour their own kin or hounded those who couldn't pay. But murder? No cottager would dare such an attack on those in authority.

'Have the cottagers been questioned?'

Jan nodded grimly. 'They have, but they're sticking together, like burrs on a dog's backside. They've sworn by every saint in Christendom he never arrived at their doors that evening. The constable's got men out searching for a gang of robbers and they may well find some too, but it doesn't mean they're guilty of this murder. But if the cottagers get away with it, and it looks like they will, what's to stop others doing the same? I warned you there'd be trouble if you raised the rents.'

'If they or you think I shall be intimidated into lowering them, you'd better think again,' Robert thundered. 'Give in to the knaves over this and next they'll be demanding I let them live there for free and pay them a king's ransom to punt my cargoes a few yards down-river. I'll speak to the sheriff and see that he questions them again, more robustly this time. In the meantime, you had better find another rent-collector. Make sure he goes out well armed and takes one of our paggers with him to watch his back. They're strong enough to hold their own against the boatmen. See to it, will you?'

'If I can find any pagger willing to go once the word spreads,' Jan said darkly.

'If any man refuses to do as he's bade, sack him! There are plenty who'd be only too willing to take his place. If you're not to send my business straight into the ditch, you must be tougher with these men.'

Chapter 15

If a person or animal is bewitched, their nail parings or hair must
be added to their urine, which must be boiled in a closed room,
but this will only break the spell if every entrance and hole in the
room has been sealed shut.

Lincoln

I drift through the marketplace, looking for excitement. But excitement comes from danger, from not knowing what lies around the corner. There is no danger in being dead. Unseen, I pull an apple from a pile and listen to the shrieks of rage as the whole stack tumbles and bounces into the street and the urchins, who will be blamed, scrabble to snatch them.

I see a butcher cheat a poor old woman by swapping the juicy chop she'd chosen for one that's as dried-out as old shoe leather. Mavet, my ferret, bites the butcher's ankle. He gives a startled howl and the knife in his hand slips, slicing his finger. That is funny, but there's no danger in it, not for me or Mavet, though I can't say the same for the butcher.

But for the living, danger lurks around every corner, and it wears the most innocent of masks. They seldom recognise it for what it is, until it's too late.

It was already dark by the time Robert left the Braytheforde and set off for home. A misty rain was falling, clinging in tiny beads to clothing and making the cobbles treacherous. Toiling up the street, Robert, though used to the steep incline, felt a heavy reluctance to face it tonight. The last of the shopkeepers were busy pushing up the counters of their stalls and fastening them over the shop fronts to form shutters. In the rooms over the shops, candles and rush lights burned and the air was thick with peat and woodsmoke, infused with a hundred different cooking smells.

Beggars drifted across the city, like flocks of ragged birds, forsaking their daytime feeding grounds around the markets for their nightly roosts in archways, alleys and church gates. Those citizens lucky enough to have homes, however mean, were hurrying to reach them, anticipating warm fires and steaming suppers. Others, weary after their day's labours, dragged themselves, in two and threes, towards the taverns and whorehouses.

Robert, aware of his dry throat and growling belly, was sorely tempted to join them. He knew he should return home to sit with his wife, but each time he saw her, it only increased his sense of helplessness and failure. Watching her cry in pain, and being unable to relieve it, was more than he could bear. He'd always been able to provide the best for her, had prided himself on it, but no matter how much he spent on cures and remedies, it was all useless, as if Edith's sickness mocked the wealth he had worked so hard for all these years. Just as he had been unable to take away her grief at losing her babies, he could do nothing now to help her, nothing. He felt rejected, shut out from her suffering, just as he had done when she had been grieving for her lost babies. He was her husband: he should be able to make her world safe, but he couldn't.

As if his legs had made their own decision, Robert found he had turned aside from his usual route and was wandering down Hungate, without any thought as to where he was going. He had almost reached the last house when he stopped. A small familiar carving of a horned imp grinned down at him from the arched door lintel.

He found himself picturing Catlin's sweet face, her smile, which greeted him whenever she saw him standing on her threshold. He couldn't remember the last time anyone had smiled in his house, much less on seeing him. A brief visit couldn't hurt. It was only common courtesy, since he was passing, to enquire if all was well. He wouldn't stay. He wouldn't even sit down.

Robert stared up and down the length of Hungate. Save for a couple of stray dogs snarling at each other as they fought for possession of some scrap, the darkened street was empty. The shutters over Maud's windows were tightly fastened against the cold, though that didn't mean she wouldn't have an eye pressed to the crack. With one final glance around to ensure that no one was abroad, Robert rapped at the door.

Diot flung it open. 'Thank Heaven you've come, Master Robert. The mistress'll be so relieved, she's in such a state.'

'Is she ill?' Robert said in alarm.

He didn't wait for an answer. He squeezed past the stout old woman into the small hall. Catlin was sitting by the fire, both hands clasped around a steaming beaker of mulled ale. Her face was pale, her lips dry.

'Robert, thank God. I've been so worried.'

Robert crossed the room in a couple of strides and, with some difficulty, knelt in front of her and clasped his hands around her own. 'What is it? What's happened? You look as if you've seen an apparition.'

He could feel Catlin's fingers trembling beneath his. Even the heat from the beaker didn't seem to be warming them. He took the cup from her and gently chafed her hands.

'I thought he'd harm you, Robert. I didn't know what to do.'

'Who? Who would harm me?' Robert was starting to feel as frightened as she looked. His rent-collector had been viciously murdered. Was someone now threatening to do the same to him?

'A friar . . . A dreadful man, with a horrible voice. He came begging at the door. I gave him what I could spare . . . but then he spoke your name, Robert. He seemed to be looking for you. I slammed the door at once.'

She clutched at his shoulder. 'Oh, Robert, I was so afraid for you and then just now Leonia went out into the yard and she found . . . she found the puppy you gave her lying dead. See for yourself.'

Reluctant though he was to leave Catlin, Robert lumbered to his feet and trudged out into the dark courtyard. The fine rain swirled in the wind, but Leonia seemed oblivious to the cold or damp. She was crouching on the wet stones prodding something that lay at her feet. Robert took a lantern from the wall and held it over the dark mass on the ground. The glassy eyes of the dog glinted in the lamplight, but he could see at once there was no life in them. He'd no desire to touch the creature, but he steeled himself to grasp a cold paw between finger and thumb and roll it over onto its back. He held the lantern lower. A dark wet stain covered the belly and throat of the dog, but it wasn't rain that had soaked its fur: it was blood.

Leonia pointed. 'Someone must have stabbed him. They did it four times, I counted. Look!'

She spread the bloody fur with her little hand and poked her finger into one of the deep puncture wounds in the puppy's throat.

'Don't touch it!' Robert snapped, and Leonia looked up at him in mild surprise, her fingers smeared with scarlet.

Robert was startled, not just by the savagery of the attack, but by the calm in the child's voice, as if she were more curious than upset. He had no time for children who cried at the slightest thing but, having no daughters of his own, he had always assumed that girls were given to shrieking at the sight of a mouse, let alone a viciously slaughtered pet.

He pulled the child to her feet, glancing uneasily around him in the darkness, but the gate leading to the lane beyond was barred and the little yard too small for anyone to be concealed in it. 'We'd better get you inside, child. You shouldn't be out here alone, not . . . after this.'

At that moment, Diot came hurrying out and enveloped Leonia in her arms, holding her tightly against her great breasts as she bustled the girl towards the door. 'Upstairs with you and I'll bring you a nice posset to help you sleep.' She turned back to Robert, shaking her head. 'I thought the fox was wicked enough, Master Robert, but what's the world coming to if they can do that to a defenceless dog?'

'He wasn't defenceless, Diot,' Leonia protested. 'He could bite. He bit me hard!'

'That makes it all the worse, then,' Diot said. 'If they can stab a dog that can fight back, what chance do we have? We'll all be murdered in our beds.'

Robert, somewhat shaken, made his way back into the hall where Catlin was still hunched by the fire. He went to the laver that stood in the corner, rubbing his hands in the water over and over again as if he was trying to wash away the image of the child's blood-stained fingers.

The old woman's words at last penetrated his mind and he turned towards Catlin. 'Diot said something about a fox.'

Catlin rose and handed him a linen cloth to dry his dripping hands. 'A few weeks ago she found a sack with a dead fox in it. It had been decapitated, and its muzzle was tied with periwinkle, or so she swears. She was convinced it was some kind of a death-threat. Edward persuaded me it was just boys playing pranks, but after today . . . Robert, I think Diot might have been right. It was a warning. It must have been the friar who did this. But I don't understand. Why would this man threaten you, Robert? Has he a grudge against you?'

111

Robert raked his hair distractedly. 'There are always men who think they had the worst of some business deal, but I can't recall having any dealings with a friar. They don't sell wool and they don't have the money to buy the quality of cloth that I sell. Nor would they wear it.' His frown deepened. 'But if it's the same man who was hanging about the warehouse a few weeks back, he may not even be in Holy Orders. I think he's one of a gang of thieves. We've had a lot of goods stolen over the past months and one of my men was found . . .' He trailed off, realising he would terrify Catlin even more if she learned that his rent-collector had been murdered. 'You saw the man at the warehouse, the first day we met. Was it the same man you saw tonight?'

She gnawed her lip. 'I didn't see his face at the warehouse, or even properly tonight – his hood was drawn low – but I'm sure the robe was the same. And I've seen someone dressed like that several times, here on this street. It's distinctive, not like the robes of the other friars who beg in Lincoln. He obviously knows you come here. Perhaps he's trying to trap you, follow you into some alley in the dark.'

Robert sank into a chair. Suppose this man and his gang had murdered the rent-collector not simply for the money he had been carrying but as a ghastly warning to Robert himself. Now he'd unwittingly brought grave danger to the door of this defenceless woman. He'd never forgive himself if any harm came to her or to Leonia.

'I'll report this to Sheriff Thomas at once, tonight, and insist his men hunt down this fiend. First thing tomorrow I intend to hire a burly manservant for you, Mistress Catlin, one who knows how to use a weapon. I shall pay his wages myself.'

Seeing she was about to protest, he wagged a finger sternly. 'No buts, Mistress Catlin, he will stay in the house at least until that felon is caught. He and your son should be able to fend off any attack. But you must not go out alone, not even to the market. Promise me that.'

'I'll see to it that my two precious angels are not left alone for a minute, you can be sure of that,' Diot said, shuffling in with a rabbit pie and a jug of wine. She set them on a small table next to Robert's chair. 'Now, Master Robert, there's nothing like a good wedge of pie to settle the stomach after a shock.'

Catlin smiled wanly at Robert as the maid waddled out again. 'Diot thinks food is the answer to every problem in the world, bless her.'

She rose, came over to the table and cut Robert a generous slice. 'But it's you I'm concerned about, Robert. It is you who needs the guard, not me. You should take an armed linkman with you when you walk abroad at night.'

Robert grimaced. 'Edith said as much some weeks ago.'

'And how is the poor creature? Is she any better?'

Not for the first time Robert marvelled at Catlin's generosity of spirit. There weren't many women in the world who, after such an upsetting encounter, would show concern for another's troubles. 'Alas, she grows weaker each day. Hugo Bayus keeps trying new remedies, but I see no improvement.'

'I'm sure he will find the right physic soon. You must try not to worry, my poor sweeting, but I can see that you do. You are exhausted. Is this news of the Lombard merchants vexing you?'

'How the devil do you know about that?' Robert stared at her. She never stopped amazing him. 'I have only just learned of it myself.'

Catlin smiled. 'I passed through the beast market this morning. I heard one of the farmers talking about the Lombards trying to buy fleeces before the shearing. Is it true?'

'It is, devil take them.' Robert drained his goblet and set it down hard. 'God's blood, those foreigners are stealing our own English wool from under our noses. As if we weren't having a hard enough time of it already, with the Flanders weavers in rebellion.'

Catlin slid out of her chair and came to stand behind Robert, tenderly massaging his temples. 'Then there is only one thing to be done. You must go out on the road yourself. You know this shire better than any Lombard merchant. You told me once you could tell which fleeces had come from which farm by looking at them. Buy them before the Lombards discover them. I'm sure the abbots and farmers would sooner deal with an honest Englishman than a foreigner, who's likely to sail away with their fleeces and their money.'

'Would that I could!' Robert caught her soft little hand and kissed it. 'But with Edith so sick, I can't leave her and I can't spare Jan to go. He's enough to deal with here. There's been some trouble with the tenants.'

'Then Jan must stay and you must go. It would be safer in any case for you to be out of Lincoln, if this mad friar is watching you. He could hardly follow you if you were on horseback, and the sheriff will catch him long before you return.'

As Robert opened his mouth to explain again why that was impossible, she pressed her finger to his lips. 'I will take care of Edith while you are gone. I nursed my dear mother and father for many years before they died. I'm not without skill in the sickroom. Besides, a woman much prefers another of her own sex to be with her when she's ill. There are certain needs that no woman can confide to a man. And no wife wants her husband to see her when she's not at her best.'

Robert, his headache easing and his whole body relaxing into a blissful stupor under her expert touch, had no doubt as to Catlin's skill. And it would certainly give him peace of mind to think that she was safely under his roof, with Tenney and Beata to watch over her, for his house was far more secure than this one.

He shook himself. What was he thinking? Edith was so unreasonably and insanely jealous of Catlin that he feared she would sooner throw herself down the stairs than let Catlin into her house.

'You're an angel, my dear, but I'm afraid Edith would never agree. She's allowed herself to be persuaded by those with venomous tongues that you and I . . . that we . . . are more than business acquaintances.'

'As indeed we are, for I've come to look upon you as a friend, a very dear friend, as I hope you regard me.'

She moved to the table, refilling the two goblets with wine. She handed one to him and stood before him, looking down at him with a sad smile. Even through her gown, he could feel the soft warmth of her leg pressing against his thigh.

'But, Robert, we know we've done nothing to reproach ourselves for, nothing that would give truth to the lies she's heard or imagined in her poor fevered brain.' She reached down and gently caressed his cheek. 'I'd never betray one of my own sex. I've felt the pain of such treachery only too sharply myself, as well you know.'

It was beyond Robert's imagining that any man lucky enough to have been blessed with such a woman as Catlin for a wife could ever betray her in another woman's bed. Not for the first time since she had confided in him, he wished Warrick still lived so that he could thrash him to death with a horsewhip. He deserved no less.

'I've told my wife a thousand times that our friendship is entirely chaste and innocent, but she refuses to believe me.'

'Then the solution is simple,' Catlin said. 'We will not tell her who I am. You will explain to Edith that you have asked a gentlewoman to come as her companion to stay with her while you're away on business. She's never seen me. I will use some other name. Why should she suspect? It's a deception, I know, but a harmless one and for her own good.'

Robert beamed at her. Then his face clouded. 'But Jan has met you. He'd recognise you.'

'Of course he would. He's a dear boy and he'll be relieved that someone is there to care for his mother. I think he'll be delighted you have shown enough faith in him to leave him in charge of the warehouse. I saw for myself that he longs for a looser rein when he is handling your business affairs and he will see this as a way to earn your trust and prove himself as a man. He'll not want to let you down. And with me there to relieve him of the worry of his mother, he'll be able to spend all the hours he needs on the business.' She clapped her hands as if an idea had just occurred to her. 'Why don't you let me speak to Jan myself, tomorrow, at the warehouse? I'm sure I can help him see that this is the best solution for both of you.'

Robert caught her hand and kissed the soft, warm palm. 'I'm sure you can. You, my dear, could persuade a man to anything.'

Catlin bent and brushed her lips against his forehead in a chaste kiss. He could smell the rose perfume between her breasts and it took all his willpower not to pull her into his lap and enfold her in his arms.

'That's settled then, Robert. Who knows? By the time you return, Edith will have learned to love me as a sister and realise there were no grounds for her suspicions.'

Chapter 16

*Whoever steps upon the grave of an unbaptised child will be
infected with grave-scab, which some call grave-merels. His skin
shall burn, his breathing be laboured, his limbs tremble, and soon
he will die.*

Beata

I thought it a queer business for a man to bring his mistress into his
house to take care of his wife, and I had half a mind to say something
to Mistress Edith, but the dear soul was so sick, I didn't want to add
to her troubles. As it was, she fretted herself half to death whenever
Master Robert was away, one moment afeared he'd been robbed and
murdered, the next that he might be in the company of Mistress
Catlin or some other woman. Her fancies had grown worse since
she'd taken to her bed for she'd little else to think about, save where
her husband and sons might be at any hour. She imagined a hundred
deaths lying in wait for them while she was not there to protect them.

Like Master Robert said, dwelling on her fears was making her
worse, sickening her stomach like a piece of resty pork. It was Master
Robert, of course, who insisted Edith shouldn't know that Mistress
Catlin had come to take care of her. He told Tenney and me who
she was, 'cause he knew fine rightly we'd find out sooner or later:
someone was bound to recognise her. You can no more keep a secret
in Lincoln than you can stop bad smells rising from a midden and,
besides, Master Jan had met her, so he was sure to say something.
Even a blind mare in the dark could have seen Master Jan was none
too pleased about the arrangement, but he'd been talked into keeping
quiet like the rest of us.

We were to call her Mistress Mariot and not utter her real name
in front of either Adam or Edith, for Adam couldn't be trusted not
to tell his mother, or so Master Robert said.

'Well, the master needn't think I'm going along with it,' I said indignantly to Tenney, as soon as we were alone. 'I'll not have my mistress deceived, not while I'm maid in this house.'

'You go saying anything to Mistress Edith and you'll not remain a maid in this house for so much as a day after the master returns. Then where will you be? Begging on the streets, is where. And if I know the master he'll see you never find another position, not in these parts at any rate. He's got a longer reach than the devil.'

'But to move his mistress in. It's not decent,' I protested, now in even more of a cob for knowing Tenney was right.

'Master says she's not his mistress, just a friend, a widow he's been helping,' Tenney said.

'And you believe that? You men all stick together. You think we women are as green as cabbage and we'll believe anything you tell us. Well, I know the master's been at that widow's house when he's sworn to the mistress he hasn't.'

Tenney groaned. 'Only 'cause he knows Mistress Edith is just like you. She's only to see a leaf fall to imagine the whole tree's about to crash down after it. You and me, we see each other morning, noon and night, even sleep in the same hall, and there's nowt going on between us. So why should there be anything 'twixt the master and this widow?'

I winced when he said that for I'd have climbed into Tenney's bed any time he asked me, and there was a time when I'd thought he might, for he seemed to have a fondness for me – but look at me: I'm nowt but a gargoyle. Once, years ago, I heard a man say they should stick me in the fields to frighten the crows and never was a truer word spoken.

But Catlin turned out to be no beauty herself. I was expecting this pretty young creature, with her breasts pushed up high, the kind of wench you see flaunting herself in the taverns, but she looked quite ordinary to me, respectable, even. She wore the kind of well-cut gowns Mistress Edith wore, though they looked far more fetching on her than they did on my poor mistress. Tenney's tongue was dragging on the ground, of course, soon as he caught sight of her. But a half-decent woman has only got to smile at a man for him to melt like butter in the sun.

I was as prickly as a thorn bush when she first arrived. I certainly wasn't going to give her any encouragement. But when I saw how tenderly she treated my mistress and how motherly she tried to be towards little Adam, I couldn't help warming to her a little. And you could see Jan was softening as well, for he was no different from any other man. They all slide into a puddle of wax when a woman flatters them.

The same couldn't be said for young Adam. He resented any stranger going anywhere near his mam, and after Catlin gently shooed him from the room, because Mistress Edith needed to sleep, Adam sulked so fierce that he'd only answer her in single words. But the widow never once lost her temper with the lad or scolded him, however rude he was to her.

A few days after Widow Catlin arrived, I came home from the market to find the yard deserted. Adam was at school. Tenney and the stable-boy had gone to collect a cartload of wood. I guessed Widow Catlin must be sitting with my mistress. I put my basket in the kitchen, then crossed the courtyard to the main house, intending to take the physic I'd collected from the apothecary straight up to the mistress's bedchamber.

But as I stepped through the door into the hall, I saw a stranger standing by the fireplace, with one of my master's best silver goblets in his hand. My heart jumped, like a frog on a baker's oven, and I gave a yelp. The man jerked round and started towards me. I grabbed the first thing I could lay my hands on, a spiked bronze candlestick in the form of a little manikin, and brandished it in front of me. Master Robert had warned us to look out for a friar known to be one of a gang of murderous thieves who had already tried to attack him. Not that this man looked like a friar, but he might have been one of his gang.

I was on the verge of yelling for help, but I didn't want to frighten Mistress Edith, who lay in the chamber directly above.

'Stay back,' I warned. 'You needn't think because I'm a woman I'll not use it. I'm well used to defending myself.'

'I don't doubt that for a moment.' He backed away a pace, holding up his hands. 'A comely woman like you must have had to fight off many advances in her time,' he said, staring at my pocked skin.

I knew he was mocking me and felt my face grow hot. 'I've sent for the bailiff,' I lied. 'He'll be here with armed men at any moment. So, if you know what's good for you, you'll give me back what you stole and get out of here afore they arrive, 'less you want to find yourself wearing the hangman's necklace.'

'I'm quite content to wait for the bailiff and his men,' he said, grinning impudently. 'I swear, upon my mother's life, I'm as innocent as the Virgin Mary.'

He had the effrontery to saunter over to the master's high-backed chair and flop into it, bold as you like, patting the chair next to it. 'Why don't you sit with me, my beauty? I'm sure there's much we could talk about to keep ourselves amused while we wait.'

I couldn't believe the man's nerve. 'If you've stolen nothing, it's only because I came in and caught you. No honest man would break into a house.'

I noticed that the flagon of wine that had been on the chest was now on the table. I lifted it to return it to its place and felt at once that it was empty. 'That proves it. You are a thief. That was half full this morning.'

He smiled. 'I will admit to taking a drink. But I trust you'll forgive a guest helping themselves to refreshment. My thirst got the better of my manners, but I'm sure your mistress would not object.'

'Guest, is it?' I snorted. 'No one's said anything to me about guests.'

He was a good-looking man, but then rogues usually are, and he certainly had the silver tongue of a trickster. I was at a loss to know what to do, for he clearly wasn't going to leave. The only thing I could think was to run out into the street and try to grab some passer-by to help me. I was on the point of doing just that when I heard footsteps crossing the wooden floor above me.

I ran towards the stairs to call a warning to Widow Catlin, but before I could reach the door, he'd sprung from the chair and clamped a hand across my mouth. With the other he grabbed my wrist and dragged me back until I was pinned against his chest. He suddenly twisted my arm, making the candlestick clatter to the ground.

I felt his breath on my ear. 'I want to surprise her,' he whispered. 'Don't spoil it, there's a good girl.'

I heard Catlin's light tread on the stairs and he pulled me back behind the door. As soon as she came through it, he kicked it shut and released me, shoving me hard away from him, so that I fell to my knees on the wooden floor.

Catlin gave a tiny cry, which broke off so abruptly, it was as if her breath had been snatched away.

'I found him here when I returned,' I told her, clambering to my feet and rubbing my bruises. 'I reckon he's one of that robber gang Master Robert warned us about—'

Catlin gave that little laugh of hers, like falling shards of glass. 'The only thing my son steals is women's hearts. Isn't that right, Edward?'

The man gave her a kiss. Then he turned and offered me a low bow, as if I were a noblewoman. 'My humble apologies, mistress. When I saw you waving that candlestick, like an ancient warrior queen, I couldn't resist seeing what you might do next to defend your master's castle.'

'You'll have to forgive my son, Beata. He enjoys playing games.'

Widow Catlin was not looking at me, but at Edward, unable to suppress a fond smile. 'Beata might have brained you, Edward, and you'd have had no one to blame but yourself. Anyway, what brings you here?' Her expression turned grave. 'Is there trouble at home? Has someone been into the yard again?'

'I came to see you, little Maman. I'm desolate without you and I wanted to see how things were progressing here. How is Mistress Edith?'

A slight frown creased Widow Catlin's forehead, and for the first time since she had come downstairs she took her eyes from her son and looked at me. 'I came to fetch Edith some of the pig's blood broth you made earlier. She thinks she might be able to swallow a little now. Would you heat some for her?'

It was as plain as the balls on a bull that she wanted to tell her son something about Mistress Edith that she wouldn't say in front of me and that straightway put me in a cob. Anything she had to say about *my* mistress should be said to me, not a stranger. And I reckoned Master Robert wouldn't be pleased if he knew this son of hers was poking around among his things.

So I took my time. I crouched to pick up the fallen candlestick, replaced it on the chest and arranged it just so, then ambled to the door leading to the courtyard. Behind me, I heard Edward whispering something to his mam. They laughed, and I knew he had made some joke at my expense. He might be good-looking, and his mam evidently doted on him, but there was something about young Edward that made me shudder, as if someone had walked over my grave.

Chapter 17

If a patient is bleeding and the flow cannot be staunched, a blood-stained bandage must be taken to the house of a known blood charmer. Let the blood charmer bless the bandage and let it be taken back to the patient and bound again about him and the bleeding shall stop.

Mistress Catlin

Without warning Edith's back arched so violently I feared it would break. The bedposts rattled as her limbs jerked in convulsions. I shouted for Beata, who came running up the stairs. Scarlet blood ran from Edith's lips and trickled down her chin as she ground her jaw. I seized a rolled linen bandage and tried to force it into her mouth to stop her biting her tongue, but I could not prise her jaws apart. Beata stood helplessly in the doorway, staring at her mistress. She looked so stricken that I feared she might swoon.

'Stinking motherwort, Beata. Is there any in the house?'

She nodded, unable to tear her eyes from Edith's thrashing body. 'Then fetch it quickly.'

I gave her a little push towards the door, which seemed to bring her to her senses, and she ran from the room.

The convulsions began to ease. Edith's body relaxed a little and she lay trembling, her eyes closed and her face deathly pale. Beata burst back into the room and breathed a great sigh of relief on seeing that the fit had nearly passed. I took the small flask from her and examined the fragment of dried plant that had been tied to it, checking that Beata had found the right oil.

'Hold her head up,' I instructed. I waved the flask under Edith's nose and, almost at once, she began to mumble and her eyelids fluttered.

'Add three drops to a little water,' I instructed Beata, 'and help me to spoon it down her.'

We managed to dribble the liquid into the corner of Edith's mouth and I massaged her throat to help her swallow. Exhausted, she lay back on the pillow. Her clawed hand shot out and seized my arm, gripping it with a strength that hardly seemed possible in one so frail.

'Great black cat . . . was sitting on my chest . . . getting heavier and heavier . . . couldn't breathe. It's her . . . it's her – she sent it!' Her shaking finger was pointing at Beata. 'It's her bid . . . It's an imp . . . imp from Hell . . . I've seen her feeding it.'

Beata gaped at her. 'Mistress, I haven't any cat. There's not been a beast of any kind come near your chamber.'

The maid moved closer to the bed, reaching out to soothe Edith, but her mistress shrank away from her, clinging to my arm and cringing against me.

'Don't let her near me . . . She's trying to kill me. Get her away! Get her away from me!'

Beata looked thoroughly alarmed, as well she might. 'Mistress, it's me, Beata. You know I'd sooner cut off my own arm than harm you.'

But Edith continued to shriek in fear and I could do nothing to calm her.

'Beata, you should leave her,' I said firmly. 'Your presence seems to distress her.'

Casting a last look at her mistress, the maid hurried into the solar beyond the bedchamber. I stepped out with her and pulled the door shut behind us. I patted her shoulder.

'I'm sure your mistress doesn't know what she's saying, Beata. I'll soak a cloth in lavender water to lay on her forehead. It'll help her to sleep. Perhaps it would be best if you stay out of the chamber for a while, just until she is in her own mind again. If she becomes agitated, it might bring on another fit.'

Beata darted another frightened glance at the door, then scuttled across the solar and down the stairs. I stared after her. Did poor Edith really have cause to fear her maid? She seemed terrified of her. Was Beata hurting or threatening her when they were alone? From now on I would ensure that Beata was never left alone with her mistress.

It was plain that Edith was growing worse by the day. Her face was so thin and yellow that it looked as if an ancient skull lay on the pillow, not a living creature. Thin dark lids were closed over her eyes, but beneath them, the eyeballs moved restlessly as if they had been transformed into a mass of scurrying insects. I had cropped what remained of her hair and tied a linen cap tightly beneath her chin, wrapping a linen band around her forehead to stop her slipping her fingers beneath. I had cut her nails almost to the quick, but still she clawed at the skin as if she was trying to tear it from her skull, crying that her head was on fire and her flesh was burning. Rusty spots of blood oozed from the sores on her scalp and stained the white linen.

I heard heavy footsteps crossing the solar and thought Beata was returning. I hastened to the door to prevent her from entering and frightening Edith again, but it was Jan who was approaching. I stepped into the solar, pulling the door to the bedchamber closed behind me.

'Your mother's exhausted. You'd do well to let her rest.'

Jan glanced anxiously over my shoulder at the closed door. 'Beata says she was seized by convulsions.'

'She was, but they've passed now. She sleeps peacefully.'

'But I don't understand.' He raked his fingers distractedly through his hair, as Robert did. 'I sent for the nuns from the infirmary of St Magdalene to care for my mother. Where are they? Why didn't they come? When Tenney took the message yesterday, the prioress told him they'd be here within the hour. I'll have to send Tenney again to fetch them.'

'The nuns came as they promised, but when they examined your poor mother they swore she has a fever of the brain, which has sent her mad. They insisted she should be kept naked without coverings on her bed or a brazier in the chamber, and doused repeatedly in icy water, which they said brings the mad to their senses.'

'My mother's not mad!' Jan shouted. 'She has a sickness of the stomach, as Hugo Bayus told us.'

'Hush now, Jan. There's no need to fret.' I pressed my fingers to his cheek soothingly, as I would with my own son. 'The instant I heard what they proposed, I dismissed them and forbade them to touch her. I'd never allow anyone to torment your poor mother. I'll tend Edith myself, as I promised your father. I won't leave her day or night.'

Jan's anger turned upon me. 'You had no right to send them away! The nuns are skilled at healing. They care for the sick every day. What do you know about such things?'

'They said your mother was mad,' I reminded him gently. 'And you said yourself that she is not. You wouldn't have wanted them to add to her pain by employing remedies that were not only cruel but useless too. I was certain if you had been here, you would have dismissed them yourself. I only did what I thought you would do, knowing how devoted you are to your mother. Forgive me if I acted without your consent, but if I had sent for you, by the time the messenger found you they would have begun to torture poor Edith. And I knew you'd never forgive yourself if you'd added to her suffering.'

.I took his hand and pressed it. 'I am guided by Hugo Bayus in all I do, and your father says there is no better physician in England. I promise I will do exactly as Master Hugo instructs. I will care for Edith as if she were my own dear sister, which indeed she has come to be these past days. You must learn to trust me, Jan, as your father does.'

March

March comes in with an adder's head and goes out with a peacock's tail.

Chapter 18

If a family member goes on a long journey, a bottle of their urine or their knife is hung on the wall. If the urine remains clear or the blade bright, they are well. If the urine becomes cloudy or the blade tarnished, they are ill or in danger. If the urine dries or the knife falls or breaks, they are dead.

Lincoln

Sparks flew from the iron shoes of Robert's horse as they struck the stones on the track. For miles he'd been staring up at John of Gaunt's castle and the cathedral squatting high on the hill above Lincoln. But that had only added to his frustration for he seemed never to draw closer to them on the long, flat road.

The message, sent by Jan to tell him Edith was dying, had taken more than a day to reach him. He'd set out at once, but it had rained hard the night before and the muddy tracks were as slippery as butter. Where the track crossed marshland, he'd frequently been forced to dismount and drag the beast forward, squelching through deep mud and over rotting boards. Whenever he passed a wayside shrine or church, he crossed himself, offering up a prayer for a miracle that would heal her.

But he'd dared not press the pace for, if the horse slipped, it might easily break its own leg or its rider's neck. He tried to tell himself that haste was useless. His wife would either be already dead, or he'd arrive at home to find her sitting up and declaring herself much better. Either way, he would be of little help to her if he was lying in a ditch with his back broken.

But when the lower walls of the city at last came into sight he was seized with panic, certain, now that he was so close, that every minute counted. He spurred his mount into a gallop, knowing that the poor beast was already on its last wind, as he was himself. But guilt drove him on in the desperate hope that he might reach home in time.

He glanced anxiously up at the leaden sky. What little light there had been was fading fast. If he didn't reach the city gates before nightfall, they'd be locked against him and he would be forced to spend the night in the guest hall of one of the monasteries or inns that lay outside the city. With rumours of unrest in the countryside over the poll tax, and every manner of robber and cut-throat roaming the roads after dark, not even a hefty bribe would induce the watchmen to unlock the gates once they were closed, and in this weather they would be only too anxious to retire into their gatehouses and warm their hands over a brazier.

His horse clattered over High Bridge. Robert sent two old women reeling back into the wall as he attempted to force his mount between them and an ox wagon piled high with kegs of salted fish. The women screeched at him as the freshly washed linen in their baskets tumbled into the mud and was dragged beneath the wagon's wheels. One tried to grab his leg, demanding he pay for the spoiled cloth. On any other occasion, Robert would have apologised and given her a few coins, but he spurred his horse onwards, scarcely registering the curses behind him.

A line of carts and wagons had drawn up before the gate in the city wall. Two of the watch were clambering onto the wheels of the carts, lifting coverings and poking among the bales and barrels with their pikes, demanding to know the destination of the drivers, how long they intended to stay and all manner of impertinent questions.

Robert knew, as did the seasoned carters, that the watch had every intention of delaying them until the bell sounded. Then they'd slam the gates, telling them they were too late to enter. A few of the watch took bribes from the inns and religious houses where travellers would be forced to pay for a night's lodging if they couldn't get into the city. But mostly it was a malicious trick they played on travellers to punish latecomers for keeping them from their supper at the end of a long and miserable day in the rain.

Robert squeezed his horse's flanks and forced his way round the stationary wagons to the front of the queue, ignoring the angry protests that he should wait his turn.

One of the watch, seeing what he was up to, moved quicker than he had all day to block his path. He reached up to grab the horse's reins. 'Get back in the line! There's others here afore you.'

Robert knew most of the watch by sight, and they him, but this man was unfamiliar. He pulled a purse from under his cloak and, without even looking at what he was holding, pushed a coin into the man's hand. 'My wife's dying in the city. I was sent for . . . In the name of charity, let me pass.'

The man gaped when he saw the glint of gold in his hand and hastily shoved it inside his clothes. He let the reins go at once and waved Robert through. Those still waiting howled in fury.

'Hold your peace,' the watchman shouted. 'The man's wife is dying. Where's your charity, you bastards?' He fingered the coin beneath his shirt.

Just then the bell sounded from the great cathedral high above and the watch grinned to each other as they hastened to the gates and began to force them shut.

'Master Robert! The Virgin be praised.' Beata's pale lips lifted into an exhausted smile as Robert burst in from the courtyard, where he had paused only long enough to fling the reins of his horse at the stable-boy.

'Edith . . . Has she recovered?' he asked eagerly.

Beata's face fell. 'No, I meant . . . I'm glad you are come. We thought the messenger might not reach you. The mistress . . . Father Remigius is with her.'

'I am not too late, then.'

Exhausted though he was, Robert took the stairs two at a time. He hesitated outside the closed door, suddenly afraid of what he would find behind it.

Catlin must have heard his tread on the stairs. Before he could put his hand to the latch, she opened it. She beamed at him and, for a moment, he was gratified to see the delight on her face.

'I told dear Edith you would come,' she whispered. 'She's sleeping.' She pointed to the thin wooden partition that screened off the bedchamber from the rest of the solar.

Robert opened the door and tiptoed in, as quietly as any man of his weight could do. Even though the evening was wet and cold, the room was hot and heavy with the smoke from the glowing charcoal in the two brass braziers placed at either side of the bed. The drawn bed hangings billowed out and back again as Catlin softly shut the door behind him.

Father Remigius knelt on a cushion before the statues of the Virgin and several saints, which were crowded on to a small table in a corner of the room. His chin was sunk onto his clasped hands. He turned his head at the sound of the door, then rose stiffly, with a groan. Hastening towards Robert, he grasped his arm and pulled him into the corner furthest away from the bed. 'My prayers have been answered,' he whispered. 'You've returned in time.'

'My wife, how is she?' Robert said, trying to pull his arm out of the little priest's grasp.

'The hour of her death will soon be upon us. We must tend her soul now, for there is nothing more that can be done for her body. Mistress Catlin has been nothing short of a saint.' Father Remigius beamed fondly at her. 'She has worn herself out caring for your dear wife night and day. She'd not even allow your maid to help her.'

Robert nodded curtly. He crossed to the bed, pulling aside one of the curtains that draped it. Had he not known it was his wife who lay there, he would never have recognised her. She seemed so very small. Her body scarcely lifted the heavy blanket that covered it. Strips of linen had been used to fasten Edith's wrists to the bedposts on either side and, to Robert's horror, he saw that her lips, black with dried blood, were stretched around a wooden block that had been forced between her broken teeth. It was held in place by a leather strap tied around her head. Her breath rasped noisily as her fragile chest rose and fell.

'God's bones, what have they done to you?' Robert seized the leather strap, trying to release the gag, but the priest caught his wrist, pulling him away.

'The block is there to protect her. At times such agony comes upon her that she tears at her flesh and bites through her lips, screaming that her head is on fire and demons are gnawing at her entrails. When the convulsions seize her, she bites her tongue until the blood pours from her mouth and clenches her teeth until they splinter in her jaw.'

Robert tottered away from the bed, flung wide the casement and leaned out into the night sky, gulping in the cold air and grateful for the cooling rain falling on his burning skin.

When he felt in control of himself again, he turned back into the room. Catlin had just lit the candles and turned to face him, her face bathed in the gentle yellow light. She was clad in a plain, elegantly cut russet gown, her skirts protected by a white apron. Her dark hair glistened beneath its scarlet fret. The gentle, anxious smile as she

130

searched his face made him almost weep at the contrast she made with the creature that lay in the bed.

'She had one of her fits shortly before you arrived, Robert. They usually leave her so exhausted that she cannot be roused for at least two hours after. You've had a long journey. You're trembling with fatigue. You should eat and rest while she sleeps. I'll watch her as I always do and call you at once when she wakes.'

Her concern for him was so tender that Robert would have taken her in his arms and kissed her, if Father Remigius had not been present. Instead, he made a formal bow. 'Mistress . . . I owe you a debt I can never repay. Father Remigius speaks no less than the truth when he says you're a saint.'

It wasn't until Catlin had mentioned it that he realised just how exhausted he was. He felt as if all the strength had suddenly drained from him and he no longer had the energy to stand. 'I think I will eat . . . But you'll be sure to call me if there's any change for better or . . . ?'

'Of course.'

Robert looked down once more at the pathetic little body in the great bed. He gently pressed the back of his fingers to the parchment skin of his wife's ravaged cheek. It was so thin and fragile he was afraid even to caress her in case he hurt her. 'I'll return in a little while, my dear,' he said tenderly. 'You rest now.'

But she did not open her eyes or give any sign that she had heard him.

Robert dragged himself across the room. As he made to close the door, he found the little priest hurrying out behind him. 'I must return to my duties, Master Robert.'

'But my wife . . . she cannot be far from death.'

Father Remigius laid a hand on his arm. Robert knew it was intended to comfort him, but it did nothing except irritate him.

'I've done all I can for your wife. I heard her confession this morning, though it made little sense. But I believe she knew, for a moment or two, who I was and what I was asking, and to that end I have taken it upon myself to absolve and shrive her. She's received Extreme Unction and Viaticum. There is nothing more I can do until . . .' He hesitated, glancing back at the closed door.

With a stab of pain, Robert knew he meant until Edith was dead and he found himself blaming Father Remigius that his wife was dying. If the priest had more faith, if the man had prayed harder, refused to give up hope, Edith would be recovering. Why had Father Remigius not demanded a miracle? That was his job, wasn't it?

The priest took Robert's arm, leading him away from the door. 'You must understand that her wits are already fled into Purgatory. She babbles of such terrors. I strongly advise that you stop your ears to anything she says. But, Master Robert, there is something else I should warn you of—'

Whatever the priest was about to confide was lost as a door banged violently below them and they heard raised voices.

Robert strode down the stairs, ready to vent his anger on whichever servant was disturbing a dying woman, only to find Jan in the hall below. The sleeve of his padded gypon was torn at the shoulder and a thin smear of blood covered the knuckles of his sword hand.

'Jan!'

'So, you're finally back, are you?' Jan said. 'I sent the messenger two days ago.'

'I left as soon as your message reached me. The roads are quagmires. Nothing is moving fast in this rain. But you should have sent for me earlier – the fits, the madness. How long has she been like this?'

'Mad? Is that what Widow Catlin told you?' Jan demanded.

'It is what *I* told your father and I hope you don't mean to quarrel with me.'

The door to the stairs opened and Father Remigius emerged from the shadows into the hall.

'My son, I have spent much of my life ministering to the dying. Many, especially the old, ramble towards the end. They return to the past, thinking their wives to be their mothers, or believing that they fought a man yesterday when it happened years ago. The past and present mingle in the dying and they wander from one to the other until it is not always easy to know where they are in their minds.'

'My mother is not old or witless,' Jan said fiercely.

'No,' Father Remigius agreed, 'she is not, and if you would have the patience to let me finish, I will explain to you why I think her mad, not wandering. Unlike the old, she babbles of things that have never happened, evil, twisted things of which she can never have had knowledge. She screams that imps peer at her round the bed hangings or crawl like snakes through the casements and knotholes. She—'

'But the worm of madness attacks only the mind, not the body,' Jan broke in. 'And she speaks of poison. I've seen her writhe and clutch her belly. I've watched her waste away. Poison would drive her to see terrible visions. Deadly nightshade, monkshood or even mandrake root would cause the agonies she feels and destroy her body besides.'

'And such poisons are fatal,' the priest said firmly. 'Mistress Edith would have died within hours had she taken those things, not lingered like this, and their effects are well known to any physician, particularly one as learned as Hugo Bayus. He would have recognised the signs at once.'

'Father, you must listen. Mother is certain she is being poisoned. She—'

'Be quiet!' Robert pushed Jan firmly aside and strode to the door that opened onto the stableyard. He bellowed for Beata, Tenney – anyone – to bring wine and mutton, then turned back to his son. 'Listen to me, boy. I will not have this nonsense spoken of again. Have you any idea what damage would be done to my business if such a rumour were to be bandied abroad? If I thought there was a grain of truth in it, I'd send for the sheriff myself this very hour, but it's the ravings of a woman in delirium.'

Beata appeared in the doorway, gripping a heavy pot in both hands, and nudged the door wider with her hip. With anxious glances at the three grim faces, she marched in and set the steaming pot of stewed beaver's tail on the table. 'Lent's begun, Master Robert. Had you forgotten? There'll be no meat now till the Easter feast.' Beata glared at the priest as if he was personally responsible for this privation.

Robert had indeed forgotten. At least beaver tails were permitted, for they were deemed to be fish, but they were certainly no substitute for roast mutton.

'Beata, you don't think my mother mad, do you?' Jan said.

A wary expression crept over Beata's face, as if she feared a trap. 'The mad don't waste away,' she said cautiously. 'I'd an old aunt who used to run about the town half naked, screaming and trying to snatch babies from their mothers, thinking they were hers. They took her to St Magdalene's and kept her locked up in there. She grew as fat as a farrowing sow in her madness. My mistress is not moon-struck like her. But . . . she's not right in her head either. 'Tis the pain, if you ask me. She's tormented so, and people say all kinds of nonsense when the fever's upon them, but that doesn't mean they're mad.'

'There! Now will you be content?' Robert snapped. 'Even Beata admits your mother doesn't know what she's saying. Let that be an end of it. I will hear not another word on the matter.'

The men watched in an uncomfortable silence as two more trips to the kitchen added leek-sops, a baked carp, bread and a flagon of wine to the table.

'Will you dine with us, Father Remigius?' Robert asked, only from obligation: he had no desire to entertain him.

The priest gazed longingly at the table, then glumly shook his head. 'I'd best be about my work.' He made the sign of the cross in front of the two men, who bowed their heads sullenly.

As soon as the door to the street had closed behind the priest, Robert strode to the table. Ripping off a chunk of bread he dipped it into the stew and ravenously shoved it into his mouth. 'Eat, boy,' he murmured thickly.

'I'm not hungry, Father.'

'Then sit down and watch me. How have things been in my absence at the warehouse?'

Jan marched to the table and poured himself a generous quantity of wine, spilling some in the process. It was only when Robert saw his hand clasping the stem of the goblet that he registered there was blood on it. He gestured towards the cut, with a piece of beaver's tail he'd speared on his knife. 'Cut yourself? You've torn your gypon too. Had an accident?'

Jan flung himself into a chair and tossed back the wine. 'It was nothing,' he said savagely. 'Florentines again. Matthew Johan and his brothers causing trouble as usual.'

Robert's eyes narrowed. 'What happened?'

Jan stared up at the great boar in the tapestry on the wall, laying its head in the lap of the Saxon princess, as if he'd only just noticed it. The gold thread of the boar's collar glinted in the flames of the fire. Jan seemed to be steeling himself to break some disagreeable news and his hesitation alarmed Robert.

'Out with it, lad!'

'Merchants from Florence left Lincoln with goods they hadn't paid for. Nigh on fifty pounds' worth of our wool and cloth, and far more besides from the other Lincoln merchants.'

'What?' The knife clattered from Robert's grasp. 'You let them run off with our goods? Why didn't you stop them?'

Jan flushed. 'I didn't know they were going to disappear. We'd traded with them before and they had a bond . . . Besides, the other merchants were selling to them. We'd have lost out if we hadn't.'

'And we have lost dearly because we did,' Robert snapped. 'How much did they take from the other merchants?'

'Nearly five hundred pounds' worth, thieving foreigners! They're all members of the Society of Albertini, the same one the Johan brothers belong to. It was the Albertini that issued the bond. I went to the mayor and told him the Johan brothers were plainly part of the fraud. He had his bailiffs seize goods and money from their warehouses and homes. Not as much as the merchants lost in total, but I went with them to make sure we got enough to cover our losses. I told the Florentines that if they wanted it back they could reclaim the worth from their own society brothers. They didn't take kindly to that.' He sucked at his bleeding knuckle.

Robert grunted. 'At least that's something. Was that where you were hurt?'

Jan shook his head. 'I met some of them in the street this evening, drunk as a wheelbarrow. Matthew started yelling it was my fault his warehouse had been raided and drew his sword.'

'Brawling's forbidden in Lincoln,' Robert said sharply. 'If the sheriff—'

'Defending yourself when a man's drawn a blade isn't against the law. Anyway, he ran off with a good deep cut across his sword arm, threatening all the vengeance of Hell, but for now he's in no state to do anything about it. The sooner we throw every foreign merchant out of Lincoln, the better off we'll all be.'

'Aye, I heard many a man say that these last—'

An agonised scream split the air above their heads. Chairs clattered to the floor as both men raced for the stairs, Beata running up behind them. Jan burst into the chamber, Robert hard on his heels.

The bed curtains were open. Edith lay motionless, her head twisted back at an unnatural angle. Her eyes were wide open and only the whites were showing. The gag had been removed from her mouth. Her hands were bound, but the fingers were twisted, as if she'd been trying to claw at something.

Catlin stood by the bed, her head lifted as if she was staring at something or someone standing on its other side. Without turning, she said quietly, 'Her suffering is at an end. It is finished.'

'No!' Jan howled.

He rushed to the bed, pushing Catlin aside with such force that she staggered and fell. He seized his mother by the shoulders and shook her, pleading with her to wake. Robert strode over and helped Catlin to her feet, holding her arm as she swayed against him. Jan was sobbing and fumbling with the linen strips that bound his mother's hands to the bed. Robert stepped away from Catlin and pressed a heavy hand on his son's shoulder, pushing him down onto his knees. 'Leave the cloth. Pray for her soul,' he said, his voice broken.

The young man crumpled, his face buried in the bed covering.

Beata stood in the doorway, tears rolling down her face. Then she moved forward, bent over her mistress and passed a hand over her eyes, trying to ease the lids down, but they wouldn't shut. Fixed and wide, they remained staring backwards into her head.

Catlin's breath caught in a little sob. Robert wrapped his arms around her and held her tenderly. She turned her face into his chest and clung to him.

'Don't distress yourself, my dear. There's nothing more any of us could have done.'

Tenney appeared in the doorway. He stared at the corpse in the bed. Then he pulled the hood from his head, twisting it awkwardly in his hands. 'I'll be fetching Father Remigius, then, and the nuns for the laying out . . . I'm right sorry to see her go, Master Robert. She could be hard to please, but she was a decent woman.'

Robert nodded.

'Will you be wanting me to fetch young Adam too?'

Robert had not registered that his younger son was missing, but now he realised he hadn't seen the boy since he had returned that evening. 'Where is he?'

Beata, her face wet with tears, picked at the knots of the linen strips that bound her mistress's hands. '*She* took him. Said hearing his mother in pain was upsetting the boy. But he should have been here to say goodbye to her.'

Catlin lifted her head and gazed into Robert's eyes. 'I thought it best, Robert. No child should have to hear his mother screaming in agony or watch the convulsions. It was too distressing for him. Much better that they said their farewells while she still knew him. I sent him to my house to spend time with my own child, under the care of Diot.'

Robert was a little annoyed. A son should be present at the deathbed of a parent, however young he was . . . Or perhaps Catlin had been right to send him away. The last thing Edith would have wanted was for Adam to be frightened. She had tried so hard to disguise her pain from him when she was first taken ill. She would doubtless have sent him away herself, had she been in her own mind.

'It was kind of you, Mistress Catlin,' he said, 'but he'll have to—'

'It was not kind,' Jan shouted, scrambling to his feet. 'She wormed her way in here when my mother was too sick to understand what was going on. Have you ever stopped to ask yourself why, Father? Why should a stranger want to take care of a woman she's never even met?'

Beata lowered her head, busying herself in tying a linen strip across Edith's open eyes in a vain attempt to close them.

'Now you listen to me, boy,' Robert bellowed. 'This good woman has worn herself out caring for your mother and—'

Jan strode to the door. 'It was not my mother she cared for, Father. Even a child can see that.'

'Come back and apologise to Mistress Catlin,' Robert roared at him. 'I'll not have any son of mine speak so to a guest in my house.'

Jan glared at him with undisguised hatred. 'She's no guest, Father. She's a leech – and there is only one thing you should do with leeches and that's burn them off your skin before they get their hooks into you and start sucking your blood.' He stormed out, slamming the door behind him.

'How dare you?' Robert strode across the room, his fists clenched, his face scarlet with rage.

But Catlin ran in front of him, barring his way. 'Let him go,' she begged. 'Grief makes people say strange things. He'll see how wrong he is, when the shock passes. It's your beloved wife you must attend to now. You have her funeral to arrange.'

Robert breathed deeply, trying to calm himself. His wife was lying there dead on the bed in front of him and he was quarrelling with his son in front of the two servants, who were listening to all that passed. He was appalled at himself. What must Catlin think of him? He ran his fingers distractedly through his hair, trying to collect his thoughts. 'Tenney, fetch the priest and the nuns, and on the way back collect Adam.'

'Let me go for Adam,' Catlin said. 'He must be told his mother has died and I think such sad tidings are better delivered by a woman and mother who can comfort him, not a servant. He'll want to cry, but he'd be too proud to do so before a man. He is growing up faster than you think, Robert.'

Chapter 19

If a witch plunges her broom into water, pulls it out and shakes it, she will cause much rain to fall.

Beata

The nuns of St Magdalene wouldn't let me touch Mistress Edith's body. They sent me to fetch water, rags and sweet herbs, then brushed me into the corner, like some scullion, to watch as they washed my mistress and laid her out in her finest kirtle of Lincoln Green wool, which made her face look like a wrinkled yellow apple. Her body was so thin it was as if the gown had been hung on a scarecrow. I fetched the gown in which she'd been wed. She was as slender as a birch tree back then. It'd have fitted her once more. But the nuns ignored me as if I was nowt but a yapping dog.

They wound a clean linen cloth round her poor shaven head, laid a crucifix on her breast and set a distaff in her hand, though she'd never used one since she was a girl. On Master Robert's instructions they placed a necklace of pearls around her throat, and rings on her fingers, for he'd not have his wife going out unadorned even into her grave. But the pearls only made my mistress's face look more ravaged, as if she'd died months before and this was some cruel mockery of her decay, like putting rosebuds in the hair of a withered crone.

As soon as they'd gone, I returned to do those things for her they'd not do. I removed the bandage that tied her bruised jaw shut and placed a coin in the cold mouth, before tying it again. I sprinkled salt on her breast, hid rowan twigs in her shoes and slipped a small iron padlock beneath her skirts over her private parts. In short I did all that I could to keep the evil spirits from entering her, so that her soul might be at peace, but what peace could there be for a woman who'd had her life so cruelly wrested from her?

I should have been with her when she died. I should have been the one to care for her in her last days. I'd cared for her all her married life, when she was sick and when she was well, when she was brought to bed with child and when she sobbed over their little dead bodies. I shouldn't have let that woman drive me out. My mistress wasn't mad, she wasn't.

Father Remigius waited for the funeral procession a short way from the church then led it the final few yards until Mistress Edith's coffin came to rest in the lich-gate. The bell-ringer began to toll the six tellers for the death of a woman, then a note for each of the fifty years of her life. When all your years are counted in the ringing of a single bell, they seem so brief, so lonely.

We laid Mistress Edith's body in a stone coffin in the churchyard for it to dry. In time, when the smell had gone and the corpse fluids run out, she would be laid to rest beneath the floor of the church and Master Robert would order a fine stone to place over it, with her likeness carved upon it – a devoted mother and faithful wife. Faithfulness, yes. Men set great store by faithfulness in their wives.

They all gathered round the grave as Father Remigius mumbled away in his Latin. Master Robert had given new black robes to twelve poor men from the parish and paid them to flank the coffin, holding great thick candles, whose guttering flames they carefully shielded from the wind – they didn't want to forfeit the coins he had promised them. No more did the choir boys, who held the lighted tapers as they sang *dirige*. It was an impressive sight and Master Robert intended it to be so. He would not have it said he had dispatched his wife like a pauper.

Nor would she soon be forgotten for he'd given pennies to the sick and bedridden to pray for her soul and several fine pieces of silver to the merchants' church. He also paid two chantry priests to say masses weekly for Edith to shorten her days in Purgatory, with a promise of more to come if they carried out their duties diligently.

But come the day of the funeral, Jan and his father stood side by side, their eyes as dry as sand in Hell. Jan had wept for his mother when he was alone. I'd seen his swollen eyes when he emerged from the bedchamber after his vigil, but not Master Robert's. Not that I'd ever seen him weep. Some men don't. They're born without tears. Besides, a man in business can't afford to show weakness, if grief can be counted as such.

Master Robert had taught his sons to bear their pain in silence too.

Little Adam walked between his father and brother behind the coffin in the procession, his eyes fixed on the ground, never once looking up at the wooden box containing his mother. When they removed her from the carrying coffin and lowered her body into the stone one, his face had been as stiff and wooden as a painted angel. He'd stared fixedly at a pair of red kites wheeling above our heads. Master Robert did not try to comfort the boy. I dare say he was struggling too hard to maintain his own stiff dignity. Once or twice I saw Jan lay a hand on his brother's shoulder and squeeze it, but neither looked at the other.

Tenney, though, is as tender as a slice of veal, not that he'd ever admit it. We'd both been so busy with visitors calling to sit with the mourners, preparing the funeral meats and running errands that we'd not had a moment to bless ourselves. I'd had no time to grieve, even at night, for I was so exhausted my eyes closed before my head touched the pallet.

But when I saw them lay the lid upon my poor mistress's coffin, shutting her up alone in the dark, and when I heard that awful rasp of stone on stone, I felt as if the skin was being ripped from my heart and I fell to sobbing. That great ox Tenney shuffled a little closer and shoved his arm about me, patting me awkwardly. 'There, lass, she's at peace. No cause to take on so,' he said.

But I heard the catch in his voice, and when I glanced up, I saw a tear running down his cheeks and sinking into his thick black beard.

The churchyard was crowded. All of Master Robert's guild brothers and their wives had come, as well as neighbours, relatives, tenants and workmen, not out of grief for my mistress, most barely knew her, but to show their loyalty to Robert. He was an influential man, and men like him had long memories and long fingers. Few would risk slighting him.

As soon as the service was over, the congregation filed past the master and his sons to murmur words of consolation. All of my attention had been on the family and on poor Mistress Edith's coffin, and in that great throng I hadn't noticed if Widow Catlin was there or not. But as the crowd began to thin, she suddenly appeared a few yards behind Master Robert, flanked by that filthy old besom, Diot, and Leonia. For a moment it gave me quite a turn, seeing them standing there so still, gazing at Edith's coffin, like three ravens watching for the chance to feed on a carcass.

As if he sensed Widow Catlin behind him, Master Robert turned towards her. He had taken a few steps in her direction when he seemed to remember he'd been talking to a fellow guild member and turned back to excuse himself before walking over to the widow. Catlin nodded to him as formally as any woman there, as if they were mere acquaintances, but it didn't fool Edith's cousin, Maud, not for a flea's breath.

Ever since the night of Mistress Edith's death, Master Robert had instructed Tenney and me to say that he was out whenever Maud came calling and he'd avoided her throughout the funeral. But there was no avoiding her now. She picked up her skirts and charged across to him, spitting and railing.

'. . . your whoring that killed her. She died of shame and a broken heart. Wicked, that's what you are . . . a fornicator!'

Master Robert spun around to face her, his arms outstretched on either side as if he were trying to shield Widow Catlin from an assassin. 'And you are a foul-mouthed old gossip,' he yelled, his face turning scarlet. 'You were forever pouring your malice into my wife's mind. If anyone killed her it was you, filling her head with fears and jealousies that had no ground. They ought to duck you in the Braytheforde.'

Everyone was goggling at them with undisguised fascination, as if this were a mummers' play. Jan ran up and tried to pull Maud away, but she was having none of it. Finally Father Remigius puffed his way over to the pair and pushed himself between them.

'These are evil words to be spoken with the Blessed Host still on your lips. Show some respect for the poor woman who lies in her grave at your feet.'

With an angry shrug, Robert stalked away, but it took several more earnest entreaties from the priest to prevent Maud running after him and berating him once more. Widow Catlin had melted into the crowd and was nowhere to be seen.

I was turning away, too, when I felt a small, cold hand slip into mine. I glanced down. Adam was standing beside me, his face as pale as whey and his jaw clenched. He stared at Robert's retreating back. 'Father didn't kill my mother,' he whispered, so low that I could barely hear him.

'Course he didn't, Adam,' I said. 'Take no notice of Mistress Maud.'
Adam's chest heaved. 'I killed her.'

Chapter 20

If a diamond-shaped crease, called a coffin, is seen in a newly ironed sheet, someone who sleeps in that bed will die. If the coffin is seen in a carelessly ironed tablecloth it foretells imminent death for one of the people seated round that table.

Lincoln

A long flight of steps and a cobbled slope run side by side up the hill from the cluster of hovels in Butwerk, outside the city walls, to the postern gate of the cathedral precincts. They call this way the Greesen. By day it is always crowded with pilgrims and ox carts, pedlars and goodwives, but at night only the foolhardy venture down it, for this, my darlings, is where the ghosts of Lincoln gather. On the cathedral side of the archway lies holy ground, but this side belongs to those who are neither alive nor dead. We ghosts loiter there most dark evenings. Some slide through the stones as if they were made of mist, which to them they are: they left life long before the walls were ever built. Others laboriously climb the steps as if they still lived.

The monk who hanged himself from the postern gate resents our gathering. He was a miserable old sod in life, and death has made him no more sociable. He seems to think that because he died on the spot, he has some claim to it, but though the creaking of his noose and his moaning may send the living fleeing in terror, ghosts are not to be deterred.

Other things swarm around the Greesen too. Creatures abandoned by their creator long, long ago. Beasts, half fish and half reptile, with jagged-toothed jaws, claw up those steep steps on their sharp fins, while ugly black birds with long cruel beaks and human eyes greedily watch the people who scuttle down the stone stairs below. A malevolent darkness flows down those steps, oozing from the tombs of

143

those who lie buried in the cathedral above. Trust me, my darlings, you don't want to climb them at night.

It was late in the evening when Jan, a girl clinging to his arm, wove his way down a narrow alley between the darkened houses and out onto the Greesen. The stairs were dark and deserted. At intervals along the walls torches guttered, sending shadows slithering between the pools of orange light. Far below, bright pinpoints of yellow and red twinkled in the distant valley, marking where boatmen far from home were sleeping on the riverbanks or shepherds warmed themselves as they kept watch.

The girl hung back, tugging on Jan's arm. 'Not down there. There's summit that grabs your ankle when you walk up those steps, pulls you back down again. My friend skinned both her knees and spilled all the fish from her basket.'

Jan giggled and flicked the girl's nose with his finger. 'If he tries to grab your pretty little ankle, I'll chop his hand off.'

He fumbled for his sword hilt, but his hand got twisted in the folds of his cloak.

'It's a woman that grabs you,' the girl said. 'Anyhow, you'll break your neck on those stairs. You're so pickled you can hardly walk straight on the flat.'

'True!' Jan said affably. 'That's why you'll have to come with me. My lodgings . . . nice warm bed. Just you and me and a flagon of wine. Forget about the whole damn lot of them.'

Slipping his hand round her waist, he drew her tightly to him, kissing the base of her throat, before propelling her towards the steps. She laughed and allowed herself to be pulled along.

Jan had made straight for the tavern as soon as he'd left the church-yard. After the row at the graveside between his father and Maud, he was not in the mood for the polite chatter of the guests as they offered their meaningless twitter of condolence. No one would mention Maud's accusations at the funeral feast, of course, but they'd be itching to pick over every detail with friends and neighbours the moment they had staggered home. Jan had stayed in the tavern until the yawning innkeeper had shoved the girl and him out of the door, and it was doubtful he'd have left then, had not the girl offered to see him safe to his lodgings.

They tottered precariously down the steep stairs. The flickering light from the torches made the descent even more perilous for the edges of the uneven steps kept melting away into shadow. Jan leaned heavily on the girl, who struggled to balance him. It occurred to him that he couldn't remember her name. Had she told him? No matter. She was pretty and willing and didn't ask questions. That was all he wanted tonight, enough wine to blunt his misery and a warm body to snuggle up against, so that he was not alone. He could not be alone tonight.

'It's the English thief!' The voice rang out mockingly from below.

The girl jerked back so quickly that Jan almost slipped off the step. Two men were standing on the steps below him. He couldn't distinguish their faces, but he caught the accent and guessed them to be Johan's men. Jan, swaying, blinked down at them. He batted at the air wildly with his arm, as if he was shooing pigeons. 'Out my way . . . If Johan wants his goods, ask the thieving bastards who stole ours.'

One of the two took a step forward, as if he intended to rush up the stairs, but his companion held him back.

'Why do you not come down here and say that, Fog-head? Maybe you are afraid to fight. You, girl, you come with us. We will show you what a real man is. This boy has to get the bailiff to fight his battles.'

Jan gave a roar and stumbled forward, but the girl held him back. The man laughed. 'No? Then we come to you.'

Jan caught the flash of daggers, as the men reached beneath their half-cloaks. His reactions were slow, made clumsier by the girl hanging on his arm. He shoved her towards the wall, meaning only to push her out of the way of the blades and free himself to fight, but the push was more violent than he intended and she crashed into the stones, tumbling down several steps as the men rushed towards Jan. One stumbled over her, falling on top of her. The other only just managed to stop himself tripping over them. He paused just long enough to see his friend get to his feet, then bounded up towards Jan.

Jan had been too appalled by what he'd done to the girl to do more than gape, but now, even through the wine fumes fuddling his brain, he saw that the two men were dangerously close. He struggled to find the hilt of his sword and draw it, but one of his adversaries lifted his dagger as if he intended to hurl it straight at Jan's eye. Jan threw himself sideways against the wall, staggered and fell heavily onto the step below, but at once realised he'd been tricked. The man had not thrown the blade and Jan, sprawled on the step, now had no chance of drawing his sword from the scabbard.

Johan's men were almost upon him, their daggers raised, ready to plunge into his chest. He tried to twist away, but the daggers were advancing on either side of him.

A black shadow slithered over his prone body and there was a low, menacing growl that sounded as if it came from the throat of a huge dog. Startled, all three men glanced up the steps above them. Something was flying down towards them, howling as it ran.

'The monk! The dead monk!' one man yelled. Grabbing each other, they slipped and slid back down the steps, vanishing into the darkness below.

Jan got to his feet, finally managing to wrench his sword from the scabbard. Below him, the girl was struggling upright, pointing and shrieking at the figure hurtling towards them. Somewhere a shutter was thrown open and a woman bellowed from an upper casement. A baby started to scream, which seemed to set all the dogs within the city walls howling.

There was the sound of running feet and two watchmen burst out of the alley and pounded down the steps, their pikes clattering as they ran. They reached the robed stranger first, but ran past him, one making for Jan, the other leaping down to the shrieking girl.

The watchman jabbed his pike at Jan's stomach. 'Drop the sword. Drop it, I say!'

Jan let it slip from his fingers and fall with a clatter onto the stones. He raised both hands to show he was unarmed.

The second watchman hauled the girl to her feet and, with his free arm about her waist, dragged her back up the steps to where Jan stood, his back pressed against the wall's sharp stones.

The watchman with the pike was a spindly youth, his eyes covered with a long fringe of greasy hair, which he jerked his head to toss aside. The man who held the girl was bald, with a neck as thick as his head.

The bald one glanced up at the open casement. 'Leave off screeching,' he shouted at the woman, who was still leaning out, complaining about the noise. 'We've got them. Get back to bed.'

She closed the shutters with a furious bang, setting the baby off again.

146

The bald one turned his attention to Jan. 'Was she trying to rob you?'

'I never!' the girl squawked indignantly. 'Two men tried to attack him. He . . . They knocked me down the steps.'

It wasn't exactly true, but Jan wasn't going to argue. He embarked on a long, tortuous explanation about the Florentines, Johan, the missing goods and the warehouse, several times forgetting what he was saying and trying to start again. The watchmen were clearly bemused.

Exasperated, the bald man brushed away the garbled tale with a sweep of his hand. 'Just give us the names of the men who attacked you.'

'Told you already . . . Johan's men,' Jan said irritably. 'Don't know which.'

The bald man pulled a face at his companion. 'We won't get a description out of him. He's sow-drunk. Wouldn't know his own mother.'

'Don't talk about my mother,' Jan burst out. 'She's dead.'

The men ignored him and the bald man glanced up the steps. 'You there, friar. You saw the attack? You'd recognise the men?'

Jan stared up. A man in tattered robes was crouching by the wall, his hood drawn low over his face. He rose to his feet. 'I saw no one,' he growled.

'That's a barefaced lie,' the girl said indignantly. 'He did see them. It was him that drove them off. I reckon they thought he was a ghost.'

The friar seemed vaguely familiar, but Jan's head was pounding. He couldn't even try to think where he'd seen the man before, though he was certain he had.

The watchman sighed. 'Amazing how half the populace of Lincoln become blind and deaf if they think they'll be called to give evidence. We could take him in, make him talk, but I suppose since there's been no harm done—'

'No harm?' the girl protested. 'I'm black and blue all over, and my gown's torn. It's new this is.'

'New to you, maybe, not to the scarecrow who had it afore you,' the bald watchman said. 'If you got any sense you'll take yourself home afore you find yourself arrested for whoring. Off with you!'

He pushed her up the steps with a hearty slap on her backside. The younger watchman sniggered.

She turned and glared at the lad. 'I'll not forget this. It's the last time you get your bell tolled for nothing. '

'I didn't . . . I don't . . .' the youth stammered, but his companion wasn't listening.

'As for you, young master, I'd find yourself a linkman to see you safe home, afore you end up running into more trouble or breaking a leg falling into a gutter.'

The two watchmen plodded back up the steps. Jan bent down to retrieve his sword and, pressing his hand to the wall to steady himself, began to edge his way down. Pity about the girl, pretty little thing and good company, but probably as well she'd gone. His head was throbbing now and all he wanted to do was lie down and close his eyes to stop the ground heaving.

'Wait!' A hand grabbed his shoulder.

He whipped round, clutching his head as the walls seemed to spin. As he tried to focus, he found himself staring into the face of the friar. Half was in shadow, but he glimpsed sallow skin pulled tight over bones and thin lips barely covering broken teeth. The flames of the torch above glittered deep within the eyes.

'We must speak.' The voice was harsh and deep. 'It concerns your father. Things you should know.'

A tiny spark of recognition blazed somewhere in the back of Jan's fogged mind. 'You . . . you were the man who followed me at Greetwell . . . on the riverbank. My horse went lame.'

'A nail, that's all. I had to make you dismount. I hoped I could speak to you before it was too late. But the children . . . those children . . .' He shuddered.

Even in his stupor, fury boiled in Jan. 'You deliberately lamed my horse? What were you doing? Trying to make me break my neck or be thrown into the river and drowned?'

'I swear—'

But Jan had already come close to being murdered once that night. This time he was on his guard. He shoved the friar as hard as he could. The man fell heavily against the stones, with a cry. Jan did not look back as he staggered as fast as he could down the steps.

'Listen to me, you fool . . . your mother's death. It . . .'

But Jan had gone.

Chapter 21

Pebbles or stones with holes through them should be hung near the doors of house and byre to protect the entrances from witches and demons. Keys should be attached to pebbles with holes through them to guard locks against robbers trying to open them and to prevent evil spirits entering through the keyhole.

Greetwell

It was already dark when Gunter and his son Hankin heaved themselves out of the punt and onto the bank. Still holding the prow rope, Gunter rubbed his aching stump to ease it, but he couldn't afford to indulge the pain for long. The punt was being dragged back by the current, which threatened to tear the rope from his hand. He could see his son struggling to hold fast to the stern rope as he tied it off on the stout post that Gunter had long ago hammered into the bank. After all the rain, the Witham was swollen and running fast. Taking the cargo downstream had been easy, but they'd had to fight the surge every inch of the way back.

Gunter strained on the rope, pulling it deep into the cut he had dug out of the riverbank. It was a snug fit, and ensured the boat was moored out of the flow. All kinds of things came floating down the river – timber from the boatyards, fallen branches, lost barrels, drowned sheep, boats that had broken their moorings. A current as strong as this would smash them against any moored craft hard enough to hole it.

The wind cut sharply across the water, rustling last year's dried reeds and sedges. Gunter stiffened as the boom of a bittern throbbed through the darkness. He'd always loathed that bird. He'd heard its melancholy call the night he'd returned home to find his mother dead and his father dying. The villagers who lived on the high cliff said an owl or raven warned of death, but the marsh-men had their own messengers.

149

It had taken his father two days to die. No one would come to help them and little Gunter alone had tried desperately to save him. On those nights when his father had lain writhing and moaning, the bittern had mocked the boy's childish, futile efforts. *You fool! You fool,* it cried, and later, *You failed, you failed,* as he tried to scrape out two shallow graves, tears and icy rain streaming down his dirty face. Inch by painful inch he'd had to drag the bodies of his parents into the pits. He'd piled the sodden earth over bloated bellies and cold grimacing faces, hideous distortions of those who had once smiled at him. It takes a long time to cover a corpse. The boy had tried hard to think of a single word of the prayers he knew must be said if his parents were not to be dragged down to Hell. But he knew not a word of Latin, and God did not understand any other tongue.

He'd lain shivering and wet in the icy cottage, waiting for the fever to come and devour him, waiting to feel the agony his father had endured, waiting to die alone and terrified in the darkness, with only the bittern's laughter ringing through that lonely night. But the fever did not take him. Come morning he was still alive. Stiff with cold, he staggered outside to find water to ease his throat, which had shrivelled from crying, and saw that the rain had washed clean the faces of his parents, who were staring up at him out of their shallow graves. For a wonderful moment, he'd thought they were rising from the dead and coming back to him. But the bittern knew the dead do not live again.

Gunter had always driven the birds off after that, destroying their nests among the reeds wherever he found them, as if they were to blame. He hadn't heard a bittern call near his cottage for years. A cold fear gripped him and he stared along the bank. In the darkness he could just make out a tiny yellow light. His wife always set a lantern outside the door to guide her husband home. It had come to be a sign between them that all was well. His fear eased a little.

'Get you inside, Bor,' he said to Hankin. 'Tell your mam I'm coming.'

Hankin didn't wait to be told twice. He was starving as usual and ran towards the cottage, as if he'd just had a good night's sleep instead of a hard day's work. Gunter smiled after him. Where did the young get their energy?

Gunter dragged mats of woven reeds over the top of his craft to disguise it from anyone on the river. They would not protect it from those who knew it was there, but if any of the thieving river-rats came this way on the lookout for anything to steal, they would hopefully pass by and take another boat instead. After the murder of Tom, the rent-collector, everyone had done all they could to protect their few belongings, though Gunter suspected the murderers were to be found rather closer to home. Not that he would have said as much to anyone, even if he'd witnessed the killing with his own eyes. River-men did not betray their own people, not even when they were as foul as Martin and his son.

Satisfied that he had done all he could to protect his livelihood, Gunter dragged his aching limbs along the rough path to the cottage. Pausing to remove the lantern, he pushed open the door. Royse and Hankin were sitting on stools, shovelling bean pottage into their mouths with mutton-bone spoons. Little Col was curled up in the corner of a narrow bed built into the side of the single-roomed cottage, the edge of a woollen blanket pressed tightly against his nose. He was already sleeping soundly, his empty bowl lying beside him.

Nonie, a cloth wrapped around her hand, swivelled the long metal bar from which an iron cooking pot swung, pulling it away from the fire. She straightened as Gunter entered. 'You're late,' she said. 'Supper's as dry as sheep droppings. I suppose you've been carousing with that alewife again.'

'A dozen of them. Couldn't fight them off.'

They smiled at each other, knowing it would never be true.

'River's running fast tonight. We had to bring her all the way from Tattershall.' Gunter set the lantern on the table and opened one of the horn panels. The candle had burned low. He licked his thumb and forefinger and extinguished the flame. His fingers were so calloused from punting that he wouldn't have felt the heat if they hadn't been wetted, but it was a habit learned from boyhood and not easily broken. 'You don't need to hang this out. I've told you a thousand times, Nonie, I could find my way home if I'd been blinded. We don't have candles to waste on lighting the river for the ducks.'

His wife pressed her lips together and pushed the pot back over the small fire, stirring it vigorously before ladling the thick, greenish-brown mess into a bowl.

'Mam thinks if she doesn't set it out something bad'll happen to you and you'll never come home.' Royse set her spoon down with a grin.

'And what if I do?' Nonie said defensively. 'That river's a widow-maker. There's many a woman said goodbye to her husband at dawn and by evening he's brought home a corpse or a helpless cripple.' She glanced at Gunter's wooden leg, as if that was all the proof she needed of the river's malice. Gunter knew Nonie hadn't intended the word 'cripple' for him. There were boatmen who'd lost both arms, or broken their backs and couldn't move from their own beds. Nonie always protested fiercely that her husband was twice as fit as men half his age with all their limbs. But the name stung, for others had spat it at him over the years and meant it.

Nonie set the bowl on the table with a savage thump. 'I've been putting that lantern out since the night I first came to your bed and I'll not stop till they carry me out in a winding sheet.'

Gunter caught her round the waist, pulled her into a hug and kissed her. She pushed him off, pretending to be annoyed, but he could tell she was trying not to laugh.

'Stop that. You'll wake the bairn.' She glanced over at her little son in the bed, but Col could sleep through a thunderstorm.

Gunter settled himself to eat. His wife handed him a chunk of coarse bread. What little wheat was in it had been mixed with dried beans and ground bulrush roots. It fell apart as soon as he bit into it and he dumped the rest in the bowl, mixing it with the pottage to soften it. He stopped chewing suddenly and pulled a little fishbone from his mouth.

'A perch,' Nonie said. 'Col caught it. Badgered me 'til I put it in the pot for you.'

'Only a tiddler,' Royse said.

'Early for them to be rising. Rain must be flushing them out. Col did well to catch it.'

'Don't encourage him,' Nonie snapped. 'I don't like him going near the river when it's up. If he falls in, like that little mite and his sister did a year back . . . I'll never forget the look on their poor mam's face. Half out of her mind, she was. I still see her sometimes searching along the riverbank for their bodies. There's no one can convince her they'll never be found now.'

She crossed herself, to ward off such evil from her own children. 'Besides, if the bailiff should catch him . . .'

'Lad knows to be careful and he's got to learn. We'll need all the fish he can catch this year, way things are going.'

152

Royse exchanged a worried glance with her mother. 'Will it be—'

'Horses!' Hankin sprang from the chair but his father grabbed him and pulled him back. Swiftly, Gunter heaved the stout wooden plank across the door to brace it shut. They all stood rigid, listening intently. Iron horseshoes clattered against the stones on the narrow track, but the riders were moving slowly, cautiously, as well they might, for the night was a dark one.

Gunter glanced at Nonie. He could see the tension in her face. Who would be riding this way so late? None of their neighbours owned horses, and merchants or monks would keep to the road, if their business was so urgent that they were forced to travel by night.

The hoofbeats came closer to the door, so close they could hear the creaking of the leather saddles. Gunter thought they were going to pass by. He prayed that they were. But then he heard the horses snort as their riders swung from the saddles, and the murmur of men's voices. There were two . . . maybe three.

As Gunter reached for his stave, he caught the look of alarm that flashed across the faces of his wife and daughter.

'They could be robbers,' Nonie whispered. 'Same as battered Tom to death. For pity's sake, don't let them in, Gunter.'

'Any man wealthy enough to own a horse wouldn't trouble to steal from a cottage as poor as this,' Gunter said, but he took firmer grip on his stave.

Although they were expecting it, the loud rapping on the door made them jump.

'Open up in the name of the King.'

'Who's out there?' Gunter's voice betrayed his fear.

'The King's commissioner. I've the King's sergeants-at-arms with me. They've the power to arrest you if you refuse to yield to us.'

Gunter spun round on his wooden stump. Dropping the stave, he crossed to the wall and pulled open a low wicket door in the thin partition between the cottage and the goat's byre on the other side of the wall. He beckoned frantically to his daughter.

'Out this way,' he whispered. 'Wait in the byre until you hear the men are inside the cottage, then keep low and run as fast as you can to the marsh. Hide until you hear me make the peewit's call. Understand?'

Royse, terrified and bewildered, for once didn't argue, but ducked obediently through the wicket. Nonie pushed Hankin towards the opening and made to grab the sleeping Col too, but Gunter stopped her. 'Lads must stay.'

He fastened the wicket behind Royse, pushing a barrel across it to hide it. Nonie stared at him, evidently as frightened and confused as Royse. Gunter thought she was about to argue, but before she could protest the thumping on the door redoubled.

'Do you want us to break this door down?'

As if to demonstrate that they could do just that, someone pounded on the door with the hilt of a sword so hard that it trembled in its frame.

Hands sweating, Gunter struggled to lift the wooden brace from the sockets. He'd scarcely laid it aside before the door burst open and a corpulent man strode into the tiny cottage, closely followed by two great hulks of men. One kicked the door shut.

Gunter did not need convincing that they were who they had claimed to be. The two sergeants-at-arms wore the King's colours on their tabards, which hung over thick padded leather gambesons, stout enough to protect their chests from a dagger thrust. The sheathed swords that dangled from their belts were clearly intended for battle, not ornament, and their scarred faces told Gunter their owners had found many occasions to put the blades to good use.

The third man was not a soldier, though he, too, wore a sword, but his had a richly ornamented hilt. His clothes were finely made and even Gunter could tell his boots must have cost more than a river-man could hope to earn in a year. Given his stout girth, it was evident that he'd grown accustomed to having others fight for him, rather than soil his own costly blade.

He fumbled in his scrip and produced a roll of parchment, glancing around for somewhere to lay it. He pushed aside the wooden bowls of half-eaten pottage on the small table, wrinkling his nose in disgust. 'God's blood, woman, take those away. The stench is enough to sour milk. What have you been cooking – swill for the hogs?' He began to unroll the parchment, running a stubby finger down a list written there.

Her face flushed with humiliation, Nonie pulled Hankin gently aside and hastened to collect the bowls. She stood with them in her hand, unable to decide where to set them down.

'I'll take them out.'

But as she attempted to squeeze past the commissioner, he shot

154

out an arm and barred her way. 'Stay where you are,' he snapped. 'I don't want you running off alerting your neighbours.' Only then did he lift his head, and what he saw seemed to arrest his attention for he stared at her. 'Stay in here, sweetheart,' he repeated, but this time almost under his breath.

Nonie darted a frightened look at Gunter and backed away a few paces until she collided with the small bed on which their son slept. Col had sprung awake and curled himself into the furthest corner, his eyes wide, gazing up fearfully at the men towering above him.

'You're known as Gunter?' the commissioner said briskly. 'A boatman by trade, is that correct?'

Dumbly Gunter nodded. Was this about Tom's murder? No, the constable or Sheriff of Lincoln would come if they wanted to question him about that. Maybe this was to do with a cargo. Were they claiming it was stolen or the tax on it had not been paid? His heart began to pound as he tried to remember each and every load he had carried these past few weeks.

'What is it I'm accused of?'

The commissioner lifted his hand from the parchment on the table, which promptly curled up into a roll again as if trained to conceal its contents. 'Guilty conscience, is it? What have you been up to? Smuggling? Creaming off some of the cargo before you land it?'

'Nothing . . . I've done nothing.'

'Yes, yes, I know you're all as innocent as the angels,' the commissioner said wearily. 'That's what they all claim. You boatmen would rob a blind monk of his last farthing, then swear you'd given him charity. You've probably broken the law so many times, they could hang you a dozen times over and you'd still have crimes left unpunished. But you needn't fret yourself this time. I'm not here to investigate your felonies. My business is the poll tax.'

Words swelled in Gunter's mouth, words so full of anger and outrage that for a moment it was all he could do not to vomit them over the man.

Nonie must have seen the fury in his face, for she whispered urgently, 'Gunter, please, don't!'

Gunter knew his wife was right to urge him to silence. Experience had long ago taught him that railing at men in authority only brought down more trouble on your head. He swallowed hard and tried to sound humble even though the effort nearly choked him. 'Sirs, I know

I didn't pay all that was due at Christmas, but with the bad weather and the rebellion in Flanders, loads were hard to come by. It's a lot to find and we had precious little notice. But with spring coming, there'll be more work . . . I can give you a little now but it's not all that I owe. I haven't got that yet . . . I just need more time. In June, at the next collection, you shall have it all.'

Even as he spoke, Gunter could tell the commissioner was barely listening. He flapped his hand at Gunter to silence him. 'Do I look like a tax-collector?' he said scornfully. 'But since you raised the matter you may as well know that, because of men like you who refused to pay what they owed in December, Parliament has brought the date for the next collection forward to the twenty-first of April. I suggest you find more work quickly for you've less than a month remaining to pay the whole amount in full.'

Gunter felt as if the man had just punched him to the floor. He saw the shock on Nonie's face. They had been able to pay only a quarter of the tax demanded at Christmas instead of the two-thirds required. Nonie had been worried enough about how they were to pay all that was owed in June, but he had kept trying to reassure her that work was bound to increase by then. But to find the rest in under a month? It was impossible.

He was dimly aware that the commissioner was still talking and forced himself to concentrate on what the man was saying.

'. . . check the records. The bailiff in Greetwell was supposed to have made returns listing all those men and women eligible to pay taxes in each household. But if this' – he flicked the roll of parchment with his forefinger – 'is a correct reckoning, then Greetwell has either been smitten by some terrible pestilence or those French pirates are coming further inland than we'd thought. According to this return, half the population of this village seems to have vanished in the last two years, and most of them women. How do you account for that?'

'I don't . . . I can't . . .'

'And neither, it seems, can anyone else in these parts. Strange, that. But never fear, the bailiff's been arrested. A few days freezing in Lincoln Gaol and I dare say he'll soon be only too eager to tell us who in the village bribed him to keep their sisters, mothers and daughters off this list. In the meantime, I've been sent to make a thorough and complete return by inspecting every cottage and searching every stinking byre and barn too, if I have to, to find these invisible women. So, let's start with your return, shall we?'

Gunter forced himself to keep his gaze fixed on the commissioner's broad chest and not to glance towards the wicket door behind the barrel, and he prayed Nonie and Hankin had not done so either. He only hoped Royse had run and hidden as he'd told her to, even if she didn't understand why.

The bailiff knew every family in those parts. He hardly needed to be told how many people lived in each croft. But suppose he hadn't written it down correctly. Gunter couldn't read. He had merely put his mark where the bailiff had instructed, trusting that his own neighbour wouldn't trick him. But he remembered the bailiff complaining about having to pay for his own family. *If they get recorded,* he'd said. Was that what he'd meant, that he wasn't going to record them?

'I told the bailiff honestly when he came here asking, just me and my wife, that's all. We've no one else living with us. No parents or kin . . . What does it say on the record?'

'Gunter and his wife Annora,' the commissioner answered, without bothering to look.

Gunter felt the tension in his chest easing. 'That's right, then. That's my Nonie . . . Annora.' He pointed to her, in case the commissioner should be in any doubt as to her identity.

The commissioner nodded. 'Gunter and wife Annora . . . Good . . . good . . .' he added thoughtfully. 'But that presents me with a problem, because it's not true that you have no other kin living here, is it? Let me see, I count one, two of your kin right here, unless, of course, they are river sprites.'

He turned to the two sergeants. 'Can you see them too or did I really drink too much of that horse piss the innkeeper in Lincoln had the effrontery to call wine?'

The men grinned. 'You want me to pinch them, see if they're real?' one asked.

'Don't you dare lay a finger on my lads.' Nonie took a step forward, the dishes clenched in her hands as if she meant to use them as weapons. 'You can see clear as well-water they're just bairns. Bailiff said we had to give the names of those over fifteen years, didn't he, Gunter? Hankin'll not be thirteen for two months yet. Even a blind man in a fog can tell he's still just a bairn. His voice isn't even broken steady yet.'

Hankin glared furiously at his mother's back and, for a moment, Gunter was afraid that he would protest he was a man, but he had the sense to swallow his pride and keep quiet.

'But we have been informed you have another child. A girl?'

A look of alarm flashed across Nonie's eyes and Gunter felt his stomach tighten.

'Royse . . . she's just turned fourteen.' Gunter tried to sound as if he was merely listing the number of bales in cargo. 'I've none other. You ask anyone.'

The commissioner gave a faint smile. 'Fourteen, is she? That's not what we've been told.'

'Who? Who told you that? They're mistaken. You can ask our priest. He baptised her. He'll have a record of it for we had to pay him the scot for it. He'll have written it somewhere in his books. He'll have put the year, won't he?'

Gunter was suddenly uncertain about what the priest might have written down. If you'd asked him yesterday he'd have sworn that every scratch and mark written on parchment must be the truth. Now, he no longer knew.

'If you imagine I have time to waste looking up the baptism of every brat in this village and the scores of others I have to visit, you're a fool. Besides, her precise age is immaterial. As the bailiff should have told you, every person over the age of fifteen must pay the tax, but also everyone who is married, regardless of their age. The law says if your daughter is married, she's no longer a child and must pay the tax, however young she is.'

'But our Royse isn't married.' Relief showed plainly on Nonie's face.

Gunter cursed himself. Every muscle in his body was as rigid as stone. He should have warned Nonie. But he'd only half believed the rumours and hadn't wanted to worry her or terrify Royse.

The commissioner snorted. 'I know that most of the commonality never trouble to marry before a priest. They merely hand-fast and often not even that. A girl simply takes up with a man and lives with him, like a vixen and a dog fox. She bears his cubs and calls herself his wife. Is that not so?'

'But our Royse's not taken up with any man,' Nonie said hotly. 'I'd never allow such a thing. She lives here with us.'

'And how do I know her mate is not away at sea or on the road? Is your daughter still a virgin?'

Nonie stepped forward, her eyes blazing with indignation. 'She most certainly is so. I've never let a man touch her, nor would I. She's still only a child.'

'And what else would a mother say about her daughter? Every woman claims her daughter is as chaste as a nun, but there's many a nun who could teach the town whores a thing or two about men. Girls have a way of slipping off and making free behind their mothers' backs. I want to question her. Where is she?'

Gunter saw Nonie's gaze flick towards the wicket in the wall, and he prayed that the King's men hadn't noticed. 'My daughter's gone away to tend an ailing relative,' he said quickly.

Unlike most men in this world, Gunter was not practised in lying. Even as a boy, his mother had always known when he was trying to cover something up and, believing her to be as all-seeing as the eye of God, Gunter had always betrayed himself even before he'd opened his mouth. A woman does her son no favours by teaching him to be an honest man.

The commissioner grinned at his two men-at-arms. 'That's the strange thing about these parts. One day the women are living here, and the next,' he snapped his fingers, 'they've vanished into the mist. So, pray tell me, when did your daughter go to visit this unfortunate relative?'

Gunter thought rapidly. 'She went this morning.' He was afraid to say it was any earlier in case a neighbour or friend had seen her near the cottage yesterday.

The commissioner raised his eyebrows and turned back to the men-at-arms. 'Another thing you should know about these boatmen is they can't count. I dare say he hasn't even noticed he's got a leg missing, since he wouldn't know how many he'd had to start with.' He gestured to the bowls, which Nonie still clutched in her hand. 'Five bowls, but strangely only four people to eat from them. How do you account for that?'

'We had a neighbour called round,' Gunter said, flushing as he realised his stupidity.

The commissioner laughed. Then, without warning, he pushed Nonie aside and grabbed Col, hauling him from the bed and holding the terrified child in the air, legs dangling, as he pushed his face into the boy's.

'Your sister, Royse, where is she, brat?'

159

'Mam!' Col twisted frantically round.

Nonie dropped the bowls and tried to reach for him, but one of the men-at-arms was ready. In his experience, women were far more trouble than men, turning into raging hell-cats if their kittens were threatened. He moved swiftly and seized Nonie by the arms before she could touch the boy.

The commissioner shook the child violently. 'Tell me the truth, brat, unless you want me to roast your backside on the fire.'

Col screamed as the man took a menacing step towards the hearth. Gunter launched himself at the commissioner, seizing his son and ripping him out of the man's hands. He set the boy on the floor behind him and sensed Hankin moving swiftly to his little brother.

But even as Gunter turned back, he felt the point of the second sergeant's dagger at his throat. Gunter was no trained soldier, and even had he not been lame, he realised that this man could cut his throat long before he could stretch out a hand to grab his stave. Nonie was still held fast by the other man, her eyes wide with terror.

Although it cost Gunter every grain of pride he possessed to surrender to these scabby bastards, he knew he could do no other to keep his family safe. When it came to defending himself or others against river-men like Martin, Gunter would have pitched himself into a fight without hesitation, but the King's men had all on their side. No common man could afford to stand against them, if he had anyone in this world he loved and feared to lose.

He held up both hands. 'There's no cause for you to speak to Royse. Record her, if you must. I'll pay the tax for her.'

The commissioner gestured to the sergeant-at-arms, who reluctantly lowered the blade. 'Come, man, you've admitted you can't even pay the sum you owe for you and your wife. Where are you going to find another twelve pennies by April?'

'I'll find it somehow,' Gunter said fiercely. 'But however we do, it's no business of yours so long as Parliament and the King gets their money. Now take your dogs and get out of my cottage. You got what you came for.'

'Oh, I wouldn't say that.' The commissioner scooped up the roll of parchment and stowed it carefully in his scrip. 'I prefer to question the girls personally. It makes for a far more entertaining evening.'

He crossed to the door and flung it open, letting in a blast of damp, cold air that set the smoke from the fire swirling round the

160

room. 'By April, remember, boatman. And I strongly advise you to pay in full and on time or the dogs they'll send next time will not be half as tame as my faithful hounds.'

The man holding Nonie bent towards her and barked in her face, laughing as she flinched away from him.

The other soldier backed to the door, sweeping the dagger from side to side as if he feared Gunter would charge at him. And he was wise to do so, for blind rage would have given Gunter the strength to rip his head from his shoulders.

As soon as she was freed, Nonie ran to the two boys, gathering them tightly to her. Gunter crossed to the door and saw one of the men snatch up the flaming torch he'd set in the soft earth. The three riders mounted and turned their horses towards Lincoln.

Gunter watched the guttering flame of the torch with its pendant of smoke moving away in the darkness. But even after the light was hidden from view by the tangle of willow and birch scrub, he continued to stand there, listening intently in the darkness to the sound of horseshoes striking the stones on the track. He wanted to make quite sure they did not double back.

He made no attempt to call to Royse. Better she should remain where she was a while longer until he was satisfied it was safe. The commissioner said someone had reported that he had a daughter and that she was fifteen. If that was true, only one man held such a grudge that he would send the King's men to a neighbour's door. Martin was behind this.

Gunter turned back into the room. Nonie was sitting on the bed, rocking Col in her arms and crooning over him as if he were still a nursling. Hankin was hunched on the opposite bed.

As soon as his father had closed the door, he leaped to his feet. 'Why did you tell them you'd pay the tax for Royse? Why didn't you just let her talk to them and tell him she's not fifteen? They'd only have to look at her to see she's not married. Nobody'd ever want to marry a mangy cat like her. Why should I have to work even harder to pay the tax for her when we don't have to?'

Gunter sank wearily onto a stool and rested his forehead in his hands. Nonie was staring at him and he knew the same question was in her mind. He shifted his weight. His stump ached and throbbed inside the wooden hollow. He longed to unstrap the wooden peg and ease it, but he couldn't until he'd fetched Royse. If he took it off he'd not get it back on tonight.

Nonie and Hankin were still watching him, waiting for him to speak. He'd have to tell them. He moistened his lips. 'They wouldn't just have questioned Royse.'

'So,' Hankin said, 'they could have talked to anyone along the river. Everyone'd say the same. She's not fifteen and she's not married, so why did you tell them you'd pay?'

Gunter didn't want to explain: Hankin was just a boy – but he would have to work three times as hard to raise the money so he had a right to know why his father was forcing him to it.

'I hear gossip, stories that would set your teeth on edge. If you believed the half of it, you'd think the poll-tax men are worse than the French soldiers who roast human babes for their supper. I don't pay heed to most of it. Besides, I was sure the King's men wouldn't be allowed to . . . I thought it was just talk.'

'Wouldn't be allowed to do what? Tell us!' Nonie sounded as angry as her son and with good cause. The shock of having armed men barge into her cottage and threaten her children would make most women cry, but Nonie was not given to tears.

Gunter studied his grimy hands. 'They said . . . some of the commissioners were taking girls whose parents claimed were not yet fifteen and examining them to see if they were virgins.'

'Asking the girls, you mean?' Nonie said, as if she couldn't believe he had meant anything else.

'No!' Gunter shouted, slamming his fist on the table. 'Not *asking* them, *examining* them. They stripped them naked in front of the soldiers and their own parents and forced their fingers inside them to see if they're still . . . untouched. Some were only eleven or twelve years old.'

Nonie's hand flew to her mouth. 'They wouldn't!'

Gunter's tone was quiet and dead. 'I said as much myself. But when I heard it was the King's men at the door, I suddenly thought, What if it's true? What if they've come for our Royse? And when I saw the leer on that bastard's face tonight, I knew there was no doubt what he'd come for.' He closed his eyes, massaging the top of his aching leg. 'They said in the tavern that fathers and brothers were simply paying up rather than put their daughters and sisters through that.'

'But that's what they want,' Hankin burst out. 'Frightening people into paying when they don't have to. We should stand up to them!'

'How?' Gunter said. 'They were armed with swords. Trained soldiers.

You think they'd have run away if you'd slung a stone at them? If I hadn't agreed to pay, they would've come back and kept coming back until they caught your sister.' His eyes blazed as fiercely as his son's. 'I tell you this, Bor. I'd harness myself to a cart and pull it like a beast. I'd sacrifice my other leg and crawl on my hands, sooner than have a man like that lay his filthy hands on my daughter or on any of my family. If I have to pay this tax ten times over to protect her, then I swear on the Holy Virgin, I will find a way to do it.'

April

March borrow'd of April three days and they were ill.

Chapter 22

At dawn on Easter Sunday, you must 'wade the sun'. Draw a pail of water and stand it beneath the skies. If the reflection of the sun in it be clear and steady, it will be a fine season and good harvest, but if the reflection be pale and trembles, then the season will be wet and cold and the crops shall fail.

Lincoln

I watch that ghost, Eadhild, crawling up the Greesen stairs behind the unsuspecting pilgrim. The pilgrim sees nothing, of course, gazing up at the cathedral, eagerly anticipating the spectacle of the Easter mass and the excitement of the thronging crowd. Until, that is, he feels a cold hand seize his ankle, bringing him crashing onto the stone. The hand drags him back down the steps, while he, terrified, tries in vain to cling to them. But even when he fearfully turns his head, he cannot see the phantasm that has seized him, or the rotting hand that holds him.

A ghost myself, I can, of course, see the wretched wraith and, more's the pity, she can see me. Eadhild is a spiteful old hag, but she seems to have taken a liking to me. She has started sidling up to me whenever Mavet and I pass that way, nuzzling up against me and trying to twine herself about me. Believe me, there is nothing more repellent than a long-dead crone who coyly flirts like a lively tavern wench. But even Eadhild's mouldering hand was warmer than Beata's mood on that particular Easter Sunday.

Beata's lips were pressed together as tightly as a sprung trap. She banged the steaming civet of hare on the table in front of Widow Catlin. The rich blood and pig's liver gravy slopped onto the white cloth, but she didn't apologise to her master or even look abashed. Diot, bustling in with a chicken crowned with eggs, wore a grin that showed she was winning the battle for control in Master Robert's kitchen.

Robert silently thanked Heaven for Catlin's sweet temper. Her serene smile didn't flicker even with Beata clattering and thumping around her. She merely gave a pleasant nod to both women. Catlin's adorable Leonia was regarding the comings and goings of the two servants with evident interest, almost, you might have said, like a gambler weighing up the merits of two cocks in the pit. Master Edward seemed as entertained as his young sister. Father Remigius, seated beside Robert, was blissfully oblivious to the tension.

Robert sighed. Beata had been as distant and moody as young Adam these past weeks. Adam was still grieving for his mother, but Robert couldn't think what ailed the serving-maid. He'd believed she would be glad of another pair of hands to help prepare the Easter feast. She was always complaining that she was worn to the bone on feast days, with only Tenney to help her and him being as much use as a husband in a birthing bed when it came to cooking. Robert, poor fool, had fondly imagined that Beata would greet the news of Diot's arrival with grateful pleasure, but she'd declared she wouldn't have the old hag within a mile of her kitchen, and railed on until Robert had been forced to remind her it was *his* kitchen, as was all else in *his* house. Since then she had gone about her duties in tight-lipped silence, banging and clattering so unnecessarily that several times he'd been forced to retreat to Catlin's home for an evening's peace.

Father Remigius beamed at the spread laid before him. The quantities of mutton and pork dishes, already ranged among savoury puddings and pastries, were enough to feed an entire monastery. He rubbed his old hands together appreciatively. 'What a feast indeed! You have certainly honoured Our Lord's rising with all your work this day, my daughters.'

Beata glowered at him, but Diot simpered as she attempted an ungainly curtsy.

'And not a fish in sight,' Jan said, cutting himself several thick slices of mutton. 'After forty days of fish, I'm so hungry for the taste of meat I could devour a whole bull, if Beata could fit it on a spit.'

Father Remigius smiled sympathetically. 'I have to confess to being a little relieved myself when the Lenten fast is over, but we should spare a thought for the poor monks. They must fast from dawn till dusk in Lent, then partake only of a frugal meal. At least, that is the rule, though it is observed in few monasteries these days.'

'Then you may count on it that I'll not be taking Holy Orders, however bad business gets. It would be just my luck to end up in one of those monasteries that do keep the fast,' Jan said.

'I hope you'd never consider such a thing,' Catlin said. 'Women would be throwing themselves into the Witham in their scores if they thought that such a handsome man as you had renounced their company.' She laid her hand on Jan's arm, patting it gently.

It was no more than any woman might do when teasing a friend. All the same, Robert found he did not like it. He caught sight of Edward staring at his mother's hand and Robert saw a spasm of hostility flick across his face as if he, too, were annoyed by the intimate gesture.

Jan withdrew his arm and turned to his young brother. 'You haven't touched a bite yet, Adam. Here, try this suckling pig. It's so tender you don't even have to chew it.'

He sliced off a couple of pieces with his own knife and tossed them onto Adam's pewter trencher, adding a good wedge of crackling, stained a rich golden-red by the honey and spices it had been basted with. The boy, his face white and drawn, stared at it as if his brother had put a dead mouse before him.

'Did you not hear the compliment Mistress Catlin paid you, Jan?' Robert said. 'At least have the good manners to acknowledge it.'

Catlin turned her gentle smile on him, while under the table she reached for Robert's hand and squeezed it. 'Don't scold him, Robert. He's tending Adam as a loving brother should. He's right. We should give all our attention to the exquisite dishes Beata has prepared.'

Father Remigius was doing just that, but he paused between mouthfuls and glanced down the table at Jan. 'Father Peter tells me there was trouble at the Good Friday service at St Mary Crackpole between the Florentines and some of your men, Jan.'

Robert glanced sharply at his son. 'I knew nothing of this. What trouble?'

Jan shrugged impatiently. 'Matthew Johan's tribe are still smarting over the goods the mayor confiscated to pay for what his fellow countrymen stole. Some of his men claim their boats were rammed and damaged by ours, and that we've tried to block their moorings near their warehouse. But if anyone's causing trouble on the waterfront it's them. If they carry on this grudge, I'll see to it that more of their goods are seized.'

169

'Why didn't you tell me?' Robert demanded.

'It was just a few punches. No one drew weapons.'

'I should hope not indeed, not in a church and on such a holy day.' Father Remigius briefly closed his eyes and crossed himself.

'They started it!' Jan said irritably. 'You've only got to look at a Florentine and he thinks himself insulted.'

'Their blood runs too hot,' Edward said, ripping a chicken leg from the carcass. 'They should be bled more often.'

'But not by my son!' Robert snapped.

There was a languidness in Edward's manner that, from their first meeting, had set Robert's teeth on edge, a dumb insolence in every gesture and expression. Even the white streak in Edward's hair irritated him. White hair should make a man look old, but somehow it only drew attention to Edward's youthful, well-sculpted face. Robert had instantly concluded that he thought he could get by in life through good looks and charm. Master Edward certainly had come to the wrong house if he thought such troubadour's tricks would work on a hard-headed merchant.

Father Remigius held up his hands. 'I'm sorry I raised the matter. I had no wish to spoil such a joyous occasion. It's just that Father Peter asked me to suggest – only *suggest* – that your men attend another church until this matter is settled. St Mary's Crackpole is not their usual place of worship, is it? And while, of course, it was Johan's men who provoked the incident, I am sure none of us would want to see it end in bloodshed.'

'You have my word,' Robert said, glaring at his son, 'that none in my employ will go near that church again.'

Father Remigius nodded. 'Then let us speak no more of it.'

The conversation died into an awkward silence. Robert was proud of how well Jan was learning the business but that had never stopped them arguing over it. It was only natural, Robert supposed, for lads to want to try new ideas, and for older and wiser men to hold the reins firmly so that they didn't bolt into foolishness. Since his mother's death, though, Jan had grown ever more prickly and hot-headed. There were days when Robert could hardly make a simple remark to the lad without him snarling. Both his sons had taken the death of their mother far harder than ever Robert could have imagined.

He glanced down the table at the younger boy. Adam had barely said a word to anyone since the funeral. He poked listlessly at the pork, raising it to his mouth, then setting it down again, as if the effort were too much. Catlin beckoned to Diot and murmured something. She immediately went out and returned with a pie in the shape of a cockerel with a little pastry hare riding on its back, complete with reins and a saddle.

'I heard Lombard pie was your favourite, Adam,' Catlin said, 'so I had one fetched from the baker this very day for you, stuffed full of chicken and bacon just as you like it.'

The boy's face had already broken into a reluctant smile at the sight of it. He examined it from every angle, but did not take a bite. His smile faded and he glanced up at Jan, anxiously gnawing his lip.

Catlin laughed. 'I know it's a pretty thing, but you can't keep it or it will spoil. Diot can always fetch you another. Why don't you enjoy that one?'

Leonia's expression darkened. She stared at her mother, her brown eyes narrowed. But Catlin was smiling at Adam.

Robert squeezed her shoulder. His fingertips briefly touched the warm skin of her neck. He let his hand drop, half embarrassed at the thrill her bare flesh had sent through his body. 'You really shouldn't spoil the boy, my dear.'

'He needs a tender hand after all he's been through these past weeks, poor motherless lamb,' Catlin murmured.

Father Remigius caught the remark and waved his knife at her, beaming. 'But not motherless for much longer, I think. We have a double cause for celebration this day.'

Jan glanced up, frowning. 'We're marking the Easter feast, but with my mother not yet cold in her grave we're not celebrating.'

The old priest looked confused. 'I meant the forthcoming nuptials. You're still in mourning, of course, and it is right and fitting that you should grieve for your poor dear mother. But Easter reminds us that after death comes life and how better to celebrate our Lord's resurrection than with the new life a wedding brings? In fact, I believe I will use that very point in my sermon next Sunday when the first of the banns is called. I trust you will be present, Mistress Catlin, to hear your banns read.'

'My congratulations, mistress,' Jan said. 'I wish you every happiness. Your future husband is to be congratulated, too.' His brow furrowed again. 'But . . . why aren't you celebrating the Easter feast in his company rather than ours? Will he not think it odd?'

171

The old priest turned to Robert, who had gone rigid and was staring grimly at the fragment of hare impaled on the point of his knife, as if it were the flesh of his worst enemy. Edward was grinning broadly.

'Have you not told . . . Forgive me, Master Robert, I was sure you must have . . .'

There was a moment of frozen silence in the room, which was shattered by a peal of bright laughter. 'But I am spending the Easter feast with my future husband, Jan.' Catlin fondled the bloodstone necklace that encircled her throat. 'Your father has asked me to marry him.'

Jan sprang up so violently that his goblet was knocked to the floor. 'Is this true?' he demanded. 'My mother's not even a month in her grave and you've already found yourself another wife?' He rounded on Edward, who was watching him with undisguised amusement. 'Do you think this right?'

Edward leaned across, took his mother's hand, brought it to his lips and kissed it. 'Your father's to be congratulated on winning the hand of the loveliest woman in England.' He looked up at Jan, still grinning. 'So, will you propose a toast to the happy couple, *brother*, or shall I?'

'I would sooner drink to my own damnation.'

Robert lumbered to his feet. 'Sit down at once, boy. Where are your manners? Have you forgotten we have guests?'

'You expect me to continue eating as though nothing has happened?' Jan said savagely. 'How could you betray my mother's memory like this? No man should even look at another woman so soon after he buried his wife. It's not decent. Did you care so little for my mother that you couldn't even grieve a year for her?'

'Mistress Catlin nursed your mother like a sister. She and I have shared the grief of her death, and that grief has drawn us together. After all, Mistress Catlin is herself a widow long before her time. Leonia needs a father to guide her as she comes to womanhood, and you've seen yourself how wretched the boy has become without a woman's care. I'm so often away on business and Adam needs a loving mother to tend him.'

Jan's face was flushed with anger. 'Do you really expect my brother to call another woman *mother* when he has only just seen his true mother laid in the grave? Or perhaps you were waiting for her to die so that you could move this woman into her bed!'

172

There was a howl from Adam. He scrambled over the bench and raced out through the door leading to the yard. Beata ran after him.

'How dare you?' Robert roared.

Father Remigius clambered to his feet, holding up his hands. 'Peace, peace. Have you forgotten what day this is? Your father is thinking of Adam, Jan. He'll recover from his grief much sooner, with the help of a good woman to—'

But Jan ignored him and strode towards the door through which his brother had fled. He turned on the threshold. 'You're always reminding me that you're a respected man in this city, a man of position. How much respect will you command from your fellow merchants, if you throw yourself into the arms of another woman before the mourning candles have even burned away? I'll not allow you to disgrace my mother's memory in this way. I demand you call off the wedding. I won't stand by and let you make a laughing-stock of yourself and this family.'

'How dare you presume to tell me what to do? I am your father and your master. Come back and apologise—'

But it was too late. Jan had already slammed the door behind him. Robert made to follow, but Catlin caught his hand. 'Let him walk it off. He'll spend the night in a tavern, and after a jug of wine it will all seem different to him. In a day or two he'll be begging your forgiveness.'

'It is your forgiveness he should be begging,' Robert said. 'I never thought to hear a son of mine speak to me as if I was an errant child to be corrected. I should take a horse whip to him.'

'I have already forgiven him and so should you,' Catlin said.

'Well spoken.' Father Remigius nodded approvingly. 'On today of all days we must follow the example of Our Blessed Lord.'

Catlin stroked Robert's arm and looked up at him anxiously. 'But I would never wish to come between you and Jan. Perhaps we should do as he asks and delay the wedding for a year or so, if he thinks it best.'

'What *he* thinks best!' Robert spluttered indignantly. 'I will not be told by a boy who is scarcely out of clouts when I may or may not marry. We'll marry as soon as the banns are read, and I will not delay by as much as a single day.'

Catlin bowed her head. 'Whatever you wish, my sweeting. My only concern is for your happiness. I will do whatever you ask of me.'

Robert, though the blood still pounded in his temples, felt his chest ease a little. That was what he adored about Catlin. Her concern was only ever for him, unlike that insolent brat he had raised.

Deep down, he knew as well as Jan did that the wedding would appear to others in the city to be conducted in indecent haste, which only made his son's words smart the more, but the truth was he couldn't wait a year to take Catlin to his bed. God's blood, it was all he could do not to carry her up there this minute, but Catlin was not the kind of woman who would ever consent to sleep with a man who was not her husband. Besides, if he waited, perhaps another man would offer her his hand. A year was a long time for a widow alone and in need of someone to protect her. She might be tempted to accept. He couldn't risk losing her.

Edward, having taken another gulp of wine, rose and stood behind his mother, hugging her and kissing the top of her head. 'Master Robert is right, Maman. Ignore Jan. You two deserve happiness after all you've both suffered. The pup will come round – and if he doesn't, who cares?'

But Robert found he did care. He hadn't realised until that moment how much he wanted the respect of his son. To see the boy he'd always taken such pride in look at him with such contempt felt like a sword slash across his face. But the pain enraged him the more and made him determined to stand his ground. He would marry Catlin now even if the whole world railed against it.

If anyone had bothered to take notice of the little girl in the room they would have seen excitement flickering across her face as if she had just watched a hugely entertaining play. But it disappeared when Robert turned back to the table. He suddenly realised the child had witnessed the whole scene. He put an arm around her and drew her close, looking down affectionately at her. 'Leonia, I'm sorry that you have had to listen to such foolishness. Once your mother and I are wed, I will treat you as if you were my own sweet child and give you all that I would have given my own daughter, had I been blessed with one.'

A happy thought struck him. He crossed to a small chest, opened it and withdrew a tiny package wrapped in green velvet and tied with a yellow ribbon. He turned back to Leonia, beaming. 'I'd intended to give this to you on our wedding day, but I think you should have it as an Easter gift, to show you how much I'm looking forward to calling you my beloved daughter.'

Robert took her hand and placed the parcel in her palm. Leonia glanced at her mother with sparkling eyes.

'Open it, child,' Catlin urged.

The ribbon was pulled off in a trice and Leonia carefully unrolled the package. A gold necklace lay inside the velvet cloth, a golden rosebud hanging from it, a single pearl set on it, like a dewdrop.

Robert chuckled in genuine pleasure at the delight that lit the child's face. She held it up to the candlelight, watching the rosebud glitter as it twisted and turned at the end of the chain.

'So you like it, then,' Robert said. 'A rosebud for beauty and the pearl for chastity. Your mother chose it. I've no understanding of things that please young girls, but I dare say I will learn. Shall I put it on for you?'

She turned while he lifted the long chain carefully over her head, then raised her black curls. He caught a glimpse of the little arched neck and smelt the sweet perfume of her skin, before letting the soft curls fall back into place. When she turned and pulled him down to kiss his cheek, Robert felt a pleasurable shiver run through him. Leonia was fair set to be as pretty as her mother, prettier even, with her golden skin and huge, long-lashed eyes. He realised he would have to guard his new daughter's virtue carefully in the years to come. He'd been a young man once and knew that a glimpse of her would be like placing a jewelled goblet before an open casement: even the most virtuous man would be tempted.

Chapter 23

If the heart, eye or brain of a lapwing is hung around a man's neck, it shall keep him from forgetfulness and sharpen his wits.

Beata

I heard the door to the house slam and came out of the kitchen, thinking it might be Master Robert come to comfort his son, but it was Jan. He was striding across the yard towards the gate, his fist clenched around the hilt of his sword as if he was itching to thrust it deep into someone's innards. 'Where's Adam?' he demanded.

I nodded towards the gate. 'He ran out as if the hell-hounds were chasing him. I couldn't catch him, but Tenney's gone after him. He'll find him and bring him back.'

Jan glanced back at the house, shaking his head, like a dog with sore ears. 'I swear my father's entirely lost his wits. He's always insisted that nothing should ever be allowed to destroy the reputation of our *respectable* family or damage our good name. The times he's blistered my ears for drunkenness or being seen with a girl from the stew-house, and now he throws all aside and announces he's going to marry within weeks of my mother's death. And to spring it on young Adam like that. When was my father intending to tell . . .'

He grasped my arm so fiercely that I squeaked, though I'm sure he didn't realise how hard he was gripping me. 'God's teeth, you don't think he's got her with child? Could she still . . . I mean can women of her age?'

'I reckon that old hag, Diot, wouldn't be able to keep her fat mouth closed if her mistress had a brat in her belly. Though you may yet have a half-brother or -sister if they wed,' I said bitterly.

I'd not thought of that, and somehow it was worse than seeing them wed. Was it because I knew my time for bearing children was gone? I felt cheated. It was strange: I'd watched my hope drip from me month after month, year after year, and felt nothing at the time, not even when I watched poor Mistress Edith's belly swell with her babies.

Once, long ago, when I still thought Tenney had a fondness for me, I dreamed one day we two might set up home together and I might dandle a babe on my knee. After all, a child cares nothing for how its mam looks, only for how much it's loved, and I had love enough in me to flood the Braytheforde. But Tenney never asked me and made no attempt to touch me, save as friend or brother. After a while I forced myself to forget my foolish fancy. Yet, no matter how often you sternly tell yourself it will not happen, there must still be a tiny corner your words can't reach, a hidden place in which you stubbornly imagine that one day you will hold your own child in your arms. And when Nature finally takes away the hope you didn't even know you carried, it hurts something fierce.

Jan was blustering on, striding up and down the yard, just like Master Robert did in the hall when he was in a lather. 'We must stop my father doing this, Beata. You've known him for years and he confides in you. Can't you reason with him?'

'He'll not listen to reason on this, Master Jan. Not with Father Remigius giving his blessing to it. And that old priest is so smitten with Widow Catlin he'd marry her himself, if it wasn't for his vows. She's leading Master Robert by the nose.'

The courtyard gate opened and Tenney hurried in. 'Is the lad returned?' he asked, as soon as he caught sight of us.

Jan took a step towards him. 'He's not come back here.'

'I suppose I must look again then, as if I had nothing better to do. Happen he's gone the other way along the river. I'll skin him alive when I get hold of him. Case you've forgotten, it's the Easter feast,' Tenney said reproachfully. 'And I've not had a bite to eat yet. What with fasting afore mass and the smell of all those meats roasting, my belly's growling like a pack of wolves. I'm supposed to be stuffing myself, not chasing through the town after spoilt brats. If you ask me, we should let the lad alone. He'll soon fetch himself back here when he gets hungry enough.'

'And what if the boy's too scared to come home?' I said. 'You saw him. He wouldn't take a single bite of that pastry Diot brought him. I dare say he thought it was poisoned.'

Jan whipped round. 'What do you mean? Why should he think it was poisoned?'

'Beata means nowt, do you?' Tenney said, glaring at me. 'Some nonsense young Adam's got into his head. Pay no heed to it. Lad's had no appetite since his mam died, but give him time.'

'What nonsense? What exactly has my brother been saying?' Jan demanded, raking his hair, just as his father did.

Behind the young master's back, Tenney shook a warning finger at me. I hesitated. Suppose Adam really had run away. Jan would have to know all, if he was to find him and persuade him to return. I decided to ignore Tenney.

'It was at the mistress's funeral, Master Jan, when your brother told me . . . told me he'd seen summit he shouldn't.'

'And,' Tenney said firmly, 'like I told Beata, lads imagine all kinds of tarradiddle at that age. Why, it wasn't so long ago he was afeared there was a monster living behind that great tapestry in the hall. But you need to have a word with him, Master Jan. Tell him what he's saying is dangerous talk. He'll listen to you. He's always looked up to you more than his own father.'

'Master Jan,' I said, frowning at Tenney, 'I've been thinking about it ever since the funeral and I've not been able to get it out of my head. Why did that creature Diot burn Edith's night linens and mattress afore she was barely cold? I reckon it was cause she was afraid something might have got spilled on it, something she wouldn't want finding.'

Tenney let out a sigh of exasperation. 'Like I told you, it was 'cos Master Robert didn't want to sleep on the mattress the poor woman died on. And no more would I. It was soiled and it stank worse than a pig with flux. You think he'd want to be reminded of her death every time he lay down?'

But Jan wasn't listening to Tenney. He was staring at me, stricken. 'You said Adam saw something he shouldn't. Are you trying to tell me he saw Diot with poison in her hand?'

Tenney shook his great head. 'Beata's not saying that at all, Master Jan. She's just repeating the nonsense young Adam told her and he's nowt but a bairn.'

Tenney grabbed my arm and pulled me away from Jan. 'Have you lost your wits?' he whispered fiercely. 'Master Robert'll have you arrested and flogged if you go around shouting murder's been done in this house.' He kept his voice low, but it was not soft enough to prevent Jan hearing.

'My father knows about this?'

'No, Master Jan. I've not dared tell him what young Adam said,' I said hurriedly. 'I wouldn't.'

'But he does know my mother swore she'd been poisoned,' Jan said. 'I told him that myself.'

'The mistress said all manner of things afore she died,' Tenney said. 'One time she was shrieking about an owl with burning eyes sitting on her bedpost. I searched her room myself, top to bottom, in case some bird had flown in, but there wasn't so much as a feather.'

'I never heard her say such things,' I said hotly. Someone had to stand up for my poor mistress, seeing as how she wasn't there to defend herself.

Tenney rolled his eyes. 'Afore you go repeating what young Adam said, you want to remember it was you who was cooking for the mistress when first she sickened. If word of poison gets round, it's you and me'll get the blame for it, no one else. You want to make sure that flapping tongue of yours doesn't put us both on the gallows.'

A cold hand clutched at my belly. Tenney was right: if poison was suspected, I'd be the first person they'd blame and how could I prove otherwise? I'd heard tell of servants being burned alive for poisoning their master or mistress, for that was nothing short of treason. I swallowed hard, trying to fight down my panic.

'Master Jan . . . I didn't mean . . . Take no notice. I shouldn't have said anything. Please don't tell Master Robert.'

But in the spring sunshine Jan's face had turned the colour of ashes. 'You did right to tell me, Beata. Rest assured, I'll not betray you to my father. But I have to find my brother. I have to hear for myself what he saw. Tenney, I'll help you search. The sooner we find Adam, the sooner you can stuff yourself.'

Chapter 24

*A turf cut from the grave of ghost and placed under the church
altar for four days will draw the unquiet spirit back into the
grave and prevent it walking.*

Lincoln

Jan trudged along the riverbank, but he was halfway to Greetwell
before he spotted his brother. He'd sent Tenney to search the top of
the city around the cathedral, knowing there were plenty of taverns
open, even on Easter Sunday, where he might quench his thirst and
appease his hunger. Then if he found Adam, he'd be less inclined to
clout him all the way home. But Jan guessed the boy's instinct would
be to run somewhere he could be alone, and there'd be few working
the river on such an important feast day.

He found Adam squatting on the bank, hunched against the cold
wind, his knees drawn up with his chin resting on them. Leaden
clouds obscured the sun, promising rain before the evening was out.
The boy was breaking twigs into pieces and tossing them one by one
into the grey water, watching the current sweep them away. He glanced
sideways as Jan approached, lowering his head again as his brother
sat down beside him, but not before Jan saw the stains of dirty tears
on the boy's cheeks.

'So this is where you've been hiding,' Jan said, with forced cheer.

Adam gave a slight shrug, but didn't raise his head.

'I don't blame you for running off,' Jan said. 'I was furious with
Father. Still am. I can't believe he'd contemplate marrying so soon.
We quarrelled . . . after you left.'

Adam groped for another twig and methodically snapped the end
off inch by inch, dropping the pieces into the water.

Jan was eleven years older than his brother. By the time Adam could
talk, Jan was already working in his father's business. Adam had always
treated his brother more as an uncle than a sibling. In consequence,

180

Jan realised he had little idea of what went on in the boy's head. And Adam was certainly offering him no quarter now, staring sullenly into the twisting eddies. Jan's belly growled, and he cursed himself for not having thought to bring some food. At least it would have eased the tension, though if Adam really did fear Diot was trying to poison him . . .

'I talked to Beata, after you ran off, about what happened to Mother . . .'

Adam flinched.

'About what you told her at the funeral,' Jan finished.

'It's true,' Adam said fiercely, flinging the whole twig into the river. 'Nobody believes me, but it's true!'

'Beata believes you.'

'Did she tell you I killed Mother? Did she tell you that?'

Jan was startled. That was the last thing he'd expected the boy to say. 'No, of course not. She said you thought Mother had been poisoned. Did you say it because Mother *told* you she'd been poisoned?'

'I said it because it was true. I saw her do it!'

Adam scrambled to his feet and ran along the bank towards a birch tree that grew between the river and the path. He kicked and pummelled the trunk, lashing out so wildly that Jan was afraid he would slip and fall into the river.

Pushing himself up, he strode across to grab the boy, but Adam shoved him away. 'I killed her! I killed her! It was all my fault. I should have protected her. You and Father weren't there. So it was up to me. I should have stopped her!' The boy was scarlet with misery.

'Who, Adam? Who should you have stopped?' Jan demanded. 'It was Diot, wasn't it? That's why you wouldn't eat the pastry she brought you today.'

The boy stared at him uncomprehendingly. 'Diot? She wasn't there.'

Jan gripped him by the shoulders. 'Then who was it?'

A fearful expression crept into the boy's eyes, just as it had in Beata's. 'You won't tell Father, will you?'

'I need to know what you saw, Adam. Tell me!'

The boy cringed away from him and Jan realised he had been shouting. He released his grip and tried to soften his tone, crouching so that their faces were level. 'Adam, I swear on Mother's grave that I won't let anyone hurt you. But you have to trust me.'

The boy glanced up and scanned the track, which was deserted.

He lowered his voice almost to a whisper: 'It was one evening, when Father was away and you were still at the warehouse. I was sitting with Mother telling her about school, but Mistress Catlin came in and said I was making her tired. She sent me out. She had no right to do that! If anyone should have been sitting with Mother, it was me, not her. Mother wanted me there. I know she did.

'So when Mistress Catlin went out to the kitchens, I crept back in to kiss Mother goodnight. But when I was in the bedchamber I heard someone coming and hid behind the screen. I could see only a little of the bed through the joint in the screen but I saw her put some drops from her flask into Mother's posset. I did! But I was too scared to tell anyone in case she told Father I'd gone into Mother's chamber when she'd said not to. I should have stopped her. It's all my fault!'

'Mistress Catlin added drops to Mother's posset?' Jan said carefully.

The boy nodded earnestly.

'But you could see only a little of the bed. You're certain it was Catlin you saw?'

'I couldn't see her face, but I saw a bit of her gown and her hands. I know it was her, Jan, I know it! She murdered my mother.'

The boy flung himself at his brother with such force that Jan was almost knocked off balance. Adam wrapped his arms round his brother, burying his head in Jan's chest, his slender frame shuddering with sobs. Jan grasped him tightly, hatred and grief coursing through his own body in equal measure.

Above them, the dark clouds burst open and fat raindrops fell, sending circles spinning across the river and trickling down the brothers' faces. It soaked their clothes to the skin, but still they clung desperately to each other under that vast grey sky, for they had no one else to cling to.

Chapter 25

To prevent a new building from falling, the shadow of a man must be secretly built into the foundations, either by measuring his shadow with a piece of rope and burying that or by tricking the man into standing so that his shadow falls on the spot where the foundation stone will be laid. The chosen victim will die within the year, because his spirit has been stolen from him and it will be compelled to guard the building for ever.

Lincoln

That vile old crone, Eadhild, is following me. I try to keep her at bay by avoiding the Greesen steps of an evening, even though it deprives me of the chance to meet the other ghosts who loiter there. When the charming Catlin and the beautiful little Leonia are safely abed, I drift instead to the Newport arch through which the Roman soldiers forever march. But they're hardly good company. I understand little of what they're saying. The Latin I dimly remember my tutor thrashing into me seems a foreign language to these fellows and, besides, they'll no more break ranks in death than they did in life. I wonder if they know they're dead.

But Eadhild has found me, sliding her rotting hand between my thighs and tilting her head coquettishly to one side, asking if I wouldn't fancy a stroll through the graveyard. I don't know how she died or why she haunts the Greesen, and I'm afraid to ask in case she thinks I'm interested in her, which, most emphatically, I am not. But I'd warrant she's been searching for a bed-fellow to share her grave for many centuries and I shudder at the thought.

I was considering where else I might hide to escape from the foul hag as Mavet and I were passing Mistress Catlin's door late one night. A youth, posing as a linkman, was leading an elderly gentleman up the street by the light of a burning torch, assuring him that it was the quickest way to the inn where the old man had lodgings for the night.

As the gentleman chattered away, the youth signalled to a slattern of a girl who was lounging against a wall further along the street. In a flash of skirts she was gone, doubtless to alert those lying in wait in a dark alley that a plump pheasant was being led straight into their trap.

I contemplated whether it would be more amusing to watch events unfold or intervene, but I felt sorry for the old man, who was earnestly thanking the youth for his help and seemed to think the nasty little blowfly was doing him a favour. Mavet, who'd had no sport all day, needed little encouragement to swarm up the youth's leg and nip him where he most deserved it. The lad squealed, dropped the burning torch and, clutching his cods, sank to the ground, where he rolled around in the filth, shrieking as if he were possessed. And that is exactly what the elderly gentleman must have feared, for he scurried away with more speed than I would have thought possible.

Chuckling to myself, I was about to set off with Mavet again, when the gate to Mistress Catlin's yard opened and a plump figure waddled out, a lantern in her hand, its light half hidden by the voluminous shawl that enveloped her head and shoulders.

She turned towards the lower part of the city. She'd removed the wooden pattens from her shoes and soft leather made little sound on the muddy track. Intrigued, I glided after her, but then I saw she was not alone. Someone was keeping pace with her, someone considerably more agile than the old woman.

A man was darting in and out of doorways, shrinking back whenever she half turned her head and running to the next corner when she disappeared from view. An experienced cut-purse never draws attention to himself. He strolls along as if he merely happens to be passing down the street on his own business. But anyone glancing from a casement would have spotted at once that this man was trailing the old woman.

Jan had not expected to see anyone leave Mistress Catlin's house at this hour of the night. For several days and nights now, he'd spent every spare moment watching it, hoping he might find something he could use to convince his father that the widow was not the angel Robert thought her. His father would not listen to tales of poison, as he'd already found to his cost, but if Jan could prove she was seeing another man, he'd certainly take notice of that. Nothing would anger him more.

But so far Jan had seen nothing he could use as a weapon against her. No man entered her house, and when she went out, it was always with one of her children or Diot. But now, for the first time, he felt he might be close to discovering something. Diot must be carrying a message for Catlin. Why else would she leave the house in the middle of the night?

Of course, it would never have occurred to a young man like Jan that a woman as old and fat as Diot might be sneaking out to meet her own lover, for the young are convinced that the old have no such appetites, but then he'd never had that withered hag, Eadhild, flirt with him.

Jan ducked into the shelter of a doorway as Diot paused to glance up and down the street. Satisfied she was unobserved, she turned abruptly into a narrow alley that ran behind a row of butcher's yards. Jan dimly remembered the passageway from his childhood explorations of the city, but he'd not had cause to go down it for years: it led only to an ancient postern gate in the south-east corner of the city wall, which was kept permanently locked. But Diot made straight for it. Raising her lantern, she let the light fall on the great ring in the old wood and twisted. To Jan's surprise, the door creaked open.

Turning sideways, Diot squeezed her massive bosom through the arch and tugged the door closed behind her. Jan darted forward and pressed his ear to the wood, trying to hear if she was moving away. He didn't want to open the door too quickly and walk straight into her, but he couldn't risk tarrying too long or he might lose her. He'd have to take a chance.

Now that Diot's lantern was on the other side of the door, there was not a glimmer of light in the alley. He ran his hand over the wood, feeling for the iron ring and suppressed a yelp of pain, as he drove a large splinter into his palm. He pulled it out with his teeth, and sucked the wound, then tried again, more gingerly this time, until his fingers connected with the cold rusted metal. He twisted and pushed the door open, just an inch or two, peering through the gap.

The door appeared to open into a small boatyard, dimly lit by the ruddy glow from a fire burning in one corner. Several broken craft, piled one on top of another, concealed the entrance from the view of anyone passing on the river, but the boats were just far enough from the door to allow someone of Diot's girth to squeeze through.

A good route for getting stolen goods or contraband in and out of the city, Jan thought grimly, remembering their own losses. He crept through the arch, pulling the door shut behind him.

Jan knew the river well enough to realise he was in Butwerk, a festering midden of cottages and huts that squatted just outside the city wall. He was used to the curious fragrance of fish, sheep's wool, ox dung and imported spices that perfumed the wharf, so much so that he didn't notice it until visitors remarked on it, but Butwerk had a distinctive odour all of its own. Rotting offal and human excrement mingled with the acrid smoke of the small cooking fires on which the inhabitants burned old bones, dried water-weed and any noxious waste they could find, wood being too scarce and precious to waste as fuel. Most of the fires burned outside the hovels, thickening the air with smoke and lighting the uneven ground with a hellish red glow, from which the huts rose up like jagged black rocks.

Jan, trying not to cough, peered through the haze and glimpsed the light from Diot's lantern bobbing up and down as she picked her way across the small boatyard. He followed, stifling a curse as his foot plunged into a deep puddle. Squelching unpleasantly, he trailed behind Diot as she wove between the lopsided huts. Their doors, or the pieces of sailcloth that served as doors, were closed and all were in darkness. A few people, rolled in blankets, were sleeping around the fires outside. Dogs lifted their heads, but didn't trouble to bark. Only the cats were awake, stalking the mice rustling in the reed-thatched roofs or hunting frogs beneath the rank weeds. Surely Widow Catlin would not have taken a lover from this quarter, unless Diot was to deliver her message to another go-between.

Diot waddled round the side of one of the huts and Jan followed, jerking back only just in time before he banged into her. He crouched down. His knee touched something wet and sticky, which soaked through his hose. He tried not to imagine what it might be.

Four women were sitting around a blazing fire. Two looked older than Diot, certainly more haggard and dishevelled. Beside them, caught in the firelight, was a girl, scarcely more than a child, with a dirty face and a wild tangle of hair, huddled close to a hollow-cheeked woman, who might have been her mother or sister.

Diot lowered her great hams onto a rough stool set ready in the circle round the fire. One of the old women offered her a wooden bowl, from which she took several deep gulps, wiping her mouth on her sleeve, then handing it to the younger woman. Jan could hear nothing of what was said, only the low babble of their voices. But he was afraid to move closer, for even another foot would bring him into the light cast by the flames.

One of the two old women nodded to the girl. She obediently rose and padded, on bare feet, into the hut. A few moments later she emerged with a small iron pot, which she suspended over the fire on an iron tripod. She filled it with a yellowish liquid from a tall clay jar. Then she carried a piece of sacking to the old woman, laying it carefully in her lap. It was heaped with an assortment of dried herbs and roots. The crone sorted through the leaves and fragments, holding each in turn close to her eyes and sniffing it, before handing her selection one by one to the girl who dropped them into the pot. A cloud of noxious steam rose and the girl coughed, wiping her streaming eyes. The old woman chuckled and sent her back to the hut. She returned, carrying a small pot, blackened with soot.

Leaning heavily on a stick, the crone levered herself to her feet. Digging her wrinkled talons deep into the pot, she dragged out a handful of greyish powder, which she flung into the heart of the fire. At once the flames prowling around the cooking-pot turned from yellow and orange to blue and green. She plunged her stick into the pot, stirring three times to the right, then three to the left, then handed the stick to the woman next to her. Each of them in turn, including Diot, rose and stirred the pot as the first had done, chanting as they stirred. Steam curled up into the ink-black sky, first white then gradually turning green.

Something was taking shape in the steam. As Jan watched in growing horror, he saw a great viper's head, with acid-green eyes and a long forked tongue that vibrated between the fangs as it savoured the foul air. The snake's head turned and its tongue flicked towards the place where he was concealed. His skin crawled, as if a thousand tiny vipers were slithering over him.

He lumbered to his feet. His shoe slipped in the liquid he'd been kneeling in and almost sent him crashing to the ground. But he managed to regain his footing and fled, trying desperately to retrace his steps towards the yard and the safety of the gate.

A man peeled himself off the wall of the hut against which he'd been leaning and hopped into the middle of the track in front of Jan, using a single crutch to balance himself. A length of cloth was wound round his head and over his face, with holes cut in it for his mouth and eyes. It was so stiffened with dirt that it looked as if it could never be peeled off.

'Now, what would a fine young man like you be wanting here, I wonder?' the muffled voice said. 'Looking for a lass, are we? Keg of wine, going cheap? You just tell Pizzle what you fancy and I'll see you right. You don't want to go trusting the thieving toads round here.'

He took another hop towards Jan, extending a filthy, rag-covered paw. 'You come along with Pizzle, young master. I know someone who'd like a word with you.'

Was he a leper? Jan didn't relish finding out. He whirled round and ran across the small clearing in front of a hut, leaping over the embers of a fire and jumping sideways to avoid the snapping teeth of a snarling dog, which lunged and strained against the rope that tethered it. As he dodged between the huts, Jan found himself running straight for the river. His heart was thumping, but he tried to calm himself. *Look for the city wall. Where is it?* But though you could hardly miss the towering bulk of it in daylight, now it merged into the night sky, as if it had melted away.

If the river's in front of me, the wall must be to the right. A stitch stabbed his side, but he dared not stop. He stumbled along a narrow path that twisted between the huts, tripping over bits of old rope and stones. Between the hovels, he glimpsed snatches of the black river. Reflections of red flames darted across the water as if fires were burning deep below. Dogs leaped at him, men hidden beneath blankets reached out of the darkness to grab his ankles, and the jagged huts reared in his path, slithering towards him, herding him into the black water.

He felt as if he'd been blundering around for hours before he found the door at the back of the boatyard, grasped the metal ring and hauled himself safely back into the city. He groped his way up the dark alley until he reached the street at the end. There, his legs gave way. He slid down the wall of a house until he was crouching on the ground, gasping for breath, his body soaked in icy sweat.

Eventually his heart stopped pounding and he felt strong enough to stand. He was levering himself up when he heard the creak of the postern gate behind him. He peered round the corner of the building. Diot was waddling up the alley towards him. He'd been too shaken to form any plan, but at the sight of her, fear turned to rage. He stepped out in front of her, trapping her in the narrow passageway. She shrieked, throwing up a hand to protect herself, almost dropping her lantern.

'So, Diot, will you tell me what happened to my mother?'

'Master Jan?' The old woman took a pace closer. 'Why, it is you.' She clutched at her massive chest and gave a nervous giggle. 'Gave me such a fright. Shouldn't leap out at a body like that. It's a wonder I didn't drop dead on the spot. What brings you here? Chasing after some lass, I'll be bound. Our Edward's the same. Out till all hours.'

'I was following you,' he said coldly.

'Why would you do that? Was there something you wanted, Master Jan?'

'I want,' his jaw was clenched, 'to know whether it was you or your mistress who murdered my mother.'

'Murder?' Diot staggered sideways, throwing out an arm to steady herself on the wall. 'Whatever put such a wicked idea into your head, Master Jan? Your mam died of an overheated liver. I heard that Master Bayus say it himself. Course, I know the poor creature was raving all kinds of wildness at the end, but you can't pay no heed to that. She'd no notion what she was saying.'

'Except that my . . .' Jan caught himself just in time. If Catlin had poisoned his mother and discovered there had been a witness to her crime, Adam's life would be in grave danger. 'Your mistress was seen putting drops from a flask into my mother's posset. I thought she was acting alone until I saw you tonight at your witches' coven, casting spells with those other hags. Who were you trying to kill this time? Me?'

'No, I swear it . . . Upon my life, I'm no witch!' Diot was clutching at her chest in earnest now, her voice cracking with fear. 'I only went to fetch a physic. Old Meggy knows all about herbs and suchlike. There's none better at curing folks than her.'

'And was it a potion from old Meggy your mistress gave to my mother?'

Diot's many chins jerked up. 'Catlin only give your mam what Master Bayus told her to. If you saw her put anything in the posset, it was the physic he sent. She had to – it was that bitter your mam wouldn't swallow it else. But it's a great pity you didn't go to old Meggy yourself when your mam first got taken sick. I reckon she'd be living now, if you had. Those physicians only know what they read in their books. Old Meggy, she learned at her granddam's knee, like her mam did afore her. It's in their blood, it is.'

'You're lying!' Jan spat. 'Your mistress is determined to marry my father for his money and she wanted my mother out of the way. And now I know who got the poison for her.'

'Mistress has money enough of her own,' Diot said defiantly. 'She don't need none of your father's.'

She had taken several shuffling steps back from Jan, though she must have seen she was trapped: there was no way she could get back through the postern gate before he reached her.

Jan advanced towards her. 'Oh, she has money, does she? Well, not for long. All the money and possessions of convicted felons are forfeit to the Crown. When you and your mistress are rotting in gibbet cages, Catlin's son and daughter will be left with only the rags on their backs. Worse than that – when my father comes to his senses and realises what she's done, I'll see to it that he brings an Act of Attainder against both her spawn, so neither they nor their descend-ants can ever own anything. They'll have fewer rights than an outcast leper. And as Catlin swings on the gallows she can comfort herself with the knowledge that her precious son will end his days carrying buckets of shit for a living, while her daughter works as a stew-house whore. Those are the only ways either of them will earn a crust of bread by the time we've finished with her family.'

Diot was slumped against the wall, wheezing, her face screwed up in pain. 'Can't hang me . . . nor my mistress. Done nothing . . . we haven't . . . nothing! Master Bayus says she wasn't murdered . . . So does the priest. They'll . . . both swear to it and you can't prove otherwise.'

'Not yet,' Jan said. 'But I'll find a way. There's a man, a friar, who's been trying to warn me of something. I thought he was threatening my father, but the first time I saw him was on the day the evil widow came to our warehouse. I'm certain now it was her he was following, not my father. He knows something about Catlin, I'm sure of it, and I'm going to find him. So you can tell your mistress from me that she'll be dancing soon enough, but not at her wedding. She'll be dancing on the end of a rope!'

Chapter 26

If a demon is suspected of raising a storm, the church bells should be rung against the wind, so shall the demon flee and take the wind with him.

Lincoln

Father Remigius bowed gravely to Robert as Beata admitted him to the hall. He seemed on the verge of speaking straight away, but stopped as he caught sight of Catlin seated beside the fire. The elderly priest glanced around, frowning. Leonia was curled up in the window-seat opposite Adam, playing a game of Nine Men's Morris with clay marbles on a wooden board.

'Forgive the intrusion, Master Robert. I had thought to find you alone.' Father Remigius massaged his shiny, swollen knuckles. 'Perhaps it would be better if I returned later.'

Catlin rose and, to Beata's annoyance, poured a goblet of wine and handed it to the priest, as if she were already mistress of the house. 'We wanted the children to get to know each other better,' she said, 'since they are to be kin. But if we are intruding on a business matter, Leonia and I will leave at once.'

'I'm sure anything Father Remigius wishes to discuss will concern us both, my dear,' Robert said pointedly, leaving no doubt in his expression or tone that if anyone was going to leave it would not be Catlin.

The priest stared at the goblet in his hand as if he couldn't for the life of him work out how he had come to be clutching it. Evidently embarrassed, he shuffled across to watch the game in progress. 'And who is winning, children?' he asked, with forced jollity, though it was plain Leonia was beating Adam soundly or that Adam was allowing her to.

Adam stared down at the board, but Leonia looked up with a smile so guileless and radiant that the old priest fondly imagined he was staring at a statue of the young Holy Virgin.

191

'Adam's won all of the other games. He's so clever.'

Adam flushed. It wasn't true. He hadn't won any of them and he knew he wasn't clever, but he didn't contradict her.

'So what brings you to my house, Father?' Robert asked, somewhat tetchily.

He'd been hoping to spend a quiet afternoon alone with Catlin, but she had paid more attention to Adam than to him, and if that weren't bad enough, Beata had been clattering about in the hall on some flimsy pretext, coming in and out so often that the banging of the door was beginning to make his head pound. He devoutly prayed the priest wasn't intending to invite himself for supper.

Father Remigius crossed back to the couple and, with an anxious glance behind him at the children, lowered his voice. 'I deeply regret that such a thing should have happened, but you must understand I cannot ignore it.'

'What is it, Father? Have my men been brawling in church again?'

The old man's watery eyes blinked at him in puzzlement. 'Brawling? I don't believe so . . . that is, no one has complained to me. I've come about your banns. The notice I pinned to the church door proclaiming your intention to marry has been . . . defaced.'

Robert frowned. 'Market brats, I suppose. They throw filth at anything. The constable needs to put a few in the pillory – see how they like to be pelted. That would soon stop them.'

'I fear it was not street urchins,' Father Remigius said. 'I would not have troubled you with such a trivial matter.' He reached into the scrip that hung from his belt and withdrew a rolled sheet of parchment, which he handed to Robert. 'This is the notice of your intention to marry, which I pinned to the door myself, but see what's been written upon it.'

Robert straightened the parchment impatiently and, as he looked down at the words, an angry flush crept across his face. 'This is an outrage!' he spluttered.

Father Remigius spread his hands in his familiar gesture of conciliation. 'I know, I know, but as someone has written it and the accusation has been posted on the church door, I am obliged as your priest to ask. . . is there any truth in it?'

'How dare you? Of course not!' Robert crumpled the parchment and hurled it into the fire. It crackled, then burst into flames.

Catlin crossed to Robert's side, took his clenched fists and lifted them to her lips, pressing tender kisses on them. She scanned his face anxiously. 'What is it, Robert?'

'Nothing,' Robert said, his jaw working furiously. 'Nothing for you to trouble yourself with, my dear.'

'But I'm afraid,' Father Remigius said firmly, 'that Mistress Catlin must be troubled with this. I cannot perform the wedding unless you both swear that the accusation is false. This constitutes a public declaration that there is an impediment to your intended marriage.'

He turned again, glancing unhappily towards Adam and Leonia, who had abandoned all pretence of playing Nine Men's Morris and were evidently listening to every word.

'Perhaps if the children were to play outside, we might discuss this matter more freely.'

Robert ordered Beata to take the children into the yard. All three glared resentfully at him as they passed, but Robert was too incensed to notice.

The moment the door had closed, Catlin turned to Father Remigius. 'What was written on the banns, what impediment?'

The old priest sighed. '*Crimen*, the impediment of crime. It was no more specific than that. Neither did the writer say which of you he thought guilty of such a grave offence.'

Catlin turned in agitation from the priest to Robert and back again. 'But I don't understand. What crime can they be talking of? I've committed no crime, and I'm sure, my dearest Robert, you could never have done so.'

It was Father Remigius who answered her. 'We cannot be sure that the writer himself has understood the implications of what he has written. The finer points of canon law on this matter are still much debated. When Pope Gregory the Ninth in his decree spoke of a promise to marry another while their spouse was still alive, are we to take it that that vow in itself constitutes adultery or that this promise becomes an impediment only if the couple are already indulging in carnal knowledge—'

'Adultery! Is that what I am accused of?' Robert bellowed.

Father Remigius flinched. 'That may indeed be what the accuser meant, but *crimen* is generally taken to refer to the crime of unlawfully killing a spouse in order to marry another. Though,' he added hastily, seeing the violent shade of puce Robert was turning, 'I am certain your accuser could not possibly have meant that.'

193

'So,' Robert said, 'I am simply accused of adultery. Nothing to concern myself with at all.'

'You spoke of "he",' Catlin said quietly. 'Do you know our accuser's identity?'

Father Remigius stared at her, clearly bewildered. 'I have no idea who would make such an accusation, but naturally we must assume a man. A woman would hardly have knowledge of canon law and, besides, how many could even write their own names?'

Catlin lifted her chin. 'I am a woman and I assure you I can write a great deal more than my name, Father. I do not think you should dismiss my sex so easily.'

'Regardless of whether it was a woman or a man,' Robert snapped, 'I demand you find out at once who wrote such a malicious falsehood.'

Father Remigius gazed despondently at the fire, which had already consumed the offending accusation. He glanced reproachfully at Robert. 'Perhaps if you had not burned the notice so hastily, we might have matched the writing.' He sighed. 'If the wedding takes place—'

'Are you suggesting we should cancel it?' Robert spluttered. 'Clearly someone is out to stop us—' He broke off abruptly. Up to that moment it had not crossed his mind that the writer of such an accusation could have been anyone other than an enemy. A merchant of Robert's standing was bound to have left a few men with grudges trailing in his wake – a fellow merchant who suspected that Robert had snatched a deal from under his nose; a brogger, who, as middleman, thought himself cheated on a price; men who were bitter because Robert had prospered while they had not. There was no counting the ways that a man might feel himself slighted or harbour murderous resentment against another. But Robert had realised he need look no further than his own hearth for the author of that vile message.

He spun on his heel to face Catlin. 'It must have been Jan who did this. He's determined to prevent our marriage out of some wretched, misguided loyalty to his mother. He doesn't seem to grasp that we're in love . . .' He looked surprised at the last word to escape his lips. But with it came the understanding that he had never spoken a word so earnestly or meant it so profoundly. He adored this woman in a way he'd never loved poor Edith. Her every gesture and look almost drove him mad with the longing to possess her.

Catlin's lips parted in a smile and, oblivious to the presence of the priest, she threw her arms about Robert's neck, kissing him so fiercely and passionately that it was all Robert could do not to surrender to the stirrings in his crotch.

Father Remigius coughed pointedly, and Catlin pulled herself out of Robert's arms with some difficulty, for he was reluctant to let her go. The priest had averted his eyes and was making a careful study of the tapestry depicting the savage boar with its head in the lap of the Saxon princess. He coughed again. 'Robert, I trust I did not give the impression that I thought your son had any part in this. Such a thought never crossed my mind. I cannot believe any son would do such wickedness to his own father.'

Robert snorted. 'You heard him at the Easter feast. When a son dares to threaten his own father openly in front of guests, there is clearly nothing he wouldn't stop at.'

Father Remigius winced. 'He spoke in haste, as the young often do, and such words are best forgotten . . . But you must know his writing. Did you recognise his hand on the parchment?'

Robert hesitated. He had been so incensed by the words that he hadn't registered how the letters were formed. He shouldn't have thrown the parchment onto the fire, but he wasn't about to admit as much. He flapped a hand irritably. 'It's impossible to match any man's writing from a few letters scrawled on a parchment when it's pinned up on a door against those he writes carefully in a ledger. And, in any case, I dare say he took pains to disguise his hand.'

'But does Jan know of any impediment?' Father Remigius persisted. 'If he does, I beg you to confess it. It may not be insurmountable. There are several occasions I recall when a dispensation was—'

'Of course he doesn't!' Robert thundered. 'Because there is no impediment. This accusation is based on nothing but malice. Jan knows Catlin and I will not be dissuaded, so he is attempting to frighten you into refusing to perform the marriage.'

Robert reached out and took Catlin's hand, pulling her round so that they stood facing the priest, looking so much like young lovers defying a disapproving parent that Father Remigius might have smiled, had he not been so troubled.

'Father, my wedding will take place exactly as planned,' Robert declared. 'And if that boy tries one more trick to prevent it, I swear I shall kill him.'

Father Remigius sighed. Weddings were supposed to be such joyous occasions, bringing families together – at least, that was what he'd believed when he was ordained. But experience had taught him that not even wars between nations could match weddings for the discord and bitterness they generated. He always reminded the couple that marriage was blessed by God, yet he sometimes wondered if it hadn't been invented by the devil. It certainly gave rise to enough mischief. He crossed himself hastily, repenting at once of this blasphemous thought, then thanked God fervently for the gift of celibacy.

Chapter 27

*To spill salt brings bad luck. To gather up the spilled salt brings
worse. Instead, a pinch of salt must three times be thrown over
the left shoulder, but never over the right. For the devil sits on
your left shoulder and you are throwing salt into his eyes, but an
angel sits on your right.*

Lincoln

I hear that putrid old hag, Eadhild, is in evil humour because I have
managed to hide from her these past few nights or so. She no longer
confines herself to grabbing the ankles of those walking up the Greesen
to bring them crashing onto the steps but walks behind those coming
down and gives them a violent shove. She likes to do it when they
have their arms full of goods to take to the market, a basket of hard-
boiled eggs or a tray of fresh loaves. But some good comes from every
ill: the beggars are delighted, for they feast well on the spoils.

Old Father Remigius, it seems, was in no better humour than Eadhild
and that evening, as soon as he had finished conducting an unusually
perfunctory service, to the bewilderment of his small congregation,
he hurried from the church and arrived, somewhat breathless, at Jan's
lodgings.

The elderly priest tried to avoid telling Jan exactly what his father
had said about him, but he was obliged to reveal that Robert suspected
his son of writing the accusation on the banns. The matter, whoever
had raised it, must be investigated and Father Remigius was not a
man to shirk his duty. 'After I spoke to your father this afternoon, I
was unable to banish the idea from my mind, not even as I said
Compline,' he added ruefully.

'What am I supposed to have written on the banns?' Jan demanded.
'That my father's future wife and her maid murdered my mother? If that
was what appeared on the parchment, it was nothing less than the truth.'

197

Father Remigius's head sank into his hands and he groaned. 'My son, why must you continue to torment yourself with such evil thoughts? I visited your mother often where she lay sick. If I'd had the slightest suspicion anyone was trying to harm her I would have prevented it. Mistress Catlin could not have been more solicitous to her or more devoted to her care.'

'But I followed her maid, that old woman Diot, and I saw her—'

'Enough!' Father Remigius heaved himself from the chair, flapping his hands at Jan. 'It was my duty to ask if you knew what lay behind the accusation that there is an impediment to the marriage, but I see you are as ignorant of its meaning as I am. That being so, unless the accuser comes forward, I must agree with your father that it is nothing more than baseless libel, born of malice, and I shall ignore it.'

'Father, wait!' Jan moved swiftly between the priest and the door. 'I swear I didn't write it, but I think I know who did. I've been searching for him these past two days and I won't stop until I find him. I'll bring him straight to you and he'll tell you what it means. He's a brother of yours in Holy Orders.'

'If he has knowledge that the law of the Church or the King has been broken or is about to be, then he should have come straight to me or the sheriff and reported what he knew,' Father Remigius said sternly. 'A man who's afraid to show himself has his own guilty secret to hide and his word is not to be trusted. I regret that many liars and rogues take Holy Orders only as a means of escaping punishment for their own wickedness.'

The priest's dry, wrinkled hand grasped Jan's arm. 'In the name of Christ, I beg you, Jan, to reconcile yourself with your father by dancing at his wedding. If the rift between you is allowed to widen any further, it may never be closed. Young Adam has already lost his mother. Do not deprive him of his only brother too.'

Shaking his head despairingly, Father Remigius shuffled from the chamber.

The moment the door closed behind the priest, Jan let out a bellow of frustration and rage. He swept his arm across the remains of his supper on the table, sending trencher, goblet and candlestick crashing to the floor. He roared curses on all priests, his father and Catlin in such savage tones that two boatmen ambling past his casement peered in, sure that a fight must be taking place.

Jan was in such a fury that, before he knew what he was about, he found himself striding round the Braytheforde, then realised he'd left both sword and cloak on the floor of his chamber. A cold wind was blowing off the water, but he did not return for them: he must find that friar. He'd search all night if he had to, but he would find him. And when he did, he would force the man to tell what he knew, even if he had to duck him in the Braytheforde and drag him by his heels to the sheriff.

Jan collided with an elderly goodwife, almost knocking her over, but for once he didn't trouble to apologise. He worked his way around the wharf. It was growing dark and rain was pattering into the water. The beggars were settling down for the night, hurrying to claim the most sheltered spots before some usurper wormed his way in. Those men fortunate enough to have money were making for the inns and alewives' houses. Jan peered into every gloomy corner and yard. The friar had first been seen near the warehouse. He might return there.

A man can be so consumed by hunting for something he is sure lies ahead that he does not notice what is behind him. Jan was so intent on searching around the warehouses that he was oblivious to the shadow that slid out from the cavern of a nearby courtyard and followed him silently, in friar's sandals, along the street. He jerked round as he felt someone touch his shoulder.

'Master Jan?' The words sounded as if they were being dragged through gravel. 'I've waited for you for far too long.'

Jan reeled backwards. The hunter had become the quarry. 'I've been trying to find you,' he gabbled. 'I've searched everywhere these past two days.'

'You could have found me easily enough, if you'd trusted Pizzle that night you were in Butwerk. I'd sent him to bring you to me. But you were intent on telling Diot you would see Catlin hanged. That was foolish. Diot does not take kindly to anyone threatening her daughter. You didn't guess? Diot is not just Catlin's maid, she's her mother.'

Chapter 28

On St Mark's Eve, a witch must walk backwards three times around Thoresway Church in Lincolnshire, then look through the keyhole and recite a charm. In this way she renews her pact with the devil. If she ever fails to do it she will lose her powers.

Greetwell

Gunter shoved Hankin out of the cottage, followed him and closed the door softly behind them. After the warm fug of the tiny room, the damp chill of the breeze from the river was sharp enough to make even a hardened boatman shiver. Hankin, rubbing the sleep from his eyes, glared mutinously at his father. Somewhere an eager cock was crowing, but the sun had not yet risen. Only a faint silvery ribbon running along the distant line of the dark marshes showed where dawn would break. Gunter heard the door open again and glanced round as Nonie emerged, clad only in her shift and fumbling to tie a shawl about her shoulders.

She thrust a package wrapped in sacking into Hankin's hand. 'A bite of bread for your dinner. See you share it with your faayther.' She looked up at Gunter. 'Can't you wait till I've heated the pottage? You both need something hot afore you start out.'

Hankin looked longingly at the warm cottage, but Gunter shook his head. 'I haven't had a load for two days. If I can get there before the others . . .'

'But you can't work on an empty belly.'

'If I can't get a load, we'll all be working on empty bellies,' he snapped. Then, seeing the pained expression in his wife's eyes, he ran his hand through his matted hair and said, more gently, 'You know we must find the money. If the King's men return, we'll not be able to hide Royse a second time.'

'But she's recorded now,' Nonie said. 'They'd have no cause to . . . examine her.'

'There's no knowing what they'd do to force us to pay up. They've seen I'd do anything to protect the bairns, so it'll be them they threaten first.'

Gunter had lain awake night after night cursing himself for what he'd done. Only a fool gave in to blackmail. Once you'd done that, they knew where your weakness lay, what to do to hurt you most. And if fit, strong men like him didn't stand up to them, what hope was there for the frail and the old?

Aware that Hankin was listening, he gave the boy a little shove. 'Start getting the reed mat off the boat, lad.'

The boy stood his ground and folded his arms. 'I want some pottage. Too hungry to work.'

Nonie glared at him. 'You heard your faayther,' she said, raising her hand as a warning. For a moment it looked as if he would defy her too, but he sulkily turned away and went down the track. 'What's got into him?' she said. 'He'll not do a thing he's told without arguing the moon is the sun.'

'We both know what ails him,' Gunter said angrily. 'He saw his own faayther give in to the King's men and agree to pay them, like some frightened old woman handing over her purse to footpads. What kind of a man does that make me in his eyes?'

'A *good* one, who'd do anything to protect his family,' Nonie said. 'Besides, they were armed. What could you have done, except get us all killed?'

What was the use of talking about it? Gunter thought. They'd been over this a hundred times, Nonie stoutly protesting that he had done the only thing he could. But words are so many fallen leaves. You never find the truth in words, only in a person's eyes. And he would carry to his grave the reproach in the eyes of his wife and son that night.

Gunter trudged along the bank to the boat. Nonie followed him a little way and stood watching, her fists clenched, as if she was struggling to find words to span the chasm that was opening between them.

Hankin had stripped the punt of its protective mat and sat inside, his head resting on his hands, his shoulders hunched. Gunter ignored him and loosened the mooring ropes. Then as he stepped into the boat, Nonie raised a hand to shield her eyes from any glimpse of him and hurried back to the house. They both knew it was bad luck for

201

a woman to watch her husband's boat depart, even on the river. It was a measure of how worried she was that she had followed him as far as she had.

Gunter pushed off and expertly turned the long punt upstream. He stood up in the square bow, pushing the long wooden quant down to the river bottom, feeling the flat iron shoe on the end pressing against the bed. Then he walked towards the stern as he poled the punt forward. In spite of his wooden leg, Gunter could balance on a moving punt as easily as other men could on dry land. Hankin was almost as skilled as his father, though being small he lacked the power to make the boat move as swiftly. Gunter glanced at him. His son was still squatting on the cross-bench making no attempt to lift the other pole. Gunter itched to cuff him out of his sulk, but he didn't.

Just a few weeks ago he'd been a hero in the boy's eyes, his father, strong as an ox, the equal of any man on the river. But in the space of an hour he'd turned into a pathetic coward. He knew Hankin despised him, not simply for his failure but for tricking him into believing his father had ever been a man.

'Eat what your mam gave you.'

Hankin's head jerked up. 'Then there'll be none for the noon bell and I'll be hungry again by then.'

'You can have my share.'

'I don't want it!'

'As you please.' Gunter tried to ignore the lad's tone. 'But if you're going to have a bite, eat fast. I need your quant in that river. We'll be coming up to the bends shortly.'

Hankin hesitated, then unwrapped the sacking. He tore pieces off the chunk of bread and shovelled them into his mouth, rewrapped the remains and, without looking at his father, took his place in the stern, dipping his pole into the water.

It was hard work pushing upstream. Through the wooden shaft of his quant Gunter could feel the currents tangling with each other as the rising sea-tide barged its way up, fighting the river water pouring down for possession of the channel. He tried to keep the boat in the upstream, but the current twisted away from him almost as soon as he found it.

Sometimes, when they were further downriver, and if the wind was blowing right, they could hoist the small square sail to help them shift a heavy cargo, but he wouldn't risk that so close to the city. The waterway was too crowded, and if a gust of wind should catch the sail at the wrong moment, the boat might ram another craft or the pillars of a jetty. Better to trust to muscle on this stretch of the river.

They pushed on in silence. A pale pink light was flooding the river and the banks were stirring to life. Men were making ready their own small boats and women were dipping pails into the water and staggering back to cottages where smoke meandered through the reed-thatched roofs.

Gunter worked the quant harder, and was relieved to see Hankin was also putting his back into it. Although the lad was not strong enough to make much difference to the speed of the craft, he helped to keep the course steady and could push away any floating debris that might crash into them, without Gunter having to break his stroke.

As they reached the outskirts of the city, the cottages huddled closer together. Those on the edge of the city, outside the walls, were thread-bare hovels cobbled together from pieces of salvaged wood, lost nails and whatever else their owners could find to keep out the worst of the weather. In the dark shadows of the open doorways, half-naked infants with swollen bellies and bandy legs listlessly threw stones at passing boats or at the gulls fighting for scraps on the water. Their older siblings were already busy with their day's work, hooking anything they could salvage from the river as it swept the city's leav-ings past them – a bobbing onion, lumps of tar, bits of wood, rope, rags, sacks of drowned puppies – anything that might be eaten, sold, burned, or used for fishing bait. Even the meanest object was a prize worth fighting over.

Further into the city the shacks stepped aside for wooden cottages, then small houses with roofs overhanging the river, shading it from the sun. You had to keep your wits about you. This stretch of water was teeming with craft. Some river-men were already moored along the bank, cooking their breakfast over small braziers, ready to trade goods from their boats as soon as the market bell rang. Gunter caught the smell of roasting herring, and his stomach growled in protest. He saw his son's head turn towards the sweet smoke.

'Keep your eyes on the boats, lad,' he warned. He needed Hankin to be alert for any craft that might swing too close to theirs and be ready to push it away.

There was a sudden splash in the water next to them as a pail of night soil was tipped out of a casement above. The filth just missed him, and Gunter gave an angry bellow. A young maid with a round face peered down at him. She blew him a cheeky kiss, grinning unrepentantly. It was against the law for citizens to empty their night soil into the river, but they did so anyway – it was easier than trailing with it to the midden.

They passed under Thorn Bridge and then beneath the great vaults of High Bridge. A couple of women were crouching on the steps that led to the water's edge between the arches, pounding their washing, though the water was so dirty that Gunter wondered if it was worth the effort.

It was cold and dank under the bridge. All around him water oozed down the walls, leaving trails of green slime, and dripped into the rushing water with an echo like a hammer hitting iron. Above him, he could hear the clatter of horses' hoofs and the grinding of cartwheels. No matter how many times he passed under the bridge he always hated it. He had lived all his life beneath great wide skies, and solid though the bridge appeared, he always feared that one day it might collapse under the weight of the wagons above, trapping him in the icy darkness of the water.

He breathed easier as the bow edged into the light again and before long the river mouth widened into the teeming harbour that was the Braytheforde. Gunter's experienced eyes scanned the water's edge for a mooring. To his relief he saw that several spaces were as yet unoccupied along the wooden jetty closest to Master Robert's warehouse, but other craft were already nosing out of the river, and several more across the other side of the harbour were pushing towards the same moorings.

'There, Bor, over there, we'll make for that one. Push as hard as you can, afore someone else beats us to it.'

Glancing back, he saw another of the flat-bottomed boats catching up fast. His heart sank when he recognised Martin and his hulking son, Simon. Martin's wife had done what every man wished for and had borne him a son first instead of a daughter. The lad was now a strapping sixteen-year-old and little Hankin was no match for him. But Gunter was determined not to be beaten this time.

Weighing up the distance between his punt and Martin's, he stepped to the opposite side and, with his next push, slewed the boat at a slight angle while still sending it shooting forward. He was gambling on Martin being alert: if he wasn't, Martin's punt would plough right into his. But the trick paid off and, with a stream of curses, Martin was forced to turn his boat and slow it down to avoid a collision.

With one swift push, Gunter had his boat back on a straight course heading for the vacant mooring closest to the warehouse. With a practised hand he brought the punt alongside. Hankin knew what was expected of him. He made the leap for the short, slippery ladder that hung down the side of the jetty, bounded up it like a squirrel, deftly caught the rope his father flung up at him and made it fast.

'We beat them, Faayther!' Hankin grinned for the first time in days.

Gunter glanced back. Martin and his son were arguing with another boatman as both tried to force their craft into the same mooring further along the jetty. Gunter knew he had the edge, but not for long. 'Make the other rope fast, so she doesn't swing out. Then wait for me on the punt. Don't go running off.'

Gunter knew the temptations of a crowded port for a young boy, never mind the excitements of the marketplace beyond. It was only too easy for a lad like Hankin to become engrossed in watching the boat-builders cutting the great logs with saws twice as long as a man, or lose all sense of time wandering among the colourful stalls, dancing bears and storytellers. As a lad, he'd done so often enough.

Gunter pressed his hand to the side of the jetty, measuring the gap between the high-water mark and the river. They were so far from the sea that the tide only made the water level in the Braytheforde rise and fall a couple of inches. But in the lower reaches of the Witham you could feel the effects of the tide's strong pull and push. By his reckoning, the tide would be high within an hour or so. If they were travelling downstream when it was ebbing, it would speed their journey.

Gunter hoisted himself up the ladder and limped along the jetty towards the warehouse. Fulk, the overseer, known behind his back as Fart, was standing at the door. He was a small, stocky man who made up for his lack of height with aggression. He lost his temper easily if forced to think about two things at once, and his attention was now focused on berating the few warehousemen who'd arrived late. But Gunter could already see the familiar figures of other boatmen wending their way round the wharf towards the warehouses. He couldn't afford to wait. If there were no loads at the first, he'd have to hurry to the next, and by that time their cargoes might already have been assigned.

Fulk was still snarling at one cowed youth when Gunter interrupted. 'Beg pardon, Master Fulk.'

'What is it?' Fulk snapped, turning away from the youth, who slid inside and disappeared.

'Any loads going out this morning?'

Fulk ignored him and peered into the dark interior of the warehouse.

'You, boy,' he bellowed. 'I've not finished with you yet. I'll see your wages docked for this. I've warned you, there's plenty ready to take your job, if you can't haul your carcass out of your kennel of a morning.' As he turned to Gunter, the men inside made obscene gestures at his back. 'There's precious little going anywhere, with the trouble those Flemish weavers are causing in Flanders. Scum want hanging, the whole pack of them.'

'But the warehouse is open,' Gunter said desperately. 'There must be something.'

Fulk tugged at his lower lip, apparently considering the matter. He derived a cruel satisfaction from making other men wait. 'There's one cargo going out today, only one, mind. Wool to be taken down to Boston.'

Gunter's stomach surged with relief. The full length of the river – that would pay well.

'But ship sails in two days. You sure you can get it there in time?' Fulk looked doubtfully along the jetty to where Hankin was sitting, swinging his legs and staring across the harbour. 'You've only a little lad with you. He'll tire afore you're clear of Lincoln.'

'He may be small, but so's a weasel and that can tackle a rabbit three times its size. Come on, Master Fulk, you know me. I've done that run since I was boy. Have I ever got a load there late?' Glancing around, he saw Martin in conversation at a warehouse further round the wharf. 'I've never lost so much as a single barrel or bale neither, not like some.' Gunter jerked his head pointedly in Martin's direction. 'Please, Master Fulk. I need this. I'll keep going all night if I have to, but I swear it'll reach the ship in time.'

Fulk plucked at his lip again. 'I suppose I could let you take it. But you'll not get paid until you bring me back the tally from the ship's quartermaster so I know he's had the full load and it's not been spoiled.'

Gunter was aghast. 'That's not right. It's always half now and half when I get back with the tally.'

206

'*Was*, Gunter. We've had too many loads delivered recently that have been short. A great many mishaps there've been, or so you all claim. Bundles disappearing in the night while the boatman sleeps, barrels falling off into the river. Of course, it's never his fault. It couldn't possibly be due to the fact that he's a thieving bastard. Anyhow, Master Robert's had enough of it. He says it's bad enough when trade is good, but when it's as piss-poor as it is at present, he'll not be robbed blind, so he's given new orders. If a load doesn't arrive on time or there's so much as a sack of feathers missing, you don't get paid at all.'

'But you know me, Master Fulk,' Gunter protested. 'You know nothing's ever gone missing from my loads.'

Fulk shrugged. 'Maybe so, but you can blame your brother boatmen not me. It's them has queered it for everyone.'

'Please, Master Fulk,' Gunter begged. 'Not half then, just enough to buy a bit to eat. If I've two days' journey ahead of me I need food and ale for me and the lad afore we set off. And if we've then to come all the way back upriver again, that's another two days' journey afore we get paid.'

'Should have brought meats with you or coins enough to buy some,' Fulk said indifferently. 'Do you want the work or not?'

Dumbly, Gunter nodded. He'd no choice. Reluctantly, he clasped the hand that was extended to him to seal the bargain.

'Right, I'll get a couple of lads to start loading the boat.' Fulk disappeared back into the warehouse.

Gunter walked back towards the jetty. He was shocked and dismayed at the sudden change in terms, but at least he'd got a load. That was all that mattered, he told himself. They'd find something to eat. Maybe, even, it was better this way: he'd be taking every penny home at the end of the job. He was so preoccupied, he didn't notice Martin until the man spoke.

'You want to watch where you're swinging that bow of yours, Gunter. If I hadn't been keeping a close eye out, I'd have rammed you broadside and that old wreck of yours would have been lying at the bottom of the Braytheforde.'

On any other day, Gunter would have come back at him hard, but he was too relieved to have found work to pick a quarrel. He clapped a friendly hand on Martin's massive shoulder. 'Come now, you were trying to beat us to that mooring even though we'd got into the harbour ahead of you. Fair game!'

'Fair, is it?' Martin said sourly, shaking off Gunter's hand. He peered at Gunter suspiciously. 'You look like a fox that's made a kill. You got a cargo.'

'That I have,' Gunter said. 'Need it badly too. Not had a load for days.' He smiled, suddenly feeling generous even to a man like Martin. 'Hope the day brings you good fortune too.'

But Martin only scowled and spat into the water.

Gunter walked back along the jetty to where Hankin was slumped, lost in thought. He prodded the boy with the toe of his shoe. 'Stir yourself, lad, we've got a load all the way to Boston.'

'Suppose Mam'll be pleased about that,' he said morosely. He suddenly brightened and scrambled up. 'Will I buy some food to take? I saw a girl walk past with a tray of pies. Hot and fresh, they were, mutton, she said. I could catch her up.'

Gunter glanced up from his son's eager face in time to see Martin disappearing through the door of the warehouse. He murmured a prayer of thanks to the Holy Virgin that he had reached the surly overseer first.

'Can I get us some pies, Faayther?' His son was holding out his hand in expectation.

'There's to be no money paid to us till we return to Lincoln. You can have your pie then.'

Hankin was as startled as he himself had been by the news. Gunter grasped him firmly by the shoulder. 'No need to put on a face like a sour pickle. You want to be grateful we've got work. If we hadn't, you certainly wouldn't be eating pie.'

'I'm not eating it now,' the boy muttered. 'Didn't you ask him for the money? Why didn't you tell him we need it today?'

For the second time that day, Gunter felt like clouting his son, but he held his temper. 'Is there any bread left?'

'Only your slice,' Hankin said sulkily. 'That won't keep us for four days.'

'It won't if you eat it, but if you save it for bait, we'll feast like kings. We'll set out a fishing line when we tie up for the night.'

'If we trailed a net, we'd not need the bread for bait.'

'It would slow us up. Never trail a net on a moving boat, unless you're out at sea. If the net snags on a fallen branch or some such under the water it can jerk a man off the punt or even sink it. We'll do fine with the line, lad, and we can always try our hand at netting a sleeping duck. We'll not starve.'

All the fowl and fish in the river belonged to those through whose lands the river flowed. But at night, well hidden from any cottage, it was a risk worth taking and it certainly wouldn't be the first time Gunter had taken it.

He felt the jetty creak and looked up to see two of the paggers bent almost double, staggering down the wooden planks towards them with large bales on their backs supported by thick straps across the men's foreheads. He tapped his son's shoulder. 'Quick, into the punt with you and be ready to help catch them as they lower them.'

He scrambled into the punt after his son and they both looked up expectantly, waiting for the bales to be passed down to them. But, to their dismay, the men didn't stop. Instead they lumbered past and on down the jetty.

'Here, it's this boat you're meant to be loading,' Gunter yelled, but the paggers didn't pause or turn.

They kept moving until they drew level with Martin's boat and dropped the bales onto the jetty. Then they began to lower them to Martin's son, Simon, who was standing in his father's punt.

'No!' Gunter scrambled up the ladder onto the jetty. 'You've got the wrong boat.'

'They haven't.'

Gunter spun round. Martin was standing behind him, grinning, showing a mouthful of crooked teeth. 'Good long run too, all the way to Boston.'

'But Fulk told me there was only one load going out today.'

'And this is it.' Martin's grin broadened.

Gunter gaped at him. 'But he promised it to me. We shook on it.'

Martin shrugged. 'Changed his mind, then, didn't he? With two real men in a sound punt, instead of a cripple and a brat in a leaking tub, he thought he'd a better chance of getting his load delivered safely and on time.'

'How much did you bribe him?' Gunter roared.

'Fair game.' Martin smirked.

Gunter's fists clenched, but the two paggers pushed between them on the narrow jetty, as they returned for another load. By the time they were past, Martin was already walking towards his boat.

Gunter felt someone race past him, but before he had time to register that it was Hankin, the boy had reached Martin. He leaped onto the man's back, pummelling him in a frenzy. 'Thief! Cheat!'

Martin staggered under the surprise and ferocity of the assault, and for a moment it looked as if both would fall into the Braytheforde. Gunter stumbled along the slippery boards as fast as he dared, but before he could reach Hankin and pull him off, Martin's son had bounded onto the jetty. He seized Hankin by the waist, swung him up and hurled him as far as he could into the thick, green water. Hankin hit it with a slap and disappeared.

Chapter 29

The spirits of drowned men return to the shore and conjure lights to lure ships to their destruction on the rocks and drown their crew.

Lincoln

Gunter stared in horror at the water of the Braytheforde where wavelets were rapidly spreading outwards in circles from the spot where Hankin had vanished. He was dimly aware of Martin's son bellowing with laughter and the cries of alarm from others who'd witnessed the boy's body arc through the sky.

Gunter dropped onto the boards of the jetty and wrenched off his wooden leg. Though he had warned his children many times never to jump into water when you couldn't see what lay beneath, he grabbed the edge of the jetty, pushed himself off the side and rolled head first into the Braytheforde. The water rushed into his nose and ears and he struggled desperately to surface, thrusting up into the air and fighting for breath, but he couldn't afford to give himself time to recover. He struck out for the place where he thought Hankin had sunk.

But now that he was in the water, it was hard to work out which direction he should swim in, never mind how far. The wind and rising tide, though by no means strong, still produced waves that kept dashing into his face making him splutter. He arched upwards and gulped a lungful of air, preparing to dive down, but just in time he heard a voice shout, 'No, to the left . . . the left.'

Gunter turned and swam a few more strokes, then taking another deep breath, plunged down. With the muddy bottom stirred up by the quants and oars of the craft that constantly ploughed to and fro, not to mention the filth pouring in from the open sewers and ditches of the city, the water was as thick as pease pottage. In the faint green light filtering down from above he could see little, except dark

211

indistinct shapes far below, which might have been anything from sunken boats to drowned pigs.

His lungs bursting, he fought up to the surface again. To his relief he saw three small boats had cast off and had arranged themselves close to him to protect him. There was always the danger of a punt or craft ploughing straight into him as he came up for air. The men in the boats were using grappling irons and poles to fish for any trace of the boy.

'Over there,' one shouted, and pointed. 'I'm sure he went down there.'

Taking another great gulp of air, Gunter flipped over and dived again into the foul soup, his arms spread wide.

Let me find him, Holy Virgin, don't let him die. Show me where he is, I beg you.

He kept searching beneath the water until he felt as if his head and chest would explode. He knew he must surface again or drown. But as he kicked desperately upwards, the back of his hand brushed against something soft and cold. With his last splinter of strength he made a grab for it and his hands closed around cloth. He yanked at it, and kicking frantically, he burst into the air, gasping and spluttering.

As the roaring in his ears subsided, he could hear people yelling excitedly, 'We got him! We've found him!'

Just a yard or two away he saw the limp body of his son being hauled over the side into one of the little boats.

'He's—' The man who had spoken broke off in a stunned silence.

The boatmen were all staring at Gunter, horror on their faces.

Panic-stricken, Gunter swam desperately towards the boat, but even as he did so he realised he was still dragging something behind him. He turned his head. There, floating just inches from his cheek, was a face, white and bloated, the eyes opaque and staring up at him, the mouth wide in a terrible grimace. On the forehead the skin was peeling away from four deep puncture wounds.

With a cry of revulsion, Gunter snatched his hand from the corpse, but it didn't sink. It floated a few feet away, staring upwards into the grey sky, its arms stretched as wide as the crucified Christ's, rocking gently on the waves.

Chapter 30

Witches can be prevented from entering a house if pins or nails are pushed into door posts or the beams above a hearth, but beware: if these same pins or nails fall to the floor, the witch may use them to harm you.

Lincoln

Robert sat facing his younger son across a supper of fried young rabbits swimming in a rich wine sauce, their tender flesh liberally flavoured with cinnamon, ginger and honey. Platters of cold mutton and pigeon pie lay beside it on the long table. Beata was still cooking every meat dish she could devise, so thankful was she to be eating flesh again after the forty long days of Lenten fish.

In many households, servants were forbidden to eat the costly spiced meat dishes they served to their masters at high table and were forced to feed any leftovers to the dogs or swine. But Edith had always permitted Beata, Tenney and even the stable-boy to eat whatever was left from Robert's table, saying it was a wicked waste for servants to cook separate meals for themselves while perfectly good food was thrown away.

Beata had never taken advantage of that by cooking great portions, not that Edith would ever have allowed her to do so, but since Easter Sunday, Robert had noticed the dishes she prepared were large enough to feed half of King Richard's army, even when only he and Adam were dining, as if she had determined to spend every last penny of his money before the wedding.

He was in two minds whether or not to task her with it but thought better of it. At least with Diot temporarily gone from her kitchen, she was speaking to him again and not clattering the pans quite so loudly, although he suspected that that happy state would last only until the wedding. He dreaded to imagine what would happen when Diot and she were permanently sharing a kitchen.

He wondered if he should ask Catlin to dismiss her maid. He could insist upon it, but he found it hard to insist upon anything with Catlin. She would obey him, he was sure, that is, he hoped, but he certainly didn't want to begin their married life by upsetting her. He couldn't understand why either of his sons should have taken against such a gentle, selfless and loving woman.

Father Remigius promised to pray to the Blessed Virgin for Robert and his elder son to be reconciled. But, from the expression on his face, Father Remigius lacked confidence that she would answer. Robert's jaw clenched. If Jan believed his father would come to his lodgings and beg him to return to work, he was either as conceited as a peacock or a slug-brained fool. If the boy didn't work, he needn't expect to be paid. He'd soon learn that pride doesn't fill an empty belly. When his money ran out, he'd come back fast enough.

In the meantime, Fulk would keep things running smoothly at the warehouse. But there was still that business with the Florentines. There'd be a hearing when the courts sat at Whitsun. He'd heard Matthew Johan was counterclaiming against the seizure of his goods. Very likely both he and Jan would be called to testify and he was not looking forward to sitting in court with his son. Such matters could drag on for days, especially when wealthy men were involved. Still, by then he and Catlin would be safely married. Jan would have to accept it and be civil. If he wouldn't, Robert thought grimly, he would have no hesitation in disinheriting him in favour of Adam.

True, Adam had never taken the slightest interest in the business, unlike Jan at his age. Neither did his younger son possess the toughness essential for the bloody cut and thrust of the marketplace, but that had been Edith's fault. She'd mollycoddled the boy and turned him against the trade. But he was determined that was going to change, and when Robert had made up his mind to something, he saw no reason to delay.

'After school tomorrow, Adam, I want you to come straight to the warehouse. You've only a few weeks left with your books and then you'll be starting in the business. Best to learn as much as you can about it before you start work in earnest.'

Adam looked alarmed. 'But Mother said I'd go to university.'

'And what good would that do, boy? Study is for men who have to make their own way in the world and find a profession. You already have one. You'll . . .'

He was about to add that Adam would one day be master of everything Robert owned, but stopped himself. He wouldn't make that promise yet. Jan had many failings, his quick temper being one of them, but he'd a good business head for all that. He'd be back . . . *Holy and Blessed Virgin, let my son come back.* Robert would barely admit it to himself, let alone others, but he sorely missed the lad, even their arguments and Jan's cursed stubbornness.

He realised that Adam was staring at him, gnawing his lip anxiously, exactly as Edith used to do. 'You can find your way to the warehouse?' Robert demanded gruffly.

'Will Jan be there?'

'Adam, I asked if you could find your way to the warehouse. Have the goodness to answer me.'

Adam lowered his chin. 'Yes, Father. I know the way.'

He had the same irritating habit as his mother of looking up shyly from under his long lashes, instead of lifting his head and meeting people's gaze straight on. When he had first married Edith, Robert had found the habit enchanting, but as she had matured it had become ridiculous. He banged the table. 'Lift up your head and look at me properly, not like a simpering girl. If you look at the workmen and paggers like that, they'll tar you and put a dress of feathers on you.'

Seeing the terrified expression on the boy's face, Robert tried to speak more gently. 'You have to understand, boy, the men on the wharf are tough. They won't show you respect because you're my son, you'll have to earn it. And in time you'll have to protect your new sister. Ensure that no man offers her any offence. You can't do that if you behave like a girl yourself.'

'My sister?' Adam said miserably. 'So Leonia *is* going to be my sister, then?'

'Your stepsister, but I expect you to treat her as a blood sister. And Mistress Catlin will be your new mother.'

Adam traced aimless patterns in the thick red sauce on his pewter trencher.

'She's a good woman, you know that, don't you, Adam? From a highly respectable family. Any man can see that in her bearing.'

His son's pale cheeks flushed a dull red and his gaze dropped to his hands, which were trembling. 'Beata said . . .'

'Beata said what?' Robert said sharply.

Adam glanced anxiously at the door. 'That . . . she didn't trust her.'

215

'You know better than to listen to the opinions of servants. Beata is put out because Mistress Catlin is bringing Diot and she doesn't like sharing the kitchen. Come here, boy.'

Adam reluctantly slid out of his chair and edged round the table, holding himself stiffly as if he expected a beating. Robert put a hand on his shoulder and lifted his chin with the other so that Adam was forced to meet his gaze. 'And what do *you* think of Mistress Catlin?'

Adam bit his lip again.

'I won't punish you for telling the truth. Speak out, boy.'

Adam stared down at his father's broad hand. 'Mistress Catlin is . . . good to me. I thought she wasn't at first, but since Mother died, she's been kind . . .'

Adam glanced up anxiously, but Robert was beaming his approval. It wasn't an expression Adam had often seen on his father's face – at least, not directed at him. He smiled shyly back.

'Kind, yes, my boy, that's exactly what Mistress Catlin is. She's fond of you, Adam. She told me the other day that she loves you as much as her own children. With a mother as handsome and elegant as Mistress Catlin and a beautiful sister, you'll be the envy of every lad at school.'

'Leonia frightens me sometimes.'

Robert chuckled. 'Believe me, my son, pretty young girls frighten every lad. You'd best get used to that. There are a great many of them in this world.'

The bell above the door pealed urgently. Robert, startled, sprang up, instinctively pushing Adam behind him. Tenney lumbered through the hall. He opened the small wooden shutter on the door and peered through the grille into the street beyond.

He turned his head. 'It's Sheriff Thomas.'

'Don't keep him standing out there, Tenney.'

His manservant slid back the stout beam that braced the door as easily as if he was drawing a knife through butter and pulled it open.

Thomas did not look at Robert or stroll to the table to pour himself a goblet of wine, which was his usual habit. Instead, he hovered awkwardly by the door, fiddling with the hilt of his sword.

'Tenney, fetch Sheriff Thomas some hippocras,' Robert said. 'He looks as if he could do with it. Bad day, Thomas?'

The sheriff waved his hand at Tenney, declining. The manservant ambled out through the door leading to the courtyard.

'I'm sorry to disturb you, Robert, at this late hour, but I thought you should know—'

'Know what?' Robert interrupted. 'Why are you standing by the door like a servant? You don't usually need to be asked to draw up a chair.'

But his guest made no attempt to move. Robert was alarmed. It was plain that Thomas had not come to call as a friend but as Lincoln's sheriff.

'Does this concern Matthew Johan?' Robert demanded.

'It wasn't his,' Thomas said quietly.

'What wasn't his?'

'The body they fished out of the Braytheforde this morning.'

'A corpse?' Robert said. 'Was it one of *my* men? Has there been an accident? A murder? Father Remigius told me Johan's men and some of my lads got into a fight at the Good Friday service. Have they been quarrelling again?'

'It could well have been the Florentines that had a hand in this. In fact I've men-at-arms rounding them up as we speak. But it's not one of your men who's been killed.' Thomas took a step forward, his face creased in misery. 'I am so sorry to bring you this news, but I thought you would rather hear it from a friend . . . The body they pulled out of the Braytheforde was that of your son, Robert. It was Jan's.'

Adam, standing forgotten in the corner of the room, began to howl.

Chapter 31

Devil's Eye, known also as Periwinkle or Sorcerer's Violet, signifies death, and if any should be foolish enough to uproot it from a grave, they shall by so doing drag up the ghost of the one who lies therein. And he shall haunt them until they fall into their own grave.

Mistress Catlin

The day they buried Jan was cruelly bright and warm. Against the glaring sunlight, it was hard to see if the candles in the hands of the black-robed men were even alight. Between the graves, and at the foot of the church wall, cowslips, ragged robin and ox-eye daisies were all in bloom, their petals stirring in the soft breeze. Swarms of St Mark's flies, their long legs dangling, drifted over our heads, and in a garden opposite, pink and white blossom had burst out on the apple tree, as if Nature were conspiring to proclaim its fecund vigour and life.

In contrast to the frozen child who had walked dry-eyed behind his mother's coffin, spring seemed to have melted Adam, too, and he sobbed uncontrollably. Beata forgot her position as servant and put her arm round him, holding him close to her as if she were his mother. She was determined to take Edith's place within the family.

I've known many servants who dream of sliding into their late mistress's bed, and I'd no doubt Beata longed to be Robert's new wife – and had harboured that secret desire from the first time she'd entered his house. It was obvious from the way she looked at him and how she deliberately brushed against him when she served him at table. I had no fears that she would turn his affections from me, for she was so disfigured that, even after all the years he'd known her, Robert could hardly bear to look at her. Poor deluded soul, did she know how ravaged her face was?

But, increasingly, I found myself wondering if Edith's suspicions that she'd been poisoned were justified and Beata was responsible. Edith was certainly terrified of her maid and had begged not to be left alone with her. Beata must have given Edith some cause to fear her. Who knows how she had tormented her helpless mistress when they were alone? Living constantly with the humiliation of disfigurement, as Beata did, can so easily twist the sufferer's mind to bitterness and hatred.

I thanked the Blessed Virgin devoutly that Diot would be sharing the kitchen with Beata after Robert and I were married. At least Diot could watch her and ensure she didn't poison me: I was sure Beata was becoming as jealous of me as she had been of Edith. I wouldn't feel safe until Robert had dismissed her.

I squeezed Robert's arm as we stood together, then gestured towards Adam and Beata.

'Do you think it seemly that a servant should be standing alongside the heir of the household on such a solemn occasion?' I whispered. 'It might appear odd to some.'

Robert turned his head at once. 'Beata, stop fussing over the boy,' he said, keeping his voice low. 'And, Adam, if you can't control yourself, have the goodness to return home and stop disgracing yourself. You're nearly a man and you'll soon be taking your brother's place in the business. The men won't take orders from you if they see you bawling like an infant.'

Adam jerked away from Beata and scrubbed his eyes fiercely with his sleeve. His fists were clenched and his jaw worked furiously, as he tried to stem his tears. But in truth there were few men present to see him cry.

No one had come to view the body in the days before the funeral. The corpse stank, having rotted in the filthy water of the Braytheforde for days, and not even the oil of myrrh with which it had been cleaned or the bunches of rosemary, thyme and bay leaves that had been tucked beneath the shroud could mask the foul odour of decay. Before being placed in the wooden coffin, the corpse had been wrapped in two layers of cloth soaked in beeswax and costly lead sheets had been folded over it, but even so the smell lingered, as though an evil spirit hovered over the coffin.

But it wasn't only the stench that kept many at a distance: it was the manner of Jan's death. Misfortune has a way of spreading. Two deaths in a family, so hard on each other's heels, might cause some to believe that family was cursed, and few would risk being touched by it.

Tragic though his death was, it was perhaps inevitable that he should come to grief. I fear he had inherited his mother's dark imagination and his father's hot temper, which, when combined, had led to madness and melancholy.

The coroner had ruled his death was an accident: that Jan, doubtless staggering around from an excess of wine, had tripped and fallen into the water in the dark. He'd probably become trapped beneath a moored boat or tangled in a rope, or was simply too drunk to swim to a ladder and climb up to the quayside. Robert refused to believe it, for no man likes to think that his son had come to such an ignominious end. He wanted to believe that the Florentines had murdered him or, at the very least, had fought with him and pushed him into the water. To his mind, the four puncture marks in his face proved it.

But, as Sheriff Thomas had tried to persuade him, they proved nothing. The Johan brothers had produced a dozen men who swore they were safe within the city walls on the night Jan had disappeared and nowhere near the Braytheforde. The sheriff admitted the Florentines always stuck together and would readily lie to protect each other, but as it transpired, the brothers had fought that night with some Lincoln men, who had grudgingly admitted the Florentines were within the city.

I betrayed nothing of what I believed. Instead I comforted Robert, agreeing that Jan must have been murdered by the Johan brothers or their men. You must support the man you love, even if the whole world should gainsay him – especially then: if he is convinced that the world has deserted him and only you fight at his side, he will cling to you the more.

Father Remigius gabbled the final words over the coffin, flinging at it holy water from the hyssop. As soon as he had finished, the few who had attended shuffled past us, mumbling commiserations, but none looked Robert in the eye and he seemed not to know how to reply. It was left to me to thank them with a gracious smile and I sensed Robert's gratitude.

My son Edward came forward and inclined his head to Robert, who received the gesture with his usual coldness towards him, his eyes only softening when Leonia approached. He patted her cheek absently, his eyes straying back to the stone coffin. It was too soon to push the matter just yet, but Robert would need a son to take over the business and it was clear that the shy, studious Adam would never fill his brother's shoes. My son was determined to step into them, but persuading Robert to give him a chance would not be easy. I must do it or I would lose Edward.

I withdrew a little as Sheriff Thomas approached, not wanting to appear that I was assuming the role of wife before our marriage. I bent down to pluck some cowslips and late primroses to lay on the coffin, the one flower denoting a bachelor, the other youth and sadness, together fitting memorials.

My attention was caught by a glimmer of light in the deep shadow of the great yew tree. The twelve paid mourners, all dressed in the long black funeral robes Robert had provided, had taken their candles back into the church where they would continue to burn for many hours in front of the statue of the Virgin, pleading mercy for Jan's unshriven soul. Now these paupers were making their way out of the church past Tenney, who was distributing the coins they'd been promised.

But one of the mourners still clasped his candle and the bright flame drew my attention as he stood beneath the dark branches of the ancient tree. He was watching me intently, and as I rose, he raised the candle so that the light shone full on his face.

I gasped and staggered backwards, sinking to the ground. Instantly Edward was at my side. 'What is it?' he asked anxiously. 'Do you feel faint? It's because you fasted before the mass.'

I couldn't bring myself to speak, but gestured instead towards the yew. Edward shielded his eyes from the sun, and peered at it. 'You know him?' Edward asked, staring at the mourner.

'It can't be . . . He's dead . . . long dead.'

I was almost sobbing from the shock. I hauled myself up on Edward's arm. The figure under the yew tree had set down the candle and turned away, walking back to join the other mourners, who were leaving the churchyard by the far gate, making for the alehouse. From behind they were as indistinguishable, one from the other, as a flock of rooks.

Edward watched them go, then put his arm around my shoulders and squeezed me. 'Seeing ghosts, little Maman? It's being in this miserable graveyard. It's a wonder the stench of Jan's foul corpse hasn't brought every spirit rising from their graves in protest at having to lie with him. Robert's son was an annoying meddler in life and is still causing trouble now he's dead.' He gave a nervous giggle and those few who remained in the churchyard glared at him. Edward ignored them. 'Come, little Maman, we need funeral meats and strong wine to banish the ghosts. See if you can't drag your husband-to-be from the sheriff. Even old Father Remigius looks as if he might start chewing the grass if he's kept here much longer, and he should be used to fasting.'

I grasped at his arm. 'He was taunting me as if he wanted me to know he was there.'

'Who? It was only a poxy beggar. God alone knows where the priest's clerk rounds them up, but half of them are as mad as a wolf at full moon. He was just leering at you. He wouldn't be the first man unable to take his eyes off you. Look at Robert.'

But I was staring at the candle, still burning under the yew tree. The tiny flame flickered and beckoned, like a light on the marsh, the soul of a dead man come to drag the living into his grave.

May

A hot May makes for a fat graveyard.

Chapter 32

If a hen crows like a cock, it must be immediately slaughtered else a death in the household is sure to follow.

Beata

Why are men so easily bewitched by women? Women fall in love, 'tis true, and foolishly run after men they know are dangerous. They often hanker for a savage wolf or cunning fox, but know them for the untamed beasts they are. They see the cruelty behind the eyes, but that excites them. Men, though, can no more see what lies beneath a woman's soft breast than the corpse buried beneath a sweet meadow.

I know what they all said about me – that I was jealous of the Widow Catlin. She even told Father Remigius that I was besotted with Master Robert and wanted to become his second wife. I'll not deny I was fond of him. How could I not be after all those years? He'd often confided in me things that he could never tell my poor mistress. But I'd no desire to share his bed. Tenney was different. I'd have climbed into his arms, but never Master Robert's. So you have to believe me when I say that I'd much better cause than jealousy to hate the Widow Catlin.

After they had pulled Master Jan out of that accursed harbour, I was sure Master Robert would think on what his son had been trying to tell him and call off the wedding. I thought, too, Father Remigius would tell him he must wait till a decent period of mourning had elapsed. But no sooner had they laid Master Jan in the coffin alongside that of his mother, Widow Catlin was whispering in the priest's ear: *Little Adam will be in even greater need of a mother to help him through the tragedy of his brother's death. Poor Robert is desperate for the support of a wife to aid him in this terrible loss.*

Terrible loss, my arse! I'd wager a barrel of gold coins she was dancing round her chamber like an imp in Hell, when she heard about Master Jan's drowning. Now there wasn't a soul left to speak out against the marriage, save me, and she knew fine rightly I had to bite my tongue for fear of dismissal or worse.

Master Robert grieved sorely for the lad, though I reckon none would have realised just how much, unless they knew him like I did: he certainly wasn't a man to shed a tear in front of anyone. But I slept in the great hall. Night after night I heard the creaking of his bed in the chamber above as he tossed and turned until dawn. Often I'd see Master Robert sitting alone, staring into nothing. He'd start up each time he heard the door, as if he expected his lad to saunter through it. Then you'd see his face crumple when he remembered it couldn't be him. Grief weighs twice as heavy on the soul when the last words you spoke to the dead were bitter.

Tenney, the great muttonhead, said a wife was just what the master needed to take his mind off things. Said the bed would soon be creaking to a different tune, and Master Robert would sleep soundly enough after he played that fiddle each night. That's a man for you. The heavens could be crashing to earth and Hell rising to meet them, but a man has only to straddle a woman for every worry to fly clean from his head. Try as I might, I couldn't make Tenney see that something was not right. But that woman could charm milk from a bull if she'd a mind to. So the master and the widow were married, and she and her brat moved in, bringing that filthy old hag, Diot, with them.

Diot shifted her arse long enough to do a mite of work when Master was looking, but the moment he left for the warehouse, she plonked herself down on her great hams and supped his wine as if she were his sister, not his maid, and Widow Catlin encouraged her. The two women would settle down to a gossip, expecting me to wait on them, though they'd always fall silent whenever I walked in. I'll own that Mistress Edith and I used to talk of an evening over our stitching, when the master was out and all the work done, but nothing was ever said between us that had to be whispered. Diot claimed she used to work in a tavern. Well, if that was true, what secrets would a respectable widow and an old tavern-slut share that couldn't be spoken about in front of me or Tenney?

The only times Diot stirred herself was when there was shopping to be done, with the master's money, of course. It was always her that went to the market. I didn't set foot out of the yard now, not even to buy the meats I was expected to cook. I'd not seen a single friend, since the wedding, save at the servants' mass, and then I'd have to hurry straight home from church to cook dinner for the family returning from their mass. And that was what I was doing on that particular Sunday when *he* turned up again.

Master Robert was away on business at Wainfleet and Catlin had taken the children to mass, insisting that Diot accompany her as her maid. As usual I had to hurry home to start baking and boiling, chopping and basting. On days like that I wished I'd been born with four arms, like that babe in one of the shacks along the river. It had four legs too, so they say. Its mam sold it to a man who wanted to take it to the fairs and charge people to gawp at it, poor creature.

The sun was a blister that day and I was sweating long afore I stoked up the fire in the baking oven. It wouldn't draw properly and I came out into the yard and went round the back to rattle a stick in the vents behind the oven and clear them of soot, so that the smoke would be pulled out better. It was then I noticed the ladder from the stable lying in the yard near the house. I thought at first either Tenney or the stable-boy must have forgotten it, but I was sure it hadn't been there earlier for it was so close to the door: we'd have tripped over it as we left for church. In any case, it would have to be moved before the family returned.

I called for the stable-boy, who was supposed to be minding the house, but he didn't appear. The casements on the upper floor had been left wide open to cool the rooms. Suppose someone had climbed in. You heard tell of more robberies every day, and the thieves were getting bolder. The more I thought about it, the more afeared I was that we'd been robbed. I ran out to the street to find someone to help, but it was deserted. Most folk were either still in church or else lingering outside to gossip in the sunshine.

I took the longest, sharpest knife from the kitchen and crept up to the door. It was still locked. If someone had broken in, they hadn't left that way. I let myself into the great hall with the key on my waist chain and stood listening. The house was quiet. The only sound was the pigeons cooing sleepily on the roof and the aimless buzzing of a fly.

I glanced around. I knew every inch of that hall for I'd swept and dusted it every day of my life since I was a girl. I could see at once that nothing was missing, not the pewter trenchers and beakers, nor the fine tapestry, which would have kept a dozen families fed and housed for a year. But the silver and jewels were upstairs, locked away in the chests. What if they had broken into those in search of rings or coins that were easier to conceal than goblets or great tapestries?

I don't make a habit of listening at doors, but I have learned that if you walk up the stairs placing your feet close to the wall, the boards don't creak – I do it only so I don't disturb the master when he's sleeping. I inched my way up, my heart pounding and the knife gripped so tightly in my hand my fingers ached.

The solar was empty. My heart began to slow a little as I examined the chests and found them still to be locked. I searched round. A few things had been moved. The silver candle-snuffer was not where I kept it, but Diot had probably left it somewhere else – she never put things back in their proper place.

I sighed with relief. The ladder lying in the yard was only the stable-boy's carelessness. Most likely one of his friends had coaxed him into a game of football. He'd sneak back before the family returned and pretend he'd been working all this while.

Family! There was me playing hide-and-seek with imaginary thieves, when there was a dinner to be cooked. I could picture Diot's smirk if they returned and nothing was ready. I took one last look round the solar and was about to run downstairs when I noticed the door to the ambry was ajar. It was where I put cold meats, cheese and pies in case Master Robert grew hungry in the night. Diot had left it open again, for all the flies in the city to crawl in.

The ambry stood next to the wooden partition that separated the solar from the master's bedchamber. As I went to close it, I happened to glance through the door of the bedchamber, which was also open a crack. By then I'd convinced myself the house was empty, so it gave me quite a fright to glimpse someone in there. Edward was standing in the master's own bedchamber, as if his feet had taken root in the floor.

'What are you doing in there?' I demanded, flinging the door wide. 'These are the master's private . . . Blessed Virgin, save us!' I staggered against the doorframe as I caught sight of what he was staring at.

The chamber was full of feathers swirling up in the breeze from the casement. For a moment I couldn't work out where they were coming from. Then I saw that the pillows and the embroidered cover on the bed had been slashed with a knife over and over again, as you might score a pig's skin before roasting. But that wasn't the worst thing. In the centre of the bed lay the skull of a seagull, with a wicked yellow beak. Two wax candles, with thorns pressed into them, were fixed upright in the sockets of the bird's eyes. It was the most evil-looking thing I ever saw, the devil's curse itself.

Edward turned slowly to face me and only then did I see a knife in his hand. I screamed and backed out of the door. Edward stared stupidly at the knife he was holding, then flung it away from himself as if he had woken from a sleep to find himself clutching a viper.

'I didn't do it!' he protested. 'The knife was lying on the floor when I came in. I picked it up. I thought . . . I didn't know. Not until I saw the bed. I've no idea who's done this. I swear it, on my life.'

He looked as pale and shaken as I felt and for a moment I almost believed him. 'What are you doing in the house anyway?' I demanded. 'The mistress is out. Who let you in here?'

'Saw a ladder propped against the casement. I thought my mother was being robbed. So I climbed in to try to stop the thief.'

'This is Master Robert's house,' I said coldly. 'If anyone was being robbed it was him. And the ladder was lying in the courtyard, not against the house.'

'It slipped when I kicked against it to heave myself over the sill. I'm not well practised at breaking in.'

'Robbers take things from houses. They don't come calling with gifts of skulls and candles,' I said, shielding my eyes with a hand. I was afeared that if I so much as glimpsed that thing again, I'd be infected with the curse of it.

'And it's a gift we must get out of here before my mother sees it,' Edward said grimly. 'Clear that mess up quickly. If the family returns I'll keep them downstairs until you've got rid of it.'

'Me? You'll not get me touching that thing for all the gold in John of Gaunt's palace. If you don't want your precious mother to see it, it's you who'll have to clear it up, Master Edward.'

He looked at me as if I'd told him to pick up dog shit. He took a step towards me and I thought he was going to hit me. But just then the outer courtyard door banged and we heard Diot yammering and Catlin's laughter as they crossed the yard below. She'd not be laughing when she saw what awaited her upstairs. Neither would Master Robert when I told him.

They'd said young Jan had all but killed himself, but I reckoned Master Robert was right: someone had a terrible grudge against this family. Whoever it was had surely murdered the poor lad and now they were coming after his father.

Chapter 33

At Andover in Hampshire, a ghost or demon pig appears at New Year, but is also seen whenever there is a violent thunderstorm.

Lincoln

Adam's back was rigid as he trudged up the narrow lane to his house, trying not to let the pain show in his face. Sweat was trickling down his nose and his tunic clung to him, but he didn't stop to draw breath. Two barefooted children were squabbling over a steaming pile of dog dung, each wanting to claim it for their pail: they would sell it to the tanners. Adam stepped around them and for a few minutes they forgot their prize, united in jeering and laughing at him for wearing a half-cloak in the heat.

'Yer mam thinks you'll catch cold, does she? Thinks her baby'll get the sniffles.'

Adam tried to ignore them. He should have been on his way to the warehouse. He'd get into more trouble about that when his father came home, but that prospect was some hours off yet and was but a pebble set against the towering heap of misery that was crushing him. He knew his humiliation would be a hundred times worse if he went down to the quayside.

He hated going there. Fulk was a pig. When Robert was close by, he'd pretend concern, showing Adam how to check the loads coming in and going out and how to assess the quality of wool, fleeces and cloth. He would pat Adam's back, saying what a keen eye the boy had and what a good head for reckoning. But as soon as his father had moved out of earshot, Fulk would sneer and mock him, deliberately giving him the wrong tally sticks, knowing they would never match, and jeering when he tried repeatedly to count the bales. Fulk would move the counting jetons on the chequerboard so that the additions and subtractions were wrong. He'd send Adam with messages to the men that would have them howling with laughter at his expense and once even locked him in the warehouse alone after dark, telling Robert, when he eventually came looking for his son, that he had deliberately hidden in there.

Adam knew that Fulk despised his father as much as he did him. He'd heard him talking to some of the warehouse men about how they did all the work and had nothing but chaff to show for it, while men like Robert lived like a king off their sweat and aching backs. But Fulk dared say nothing to Robert's face so he made sure his son suffered for it.

Tears burned in Adam's eyes and he scrubbed them angrily away with his sleeve. Fulk would never have dared to torment him if Jan was still steward. His brother would have thrashed Fulk and dismissed him, but Jan was dead, murdered by those Florentines. He missed him even more than he missed his mother.

Adam knew what would happen if he went to the warehouse today. It was stiflingly hot and the stinking stacks of fleeces would make it suffocating inside. The paggers would be stripped to the waist and Fulk would be working in his short sleeveless tunic. Even on a freezing winter's day, Adam would have been jeered at for wearing a cloak in the warehouse. On a day as hot as this, they'd most likely have ripped it off him. And then they would have seen the blood on the back of his tunic. They'd know what had been done to him. He felt sick at the thought. If he could just get home and wash his tunic without anyone seeing . . .

He edged into the stableyard. It was deserted. One of his father's horses was tethered at the far end of the stables, dozing in the heat. But there was no sign of either Tenney or the stable-boy. He tiptoed across the yard, keeping close to the house wall so that he couldn't be seen from the windows, and peered cautiously through the open door of the kitchen, a small stone building to one side of the yard. Beata wasn't in there. She usually was, these days, even when there was no cooking to be done.

She slept there some nights too, saying she'd rather be with the mice than the hog. He knew she meant Diot who, she complained, snored so loudly, it was like sleeping in the bell tower of the cathedral on a feast day. Adam had heard her telling Tenney that she couldn't be in the same room with that slattern without wanting to brain her with a pan, and begging him to stop her if he ever saw her near Diot with a knife in her hands: the temptation would be too great for even a saint to bear.

232

Adam heard laughter coming from the open casement in the house. Diot was inside with Leonia, and as the voices drifted out on the hot, still air, he thought he heard Catlin's laughter too. He always thought of her as Catlin. He was supposed to call her 'Mother' now, but usually he tried to avoid calling her anything.

He couldn't go in. They'd want to know why he'd come straight home from school and not gone to the warehouse. If he said he was sick, Catlin and Diot would insist on putting him to bed and then they would see the tunic. He couldn't bear them to know, especially Leonia. That would only add to his shame. And Catlin was bound to tell his father.

He slipped into the stables and crouched behind the partition. He could go to the river, but it would be crowded with boats. Suppose one of his father's men saw him or the boys from school. Some, like him, had to help in their parents' shops or businesses after school, but many would be swimming on a day like this.

Then he noticed the pail of water at the far end of the stable for when his father came home. He always insisted the water for the horses be drawn early and left to stand, so any horse still hot from being ridden wouldn't get colic by drinking it ice-cold from the well.

Adam unfastened his cloak and sighed with relief to be rid of the weight. Then he tried to remove his tunic, but the blood on it had dried, gluing the cloth to the wounds on his back. He groaned as he tried to peel it off, but realised he would only start the bleeding afresh if he persisted. He crossed to the bucket and began dabbing water with his fingers onto the small of his back, hoping to soak the cloth free. But it was awkward to reach and every backwards movement of his arm made the stiffening lacerations smart afresh.

The boy he'd punched was Henry de Sutton, an arrogant, spiteful child, who never ceased reminding his schoolfellows that John of Gaunt himself was his father's patron. Even the schoolmaster toadied up to him because of it. His father had had John's crest installed on their fine stone house, proclaiming to all the world that the King's uncle was their protector. And there was no more powerful man in the country than John of Gaunt, as Henry was forever telling everyone. He was even hereditary constable of the great Lincoln Castle which – according to Henry – meant the whole city practically belonged to him.

Adam and Henry had never been friends. Henry was lazy and

233

stupid, but he always got away with it because there was no shortage of boys willing to copy his lessons for him, in the hope of being admitted to the privileged role of friend. Unfortunately for Adam, the boy whom Henry usually picked on to do his Latin preparation had not come to school that morning so Henry, knowing Adam was a good Latin scholar, demanded that he hand over the parchment he had so painstakingly written. Adam refused so Henry had tried to snatch it from him, tearing it in two and taunting Adam with the half he'd managed to grab.

Adam had never before got into a fight. His anger always turned in on himself. He'd hide and beat his fists against a wall in frustration rather than against another boy's head. And even under this provocation, he would probably have turned away had not Henry begun to taunt him about Jan.

'My father says your brother was so drunk he tripped over his own feet and fell into the Braytheforde.' Henry crossed his eyes, lolled out his tongue and made a grotesque mummery of a drunkard staggering. The other boys standing around him howled with laughter. 'Jan, Jan, drunken man. Couldn't piss straight in a pickling pan.' Henry lurched about, pretending to grasp hold of his own prick, while the grinning boys took up the chant.

Without thinking what he was doing, Adam launched himself at Henry. The boy, assuming that no one, especially not that little squab, would dare to attack him, was caught unawares and, more by luck than skill, Adam's flailing fist caught Henry squarely on the nose. The blow sent him tumbling backwards, scarlet blood gushing down his face. Adam did not follow up the attack. He stood there, more stunned by what he'd done than Henry was by his assault.

Before either boy could say anything, a hand grabbed Adam's ear and he found himself staring up into the furious countenance of his schoolmaster. 'Well, boy,' he thundered, as Henry's friends helped him to his feet, 'why did you attack Master Henry? And don't dare lie to me and say he struck the first blow. I could see you both from the casement and it was plain to me Master Henry had done nothing to warrant such a punch. To attack someone without provocation is the act of a cur and a coward. I'm waiting! What is your explanation?'

He pinched Adam's ear so hard it brought tears to his eyes, but before he could even utter a word, Henry stepped forward, holding

234

out the torn parchment covered with his blood. 'Please, sir,' he said thickly, 'Adam tried to steal my Latin copy from me, and when it ripped, he lost his temper.'

'No, it was—' But Adam was not given a chance to finish.

'Is that what happened?' the master demanded, turning to the boys gathered round. A few shuffled their feet and studied the ground, but Henry's friends nodded vigorously.

Adam was forced to strip in front of the whole school. He was given three times the usual number of strokes of the birch for he had, or so the master roared, committed not one but three heinous crimes: failing to do his Latin copy, attempting to steal that of another boy and carrying out a vicious and unprovoked attack on a fellow pupil.

Adam had rarely given anyone cause to punish him, let alone birch him. He was completely unprepared for the searing pain and humiliation. Henry, after he'd had the satisfaction of witnessing the flogging, was sent home to nurse his injured nose, but Adam was not permitted to run away and cry. He was forced to sit the whole day at the front of the school wearing the fool's cap, as his cuts and welts burned and throbbed, Henry's friends grinning and pulling faces at him each time the master's back was turned.

His eyes screwed up in pain, Adam pulled the sodden tunic over his head and plunged it into the horse's drinking pail. Blood ran out, staining the water red, yet when he pulled it out there still seemed to be as much dried blood on it as before and, if anything, the wetting had only made it spread. He put it back into the water, rubbing it clumsily.

'You'll never get it out dabbing at it like that.'

He spun round, wincing as he did so. Leonia was standing by the horse stroking his nose. Adam stood up, backing away into the corner. Leonia came over and peered into the bucket. Wrinkling her nose, she plucked a corner of the tunic between her thumb and forefinger, and inspected it before dropping it back into the water. 'Dried in. You'll need to soak it, then scrub it to get it out.'

'Go away,' Adam said. 'It's nothing to do with you.'

'And how are you going to dry it? Take ages if you can't put it out in the sun.'

'Leave me alone,' Adam muttered, through clenched teeth.

But Leonia didn't move. 'Want me to fetch you a clean tunic? I can do it without them seeing and we can bury this one. If they notice it's missing, Beata'll blame Diot for losing it and Diot'll blame Beata. They'll argue about it for weeks.' She smiled, as if the prospect amused her. 'Well, do you want me to fetch a tunic or not?'

Adam hesitated. 'Are you going to tell . . . ?'

'Why should I? There's lots of things I don't tell.' She smiled again. 'I'll be back as quickly as I can. Bury that tunic under the straw in the corner. The stable-boy never mucks out properly, not to the edges. If they find it before the mice eat it, it'll be so filthy they'll think it's just an old rag.'

Using the rake to scrape back the soiled straw down to the beaten-earth floor below, Adam threw the sodden tunic into the hole, then heaped the straw back over it. He'd only just finished when Leonia slipped back inside and brought out a folded tunic from under her skirts. He held out his hands for it, but she shook her head.

'Let me look at your back first.'

'No!'

'Don't be silly, I know you've been whipped. Marks are all round your sides. I only want to see if they've stopped bleeding. If they haven't you'll just spoil another tunic.'

He felt his face grow hot with shame, as he saw again the faces of the laughing boys.

Leonia shrugged. 'All right, I won't look, but wrap this round yourself first, so you don't bleed on the clean tunic.'

She unfolded the tunic. Inside was a long strip of linen, which she handed to him. He tried to wrap it around himself, but the welts and cuts made the twisting and turning needed impossible and, besides, his hands were too clumsy to wrap the linen smoothly. In the end he was forced to let her help him. He expected her to wince and murmur when she saw the welts on his back, as his mother and Beata had always done when dressing a cut finger or a bruised knee. But she said nothing.

'There's lots of dry blood on your breeches too, but the tunic'll hide it till you can change them. You'd better bury them too when you do.'

She handed him the tunic. It was warm and he blushed as he pulled it on, knowing that it had been next to her bare skin. She crossed to the barrel that held the oats for the horses' feed, swung herself onto it and sat there, her legs dangling. The sunlight, streaming over the top of the partition, haloed her black curly hair, making it gleam.

236

Adam noticed it wasn't really black at all in the light. It was almost purple, like ripe plums.

'Schoolmaster do that to you?' she asked casually.

'What if he did?' Adam snapped.

'What did you do to make him so angry?'

Adam's gaze dropped at once to the floor and he crouched, picking up a piece of straw and twisting it round his fingers. 'Nothing. I punched a boy.'

'Bet he deserved it. Did your master beat him too?'

'No, he didn't!' Adam said furiously. 'He's Henry de Sutton. His father has John of Gaunt as a patron. Henry could burn the whole school down and they'd pat him on the head and say it was mischief.'

'Who do you hate most? Henry or your master?'

Adam stared miserably at the piece of straw he was twisting in his fingers.

'I think we should punish the master first,' Leonia said. 'He's most to blame, because he's an adult. They have to be punished the hardest.'

'Can't punish masters or any adults,' Adam said. 'But I wish I could. I'd make him smart!' For a moment, a wonderful image came into his head of his master lying bare-arsed over the whipping bench. He could hear him howling for mercy, as the birch descended over and over again. Even shitting himself, maybe. He'd known small boys do that in their terror.

'Then let's do it.'

Adam snorted. 'Don't be daft. We couldn't whip him. Can you imagine what he'd do if we asked him to drop his breeches?'

'We don't have to ask him,' Leonia said. She slid off the barrel and picked up a handful of straw. 'Find me some long pieces. These are too short.'

He didn't really know why he did as she asked, except that it didn't occur to him to say no. He searched through handfuls of straw, handing her the longest as he found them. She carefully laid them side by side on top of the barrel. He hunted for the straw for a long time yet he wasn't bored. If anything, he was enjoying being alone with her. If he found an extra-long piece, she nodded her approval and he found himself wanting to make her smile. Curiously, in spite of his pain, he felt happier than he had since the day his mother had fallen ill.

'Will this do?' She held something up in the light. She'd folded the clump of straw in two, twisting a piece round the neck to make a head. Another twist held the torso together at the bottom. Then she'd divided the ends of the straw into two plaits, which made the legs. A twist of straw poked horizontally through the body formed a pair of crude arms. As a final touch she poked two little burrs into the face to make eyes. But no mouth. She hadn't given it a mouth.

'You've made a silly poppet to play with.'

There was no disguising the disgust in Adam's voice. She was laughing at him, like all the others. He was on the point of running out of the stable, but she moved swiftly in front of him, blocking his way. She held up the doll again. 'This poppet is called Master . . . What's your schoolmaster's name?'

'Warner,' Adam said sullenly.

'Master Warner,' Leonia repeated slowly. 'We must baptise him properly if he is to have a name.' She carried the poppet over to the pail of bloody water. 'Come here. You shall be the priest.' She held out the doll to him and Adam found himself taking it from her. He held it awkwardly, sure she was mocking him, but uncertain what she meant to do.

'Go on, Adam, dip the poppet into the water three times, right under. Then say his name. Say, "I name you Master Warner."'

Adam plunged the straw figure into the bloody water. 'Master Warner,' he mumbled.

'No, you must say "I name you" or it won't work.'

Adam felt utterly foolish, but sensed she would not stop tormenting him until he repeated the words exactly as she'd instructed.

The first time he said it was almost under his breath, but by the third time he found he was laughing. For some reason he could never have explained, he was suddenly elated, as if he really was ducking old Warner himself under the water.

Leonia was laughing too. When he'd finished, she tipped the scarlet water away in the corner. 'Don't want anyone finding that and asking questions.'

Adam gazed at her with admiration. He'd never have remembered to do it. She took the wet poppet from him and placed it on the top of an oat barrel, standing the little straw manikin upright so that a little puddle of bloody water pooled at its tiny straw feet.

'Now, Master Warner, how shall we punish you?'

'We could hang him,' Adam said eagerly, entering into the game. He was already casting about for a piece of cord.

'He'll die in time, but you don't want to kill him yet. That's too quick. You want to hurt him first.' Leonia searched the stable floor, scattering the straw with her shoe, then pounced on something. 'I knew there'd be one somewhere.'

It was an old iron horseshoe nail, bent and rusty. It had evidently lain in the straw for some time. Leonia was right: the stable-boy didn't make a good job of mucking out. She handed the nail to Adam. 'Choose where you want to stab him. Not in the heart, though.'

Adam glanced up, aware that it was growing dark. The air was still as hot as Beata's baking oven, but thick clouds were rolling in, obliterating the sun. Leonia's eyes were glittering in the strange sulphurous half-light and he felt uneasy. It was as if she really believed they could kill old Warner. 'I think it's going to rain. We should go in before we're missed.'

'No!' Leonia was not smiling. 'Adam, remember what he did to you. Think about what it felt like when you were lying there as he flogged you. Think about how much he hurt you when you'd done nothing. You have to go to school tomorrow and they all saw you being whipped. They all know. What do you want to do to him now?'

Blood rushed into Adam's cheeks as he relived being forced to take down his breeches in front of the whole school, being made to lie across that bench, shaking as he waited for the first blow to fall and the next and the next, biting his hand so he wouldn't disgrace himself and cry. Warner hadn't let him explain. He should have listened. He should have listened!

Seizing the nail in his clenched fist, he threw the poppet face down on the barrel. He raised the nail as high as he could, then plunged it into Warner's buttocks, his legs, his arms, his back. It was not the straw he was stabbing, but flesh – flesh that could hurt and flesh that could bleed. Adam stabbed again and again, until he was exhausted.

Somewhere in the distance he heard the long, slow rumble of thunder.

Chapter 34

A cat's heart or a frog, pierced with pins then dried and hung in a house, is a remedy against witches.

Lincoln

One of the delights of being dead is watching men and women torment themselves over the petty irritations of life – the bread that won't rise, the horse that's gone lame, the pots that crack in the firing, the shopkeeper who passes them a bad coin. It takes but a handful of these mischiefs to make a man fancy he is having a bad day or even year. And all the while their eyes are fixed on their broken shoe-lace, they don't notice the great mountain teetering above them, ready to crash down on their heads.

But that sweet child, Leonia, had learned long ago never to fret about what annoyed her. She simply resolved to remove the source of the irritation when the time was right. In consequence, her sleep was never troubled by the puny coughing of a mouse, unlike the rest of the household, whose days and nights were constantly troubled by the pitter-patter of their own thoughts and the gnawing of their own imaginations.

It was Tuesday evening when Robert finally returned from Wainfleet, tired, dusty and decidedly irritable from the long ride. His business had, he supposed, gone tolerably well, for he would never allow another man to get the better of him in a deal, but he'd been anxious to reach home before dark. You increasingly heard tales of travellers being attacked by gangs of robbers who, relying on numbers, didn't even bother to conceal their faces, but simply swarmed out from the trees or rushes and overwhelmed their victims, beating them half to death even after they had surrendered their valuables.

After Jan's death, Robert found himself him more nervous than he'd ever been previously. If a fit young man, who was skilled at defending himself, could be overpowered, then anyone could be struck down. Robert was painfully conscious that his sagging body was ageing and was no longer as quick or agile as once it had been.

He still could not believe that a lad with so much life in him should be rotting in his grave. It happened, of course, to countless others, but not to his own son. He refused to accept it had been a foolish accident. He didn't want to believe it. He didn't want others to believe it either. He couldn't bear the thought of half the city gossiping that he had raised a drunk and a wastrel. Even as he grieved for his son, he found himself seething with rage against him. If the lad hadn't been so stubborn, he would have been safely enjoying a supper with his family that night, instead of wandering round the Braytheforde putting himself in mortal danger.

Robert had not stopped at any of the inns on his way home. He'd eaten a few roasted snails and some dried meat as he rode, which had only served to give him a thirst and his leather bottle of ale had been drained to the last sour drop long before he reached the city gate. He'd been eagerly anticipating a quiet meal with his new bride, just the two of them, Catlin pouring him a goblet of hippocras, massaging his temples and asking with soothing concern about his arduous journey. In consequence, he found himself unreasonably annoyed by the sight of his family sitting at the table in his great hall, finishing the last of their meal.

Why had Catlin not waited for him before dining? Edith always had for, as she used to say, it was what a dutiful wife should do. Now he'd be forced to eat alone from pies already cut and meats that been cooked too long. No one could have known the hour of his arrival, or even the day on which he was returning but, angry, he dismissed that.

The moment the door opened, Leonia ran to him and flung her arms about him, pressing her face into his chest. He ran his fingers through her long silky curls, and kissed the top of her head. He was gratified by her delight, but it emphasised his new wife's failure to come running the moment she had heard his horse in the yard. Indeed, he doubted she had heard it at all for as he entered he'd seen Catlin's head inclined towards a young man, so engrossed in conversation, that the house might have burned down around them and they wouldn't have noticed.

The man was three-quarters turned away from the door and Robert's heart gave a little jolt. For a moment he believed it was Jan, sitting in the chair he had always occupied since he was a little boy. But instantly the image of his son vanished like a wraith at cockcrow to be replaced with the face of Catlin's son, Edward.

Catlin rose and came towards him. 'Robert, you're home. We didn't expect you until tomorrow at the earliest.'

'Evidently,' he snapped.

Catlin seemed not to notice the curtness in his tone, or his stiffness as he received, but did not return, her tender kiss. 'I hope your business was concluded well, my sweeting.'

'Well enough.' Robert strode to the laver set ready in the corner and washed his hands in the bowl of rose-scented water, splashing some over his face. Beata, who could move faster than Diot, handed him a clean linen napkin to dry his hands, smiling triumphantly at the tiny victory over her rival. Catlin poured her husband some wine, handing it to him as gracefully as a virginal bride on her wedding day, but he offered no thanks to either woman. Beata was used to that, but a frown creased Catlin's brow.

Robert strode to the head of the table, still clutching his goblet of wine and flopped into the great carved chair. The wooden joints groaned under his weight. Edward rose and made a courteous enough bow, but Robert was indignant that he resumed his seat without waiting for the master of the house to give him leave, as if he thought he was more than a guest. Robert hadn't agreed to Catlin's son taking up residence in his house.

Adam and Leonia glanced at one another. Leonia's eyes were glittering with excitement. The boy sensed she knew some secret, but wasn't going to tell, not yet. He was quickly learning that Leonia enjoyed playing a watching game. He hugged himself in a thrill of anticipation.

Robert helped himself to a large portion of veal pie and ate in silence for a while. Then he turned to Edward.

'I'm surprised to find you here, Master Edward. I'd thought that since you no longer had to care for your mother and sister you'd be eager to seek your own way in the world, perhaps returning to your father's kin. That is customary for a son.' Not, Robert thought sourly, that there had ever been much evidence of Edward ever doing his duty by his mother. Rather, he had dangled from her, like some bloated river leech.

Edward opened his mouth to speak, but Catlin motioned him to silence with a slight shake of her head. 'As I told you, Robert, after the evil my late husband, Warrick, committed, I couldn't allow my children to remain there and suffer the cruel tongues of our neighbours. Even when sons are innocent they are always blamed for the wrongdoing of their fathers.'

And fathers for the behaviour of their sons, Robert thought bitterly.

Adam glanced curiously at Leonia from under his long lashes, desperate to ask her what her father had done, for it must have been something terrible. But he knew he couldn't ask her, not even when they were alone. Leonia did not like to be questioned. She bestowed her secrets as a queen rewards her servants with gifts, only when they had pleased her.

'There's something else,' Catlin said, leaning forward, 'though I hadn't intended to tell you so soon after your return, knowing it would distress you. While we were at mass on Sunday, someone entered our bedchamber. Beata insists that whoever did it must have broken in, climbed up a ladder and through the casement. It might have been the Florentines or even that friar who was watching the warehouse. They slashed our bed, Robert. And I'm sure it was meant as a threat against us, a warning that they could break in and murder us as we sleep.'

Robert's knife clattered to the floor as he stared at her in shock. It was one thing to fear an ambush on the darkened street or out on the open road, but for someone to break into his own bedchamber, the one place he had thought himself safe . . . 'Did they steal anything?'

Catlin shook her head. 'They did nothing but slash the bedding.'

'They did far more than that, Master Robert!' Beata interrupted. 'The worst of it was that evil thing they left on the bed. Tell him about the skull and candles, Mistress. It still gives me the shivers just to think of such a curse in our house. It was witchcraft, that's what it was.'

'What?' Robert demanded, now thoroughly shaken.

But Edward and Catlin were staring at Beata as if she was raving.

'There was no skull, Beata,' Catlin said gently.

'There was! You saw it same as me, didn't you, Master Edward? A seagull's skull with two candles wedged into it all stuck with thorns.'

Edward shook his head. 'I saw nothing like that.'

'And I came in shortly after you discovered the damage,' Catlin said. 'I should have been terrified if I'd seen anything so hideous but, as Edward said, there was no skull or any candles, save the usual ones Diot had set on the spikes and trimmed ready for the night.'

Diot had been staring fixedly at Catlin, bewilderment and alarm on her plump face. Now she jerked, as if woken from a trance, and nodded vigorously. 'Candles . . . on spikes . . . set them there myself, same as always. I always tend my mistress's chamber. I know how she likes things arranged. Wouldn't trust it to no one else.'

Beata looked in puzzlement at the faces round the table, as if they were babbling in some foreign tongue. 'The accursed thing was there, Master Robert, I swear it,' she protested. 'I saw it with my own eyes, right in the middle of the bed.'

'Are you calling my mistress a liar?' Diot said indignantly. 'Witchcraft, curses, my mistress knows nothing about such things, nothing!'

Catlin grabbed the old woman's hand, squeezing it so hard that Diot's eyes opened wide in pain. 'I will tell you if and when I require you to speak remember!' The old woman looked as if she was about to retort, but was silenced by a furious glare. She waddled out of the hall, massaging her hand. Her lips were compressed into a sullen pout, but there was a trace of fear in her faded eyes.

As if the exchange with Diot had never taken place, Catlin turned to Beata, with a kindly smile, her tone gentle and patient. 'Your confusion is understandable, Beata. It must have been a terrible shock finding the bed slashed. Perhaps the feathers from the pillows drifting about made you think of birds. In your distress you might easily have mistaken a shadow or a twist of the bedcover, for something more sinister.'

Beata began to protest again, but Robert held up a hand to silence her. 'My wife is quite upset enough as it is by someone breaking in, without you making it worse with wild stories. And I forbid you to frighten little Leonia.'

Leonia looked anything but fearful, rather as if she was hugging the dark image to herself in excitement.

'Beata, would you be so good as to fetch some pickles for your master?' Catlin said.

Robert was on the point of saying he didn't want any, then realised that this was Catlin's way of getting Beata out of the room. Beata knew it too and banged the door unnecessarily hard as she left.

Catlin lowered her voice. 'Robert, I am concerned about Beata. The way the bed was slashed was horrible . . . as if whoever had done it was mad or possessed by a fit of uncontrollable jealousy.' She hesitated, glancing towards the closed door and tugging her lip with her sharp white teeth. 'Beata was alone in the house at the time and you've observed her hostility towards me, how possessive she is towards you and Adam. I confess I wondered if she might have . . .'

'No!' Robert flapped his hand in irritation. 'All women are given to strange fancies from time to time, Edith certainly was, but Beata's been with us since she was a girl and I've never known her to attack anything or anyone. I can't believe she'd do such a thing.'

Catlin gave an anxious smile, fingering her bloodstone necklace. 'Poor Edith was so afraid of her and begged me not to let Beata near her when she was sick. It made me think . . . But, of course, you know your own servants. If *you* trust her, Robert, then it must have been someone from outside the household who broke in. But, in any case, you will understand that I was greatly alarmed, especially for our children's safety. I pleaded with Edward to move in with us. I knew you'd never want us to remain unprotected and defenceless.'

Robert nodded curtly at Edward. 'You have my thanks. I'll speak to Sheriff Thomas in the morning, insist his watch patrol this street day and night. You may rest assured, Catlin, my dear, I'll not allow anyone to get inside again.'

Catlin dressed her face with one of her most winning smiles. 'It's such a comfort for me to have my son close. I would fret so if he was in another city and I didn't know if he was sick or well. We foolish women worry so about our children, don't we?' She reached out and squeezed Robert's hand. 'And I was telling Edward I was sure you could find him a good position in your employ.'

Robert could understand Catlin trying to advance the cause of her son. He supposed Edith would have done the same, but Edward was hardly an orphan child to be found an apprenticeship. Besides, even though he was Catlin's son, Robert could not bring himself to like the fellow, or see why he should. He wanted Edward gone. Robert'd had the pleasure of his new bride for just a few weeks, and the last thing he wanted was her attention diverted from him to fussing over her son.

'I've no work to offer Edward, my dear. As I've explained to you many times, our profits are falling and will continue to do so as long as the Flemish weavers remain in rebellion. With that and the huge sums those Florentine swindlers stole from us, I shall be hard put to

245

pay the wages of those men I already employ, never mind take on another. Besides, I need experienced men who know about wool and cloth, selling and shipping. I can't let a squab loose in my warehouse. He'd ruin me in a week.'

'I'm no squab!' An angry flush spread over Edward's face and his hands clenched into fists.

'Edward,' Catlin said warningly, 'Robert meant that you know little about the wool trade, which you must own is true. You will have to learn that people in Lincoln are plainly spoken.'

It was Robert's turn to take umbrage. Was she accusing him of being uncouth in his speech? He prided himself on his manners.

Catlin turned the full light of her smile once more upon her husband. 'My son knows he's much to learn and he's eager to do so. He's willing to start in a humble position until he's proved his worth. For my sake, my sweeting,' she wheedled. 'He is my only son.'

But Robert had caught the sulky expression that flashed across Edward's face, when Catlin had mentioned a humble position. He'd been in business long enough to know that giving a man a job he considers beneath him is like putting a rotten oyster into a barrel of good herring: it will corrupt the whole mess of them. So, for the first time since he'd known her, Robert refused to surrender to Catlin's coaxing.

'I've nothing to offer him.'

He heaved himself to his feet and turned towards the stairs, but not before he'd caught the furious glare Edward directed towards Catlin. Far from being dismayed, Robert found himself positively gloating as he laboured up the steps. He prided himself on being able to appraise the quality of a man as well as he could read that of a fleece. And the moment he'd clapped eyes on Edward he had concluded he was third-quality wool, taken from the legs of the beast, kempy and fouled with dung. Such wool will never take the master's dye, no matter how long it is immersed: better to waste no time on it.

Robert was confident that as soon as Edward realised there were no fat purses to be wheedled out of his mother's new husband, all they'd see of him was the cloud of dust at his heels as he marched out of Lincoln.

Chapter 35

A man who desires to know which of his family and neighbours will not live another year must stand in the church porch at midnight on Midsummer's Eve. Then he shall see the spirits of those who are about to die come in solemn procession to the church.

Lincoln

The wool-walker hung back until he saw the women leave the house. Diot, clutching a basket, waddled out of the yard, dragging Leonia by the hand. The wool-walker, thin as a weasel, slid into the shadow of the doorway as they passed. Diot, chattering to the girl, wouldn't have noticed if half of the King's army had been concealed in the archway, but Leonia turned and stared straight at him. The child's face was expressionless, but there was a flash of recognition in those gold-flecked eyes. The wool-walker thought she might draw the maid's attention to him, but she said nothing, only frowned a little, then twisted round to look behind her, as if she were listening to someone. So intense was her gaze that the wool-walker, too, turned his head, expecting to see someone behind him, but the street was empty.

As soon as Diot and Leonia were out of sight, the wool-walker turned his attention back to the heavy gate in the wall that led into the courtyard. He'd lingered outside Robert's house for days, waiting for the right moment to approach. But so far, whenever Diot and the girl were out, Catlin was at home, or if she was out riding, the children were playing in the stables. He didn't want to approach the house when any of the women were there.

He'd watched and listened for so many hours that he knew the names of each person who lived in that house as they were shouted from open windows and called across the yard. Several times, he'd followed Robert, hoping to speak to him at the warehouse, but it had been impossible. None of Robert's men would let him near the warehouse, thinking he was a beggar or a thief, and when he'd tried to waylay Robert in the street, the merchant had reacted as if he was an assassin intending to cut his throat. Robert had bellowed for the watchmen and attracted so much attention that the wool-walker was forced to take to his heels for fear of being arrested.

He heard the courtyard gate open again and, to his relief, saw the mistress of the house come riding out on her palfrey. This was the moment he had been waiting for. She turned her mount away from him and trotted towards the river.

Tenney stood in the open doorway, staring after Mistress Catlin. He was beginning to smell a bad odour around that woman. Master Robert was seldom at home during the day and was therefore unaware of just how often she went off on these jaunts. But it was a mystery to Tenney that he'd failed to sense something was afoot.

He shook his head impatiently. Maybe he was imagining it. Mistress Edith had been a homebody and couldn't abide riding, but not all women were like her. He was probably looking for trouble where was none. That was what came of listening to Beata, mithering on morning, noon and night about her distrust of Catlin. He was catching her strange fancies and all the saints in heaven knew she was full of those. When one woman took against another, there was no reasoning with them. But Tenney had repeatedly warned Beata to say not a word about Catlin to Master Robert, if she valued her job. 'Like my old mam used to say, see nowt, hear nowt and say nowt. Then they can hold nowt against you.'

But even though he tried to convince himself it was all in Beata's head, he couldn't entirely shake off his growing unease about Mistress Catlin. As for that son of hers, he was not a man you'd ever want to walk alone with, or not without keeping a good grip on your purse and your knife.

Sighing, Tenney began pushing the heavy gate shut, but felt someone pushing against him on the other side. If he'd not been so distracted he would have reacted more swiftly and rammed the gate closed but, like a shadow, the dark figure had slipped through before he fully realised what was happening.

The wool-walker stood in the courtyard, panting a little, having come within a whisker of being squashed between door and frame.

But the last few years spent living by his wits had given him a nimbleness that usually only street-urchins possessed.

'What do you think you're doing?' Tenney demanded. 'You can't come barging in here. You want alms, beg in the marketplace with the rest.'

The man's ill-matched clothes looked as if they had once belonged to men both bigger and smaller than himself, which indeed they had, for they had mostly been stolen from bushes where they'd been left to dry. A shirt here, a pair of breeches there, in the hope that the goodwives would think them blown away or snatched by dogs. But the sleeve of the right arm of his over-large jerkin hung down at an odd angle and Tenney guessed the hand beneath was either missing or wizened and useless.

'I'm not here to beg for alms,' the wool-walker said. 'I must speak with your master. I seek work . . . as a fuller.'

Tenney involuntarily took a step back. Fullers or wool-walkers spent all the day up to their knees in vats of rancid piss, treading the woollen cloth to thicken it. It was foul work and they carried the stink of it with them, even when the day's labour was over. In summer they carried their own cloud of flies, too, drawn by the lingering smell, although Tenney had to admit this man seemed somewhat fresher than most in his trade. He'd obviously not worked for some time. 'If it's work you're after, you'll have to see the steward . . .'

Tenney checked himself. He kept forgetting there was no steward now, not since Jan's drowning. He missed the lad, kept expecting him to stroll back in, ready with the latest joke from the quayside, and pretty bawdy most of them had been. He smiled ruefully, remembering. 'They've no steward at present. You'll need to speak to the overseer. Fulk, they call him. You'll find him at the warehouse on the quayside – leastways, that's where he's supposed to be, but if he's not there, try any of the taverns by the Braytheforde. Between you and me, I'd start with the taverns, save yourself a bit of time and shoe-leather.'

'It's Master Robert I must speak with. Please, I beg you, tell him—'

'Tell me what?' Robert came out of the open back door and strode towards them. 'What is he doing in here, Tenney? I thought you'd have more sense than to let strangers in after that business of the bed being slashed.'

Tenney shuffled uneasily. If he said the man had forced his way in, Master Robert would think he was getting too old for the job, that he needed to employ someone younger and fitter. Better to let the master think he'd freely admitted the man.

'He's looking for work, Master Robert. Says he's a fuller by trade. Not many wanting that kind of work, these days. I thought you might be needing a skilled man. He's certainly keen enough anyway,' Tenney added, trying to put in a good word for the wool-walker who, judging by the sharp bones of his face and the dark hollows around his eyes, was surely in desperate need of some means to put food in that shrunken belly.

Robert's eyes narrowed as he studied the stranger. Then he took a hasty step backwards. 'He's no fuller! Look at his feet.'

Tenney stared down. The man was wearing leather sandals with thick wooden soles. His feet were filthy and the toenails long and black-rimmed, but they were no worse than those of any man who wore sandals in the dirty streets.

'His feet would be bleached white and the nails eaten away from standing in piss all day.'

The man shuffled, as if he was trying to bury his toes in the stone of the courtyard. 'I've not had work these many months.'

'You've not had work as a fuller at all. If the nails do grow back, they're misshapen for life. And your eyes. If you were a fuller, they would be raw from the fumes. Why are you really here? Are you working for Matthew Johan? Do you think to do to me what those Florentines did to my son?'

'I'm no Florentine. You must hear me, Master Robert.' The man took a step towards Robert. 'I came to warn you.'

Robert's eyes widened in alarm. 'Get him out! Get him out and bar the gate. Tenney!' he yelled, backing towards the door of the house. 'I told you to throw him out.'

'You're in grave danger,' the man said desperately. 'You must—'

But Tenney had seized him by the back of the neck and was bundling him towards the street. The man twisted round, thrusting out his foot and jamming the wooden sole of his sandal in the gate. 'If you care anything for your master, make him listen to reason before it's too late. That woman he married is not what she pretends to be. Beg your master to come and find me. I'll tell him everything.'

Tenney glanced behind him. But Master Robert had retreated into the house and secured the door. He turned back to the wool-walker and lowered his voice. 'I'm making no promises, mind, but supposing he does want to talk to you, where will he find you?'

'Look for me at the church of St John the Poor,' the man said. 'But urge him to come soon or, before the summer is out, he'll be lying alongside his wife and son in that graveyard.'

Chapter 36

Witches are unable to shed tears in the presence of judges.

Beata

'What are you two whispering about?' I said, coming up behind Adam and Leonia in the yard.

Adam jerked away from the girl as if I'd caught them out in some mischief, but Leonia glanced up, a look of annoyance in her face, which plainly said, how dare I, a mere servant, interrupt her? She was as arrogant as her mother, not that Master Robert could see that. As far as he was concerned the girl pissed rosewater. It cut me to the quick to see the way he spoiled her, yet rarely spared so much as a kind word for his son, who'd lost mother and brother.

'What's that you got?' I'd seen Adam push something hastily into Leonia's hand. I'd not watched Jan grow up without learning that if a lad were concealing something, it was bound to be something he shouldn't have. Adam glanced at Leonia, but neither child answered. I didn't like it. Adam had always been such an open, honest boy, but in the past few weeks he'd become sly and secretive. I tried not to think badly of him. What could you expect after all that poor boy had been through? But the less time he spent in that girl's company, the easier my mind would rest.

'If school's finished, your father'll be expecting you at the warehouse. He'll not be pleased if you're late. He gave orders you were to go straight there.'

Adam immediately looked stricken and made towards the gate, but Leonia held him back.

'Adam won't be late.' She gave me one of her knowing smiles, so cold it fair froze the breath in me. 'Everyone was sent home early from his school today, weren't they, Adam? So he won't be expected at the warehouse yet.'

'Master Warner must be in a good humour to let you out early. He usually keeps you late. Courting again, is he?'

The schoolmaster was well known for being as peevish as a bear except when a young woman took his fancy. Then you'd think he was a lovelorn youth of fifteen, instead of the five-and-fifty he was. For a few brief weeks when he was chasing her and showering her with gifts, he was as sunny and jovial as a beggar who'd found a gold piece. But it always ended the same way, for the girls he pursued were young, beautiful and far too wealthy for their fathers ever to consent to them wedding a schoolmaster. Before long Master Warner's face would be as sour as a pickled herring again.

Now Adam looked at Leonia, as if he were asking her permission to speak. Again, she answered for him: 'Master Warner had a pain, didn't he, Adam?'

'You were there, were you, Leonia?' I said tartly. 'I didn't know they'd started to admit girls to school. Who will they take as pupils next? Beggars and stray cats, I shouldn't wonder.'

The look she gave me was so venomous it would have brought a bull to its knees, but I wasn't going to take any nonsense from Widow Catlin's brat. 'You'd best run along, Adam, because if your father hears the school was closed early, and he will, the way news spreads in this town, he'll still want to know why you didn't go to the warehouse at once.'

Adam turned towards the gate and Leonia followed as if she had every intention of walking with him.

'Adam can find his way without your help, Leonia. You stay here. Your mother may have let you go wandering about town on your own, like a tanner's urchin, but you live in a respectable household now. Master Robert has a position in this city and he'll not be best pleased if you disgrace him.'

That was her told. I didn't wait to see if she would heed me but marched back to my kitchen.

I'd barely finished skinning and gutting a brace of hares when there came rapping at the gate and as Tenney, as usual, was nowhere to be seen, it was left to me to wipe the blood and mess from my hands and unlock it. Master Edward, Catlin's son, pushed his way in without so much as a by-your-leave, and strode towards the door as if he was family. He might have been Widow Catlin's kin, but he was certainly none of Master Robert's, as far as I was concerned.

I'd never forgive him for making me out to be a fool in front of Master Robert. He and that mother of his had seen the bird's skull as plain as I had. Widow Catlin herself had bundled it in a cloth and taken it away, though God alone knows where she threw it. After she denied she'd seen it, I went looking for the skull to prove to the master I wasn't going mad, but I couldn't find any trace of it on the midden. Even Tenney thought I'd imagined it for, as he said, what cause would they have to tell the master about the slashing, but pretend they'd not seen the curse? It made no sense. I could no more explain it than him, but I knew one thing for certain: from now on, I wouldn't turn my back on that woman or her brats for fear of getting a knife in it.

When Master Robert was at the warehouse, Edward was usually to be found in the solar with his mother, plotting, no doubt, how to get his hands deeper into the master's coffers. In the evenings, he took himself to the tavern and you can be sure it wasn't his own money he was spending. I even saw Catlin give Edward that lovely little rosebud necklace, the one Master Robert had given Leonia. I said nothing. It was no concern of mine if the brat lost it. The master should never have given anything so fine to a child, and one who was not even his own. But what kind of mother steals a necklace from her daughter and gives it to her son to drink away? Master Robert was being robbed under his very nose only he couldn't see it.

Once I'd seen Adam off to the warehouse and had set all the pots simmering for dinner, I went into the great hall to collect the pewter trenchers and goblets to rinse. Although Tenney had cleaned them the night before, all the casements were flung wide in the heat and the dust had settled on everything. Edward and Catlin were up in the solar. I could hear them murmuring and might have been tempted to creep up and listen, except that Leonia was sitting on the window seat in the great hall. I was gratified to see she had minded me and not followed Adam.

She didn't look up as I came in, deeply absorbed in some game that lay beside her on the seat. A first I thought she was playing knuckle bones for some bones were arranged in a circle on the seat, but she was not tossing them. Instead her hands were cupped around something. Curious, I moved closer. Still, she ignored me. There were not just bones in the circle, but a shrivelled brown apple core, a piece of dry bread with a bite out of it, and several other bits of rubbish that she might have fished out of the midden.

Leonia opened her hands and a large black spider ran out between her fingers straight towards one of the bones. As soon as it had scuttled across it, Leonia, pouncing as swiftly as a cat, caught it again and placed it back in the centre of the circle. She let it escape once more and I watched it run towards a piece of broken comb. I suddenly realised it was my own comb. I'd accidentally snapped it in two only the week before and had thrown it away.

Course, I know children'll hunt out any old piece of rubbish to turn into a toy – a fragment of glass becomes a princess's jewel and a bit of stick a knight's sword – but, still, the sight of that spider crawling across my old comb made me shudder as if it were in my own hair. I found myself tearing my linen cap from my head as I hurried from the hall and scrubbing at my hair, for my scalp was itching as if a nest of spiders had hatched out in it and were running all over me.

It was a good half-hour before I could stop scratching long enough to rinse the pewter. I carried it back to the great hall ready to set the table. I opened the door a crack and peered at the casement seat at the far end of the hall but it was empty. I thought the hall was, too, until a movement caught my eye as I pushed the door wider and stepped in.

Catlin and Edward were standing in the corner behind the door. Catlin was pushing the stopper into the flask of hippocras, the spiced wine that was always kept on the oak chest especially for Master Robert. He often had a measure after his dinner, for he said it settled his stomach – at least, that was his excuse. It was expensive even by Master Robert's standards. Surely Catlin wasn't serving it to that good-for-nothing son of hers. The master wouldn't take kindly to that. But then I saw that neither Catlin nor Edward had goblets in their hands.

I grinned to myself, making a huge bustle of laying the table. At least I'd prevented Widow Catlin pouring any wine for that wastrel. Not even she'd have the gall to do it in front of me and I'd make quite sure I never gave her the chance. I was determined to keep my promise to poor Mistress Edith that I'd watch over Master Robert and her sons. I'd not been able to protect Jan, but I'd make certain that scheming harlot didn't hurt Master Robert and Adam, not while I still had breath in my body.

Chapter 37

Monkshood and dwale belong to Hecate, the moon goddess of the witches, and by their use are witches able to fly.

Lincoln

The night air was as hot and thick as pottage. The midges and biting gnats swarmed over the stinking ditches and sewers. Women and many men wafted bunches of mint to keep them at bay, or pinned sprigs of lavender, rue and fleabane to their clothes till they resembled walking bushes. But the hardy paggers and boatmen merely slapped their itching arms and faces and hurried towards any of the inns that were close enough to the Braytheforde to catch the night breeze.

After the long trudge up Steep Hill, grime and sweat were running down Tenney's face – he looked as if someone had thrown a bucket of slops over him. He was sorely tempted to go back to Braytheforde and join the paggers in the Mermaid, but he forced himself to keep climbing. He'd not been able to stop thinking about that wool-walker.

He'd said nothing to Master Robert about the fuller's warning. What would have been the point? Given the rage he'd fallen into when Jan had tried to warn him against Catlin, Tenney knew his employer was not going to toil up here and seek out some stranger to listen to tales against his wife. And there was always a chance the man was working for the Florentines, as Master Robert feared. After what had happened to Jan, Tenney certainly wasn't going to risk helping them to spring a trap to catch Robert. If there was danger to be faced, better he walk into it than his master. Besides, Tenney reckoned he could put up a better fight than Master Robert any day. He touched the hilt of the freshly sharpened knife in his belt and took a firmer grip on the stout wooden staff.

Tenney searched the faces of the half-dozen or so beggars lying listlessly beneath the alms window outside the church of St John the Poor. A couple lifted their heads and held out their bandaged hands, but it was a half-hearted gesture. Any seasoned beggar could tell by the way Tenney studied them that it was not charity that had brought him here. He was looking for someone. They'd seen that intense expression before on men's faces and turned away. They weren't about to rat on their own, unless he offered a good purse, which Tenney certainly didn't look as if he could afford.

Tenney prodded the nearest beggar's foot with his boot. 'I'm looking for a man who says he's a wool-walker. I reckon he's lost his right hand.'

'Found it for him, have you?' The beggar sniggered. He held up the stumps of his own two arms. 'Find mine 'n'all, can you?'

The others laughed. Dozens of men in Lincoln were missing one hand or both, some lost in battle or in accidents at work. Others had had them amputated to save their lives when a cut had turned foul. Possessing only a single hand was hardly enough to identify a man and, in truth, Tenney didn't know for certain that the fuller's hand was missing. It was only when he tried to recall what the man looked like that he realised he could remember little about him, except the manner in which the sleeve of the shirt hung down at the end as if there was nothing beneath it.

Tenney was turning away, when a bundle of cloth lying in the far corner of the churchyard uncurled into a man who struggled to his feet. The movement caught Tenney's attention. The wool-walker immediately recognised him, even if Tenney could not have picked him out of a crowd. The man made his way towards him over the twisted bodies of the beggars.

'Where's your master?' the wool-walker demanded, as soon as he drew close.

'Let's hear what you've got to say first. See if it's worth troubling Master Robert with it.'

Seeing the scowl on the man's face, Tenney added, 'If you were hoping to tap him for a heavy purse, you're a fool. He'd not pay for information at any time, but especially not against her. You'd be more likely to find yourself whipped out of town at a cart's tail. So be grateful it's me you're speaking to, not him. I'll share a flagon with you, but that's all the payment you're getting.'

'I don't want his money or yours,' the fuller growled. 'Can't you see I'm trying to save your master's life, you numbskull?'

Tenney shrugged and gestured towards an inn, whose door lay open, spilling a pool of candlelight and chatter into the darkening street. They walked to it in silence, which neither attempted to break until they were sitting in one of the far corners with a large flagon of ale between them on the table. Both men drank deeply, but Tenney set down his leather beaker first.

'When you came to the house you were blethering about the master's new wife putting him in a grave. I reckon she's set to break his heart, but can't see her sticking a knife in it.'

'If you thought she was no threat, you wouldn't have come.' The man's voice was unnaturally low and grated, like a stone coffin lid being dragged into place. 'You know what she is,' he added.

'I know nowt,' Tenney said. 'And I warn you, if this is just a trick to get near my master and do him harm, I'll not be throwing you out this time, I'll be throwing you in – into the Braytheforde with your back snapped in a dozen places.' He clenched his great hand into a fist on the table just in case the stranger should be in any doubt. But the man didn't flinch. 'You got a name?' Tenney demanded.

'Godwin, though there isn't a soul in the world who calls me that now. When you no longer own a name, that's when you know even the devil has turned his back on you.'

Tenney could hear him wheezing and began to worry that he might have a fever. He leaned away from him. 'Out with it, then,' he said. 'What is it you've to tell me?'

Godwin drained the last dregs from his beaker and waited for Tenney to refill it.

'To look at me now you'd never think it but I was once as wealthy as your master, at least, my father was, and as his eldest son, I would have been in time. My father owned a manor in the north not far from the port of Whitby. Every day as a child I'd ride to the top of the cliffs, and while my horse grazed, I'd spend hours lying on my belly on the grass, gazing down on the sailing ships carrying cargoes of spices and wines into port, and the warships, crammed with men, sailing out to glorious deeds of battle. Never did I imagine, during those long summers, that I'd end my days in rags, begging for coins from strangers who don't deign to look at me as they drop them in the dirt.'

'Aye, 'tis as well we don't know what lies ahead of us else half the world would cut their own throats while they were still in clouts,'

Tenney said, not unsympathetically, for what man didn't fear ending his days begging for alms?

Godwin continued, 'My father, a man called Fycher, traded in spices and frankincense, which he sold to churches and monasteries. He even supplied the table and chapels of the Archbishop of York. My mother, Clare, was much younger than him and was little more than a child herself when she was brought to bed with me. Two more children followed, both girls, but as she carried the last in her belly she became sick. Her legs were so swollen that she could barely walk and she died within hours of my youngest sister's birth. My mother was a beautiful woman, Master Tenney. My father used to say she was too gentle and good for this world. He was heartbroken, but as the years passed her memory wore smooth, like a well-loved bench, and no longer pricked us as it once had. And that was when the witch struck, though we had no way of knowing what she was then.

'Pavia was a young woman, not much older than my mother had been when first she and my father met and in many ways much like her to look at. Perhaps that's what attracted my father to her. She'd come to stay with us as the companion of an elderly cousin of my father's, and when the old woman took a nap, which she did often, Pavia would persuade my father to walk with her along the cliffs or take her riding. I confess, I was as enchanted by her as my father, for she cosseted me and my two little sisters and gave us the mother's love we craved, having been deprived of it for so long.

'In due course, my father proposed marriage. It was rumoured Pavia had no money of her own, that even her clothes had been bought for her by my father's cousin. But my father was wealthy enough in his own right and in taking a second wife had no need to marry for land or money. It was a match made in Heaven, he said. But if he had known what was about to befall him, he would have thought it a match forged by the devil himself.

'Pavia was always slipping out to take a basket of meats to some ailing crone in the village or physic for a woman who had the fever, often going out in the middle of the night, if word came she was needed. My father said she was a saint, exhausting herself with charity, for he saw only Clare's reflection in her.

'There was much trouble in the village at that time. Bonfires were seen burning on the cliff tops at the time of the old pagan festivals. A child's corpse went missing from its newly dug grave. Bunches of

260

Hecate's herbs were found tied to the body of a fox floating in the sea. The parish priest was angry and blamed the disturbances on a woman who'd not long arrived in the district and was living alone on the seashore. He said she was leading the village women back into the elder faith, and instructed the men to keep their wives home at night. But the men were growing afraid of their wives. They refused to sit at home keeping watch over them and enduring their cold fury when they could be spending their evenings in the welcoming taverns. So, the bonfires continued.

'In the meantime I was growing into a young man and still watching those ships sailing away to distant and exotic lands, where the spices grew and the frankincense trees blossomed. Pavia often invited a guest to dinner, a man called Peter de Ponte, an envoy who travelled between England and countries across the world delivering documents, treaties and valuables for any man wealthy or powerful enough to need his services. My father didn't much like or trust the man. I think he was a little jealous of the attention Pavia paid to him, but Pavia would encourage de Ponte to tell me tales of the sea, and I would sit for hours enthralled. He made life at sea seem the most exciting adventure that the world could offer.

'Naturally, I begged my father to let me go to sea, but he refused. I was his heir. He wanted me to stay at home to learn the business. But what lad wants to be sitting in a shop in the same town for the rest of his life, counting coins and pounding cinnamon, like a goodwife, when he could be out there among the mermaids and sea-serpents, discovering cities built of solid gold and whirlpools that can swallow a mountain, men with the heads of dogs and women with faces in the middle of their chests? You see, I'd devoured all of de Ponte's tales.

'I went to Pavia and begged her to plead my case with my father. At first, she appeared as reluctant as he was to let me go, saying she had come to love me as if I was her own son and would worry so about me if I was away at sea, but eventually I persuaded her and she worked her charm on my father. Peter de Ponte found a captain willing to take me on and, barely a month later, I found myself standing upon a rolling deck, watching the cliffs of my home recede and listening to the gulls scream warnings against our departure.

'The night before I sailed, Pavia threw a great banquet for me, with a roasted boar's head in pride of place upon the table and wine flowing like the tide to toast my safe return. As a parting gift my father presented me with a gold ring in the form of an ouroboros, a snake devouring its own tail, in which a serpent's tongue was embedded to protect me from poison. But to my consternation, when I awoke with a throbbing head the next morning, I discovered that the ring had slipped from my finger and was lost before I'd even left the shore. I begged my gentle stepmother to look for it, for I was afraid to upset my father. She assured me she would search for it and quietly return it to me as soon as I came home, without my father ever discovering its loss.

'I quickly learned that life at sea is not nearly as adventurous as the sea-wolves would have you believe. Mostly it's wretched, back-breaking work, with foul food, worse weather and nothing to see, except the hazy line of some far-distant shore. Though there were compensations to be had in the ports.'

Godwin gazed into space, his eyes soft and his mouth curving into the semblance of a smile. Tenney guessed he was picturing some enchanting girl long abandoned on a foreign shore. Every man had his dreams and regrets, but Tenney hadn't come here to listen to Godwin's life story and he couldn't begin to see what any of this had to do with Catlin. He nudged Godwin irritably with his foot. 'If you've something to say about my master's wife, spit it out, man. Tales of the sea are a penny a dozen down by the waterside and all of them far more exciting than yours.'

'Excitement? I can't give you that.' Godwin scowled. 'I'd not describe years rotting in a French fortress as *exciting*. For that's where we ended up, captured by French pirates. They took us by surprise, two swift galleys hiding in a bay round a headland and attacking at dusk, one diverting us on our port side while the other crept up on the starboard. It was trap, not a chance encounter, as if they knew where we'd be. The ordinary seamen and ship's boys who survived the battle were shackled in irons to be sold as slaves in the markets of the Holy Land or, if they were injured or maimed, tied together and tossed overboard to drown. Those of us whose families had rank or wealth were thrown into the oubliette. You know what that means, do you? "The forgotten place", for that's what we were, or I was, at least.

'One by one my companions left for home as their families settled their ransom demands, but not one word did I receive from my father. I didn't know whether he'd not received the demand or if he'd sent the ransom and it had been stolen. But I told myself that eventually it would come. Fool that I was, I never stopped believing so. As the weeks dragged past, the French grew impatient. They thought I was lying to them about my father's wealth or else I was a spy. So they questioned me.'

Godwin pulled back his sleeve and held out the stump of his arm towards Tenney. 'They crushed my hand slowly in a press till it was nothing but pulp and splinters of bone. And after that they amused themselves by doing this.'

With his teeth and practised left hand, Godwin unfastened the cords that tied together the front of his shirt. Tenney gasped and winced – he could almost feel the agony of it himself. He was staring at a painting, like those on a church wall. But what was on the man's body had not been made by paint and brush. Godwin's chest was covered with raised black welts. The scarred skin had healed so tightly over his ribcage, it was a wonder he could move his ribs enough to breathe. Lines had been painstakingly etched to form a picture of two fighting ships, one of which was in flames and sinking, while all around men drowned in the sea or were devoured by monsters and scaly sea-serpents, whose long tails coiled round Godwin's sides.

'It's to remind me and all who see me that the French will defeat the English,' Godwin said dully, pulling his shirt closed. 'You want to know how it's done? Each line was first carved into my flesh with a knife. Then hot wax, soot and sulphur were dripped into each wound and set afire, so that the marks would be etched deep. It took many . . . many weeks to accomplish every last detail.

'There were days when I feared I should never see another night, and nights when I prayed I would not live to see another day. But dawn must come even to the eternal night and finally there was another ship taken. This time it was one of the King's own ships. The Crown paid the ransom for all the officers, and the French soldiers who came to escort them to the port, through carelessness or ignorance, swept me up with the rest and herded us aboard a vessel bound for England.

'As soon as we had landed, I set off at once to my home, knowing that my father would be overjoyed to see me, but when I arrived I found strangers there. "Master Fycher's son is long dead," they said, "and his bones are buried in the church."

'They threw me out of my own manor. I thought it was some kind of cruel trick to deprive me of my lands until I went to the church and stared down at my own tomb, with my own effigy carved upon the stone – *Here lie the mortal remains of Godwin de Fycher.*

'I discovered that an old servant by the name of Aggy still lived in the village. She'd been wet-nurse to my sisters, and in my face she recognised the vestiges of the beardless youth who had sailed away so long ago. As she said, I was now so much like my father, I could have been his ghost. It was a miracle old Aggy didn't drop dead on the spot when she saw me, for she had watched my remains laid in the church.

'When she recovered from the shock, Aggy told me that the ransom demand had indeed reached my father and he had quickly despatched the messenger back to France with the considerable sum demanded. Pavia had waylaid the messenger as he left and handed one of her jewels to him, which she told my father was to buy me fresh clothes, good food, physic and anything else I might need to make my journey home more comfortable. My father kissed her and told her she was the most generous and tender of women. Pavia eagerly began to prepare to welcome me home with great festivities.

'But some weeks later, when my father returned from his business, he was met by Pavia and his two little daughters in tears. They led him into the hall where a casket lay on the table. Pavia gently broke the news to my father. The ransom had arrived too late. I had died of prison fever just days before. But the French had honoured the payment by returning my bones to my family. As is the custom when a man dies far from home, they had buried my heart and innards in a French churchyard and boiled my skull and bones clean before wrapping them to be sent to England. In the bone-casket they had also placed the ring I was wearing when I was captured, as proof of my identity.

'As soon as he saw the ring my father recognised it at once and fell to weeping, for it was the very ring in the form of a serpent that he had given to me the night before I sailed. The one I had confessed to Pavia I had lost.

'My father fell ill shortly after. He was gripped with violent pains of the belly and began to waste away. His hair and nails grew brittle and fell out and at times he scarcely had the energy to draw breath. The local physician said it was the green sickness, which often follows grief, but Aggy refused to believe it.

'She told me she had learned that Pavia was the daughter of the woman who lived on the seashore, whom the priest had accused of leading the village woman back to the old ways. But it was not her mother who led the women when they went out to dance about their bonfires on the cliffs. It was Pavia. She had learned all her mother had taught her and far more besides, for unlike her mother, an unlettered woman, Pavia had learned to read.

'It was Pavia who taught the women how to make candles from human corpse fat and call out the names of all those men they wanted to harm. She would pronounce the great sentence of excommunication against their victims to stop their mouths, so they couldn't confess their sins to a priest or swallow the sacred Host. Then the women lit the candles, pierced them with thorns, and let them burn. Those they'd named would feel as if their very flesh was afire and running like wax from their bodies.

'Aggy said that if Pavia gave the candle the name of a person and let it burn down till it went out, the person would surely die and nothing could be done to save him. She swore Pavia was at the bonfire on the cliff top with her mother the night they sent for the priest to give my father the last rites. And he had died at the very hour she named him.

'I am convinced that it was Pavia who, through de Ponte, ensured that the ship was captured, for he was well placed to see that the information of its whereabouts and cargo would reach the French pirates. And I am certain Pavia obtained the bones they buried in place of me. Who knows? She might even have boiled down a corpse herself to get them. God's blood, I'd swear she was capable of doing so, without so much as a shudder.'

Godwin stared down at the table, his face twisted in grief.

Tenney shuffled his great buttocks awkwardly on the bench and averted his eyes from the man's misery. He still couldn't see what any of this had to do with Mistress Catlin and was beginning to think that Godwin was one of those demented creatures who insisted on telling their story to any stranger who'd listen, when their friends had long grown weary of it. Not that he felt anything but pity for Godwin. The torture those foreign dogs had inflicted on him would be enough to turn the wits of the most battle-hardened soldier. Now he knew for certain that, if those French bastards could do that to an ordinary seaman who'd never done them any harm, there wasn't a man, woman or child in England who'd be safe if King Richard failed to stop the French invading.

265

Tenney eased himself sideways along the bench, intending to slip out while the man was still sunk in his own thoughts, but Godwin grabbed his arm to stay him. 'I've not told you all yet.'

Had any other man been bent on cornering him, Tenney would have made some excuse about the master wanting him at home and walked away, but he couldn't wipe from his mind what he'd seen beneath the man's shirt. Sighing, he settled himself down to humour Godwin just a little longer.

'Aggy told me that since my father believed me dead and had no other close male relatives, he'd left most of his money and his estate to my two little sisters for their future dowries. His beloved and trusted widow, Pavia, was to be given an allowance so that she should not be in want and was to act as guardian for her stepdaughters, managing their portions until they were of age. But the wreath on his grave had not faded before Pavia sold everything and left the manor, taking my sisters with her.

'As soon as I learned that, I set off to find them and confront Pavia, for if even a tenth of what the old woman had told me was true, I'd no wish to leave those two helpless girls in her care. And, yes, I freely admit I went to claim what was mine. Since I'd returned alive I was certain that the Consistory Court would overturn my father's will and grant me my inheritance.

'I'd little idea of where to start looking, but I went through the village, cottage by cottage, asking everyone if they knew where Pavia had gone. The women refused to tell me anything, though I suspected they knew, and her mother's hut on the seashore had long been abandoned. Eventually I came across a wagoner who thought he'd seen Pavia a year or so after my father's death at the Thirsk fair. He'd recognised her, for she was a striking woman who stood out in the crowd.

'So I set off at once for Thirsk. No one there had heard of a woman called Pavia, but I described her to everyone I met and it seems a woman resembling her, calling herself Margaret, had arrived there shortly after my father's death and married a local landowner, Sir Richard, who had a manor in those parts. They said she had come to Thirsk alone, accompanied only by a maid, a woman old enough to be her mother. There were no little girls with her. I was certain then that she'd cruelly murdered my sisters somewhere on the road so that she could keep all of my father's money.'

Tenney shook his head in exasperation. The tale had grown wild beyond belief and Godwin was sorely trying his patience. 'Even if it was the same woman, your sisters could have died of the Great Pestilence that took so many young ones when it returned, or some other sickness. You've no proof that murder was done. Besides, the description of one woman may fit a dozen, a hundred, even. Why should Margaret and Pavia be the same woman? It seems more likely she wasn't, if she had no children with her. Did you see her, speak to her?'

Godwin, without waiting to be invited, refilled his beaker, emptying the flagon to the last drop. 'Sir Richard had died long before I arrived in Thirsk and his wife had vanished shortly after. But the proof is this.' Godwin leaned forward eagerly, his eyes blazing in their dark hollow sockets. 'Sir Richard also died of the green sickness and it took exactly the same progress as my own father's.'

'As well it might,' Tenney said, 'if it was the same sickness.'

'Just listen to me!' Godwin snarled, his face twisted into such hatred that Tenney was afraid he would attack him. 'I discovered another husband after Sir Richard who died at that witch's hands, a man called Warrick. She bewitched him into madness, so that he killed himself by riding into a tree.'

'Men die every day after being thrown from a horse,' Tenney said. 'There's no witchcraft in it, only the carelessness of the riders. You should have seen the way young master Jan used to ride, especially after a night in the tavern. His poor mother used to fear every day he'd be brought home on a bier.' He crossed himself, thinking it was a blessing Mistress Edith hadn't lived to see her son dragged out of the Braytheforde.

Godwin groaned. 'What will it take to convince you? I followed Pavia's trail here to Lincoln and this time I caught up with her. I've seen her with my own eyes, not once but many times. I watched her until I was absolutely sure, not trusting to looks alone, for it has been many years since I laid eyes on her, but observing the way she walks, her gestures, her manner. Those things don't change in a woman, though her face may age. I even called at her door once, begging for alms, so that I could hear her voice. I would swear upon my life, upon every saint in Christendom, that the woman who now calls herself Catlin is my father's wife, Pavia. And Catlin's maid is the woman who lived on the seashore, Pavia's mother. If Catlin and Diot are those two witches, then your master's life is in grave danger, his son's too.'

Tenney tugged his thick beard. 'If you're that certain of it, you should take this tale to the sheriff. See what he makes of it. He's a great friend of the master. He'd act soon enough if he thought his life were in any danger.' Another thought struck him. 'And that's another thing that makes no sense. You said you wanted your inheritance so why didn't you go straight to the justices as soon as you returned? Tell'm you were still alive. I've heard of men that were thought certain dead in battle, returning months, even years later and reclaiming their lands. This Aggy would surely have stood witness that you were who you claimed to be.'

Godwin gave a bitter laugh. 'You think that wasn't exactly what I intended? But I'd underestimated Pavia, as all men do. Aggy told me that, shortly after I set sail, a young girl's body was found down a well, battered beyond recognition. They only realised the corpse was down there when people started getting sick and complaining about the stench of the water they drew up. The girl was probably a beggar or traveller's brat, for no one from the village had been reported missing, else they'd have searched long before.

'The hue and cry was raised, but there were no clues as to who'd killed her and no relatives to press for justice, so the search was abandoned. But at my father's funeral, Pavia broke down sobbing, saying that as he lay mortally sick my father confessed to her that I'd raped and murdered the girl. He'd discovered what I'd done and that was why he'd sent me to sea, so that he'd be spared the shame of having a son convicted of murder.

'Aggy, bless her, didn't believe a word of it, for she'd known me all my life, but who listens to an old woman? Everyone in the village suddenly remembered wondering at the time why a wealthy merchant should send his eldest son and heir to sea. To them the explanation made perfect sense. They were convinced of my guilt.

'Since everyone assumed I'd died in a French dungeon, there was nothing more the bailiff could do about it, save say that God had meted out His own justice. But if I were to turn up claiming to be Godwin, I'd be arrested for the girl's murder with no way to prove otherwise. It would be my word against the deathbed confession of my own father. Pavia was clever. She'd made quite certain that if, by some miracle, I survived, I could never go to the justices anywhere in England for I'd be a wolf's head, an outlaw.

'I had to track her down myself. I tried to stop her marriage to your master by scrawling a message on the banns nailed to the church door. And I warned Pavia her secret was discovered by leaving her own curse on her marriage bed, the same one she had used to murder my poor father, the candles stuck with thorns.'

'Hold up!' Tenney said. 'Then it was you who broke in and slashed the bed.'

'To frighten her away.'

'Beata swore there were candles and a bird's skull left in the chamber, but Edward and Mistress Catlin denied it and Master Robert wouldn't believe my poor lass.'

Godwin grasped Tenney's wrist fiercely. 'But you must believe Beata and you must make your master believe before it's too late. The woman you call Catlin is a witch, like her mother, only far more powerful, and her own daughter has learned from the pair of them. I've been watching her. That child is growing up to be as evil and ruthless as the dam, perhaps more so. Leonia is bewitching Adam, as her mother enchanted my father and your master. And Leonia will destroy Adam, just as surely as her mother murdered my father. I beg you to believe that. The mother and daughter have fastened their talons around father and son and they will devour them both, unless you stop them.'

Chapter 38

Sorcerers and witches are able to inflict the falling sickness on their victims by burying an egg in a grave with a corpse who was of one of their own kind. When the egg is dug up, it is concealed in the food or posset of the person they wish to harm, and charms are recited under the breath as the victim eats it. Then the falling sickness shall come upon them and they will be seized by fits whenever the witch wills it.

Lincoln

'But, Tenney, you'll have to tell the master,' Beata said. 'You must find a way to get him alone, away from them.' She peered out of the stables across the dark courtyard. The lights in the hall had been extinguished, but the glow of candles in the solar upstairs showed that the family had not yet retired to bed. 'I knew there was something evil about all three of those women. I told you, Tenney, but you wouldn't have it, you stubborn old goat. "Master Robert needs a new wife to take his mind off his troubles,"' Beata mimicked Tenney's gruff tones. 'Well, he's more troubles than a chicken in a foxes' den now. If you'd listened to me—'

'Supposing I had,' Tenney grumbled, 'what difference would it have made? The master would've no more taken notice then than he will now.'

Beata pounced. 'Aye, but it's different now. What this Godwin told you – that's proof, that is. He'll have to believe it.'

Tenney shook his great head. 'Believe what? Some fanciful tale spun by an outlaw the master already thinks is out to rob or murder him? I don't even think I believe it. And even if any of it's true, we've only Godwin's word that Catlin and Pavia are one and the same. Remember your old aunt who kept thinking other women's bairns were her own? She even came up to you in the marketplace when Master Jan was little, saying he was her babe stolen away from her. Swore blind she recognised him, even though you'd cut Master Jan's cord with your own hands. No amount of telling her convinced her, though, did it? And if you'd seen what those French did to that poor wretch of a man . . .' Tenney shuddered. 'No one'd be in his right mind after that.'

'*I* believe Godwin,' Beata said stubbornly. 'I've seen what that little imp Leonia can do. Aye, and felt it too. And I can see how she's witching young Adam. Haven't you noticed the lad's changing? He's getting sly and spiteful.'

'He's growing up,' Tenney said.

'It's more than that. I saw them the other night after dark, here in the stables. I couldn't see much of what they were up to, but they weren't playing sweethearts, that's for certain. She'd a bowl in front of her and a lit candle. Both of them were peering into it. They'd caught some creature or other. I couldn't see what it was 'cause they were bent over with their backs to me. But I could hear the poor thing shrieking in pain. It was enough to set your teeth on edge. Made me feel sick it did. I was in two minds whether or not to go in and demand to know what they were doing, but . . . I couldn't seem to step inside. It was as if there was a solid door there. It fair gave me the shivers, I can tell you. I ran straight back to my bed. Lay awake half the night, as chilled as if a corpse were lying atop me.'

Tenney sighed. 'If I go saying anything to him about his wife or Leonia, I'll find myself turned out on the road, afore I can say, "Bless me."'

'If you won't tell Master Robert,' Beata said, 'I will. I promised the mistress I'd watch out for her husband and her son and I'll not break my word to a dying woman.'

Tenney groaned. When Beata took that stance, arms folded and lips pursed, not even an angel with a flaming sword could turn her away from what she'd made up her mind to do.

A piercing scream split the darkness and Robert found himself staggering out of bed for the third time that night. Had Johan's men broken in? His heart thudding, he stood listening until he heard Tenney's voice calling up from below.

'It's only Beata again, Master Robert. Don't you fret. I'll see to her.'

Robert peered down into the dark stableyard below. Tenney was making his way to the kitchen, a lantern swinging in his hand,

271

sending shadows slithering up and down the courtyard wall. Robert slammed the shutter. It was a damnably hot night, and they needed every breeze they could capture to make sleep possible, but better they roast than listen to those shrieks. He crossed to the ambry where the food and drink for the night had been left and poured himself a goblet of wine, drinking it in thirsty gulps. He knew it was foolish. He'd wake in a few hours with a sour stomach, but rather that than lie tossing and turning for the rest of the night.

He climbed back into bed next to Catlin, groaning as he tried to find a comfortable position in the sweat-soaked sheets.

'You'll have to dismiss her in the morning,' Catlin murmured in the darkness.

'She's been with me for years,' Robert said. 'Can't send her packing just because she has nightmares.'

'No normal woman has nightmares like these. And have you forgotten that nonsense when she imagined she saw a skull and candles on our bed?'

'Jan's death has unsettled Beata, that's all,' Robert said.

But in truth he was beginning to worry that Beata was rather more than *unsettled*. Only the other day, when Catlin had poured him some of his favourite spiced wine from the flask that was always kept for him on the chest in the hall, Beata had suddenly turned as white as whey, flown across the room and dashed the goblet from his hands. Before anyone could stop her, she was pouring the contents of the flask onto the floor, babbling about Catlin putting poison in it. Poor Catlin had been forced to pull the flask from Beata's hands and drink from it herself just to prove to her that the wine was untainted.

Suppose his wife was right after all and Beata had slashed the bed. Hadn't she said her aunt had been mad? Such things tended to run in families. Robert wondered if it really was time to dismiss her, though he resented being told to do it.

'And what are we to say to the neighbours?' Catlin said tersely. 'I saw Mistress Ann peering through her casement earlier tonight as if she feared there was a demon in our courtyard. It will not help your business if the rumour spreads you're employing a woman who's possessed.'

'I'll deal with it,' Robert snapped. 'Don't turn into a scold like Edith!'

He heard a sharp intake of breath as if he had slapped her and was instantly remorseful. He reached for her hand in the darkness, stroking the back, marvelling, as he never ceased to do, at the delicate softness of her skin. 'I'll speak to Beata in the morning, my dear. Now please can we try to sleep while she's quiet?'

Early-morning sunlight flooded through the casement, promising another cloudless day, which was more than could be said for the mood of those gathered around the table in the hall for breakfast. Robert, Catlin and Edward had the puffy faces and dull eyes of those who had slept ill, while Tenney and Diot were as bad. Only Leonia looked as fresh as a rosebud. Nothing had troubled her sleep.

Robert gazed at his stepdaughter. A black curl swung against her soft cheek, iridescent in the sunlight. Was it his imagination or had her breasts filled out a little in these past few weeks? Rounded little mounds peeped over the embroidered neckline of her dress. It was a credit to the child that, even at this hour, she had taken care to dress pleasingly, which was more than could be said for her mother.

Catlin was clad only in her dressing robe of russet fox fur, her legs flashing bare and white beneath it as she shifted in her chair. It irritated Robert to see her so, especially with her son in the house. It was vulgar and unbecoming for a woman of her rank to be dining half naked in front of her son – her stepson too, come to that. He caught Catlin and Edward exchanging another of their knowing glances and felt disquieted, as if they were anticipating something of which he had no knowledge.

Robert dipped a sop of bread into his ale and pushed it into his mouth. In truth, he was so weary he could barely face breakfast, but he hoped that food might rouse him a little. It had better, or he was likely to fall asleep where he sat.

The door opened and Beata entered, placing a dish of boiled herring on the table. Her hands were trembling, making the dish rattle against the wood as she set it down. Robert did not much care for herring at any time, but today, with those white boiled fish eyes staring up at him, any vestige of appetite that might have been stirring was instantly quashed.

Catlin coughed pointedly, catching Robert's eye. For a moment, he couldn't think what she wanted. Then he remembered.

'Beata?'

She flinched at the mention of her name and darted a frightened glance in his direction. Robert was shocked to see the change in her. She was no beauty at the best of times. The pox had been cruel to her, leaving her with a deeply pitted face and drooping eyelids. But today she looked positively hag-ridden. Her face was pale, with dark smudges under her eyes – she might even have been punched. The memory of Edith floated into his head. Was Beata afflicted with the same sickness as had taken her mistress? No, it was not the same, he could see, yet the rapid change in her perturbed him.

All the faces at the table had turned to him, waiting for him to speak, but he couldn't bring himself to talk to her in front of them, when she was obviously so distressed.

'Beata . . . I wanted a word with you. I'll come to the kitchen presently.'

To his surprise, she seemed desperately relieved. 'Yes, I must speak with you, Master Robert. Please come soon.' Lowering her gaze, she scuttled out.

Robert took a last swig of the ale and rose.

Catlin reached out to touch his hand. 'You will tell her she must leave. I can't stand another night of this and the children will be ill if they're continually disturbed.'

'The children are well enough, my dear. I wish I had their resilience.' He pinched Leonia's cheek, smiling tenderly, in spite of his tiredness. 'In fact I would say our daughter is positively glowing with health. What is your secret, my dear? An innocent soul?'

Leonia giggled. 'It's because I always feel safe when you're here, Père. Nothing disturbs me because I know you'll protect me.'

She stood up beside Robert, throwing her arms around him, and arching her back as she lifted her face to be kissed. From this angle, Robert observed that her breasts were definitely swelling into the sweetest little peaches he'd seen on a girl in a long time. She would need careful guarding. There were many lads and men out there who'd be only too eager to steal over the wall to pluck the fruit from such a tree and she was such an innocent.

When Robert pushed open the door to the kitchen he found Beata sitting on a stool, rocking back and forth amid a chaos of unwashed pots and half-prepared food. She lifted her head only long enough to see who had entered, then lowered it again without meeting Robert's gaze.

Robert had never hesitated to dismiss any man, young or old, if he wasn't performing his work as well as he should, but dismissing a woman, and a woman who had been part of his household for so long, that was different. He'd no idea how to begin this.

'Beata . . . the nightmares . . . You wake the whole household repeatedly. It can't continue. If it was simply a question of disturbed sleep, Hugo Bayus would be able to prescribe you a draught to help, but this is more—'

'I don't ever want to sleep again.' Beata stared up at him, her reddened eyes full of fear. 'Each time I do it's the same. I'm in the river, under the thick green water. I can't reach the surface. Something has hold of my ankles, pulling me down. Then I see them swimming towards me. Long black eels with rows of teeth. I feel their fat slimy bodies twisting round me, pinning my arms so I can't move. They're strangling me. Eating me alive. Eels with human faces. Eels with Jan's face!' She gave a great sob and buried her face in her hands.

Robert closed his eyes, shuddering at the memory of his son's bloated body, dragged from the water. 'You were . . . fond of Jan, I know. The shock of his death, it . . .'

She shook her head, glancing fearfully out of the open door. Then she leaped to her feet, pushed past him and dragged it shut, plunging them into darkness. The only light came from the deep, ruby glow of the embers in the oven. She drew so close to Robert that he could smell her sour breath. For an insane moment he thought she would attempt to kiss him. Alarmed, he tried to back away, but succeeded only in knocking over a pile of pots.

'Did Tenney speak to you?' she whispered urgently. 'Did he tell you what Godwin told him about Widow Catlin and Leonia?'

Robert was bewildered. 'Godwin? I know no one by that name. Beata, we need to decide what's to be done with you. You've given good service to my family, but—'

'You must listen, Master Robert. Leonia is enchanting Adam. It's already begun.'

A fond smile crossed Robert's lips. 'Leonia has the gift of enchanting everyone. It's good if she can coax young Adam into better humour.'

'It isn't good at all! Adam is no more than a nestling, but Leonia, she's a woman. She can seduce—'

'No!' Robert's face flushed with indignation. 'She's just a child.'

Even as he uttered the words he knew deep down that they weren't quite true, but that only made him the more annoyed.

He tried to remember that Beata was sick and attempted to keep the anger from his voice. 'If Leonia is kind to Adam, it's because she's a tender, motherly girl and naturally feels pity for the boy, that's all. But, of course, if you have proof otherwise, you'd better tell me at once.'

'I do have proof,' Beata gabbled, then turned her head, staring wildly at the wall, as if she were addressing someone Robert couldn't see. 'I will speak, I will . . . You can't stop me! All three of them—' She broke off with a strangled cry, her hands clutching at her throat, then fell to the floor, her back arching, jerking violently.

Robert ran to the door, flung it wide and shouted for help. He glanced around and, seeing a beaker of small ale on the table, he snatched it up and dashed the liquid into her face, but still she convulsed. Tenney came running across the yard, closely followed by Diot.

'Look at her! It's as plain as a pig's arse, she has the falling sickness,' Diot announced triumphantly. She hurried back towards the house as if she couldn't wait to apprise her mistress of every detail.

Beata's jerking gradually subsided and she lay still, as white as a shroud. Robert strode across the yard, beckoning Tenney to follow. He kept his voice low, not wanting to distress Beata and bring on another attack.

'When Beata has recovered sufficiently to be moved, put her in the cart and take her to the infirmary at the convent of St Mary Magdalene. Give them this for her admission.' He fumbled in his purse and brought out a gold coin, which he handed to Tenney. 'If they can make her well, they may take her in as a lay servant but tell them she cannot return here. If she should be overcome near a fire or on the stairs, she could kill herself. The nuns will know to set her to work where she risks least harm, in the gardens, perhaps.'

Tenney tried to thrust the coin back at Robert. 'Master Robert, it's not the falling sickness, I'm sure of it. It's grief over Mistress Edith and Jan, and now she's fretting herself sick over you and young Adam. If she could but sleep without dreaming . . . I'll ask the nuns if they have a potion to help her. I know if she could just rest—'

'There is no sleep without dreams,' Robert told him firmly. 'I'm sorry, Tenney. I know you're fond of her, but I cannot have the curse of the falling sickness in my house. I'm master of the Guild of Merchants. With business already as bad as it is, if this should become known, I'd be ruined. No one would trade with me for fear of it and then I'd have to part with you and Diot too. Besides, it's not just the sickness. It's her insane accusations – poisoned wine and skulls! Beata herself admitted that her aunt had run mad. I fear she's afflicted with the same tainted blood, and what if she should attack Catlin or Leonia? I'd never forgive myself.'

But Tenney would not give up easily. 'Please don't shut her away, Master Robert. I'll ask her to wed me. I've been meaning to for years, but never got around to it. We could rent one of your cottages. I'd keep her out of harm's way. I know she's not the fairest lass in the cabbage patch, but I'm not the best-looking man either and she's a good soul. She doesn't deserve to be walled up.'

'No one who has the falling sickness can marry. The Church forbids it and I forbid it,' Robert said. 'She'll have a good life in the nunnery, plenty of women to gossip with and people to care for her. You will take her to Magdalene's this morning, Tenney. I'll not be dissuaded from this.'

He turned away towards the house, but for the first time in his life, Tenney laid hold of his master's arm and pulled him back. Robert stared at him, as if he, too, had run mad.

'Beg pardon, Master Robert, but Beata was right. There's something I have to tell you. Maybe if I'd come straight out with it and told you soon as I got home, she wouldn't . . . It's like this. I got talking to a man—'

Tenney froze, staring at something over Robert's shoulder. A look of fear passed across his face. He quickly averted his eyes, and strode back to the kitchen. Alarmed, Robert turned to see what had frightened him, but saw nothing untoward, only little Leonia standing in the open doorway, her lips parted in her usual beguiling smile.

Chapter 39

If a man or woman is sick, take the water that has been used to wash them and fling it on the track outside. The first living creature, human or animal, to pass over the wet ground shall take the illness upon themselves and the sufferer will recover.

Beata

I rushed at the door of the infirmary as soon as it opened, but Sister Ursula and the two lay sisters who flanked her were on their guard. Afore I even reached the door, they'd grabbed my arms. I yelped as their fingers dug again into the bruises they'd already made. They steered me back to the little bed. The twenty or so patients in the long chamber watched me warily as if they thought I might start screaming or biting, like they did.

My bed, like the others, was enclosed on three sides by high wooden panels. There was even a fourth panel, which could be bolted to the remaining side, like a cupboard door, to lock the patient inside for hours, as I knew only too well.

The lay sisters were spiteful cats, especially when the nuns weren't around. They were always grumbling about the filthy work they were forced to do because they were low-born or bastards, while the daughters of wealthy families had dowries to buy their way into an easy life at the convent. The lay sisters dared not complain to the nuns so they took it out on us. It was no good appealing to them, but a nun would surely listen to reason.

'Sister Ursula, please, I must speak with Master Robert. I'm so afeared for him. He doesn't know how wicked she is. She'll destroy him and poor little Adam, else send them mad. They're both such innocents. I have to warn him.'

'I am quite certain,' Sister Ursula said sternly, 'that a wealthy merchant like your master is far from innocent in the matter of women and more than capable of dealing with any female who has designs on him.'

'But he isn't,' I protested. 'You must let me out. I have to talk to him, tell what we've learned, for Tenney's too afeared to do it. I swear I'll not linger, not if he doesn't want me there. I'll go as soon as I've made him understand.'

The two lay sisters smirked, as if I had told a bawdy joke. 'You'll not be going anywhere, will she, Sister?' one said. 'In here for life, that's right, isn't it?'

'That will do,' Sister Ursula snapped. 'Amice has soiled herself again. She needs her bed linen changing.' She nodded towards an ancient, toothless woman, who huddled naked on the edge of the bed, rocking and whimpering to herself.

'Wh-what did they mean, for life?' I said, panic rising.

Sister Ursula wouldn't look at me, but occupied herself with trying to draw the sheet up around me as if I was a bairn she was tucking up for the night.

'Some of the sick we can cure,' she said, 'but others will always be in need of our care. It's rare that those with the falling sickness are completely cured, though we pray daily for miracles, and if it is God's will—'

I tried to struggle out of the bed again. 'But I don't have the falling sickness. I've not fallen into a fit once since I came here, you know that. It's the girl. She casts the evil eye. She makes me see things, sends demons to torment my sleep. When I'm away from her I'm well, but if she's near, she strikes me dumb, so I can't name her.'

'Then you'll be safe in here, won't you?' Sister Ursula said, as if I was a simpleton who needed to be calmed. 'Whoever you fancy is trying to harm you can't reach you in here, not while you're surrounded by the protection of the blessed St Mary. And, besides, where else could you go? You should be giving thanks daily to the Holy Virgin that your master found you a place here. For you've no work and no family. What would become of you if we cast you out? You'd become a beggar or a harlot.'

'Not much danger of her becoming a whore with that face, Sister,' one of the lay women called over. 'You want to think yourself lucky, Pock-head. At least you spent half your life outside. Old Amice has been in here since she were a girl, and she'll die in here, won't you, you filthy old gammer? And not before time.'

'No!' I scrambled out of bed, shoved Sister Ursula aside and fled to the door. 'I'm not sick. I'll not be kept in here. It's that witch who should be locked up.'

279

I pushed against the door with all my strength, pounding on the wood and twisting the iron handle, but it wouldn't yield. Even as I tried to smash my way out, the two lay sisters grabbed me again. They glanced back, waiting for instructions from Sister Ursula, who came hurrying up.

'She needs a bath to calm her,' Sister Ursula said.

My legs buckled beneath me. 'No, please, not that again,' I moaned. 'I'll be quiet. I'll sit still, I promise. Please!'

It took four of them in the end to drag me into the small, window-less chamber, and force me, naked, into the deep wooden tub filled with cold water drawn from one of the many dark wells. I fought them every inch of the way, bruising myself as I struggled and kicked, scraping my arms on the wood. I thought I was strong from years of hard work, but the lay sisters were stronger and they forced me down. One held my head in the lock of her arm until the two halves of the wooden lid of the tub were bolted around my neck, sealing me into the icy water, leaving only my head poking out of the top.

Two of the women took turns pouring water from a jug over my face to cool my brain, till I thought I would suffocate. I screamed, choked and swore at them, beating my fists against the wood, trying to break free, but they continued until finally I sat still, defeated and sobbing. I couldn't win. I couldn't fight them.

They left me, locked in the freezing water, numb with cold and fear.

'There's nothing to fret about. With the lid fastened around your neck, you can't drown even if you wanted to. You'll come to no harm,' they said. 'What's there to be afraid of? You're safe here.'

They closed the door and left me, shivering, alone in the darkness – alone, that is, until the eels came swimming out of the thick green water.

June

If June be sunny, harvest comes early, but a leak in June sets all in tune.

Chapter 40

*If a spell is cast over a flock of chickens causing them to sicken,
or the cows' milk to dry up, then roast alive a bird from that flock
or bury a calf from the herd alive and the spell shall be broken.*

Kirkstead Abbey

Gunter crouched in the punt and leaned over the river, dashing
handfuls of cool water over his sweating face. He and Hankin had
carried a load of timber downriver to Kirkstead. It was needed as
scaffolding for the repair work at the abbey. It wasn't a great distance,
but the loading and unloading had been time-consuming and hard.
The river was low, and heaving the heavy poles and planks upwards
onto the bank had not been easy. The lay brothers sent to fetch the
wood from the jetty had been an idle and insolent pair, who'd made
it plain they did not regard it as their responsibility to lift so much
as a splinter until the cargo was on dry land. So Gunter and little
Hankin had been forced to unload the wood between them while
the lay brothers sat on the back of their wagon, swigging ale and
watching them work.

Gunter had been hoping the abbey would have a load to send
down to Boston or back up to Lincoln, but the lay brothers' wagon
had arrived empty and he knew that so late in the afternoon there
was little chance of obtaining another cargo elsewhere. So, he'd decided
to draw breath and eat a bite or two before punting back upstream.

He shifted his weight back into the centre of the boat, frowning
as the boy grabbed the edge of the punt when it rocked with his
motion. It pained him to see Hankin so afraid of the water that he'd
once treated as a second skin. This time last year, if they'd stopped
to eat in the heat of the day, the lad would have torn off his clothes
and dived over the side before Gunter had even settled himself down,
plunging and rolling in the water, like a young otter, for the sheer
pleasure of it. But since his near-drowning in the Braytheforde, the

283

boy was as anxious as a minnow in a pool of pike when he was anywhere near the river.

Gunter tried to tell himself it was as well that the scare had made him understand the danger and respect the river. Like most boys his age, Hankin had treated the water with a careless indifference, certain he was invincible. Gunter told Nonie it would do the boy no harm to learn that the river could turn from friend to enemy in a heartbeat, but he could not convince himself of that.

Hankin had been ill with a fever for nearly two weeks after the ducking. The water had got into his lungs and he coughed it up day and night. Nonie had made warming poultices to lay on his chest and given him a decoction of herb of grace to drink, which she'd picked from their own small vegetable patch. A neighbour had offered some precious syrup of marsh poppy to ease the pains of his fever and help him to sleep but he'd woken screaming and flailing as if he were still under the green water, trying to reach the air. Sometimes Gunter had the same dreams. A man with a blanched face and sightless eyes had a hand round his throat and was dragging him down into the cold, dark depths.

He still could not believe that the man they'd dragged from the Braytheforde was Master Robert's son. It seemed inconceivable that the peeling lump of white flesh had once been the vigorous young man he'd seen only days before striding from the warehouse. They'd arrested some of the Florentines for murder, including Matthew Johan, but they'd had to let them go. There was no proof, except that Matthew had had a grudge against Jan, but not even the sheriff of Lincoln could detain a man for holding a grudge.

Gunter wondered if they shouldn't be looking closer to Master Robert's own warehouse for Jan's killer. If Jan had discovered that Fulk was taking bribes from Martin, and challenged either of them at the warehouse, he'd have been highly likely to take a dip in the Braytheforde, just as Hankin had done.

Witnesses said they'd heard Jan shouting and crashing about in his own chamber, and others swore they'd seen him striding round the Braytheforde in such a temper that he'd knocked an old goodwife into a wall and cracked her head open, then cursed her roundly for getting in his way. The coroner and the twelve jury men who had examined the body could make little of what they saw. There were no marks on the body, save the four puncture wounds on the face.

284

Jan wouldn't have been the first man to drink too much and trip over a mooring rope in the dark, or slip on some fish guts and pitch into the water. The marks, so the coroner directed the jury, were doubtless made by the iron shoe at the end of a punter's quant when the body was trapped under water, by an oar or an anchor, even.

Later, several of the jurors, after they'd supped a mug or two of ale bought for them by curious friends, said that if the coroner had learned anything about boats, which he plainly hadn't, he'd have known there wasn't a quant or anchor on the river that would make wounds like that. But since they'd had no better explanation to offer they'd gone along with what he'd said, not least because every hour they went on debating the matter was an hour they weren't out earning a living. It was agreed by all that if you were forced to serve as a juryman it was best to accept any verdict the coroner suggested, no matter how addle-pated you thought him, just to get the whole business over as quickly as possible. So, an accident it had been.

But within hours the rumours began to spread. Friends recalled Jan telling anyone who'd listen that his mother had been poisoned by the harlot his father was to marry. But, at the time, not even his friends had thought it more than the ravings of a grief-stricken son. After all, every son regards any other woman his father takes up with as a scheming bitch. But Master Robert had wed so indecently soon after his poor wife and son had gone to their graves, which made you wonder, didn't it?

'Wait, hold hard there!'

Gunter looked up in surprise as a man came hurrying towards the mooring. He was scarlet in the face and dripping with sweat, as if he had been basted over a spit. He doubled up, panting, flapping his hand at Gunter to indicate he would speak when he'd found enough breath to do so.

Gunter pulled a leather bottle of small ale from under the cross-plank where he'd placed it out of the sun and handed it up to the man. He took a long, thirsty gulp before returning it, his face screwed up in distaste. 'Going sour, but my thanks. Anything's welcome on a day like this, so long as it's wet. Which way are you bound?'

Gunter jerked his head. 'Back up stream as far as Greetwell.'

The stranger looked blank.

'On the way to the city of Lincoln.'

285

'Lincoln?' The man beamed at him. 'That's where I'm to go. I'll give you twopence to carry me.'

'Fourpence, if you want to go all the way into Lincoln. It's well beyond Greetwell.'

It wasn't, but clearly the stranger didn't know that. Besides, Gunter reckoned the man could afford it. Though he was travel-stained and covered with dust, his clothes were of good quality. This was no cottager bound for market.

'Threepence.' The stranger held out a hand and they shook. 'William de Ashen . . . from Essex,' he added, seeing the name meant nothing to Gunter.

Gunter spread a couple of sacks on the wooden cross-seat and steadied the stranger as he stepped down into the punt. He wobbled dangerously, like a cow on ice.

'Essex? You're a long way from home. You planning to walk all the way to Lincoln, were you?'

'I was beginning to fear I might have to,' William said, looking at little less alarmed now that he was seated. 'My horse collapsed under me, poor beast. I'd ridden her hard and should have changed mounts miles back, but I couldn't find an inn.'

'Precious few of those hereabouts.'

William nodded ruefully, as if he could testify to that.

'Some lay brothers passed me with a wagonload of timber. I asked them for a lift, but they were only bound for their abbey. I thought of going there to ask for a horse, but they said a boat was just leaving, and if I hurried I might catch you.'

Gunter motioned to Hankin to cast off the mooring ropes, and braced the punt with his quant, keeping it tight to the bank, so that the lad didn't have to leap a gap to get on board. Hankin was nervous about doing that now, though he'd always jumped with reckless bravado before the ducking.

'I doubt the abbey would have sold you a horse. They were badly hit by the last murrain. Lost a good many beasts and men too.'

'I could have commandeered one.' William patted his leather scrip.

Hankin looked up sharply from the stern. Gunter knew what he was thinking. If William de Ashen had the authority to commandeer a horse, he could seize a punt too. He was lucky the man had agreed to pay anything.

'I travel on the King's business,' William said proudly. 'I've never

286

been sent on such a journey before, but men are being dispatched with urgent news to all the towns the length and breadth of England. There weren't enough of the regular messengers to go, at least not from Essex.'

'Have the French invaded?' Hankin said eagerly. 'Are we to defend the towns?'

William swivelled round, smiling indulgently. 'Raring to fight, are you, son? I don't blame you. I was the same at your age. But if there's fighting to be done it'll not be the French you'll be up against, but Englishmen.'

Hankin drew himself up indignantly. 'I'd not fight my own countrymen. No man would.'

William grunted. 'That's the tidings I bring for your city fathers. Essex is on the march. Essex men are raising a rebellion against Parliament. They're pouring out of the villages all over the county and whipping up more support in every town and hamlet they pass through . . . Aah! Steady on!'

William made a grab for the side as the punt gave a violent lurch. The corner of the bow collided with the bank, and both Gunter and his son teetered perilously before righting themselves. Gunter fought to regain his stroke and push them back into midstream.

'Won't happen again, Master William,' Gunter said gruffly, furious with himself and grateful no other boatmen were passing to witness his clumsiness. 'It was what you said . . . I never thought to hear . . .'

'I don't wonder it put you off your stroke,' William said. 'I never thought to see such a thing either. I was there when it all started at Brentwood, though I never dreamed it would come to that. Sir John de Bampton and Sir John de Gildesburgh were there to preside over the Whitsun Assizes. I wasn't in the court myself, but from what I hear there was a man called up from one of the villages, Baker his name was. Bampton said he'd not declared all the people in his household eligible to pay the poll tax and that he must pay what he owed there and then.'

His gaze fixed on the river, Gunter's jaw clenched. He was reliving the night he'd been accused of the same thing. He dared not turn, but he guessed Hankin was remembering it too. William carried on blithely with his account, apparently failing to notice the effect his words were having on Gunter and his son.

'Baker said he'd already paid what the taxmen had asked of him and they'd accepted it. He wasn't going to pay any more. You can imagine how the King's commissioner reacted to that. They don't take kindly to being told no by a commoner. So he ordered the sergeants-at-arms to arrest him. There were near a hundred men or so at that court, not just from Brentwood but all the villagers around who'd been summonsed. When the sergeants-at-arms went for Baker, they just pushed between him and the sergeants, to shield him. They wouldn't let them take Baker, and the more Bampton threatened, the more belligerent they got. In the end the whole lot of them declared they'd not pay a single penny they owed in poll tax and they'd not recognise his authority either.

'So Bampton ordered his sergeants to arrest the ringleaders. Have you ever heard anything so cod-witted? It might have worked if he'd had a whole troop of men with him, but he had only two sergeants. Even a drummer boy could have told him they were no match for a hundred riled men.

'The crowd attacked them, drove Bampton, Gildesburgh and their two sergeants out of the town. I saw that part with my own eyes, the royal commissioners galloping away as if the hounds of hell were at their heels, a great mob of men and women brandishing staves and firing arrows at them. It's a wonder none of the townsfolk was hit, the way those arrows were falling. Their blood was running so hot that if they'd caught up with the commissioners they'd have beaten them to death.'

'Have the villagers been arrested?' Gunter asked. He shuddered to think what punishment would be meted out to the men and their families who'd turned on a royal commissioner.

William shook his head. 'They spent the night hiding in the woods. I suppose they thought armed soldiers would come looking for them, but none did, and after word spread, other villagers declared they'd pay no poll tax either, but that's the least of their demands now.'

'Is no one stopping them?' Hankin asked, from the stern.

'Parliament'll send men soon, lad. They must. The men-at-arms in the places the rebels are marching through take one look at them and flee. The mobs are just too large for a handful of men to deal with. I even heard that some of the men-at-arms are deserting their posts and joining the rioters. Anyone who tries to stand against the rebels gets their workshops and houses smashed up. They're even attacking abbeys, forcing them to pay a fine to be left in peace. Parliament will have to do something, but I don't know what. They say half the fighting men are occupied with the French and the rest are with John of Gaunt up north, trying to parley with the Scots. If Gaunt was here, he'd soon have every rebel dangling from the gallows, but I doubt word's even reached him yet.'

'Is Lincoln to raise men against them? Will we be sent to fight the Essex men?' Hankin asked.

William craned around again. 'I know nothing of that, boy. I'm sent to bring news of the rebellion to Lincoln. Warn the city fathers and royal commissioners in these parts that they've to make ready in case the same thing happens here. They've to put the guards on alert and organise the good citizens to defend their streets and property, 'cause if this takes hold the whole country'll go up in flames.'

Chapter 41

Let any who have been cursed with the falling sickness mix grated bone from a human skull with their food or else drink from the skull of a suicide, and they shall be cured.

Lincoln

They say that a naughty imp once flew into Lincoln Cathedral to make mischief. When he refused to leave he was turned to stone and forced to listen to every dreary sermon preached in that great edifice until its walls come tumbling down. And that must be counted as the harshest of penances even by the sternest judge. But if the wicked imp was listening on that particular day in June, he would, for once, have heard gossip to gladden his little black heart for there was only one topic on everyone's lips that day – the great Essex rebellion.

In the cathedral and all the churches of Lincoln the clergy pointed to the wall paintings of Christ as King surrounded by saints and angels and below them the souls of the righteous men who gazed up at them in adoration. They sternly reminded their congregations that the social order on earth, with its kings, archbishops and bishops at the head, was the earthly reflection, in every particular, of heaven above. To rebel against King and Parliament was to rebel against God Himself. Look at the wretched souls being tormented in Hell. That was what lay in store for those who sought to overturn the divine order on earth. Did they want to see blood run in the streets, their women raped, their children spitted on pikes?

The townsfolk and choir boys who attended the daily services were so busy discussing the latest rumours with their neighbours that they heard only odd phrases from these sermons, and were left baffled as to whether the rapists and baby-slayers were the invading French, the damned Scots or the foolish Essex men. But since they all counted as foreigners, what else could you expect from them but savagery?

290

If Robert had been in church that Tuesday morning in June listening to one of those sermons he might have been even more worried than he was, but instead he was packing, or Catlin was packing for him, anxious to set out as soon as he could. He wanted to reach his favourite inn before dark. He'd travelled to London often enough to know how long each stage would take, and if you left too late you might find yourself forced to spend the night in some wretched lodgings, where the pallets were crawling with lice, the wine bad and the food worse. Even if you could manage to snatch a wink of sleep between groaning with bellyache and your neighbours snoring, you'd have to do it with a knife in your hand for fear of being robbed of everything you had, including your clothes. The prospect of going to London was bad enough, without being dragged through every anteroom of Hell on the way.

Leonia slid into Robert's lap, slipping her arms about his neck. The barber had been summoned at dawn to cut his hair and shave him. He was glad of it as she pressed her tender cheek against his.

'Why do you have to go away, Père?'

He liked the name she'd chosen for him and the way she threw her arms around him in tender affection. It was new to him. Boys didn't hug their fathers, or fathers their sons. Robert felt the sudden hollow ache of grief. For a moment he saw Jan running into the sun-lit hall, an excited little boy again. He longed to sweep him up and hug him tightly. Had he ever actually told Jan how much he meant to him? He couldn't recall a single occasion on which he had. But he must have said it, surely. Besides, Jan had known without needing to be told, hadn't he? He must have.

Robert cleared his throat. 'I've important business in London, child. The merchants have asked me to take a petition to the Savoy Palace for John of Gaunt. There're not enough guards at the castle in Lincoln to defend the city if there should be an uprising here. We must have more and, as constable of the castle, it's his duty to send his men to protect us.'

'Uprising?' Leonia frowned. 'Why would—'

Catlin descended the stairs and entered the hall, Tenney hard on her heels, two great packs slung across his shoulders. The smile on his wife's face dissolved at the sight of Leonia sitting in her husband's lap, snuggled into his neck.

She strode across, grasped the girl's arm and yanked her off. 'Is that any way for a young lady to behave? You're not an infant,' she snapped, digging her long nails deep into Leonia's tender skin.

Robert winced for her, but not even a flicker of pain showed in Leonia's face.

'I was only telling Père how much I'm going to miss him,' she said innocently. 'I do wish he didn't have to go.'

Catlin released her grip on her daughter's arm. 'We all wish that, Leonia. But to be chosen to represent the city is a great honour and responsibility. The safety of all of us and Lincoln itself depends on him.'

'Are we going to be attacked?' Leonia asked. There was no fear, only curiosity, in her voice.

Robert had no wish to alarm Leonia, but he'd never seen any reason to pretend to children that life was all honey and cream. 'In the south, some villagers stirred up by a preacher called Ball have attacked the property of their masters and even monasteries.'

'Why don't they hang them?' Leonia demanded.

'They will, my dear, but the authorities were taken unawares and didn't act quickly enough. If a house catches fire, and people straightway pull down the thatch with grappling hooks and stamp on the sparks firmly, then the flames have no chance to spread. If they don't a whole town can be set ablaze. But the rebellion'll not spread here. We'll ensure there are well-armed men to arrest any rebels at the first whisper of trouble.'

He was determined to sound assured, particularly in front of the servants, but he was far from convinced of what he'd said. If even half of what William de Ashen had reported to them was true, the merchants in Lincoln would be hard put to find enough armed men to defend their homes, never mind their shops and warehouses.

'Let me ride with you, Master Robert,' Tenney said. 'If there's folks roaming abroad, looking for trouble—'

'And leave us unprotected?' Catlin sounded as shocked as if he had suggested she dance naked in the streets. 'When my husband was last away someone broke into our bedchamber, as you well know. Besides, Robert isn't a lord or abbot. He's in no danger in London.'

In truth, Robert would have been glad of Tenney's company. Rumours were buzzing around the town, like flies in the meat market. Every hour brought fresh alarms, and no one knew what was true. Suppose he encountered some of the rebels on the road. But he couldn't very well leave the women undefended after all that had happened. He really shouldn't be leaving them at all . . . 'Your mistress needs you here,' Robert reluctantly agreed.

'But, Master Robert, it's not safe you riding alone,' Tenney said desperately. 'Let me come along to watch your back and keep you company. You could easily get a couple of strapping lads from the warehouse to sleep here of a night and keep watch on the house.'

Catlin's eyes narrowed. 'I thought you prided yourself on your skills as a manservant, Tenney. Are you admitting that any common labourer could do your job?' She gave one of her brittle, tinkling laughs. 'Why, Robert, I do believe Tenney is suggesting you could save yourself a fortune by dismissing him and employing a pagger to serve you at table instead.'

Tenney flushed. 'I only meant . . .' He trailed into silence.

Catlin gave a satisfied nod, as if she were a queen graciously pardoning her fool on condition he did not offend again. 'With poor Beata gone for good, we certainly don't want to lose you as well, do we, Leonia?'

An identical smile crossed the faces of mother and daughter. Tenney's skin crawled, as if a spider had run down his back. Staring miserably at the floor, he heaved the great saddle packs across his shoulders again and shuffled from the hall.

Robert gazed after him in dismay. 'Am I taking all that? I've no wish to be in London for more than a day or two, if I can help it. I must return as quickly as I can.'

'If you're to be received at the Savoy Palace, you must look as though you are a man of substance,' Catlin said. 'You can hardly turn up in clothes dusty from the road – and suppose you're invited to dine, Robert? I've packed only what you need, I assure you.' She bent over him, kissing him passionately on the mouth. A few weeks ago that would have excited him but, for some reason he couldn't understand, today her touch stirred nothing in him. 'I'm so proud of you, my dearest, for offering to represent the city. All Lincoln will be in your debt.'

Not for the first time Robert wondered how he had come to be undertaking this journey. He and Catlin had been dining with Sheriff Thomas and several of his fellow merchants and their wives. Catlin had been seated next to Thomas, who couldn't keep his eyes off her for, as ever, she was charming to all the men around her.

The talk had been of the rebellion and the plans to defend their own businesses, should it spread. John of Gaunt had left only a handful of troops at the castle, mostly untried boys or ageing men who could be spared only because they would be of little use in battle. Someone had proposed going to London to convince Gaunt's steward he must reinforce the castle, but quite how Robert had been chosen for the expedition, he couldn't for the life of him recall.

Sheriff Thomas had been liberal with the wine during the meal, at the city's expense, and after the food was cleared away Robert had enjoyed several goblets of hippocras. He dimly remembered Thomas thanking him, and Catlin smiling modestly as Thomas kissed her hand, holding it far longer than courtesy demanded. His fellow merchants, looking most relieved, had thumped him heartily on the back. He couldn't remember offering to go, though he could hardly admit that to anyone.

The door leading to the stableyard opened and Adam raced through it, stopping dead as he saw the gathering in the hall, which he had evidently expected to be empty at this time.

'Adam? Why aren't you at school?' Robert asked sternly. 'Are you playing truant?'

The boy shook his head. 'School's closed. We've all been sent home till they can find another master to teach us. Master Warner . . . he's got worse.'

Adam glanced swiftly at Leonia, before dropping his gaze and staring at the legs of the table. Robert recognised fear in the boy's face and rose swiftly from the chair, to grasp his son's shoulders. 'Worse, boy? What do you mean? Has Master Warner been stricken with a contagion?' He looked at Catlin, his expression as anxious as his son's. 'If he's been teaching the boys when he's suffering from a fever . . .'

Catlin came across, put an arm gently around Adam and led him a few paces away from his father. 'Tell us, Adam, is Master Warner sick? Do you know what ails him?'

Again the boy cast a frightened glance towards Leonia, but this time Catlin caught the look. She turned swiftly to her daughter. 'Did you know the schoolmaster was ill? Why didn't you tell us?'

A tiny smile of triumph hovered around Leonia's mouth, so fleeting that Robert thought he must have imagined it. 'Adam said his teacher had pains in his back. He was limping, you said, didn't you, Adam? Could hardly sit down, or stand up again. Couldn't even raise his arms. But I'll pray for him. We both will, won't we, Adam?'

Catlin stared long and hard at her daughter. But Robert smiled, much relieved.

'Then it's no contagion. I dare say he's suffering from some inflammation of the spine. I had an uncle who was struck down with that after a fall. A paralysis crept over him, but though he couldn't move his limbs, he was in agony for the rest of his days. I trust it will not be so for poor Master Warner.'

Adam had turned very pale and was holding himself rigid, gazing wide-eyed at Leonia. Robert felt a surge of irritation. Why couldn't his son be more like the girl who was looking up at him with such an adoring smile? 'Well, Adam. As long as the school's closed, I expect you to work all day in the warehouse with Fulk. I don't want you idling your time away.'

'But Fulk is . . .' Adam hesitated, staring wretchedly down at the floor. 'What I mean is . . . when are we going to get a new steward, Father? The men say we need one and . . . I think so too.'

'You think we need a new steward?' Robert shouted. 'Who are you to decide such matters? You wish to replace your brother, just like that. Did you care nothing for him? I am still grieving for my son and you dare to talk to me of stewards!'

'Hush, Robert,' Catlin said. 'The boy's only repeating what the men are saying. No one can ever replace Jan as your son, but you need a man to lift some of the burden from your shoulders or you'll wear yourself out.' She sidled over to him again, running her soft fingers down his cheek. 'I was hoping that, once the nonsense in the south is brought under control, I would see more of you at home. Remember how things used to be, our pleasant evenings . . .'

Robert flushed, darting an anxious glance at Adam, but the boy was staring like a mooncalf at Leonia and didn't appear to have heard.

'I'll consider the matter when I return.' He had no intention of doing any such thing, but he knew the easiest way to stop women nagging was to pretend to think about it.

'I'll miss you, Père.'

Robert smiled fondly at his stepdaughter, his irritation dissolving at the sight of her pretty smile. 'And what shall Père bring back from London for you, my dear?'

'Only yourself, safe and well.' She lifted her face to be kissed.

Robert chuckled. 'You, child, are the sweetest little angel on earth.'

He was still smiling to himself as he strode across the hall towards the stableyard, entirely oblivious of the steel-cold glitter in his wife's eyes.

Chapter 42

The monk, Gregory the Great, tells how a nun, in her greed, ate a lettuce without first making the sign of the cross to protect herself against the evil spirits that hide between its leaves, and so she became possessed by a demon.

Greetwell

Have you noticed how often the living claim an evil spirit made them do it? A demon possessed them, the devil tricked them. As if demons didn't have something far more important to do than make a child smash an old woman's pots or force a man to fornicate against his will. If I were a demon, I'd think myself ill-used to be sent on such a piddling assignment when I could have been stirring up wars or tormenting popes.

But, then again, the actions of the most insignificant men or women can be as a single raindrop that rolls a pebble that dislodges a clod that tumbles a rock and, before you know it, the whole mountainside has crashed down, sweeping palaces and pigsties, princes and paupers into the sea. So maybe there are demons at work, even in the smallest mischief.

The punt glided towards Gunter's cottage in the late-evening sunshine. Hankin shaded his eyes, peering towards the clearing in the willow scrub. 'Why's Mam doing that now?'

Gunter was wondering the same thing. Nonie was kneeling at the washtub scrubbing some linen. Little Col was pulling on her arm, sobbing, his face scarlet and stained with tears, as if he'd been crying, uncomforted, for a long time.

There was nothing unusual in seeing Nonie wash clothes. She'd always prided herself on keeping the cottage as clean and neat as any woman could. But it was evening. Nonie never washed clothes in the evening. They wouldn't dry before dark and she wouldn't leave them out overnight with the risk of them being stolen or mauled by an animal. At this hour she was usually to be found inside the cottage, stirring the cooking pot or trimming the candle in the lantern, ready to set it outside to guide her husband home.

Unease gripped Gunter. He edged the punt into the gap in the bank and hastily tied off the prow rope. Hankin had already leaped ashore and was glancing anxiously at the cottage as he fumbled with the stern rope. Gunter could see he was about to race off. He pulled him back.

'I'll see to your mam. You make the punt fast and cover it.'

Gunter limped towards the cottage and swept the bawling Col into his arms. The little boy clasped his hands around his father's neck and pressed his tear-smeared face into Gunter's shoulder. Nonie's face was dripping with sweat and flushed with exertion. She was breathing in shallow, rasping gasps.

'Nonie,' Gunter said. 'Nonie, are you sick?'

But she didn't rest or even look up. She just kept rubbing the clothes in the tub, rocking backwards and forwards on her knees, as if Gunter was no more solid than the wind at her back.

'Nonie? What is it? What's amiss?' Then a sudden fear gripped him. 'Has something happened to Royse? Where is she?'

He looked at his little son in his arms. The child's sobs had given way to hiccups.

'Col, where's Royse? Where's your sister?'

The boy pointed towards the open door of the cottage.

Hankin came running up and Gunter thrust the child at him. 'Stay here and take care of your brother.'

His heart thudding, Gunter lumbered towards the door and froze on the threshold. For a moment, he thought he must have stumbled into the wrong cottage. The table and stools that normally sat in the centre of the tiny room were gone. The shelves where Nonie kept an assortment of wooden trenchers, beakers, jars and boxes were bare too. All that remained were the straw pallets and blankets on the two plank beds that ran along each side of the room, with a single cooking pot.

Royse sat on the floor with her back to the rough wall, staring blankly ahead. She gave no sign that she was aware her father had come in.

'God's bones, what's happened here?'

She didn't move or look at him.

He bent down and grabbed her shoulder. 'Answer me, lass. Who did this?'

Royse scrambled to her feet, tears glinting in her eyes. 'I did it! It's all my fault. That's what Mam thinks, and Hankin and you. The goats are gone, Mam's goats. You should have let them talk to me. You shouldn't have sent me away. You all blame me!'

Gunter put out a hand to try to calm her. 'Royse? What—'

But she pushed him away and darted outside. Gunter blundered after her, but she was racing along the riverbank as if she was trying to outrun her own shadow.

Gunter caught Nonie by the arms, forcing her to stop washing, and dragged her to her feet. 'Did someone attack the cottage? Have we been robbed? What's happened?' He shook her. 'Nonie, for God's sake, tell me!'

She pulled stiffly out of his grasp and gazed across in the direction of Lincoln, its sumptuous cathedral and castle towering high above them on the hill. Her voice, when she finally spoke, was as flat as the fens.

'King's men came for the poll money we owed. Said people in Essex had refused to pay so they'd been told to collect ours before we had a chance to do the same. King needs the money, they said.'

'But I told them I'd pay. I just needed time,' Gunter said.

But Nonie was still talking as if to someone only she could see. 'Said they'd instructions to take goods to the value of what we owe and more for the fine for not paying on time.'

Gunter groaned. 'But they've taken everything. It's worth far more than we owed.'

'Had to, they said. They have to sell it to get the money and they said what we had wouldn't fetch much, too old and battered. And with other cottagers having their things seized, there'd be so much to sell, our bits would be worth even less. They'd been told to leave just what we needed to live, that's all . . . That's all we need, they said, a pot to cook in and a place to sleep, that's all we need . . . The lantern, they took the lantern. How am I going to bring you home? How . . .' She started to sob.

Gunter slammed his fist into his palm. 'Filthy, miserable cowards! They knew all the men would be away at work and there'd be only women at home who couldn't fight them.' His jaw was clenched so hard his teeth ached. 'This is all the fault of that Essex man. Should have drowned the bastard when I had him on my punt. Should've made sure he never reached Lincoln alive. If they hadn't got wind of the rebellion in Essex . . .'

'If, Gunter, *if*!' Nonie said furiously, as the tears streamed down her face. 'What's the use of wishing? It doesn't matter how hard we work, they can just take it away from us in a snap of their fingers. And we can't do anything to stop them. What's the use of even trying any more?'

Hankin's face was contorted in fury and excitement. 'That Essex man said there's whole armies of people rising and chasing the commissioners out of the villages. And I heard a man on the quayside say they were forcing the abbeys and the lords to give them money, else they'd burn and smash their houses. We should do that. We should do it to the sheriff. Burn his house down, see how he likes to lose everything.'

'And get yourself hanged!' Nonie shouted. 'Don't you think I've lost enough? You think Royse and Col want to stand there and watch their brother strangling on the end of a rope? You really think that's going to help us, do you?'

'They're not hanging them in Essex,' Hankin said sullenly. 'Nor in Kent neither. The man said so. He says no one can stop them. Maybe everyone in England is rising and refusing to pay the poll.'

'Not here, they're not,' Nonie said bitterly.

'Only 'cause they don't know who'd stand with them,' Hankin said. 'But if someone went to find the men who are rising and brought 'em back here, if there was a great army of them came to Lincoln, everyone here'd join in. I know they would. I've heard them talking on the quayside about how they hate the poll.' Hankin turned eagerly to Gunter. 'We could go, Faayther, you and me. We could find them and tell them to march on Lincoln to help us.'

Nonie took the boy by the shoulders and shook him furiously. 'Have you frog spawn for brains? Do you think for one moment I'm going to have my bairn joining some mob rampaging round the countryside, like the French army, burning, looting and God knows what else besides?'

Hankin tore himself out of his mother's grasp, tears of fury in his eyes. 'I'm not your bairn any more. I'm the one that has to work to pay the taxes. I do a man's work. And a man doesn't let people walk into his home and take everything. A man doesn't just give in and pay up 'cause someone's threatened him. I'm not a coward like him!' He pointed contemptuously at his father.

Nonie slapped his face with such a resounding crack that the starlings, settling to roost in the nearby trees, rose chattering in alarm.

'You'll never be half the man your father is if you live for a thousand years. You think I don't hear the rumours too? You think I don't talk to the boatmen and their wives? You tell me that a real man wouldn't sit there and let someone take his property. So what do you imagine the abbots and lords are going to do when the mob comes onto their lands? You think they'll stand aside and watch someone burn their houses? Sooner or later the King will send battle-hardened soldiers in and cut those villagers down in their hundreds. And those that get taken prisoner'll be tried for treason, for that's what rebellion is, treason. You think you'll feel like a real man when you're lying in front of a jeering crowd as they slice open your belly and draw out your guts and burn them in front of you while you scream in agony?'

Hankin's eyes blazed with a hatred Gunter had never seen in his son's face before.

'I'd rather die hanged, drawn and quartered 'cause at least then I would have tried to stop them, instead of spending the rest of my life hiding in a hole, like a rat afraid to come out because of the dogs.'

Chapter 43

If anyone fears theft, let him scatter caraway seeds among those things of value and if a thief should try to steal them he shall be held in that place. Likewise, if a woman fears her husband may stray she should sew caraway seeds into his clothes, so that no other woman may steal him away from her.

Mistress Catlin

I waited for him in the small chamber at the top of the tower, staring down through the slits at the grey-green river crowded with boats. How many of them were carrying goods to and from Robert's warehouse? The boatmen were too busy thumbing their noses at each other or trying to push their craft through impossibly narrow spaces to glance up to where I stood. I couldn't bring myself to look through the slits on the opposite wall, from which I would be able to see the street that led to the door of the tower. I was afraid I wouldn't see him walking towards me. Afraid he wouldn't come. I was always afraid that one day he wouldn't come.

Even though Robert was on his way to London, we couldn't meet in the house. Leonia had a habit of creeping round the place as silently as a cat. You'd think she was out and then turn to find her watching you from a corner without any idea how long she'd been there. She was always as sweet and blithe as Sunday's child whenever Robert was close by. But she was growing wilful, and increasingly I glimpsed that cunning smile on her face and the excitement in her eyes whenever Robert and I were together, as if she knew that, with a snap of her fingers, she could cause a chasm to open between us and all the fires of Hell to come leaping out.

Do all mothers become afraid of their own daughters? It's as if a maggot is buried deep within them, growing and changing by stealth, until finally it emerges, a flying hornet ready to sting. Suddenly that innocent child becomes a young woman who thinks she has the power

302

to command the whole world and no one can stop her. But she would soon learn that the world was not so easily broken to her will.

It was Diot who found me the tower and bribed the watchman for the key. It was rarely used, except to store kegs in the bottom. The upper room was bare, save for the sheepskins Diot had spread on the dusty boards. The chamber was squalid, but nothing compared to what it looked down upon. For the tower stood by the east wall of the city, right on the riverbank, overlooking the city on one side and the midden they call Butwerk on the other. Diot knew it well. She went often to that cluster of hovels, though she thought I didn't know she was sneaking out at night, or what she was doing. She was terrified I would discover her secret visits to those filthy old hags.

Diot would do anything I asked to be allowed to remain with me for she knew only too well the world could be a cold, cruel place for a penniless old woman alone. And it was safer to keep her close. Simple women, like her, have a habit of babbling foolish things that can so easily lead them into trouble. I had to keep her from harm.

I heard the wooden stairs creak behind me and knew it was him. I felt the jolt of relief and exhilaration that always surged through me at his coming. I turned to face the open trapdoor so that the light from the window would halo my hair. In sunlight my hair shone purple and iridescent as a starling's wing, which he always loved.

His head emerged, then his shoulders. He scrambled through the gap and in two strides had clasped me about my waist, lifting me and whirling me round, before kissing me. As we pulled apart, his smile faded and he wrinkled his nose.

'We'll have to find somewhere better than this,' he complained, flicking the sheepskins on the dirty floor with the toe of his boot. 'Isn't it bad enough that your husband stinks of sheep? Do you want me to smell like one too?' A mischievous grin flashed across his face. 'Or does the smell excite you now?'

Delicately he plucked at the laces that fastened the front of my kirtle. I made no attempt to help him, though I was desperate to tear off my clothes and his, and feel the warmth of his bare skin pressed to mine. But he liked to unwrap me himself, savouring and caressing each part of my body as he exposed it.

'I want to lie you on sable. Roll you in white fur,' he murmured, as he kissed my breasts.

I laughed. 'I can't very well ask Diot to smuggle the furs out of my husband's house and bring them here. I think even Robert would notice that.' I ran my fingertip across his full, soft lips.

He kissed me again and we sank to our knees on the skins, our hands fervently caressing each other's bodies, our mouths pressed to each other's hot flesh. He, almost too impatient, dragged my shift over my head, then slid me naked onto the sheep's wool. Before I could draw breath, he was on top of me, pushing himself into me.

Afterwards, I watched him as he slept, his arm thrown back behind his head, his face beaded with sweat. A narrow shaft of sunlight sliced across his pale belly and across my breasts as if a single spear had impaled us both. I pressed my nose close to his neck, revelling in the smell of his skin.

The separation we endured between these secret meetings only made me ache for him the more, as did the terror in me that he would become bored and find another woman to replace me. Maybe he already had and I was now the dalliance, not the love. But I'd know if he had: I'd see it in his eyes, feel it in his touch. Besides, no matter who he flirted with, he always came back to me. He could do no other. No more could I. There are some souls who are born to be together. The same breath that created them bound them one to another at the dawn of the world. Even if they should be separated by an ocean, the chain that links them is so strong, sooner or later they will be drawn to one another, though every demon in Hell and angel in Heaven should strive to keep them apart.

Chapter 44

Witches have the power to raise storms by whistling or shaking out their hair. Others do it by christening a dead cat, then tying parts of a human corpse to it before flinging it into the sea.

Lincoln

'Off to the warehouse so early, Adam?' Catlin called from the stairs.

The boy paused at the door leading to the stableyard, his hand on the latch, and looked up at her. His stepmother's dark hair hung loose down her back. She clutched her robe of russet fox fur tightly about her body. It was half slipping from one shoulder, and as she stepped down the last few steps, he caught a glimpse of her bare calf. He knew that under the fur she was naked and blushed as hard as he would have done had he seen her bare body, perhaps more so, for he felt guilty at even imagining it.

'Have you eaten?'

'Bread and cheese . . . Tenney gave it to me,' he added, as if she might accuse him of having stolen it.

'Tenney.' She repeated the name as if she was biting the letters off it. 'You don't need to go bothering him for food. That's Diot's job. Tomorrow I shall ask her to cook you some fish. A growing boy needs more than yesterday's bread and cheese if he's to do a full day's work. Your father would be proud of you, Adam, to know you're working so hard in the business.'

Adam mumbled something incoherent and fled out into the early-morning sunshine. Why had she said that about his father? Was she trying to catch him out? Setting a trap? Did she know he hadn't been going to the warehouse? He ran across the stableyard to the gate beyond, only stopping when he was in the street outside. He stood in the shadow of the wall, where he knew he couldn't be observed from the house.

Adam hadn't gone to the warehouse once since Robert had left for

305

London. When his father returned, he would shout at him, maybe even punish him, but that would not be today. Today Fulk would be waiting for him with his gibes and torments.

When any boy is faced with a choice of two things he fears, he will always avoid the one that is most immediate. He hopes, even though life has taught him otherwise, that something will happen to save him from dealing with the other threat. I say *boy*, but we are all boys when it comes to dealing with our fears, however old we grow. Adam was no exception. As long as he didn't have to face Fulk today, he could push the menacing shadow of his father's wrath from his mind.

He was making up his mind where to hide himself when he sensed he was being watched. Alarmed, he spun round to a see a gaunt man, dressed in a rag-bag of ill-fitting clothes, standing just a few yards away. Adam knew at once the man's glance had not been casual. As soon as their eyes met, the man beckoned urgently to him. But before Adam could react, the stranger turned abruptly away.

Adam jumped as he felt a light touch on his arm. Leonia was standing beside him. 'Where are you off to?'

'Work, of course,' Adam muttered. 'Anyway, what are you doing up so early? Your mother isn't even . . .' He had meant to say 'dressed', but the image of his stepmother's naked calf was seared on his mind and he felt himself blushing again, which only added to his discomfort.

'*Our* mother,' Leonia said carefully, as if the shared possession of Catlin mattered to her.

'I have to go. I'll be late at the warehouse.'

'But you're not going to the warehouse. You didn't go yesterday or the day before.'

'I did!' Adam said furiously.

Leonia smiled. 'Don't worry, I won't tell Catlin. I won't tell anyone. Come on, let's go down to the river before Tenney or one of the women sees us.'

Adam felt Leonia stiffen beside him. Suddenly she turned her head, as if she, too, had sensed someone taking an interest in them. Adam followed her gaze. The man was still there, apparently engrossed in examining a stack of pots. He darted another glance in their direction, before walking rapidly away. Leonia shook herself, as if trying to get rid of an irritating fly.

306

'Do you know him?' Adam asked. 'I think he wanted to say something to me.'

Leonia giggled. 'Maybe he fancies you. Some men like touching boys instead of women. If I were you I'd run, if you see him again, before he tries to put his hand down your breeches.'

She grabbed his sleeve and they raced down the hill towards the river, turning the opposite way from the Braytheforde. When they knew there was no chance of being spotted by any of their neighbours on the way to market, they slowed and ambled along the bank, watching the boats pushing and jostling to get past one another. The cottages here stank of stagnant water and burned beans. Some of the boats were moored, their owners already hard at work selling woven reed baskets, kindling wood, dead hares, live river fish swimming in buckets and hunks of meat, black with dried blood and flies.

Trading had not yet begun in the markets and such sales were against the law before the bell had sounded, but neither the sellers nor their customers were taking any notice of that. Other things changed hands too, objects wrapped in sacking, slipped beneath the bread in a basket or under a tunic. But though a dozen eyes looked on from the squalid little houses around, no one would send for the constable, that was for sure.

'Do you hate working in the warehouse?' Leonia asked.

Adam shrugged. 'I don't mind it. At least, I don't think it would be so bad if . . .'

'If Fulk wasn't there.'

'How do you know?' Adam was startled. He'd never complained about Fulk to her, to anyone.

'I could tell you didn't like him when you tried to speak to Robert about getting a steward.'

'Don't you mean *Père*?' Adam said spitefully.

'He's not my father!'

Adam was startled. 'I thought you liked him. You're always kissing him.'

'He likes me. That's what you've got to do with adults, Adam. Make them like you, then you can make them do anything you want. That's what Catlin did and Robert married her. But if you start liking them back, it makes you as weak as them.' She laughed, but her fists were clenched. 'Anyway, why didn't you tell Robert about Fulk?'

'What's the point?' Adam said bitterly. 'He'd never listen.'

He kicked a stone into the river, narrowly missing a boatman, who swore at them. Leonia made an obscene gesture and ran off along the bank, with Adam following. She threw herself down at the river's edge, plucked a daisy and tore the white petals from it one by one, dropping them into the current and watching them sail away. Adam sat beside her, careful to keep a small space between them. He wanted to press himself close to her, but he was afraid she'd recoil in disgust.

'Fulk'll tell Robert you haven't been to the warehouse. You know that, don't you?'

Adam nodded miserably. 'He'll enjoy doing it. But Fulk doesn't want me there. I think it's his fault these barrels and bundles are going missing. Once I saw him dividing up money with one of the boatmen. He caught me watching and pushed my head into the horses' drinking trough. He held me under till I nearly drowned. He said if I started telling tales at home I'd be going for a swim, like – like my brother.' Adam swallowed hard. 'But I don't know why he bothered threatening me. Fath— *Robert* would never listen to anything I say anyway.'

'Do you want to make another poppet?' Leonia asked, as if she was offering him an apple.

Adam sprang to his feet. 'No, I don't!' He'd tried to push out of his head the guilt and fear over what he'd done to his schoolmaster, but at night when he lay in the dark, it came flooding back. His father had said he'd known men to become paralysed from pains in the back and never recover. Master Warner was getting no better. In fact, Tenney had heard he was much worse. Was he going to be paralysed? Adam had never dared talk to Leonia about the poppet, not after that day in the stables. As long as they didn't speak of it, he could try to convince himself it was nothing to do with him. But now she'd spoken the words, he had to know.

'Did we . . . did we hurt Master Warner?'

'You wanted to hurt him, didn't you? Remember how he beat you when it was the other boy he should have punished? He whipped you in front of the whole school. He had to be punished.'

'But I didn't want him to be paralysed . . . not for ever,' Adam protested.

'You stabbed the nail into him. He can only be as hurt as you wanted him to be.'

Adam turned away from her, feeling wretched. He wanted to ask her how he could make the schoolmaster's pains stop, how he could make him well again. But he knew before he asked that she'd only laugh and tell him it was too late, far too late.

'I don't want to make another poppet,' he whispered.

'Then we won't, but we don't want Fulk to tell Robert you weren't at the warehouse, do we?' She rose gracefully to her feet and smoothed out her green skirts. The sunlight glinted on her long, shining black curls. 'Fulk is a wicked man, isn't he?'

Adam took a pace back, gazing at her anxiously. 'What are you going to do?'

She held out a hand to him and smiled. 'You'll see.'

Chapter 45

*A witch may take the form of a magpie, for it would not enter
the Ark with Noah, but remained outside to cackle in glee at the
drowning world.*

Smithfield, London

The flames from the blazing torches writhed in the darkness, making
the eyes of the great crowd of men glitter like a thousand jewels.
Hankin stood in the centre of the track, legs astride, and faced the
armed man squarely, though his head came up only to the man's chest.

'With whom holds you?' Hankin demanded.

'With King Richard and the True Commons,' the man bellowed,
loudly enough to be heard all the way over the city to London Bridge.
He punched the air triumphantly to the cheers of all those crowded
around him, then broke into hearty laughter, clapping Hankin on
the shoulder. 'Well challenged, lad, well challenged indeed. I see we
have a true commoner here, Giles.'

'That he is, Thomas,' said a gruff voice behind Hankin. 'We found
him on the road. From Lincoln he is, come all the way by himself.
Wanted to join in the fight in Essex, but we told him that was already
won. It's London we take next. Isn't that right, lads?'

There was another answering cheer from those standing close by.

Giles gave a grin. 'Meet Thomas Farringdon, lad. He's the man
who leads us.'

Hankin was too awestruck to speak. Farringdon was a name he'd
heard uttered many times since he'd joined the Essex men on the
march to London, but among so many thousands of men he'd never
thought to meet him. He made a clumsy half-bow, but snapped up
straight as he heard several men laughing at him. But, to his relief,
he saw Farringdon wasn't among them. Instead, the man gravely
nodded his approval. 'Brave lad. It's men with your mettle that England
needs. Are they rising yet in Lincoln?'

'They will if you were to go there,' Hankin said eagerly. 'I know it. I've heard them talking. They'd rise up in a minute if you were to lead them.'

Farringdon smiled. 'After tomorrow, we may all go back to our homes in peace and there'll be no more need for any rising in Lincoln or Essex.'

Hankin felt as if his stomach had just fallen into his shoes. All this way, so many men, and they were just going to give up?

Farringdon chuckled. 'You look as if you were promised roast hog and given burned peas. We've won, lad, or we will have by this time tomorrow.'

A murmur of excitement ran through the crowd as his words were passed back to those who weren't close enough to hear. The men pressed forward, almost trampling Hankin into the ground, so eager were they to hear the news. Giles grabbed him just in time and wrapped a brawny arm around his shoulders to brace him. He turned to face the crowd, shouting over their heads, 'Make way. Let Thomas through to that old wagon, so you can hear him speak.'

After a deal of confusion the men parted just enough to allow Farringdon to squeeze his way through them. He was lost to sight, until finally Hankin saw his head and shoulders rise above them. Farringdon motioned them to sit, and there was a great deal more shuffling as they each found their own patch of grass. Hankin looked round for Giles. There were thousands camped here at Smithfield and he was desperate not to lose sight of the few men he had come to know.

'So many here, they'll never hear him,' Hankin said.

'Don't worry, lad,' Giles said. 'Any news he brings will spread through the whole camp quicker than fleas in a pack of hounds.'

Hankin squeezed into a narrow gap and sat down next to him, then wished he hadn't: he was on a thistle. He quickly rocked forward into a crouching position.

It had been early evening when they'd arrived. They were heading for Aldersgate, one of the great gates in London's fortified walls, but it was firmly barred against them. At the head of the procession, men were arguing with the watch that the curfew bell had not yet rung and the gate should be open, but it remained shut. Dozens of arrows had suddenly appeared, poking through the slits of the two round bastilles on either side, with the threat that they would be loosed if

311

the Essex men attempted to smash their way in. Not that they could have done, for even Hankin could see that nothing short of a battering ram would force those great gates to yield, but the arrows were real enough and there was panic as those at the front tried to scramble back through the crowd pressing behind them to get out of range.

The men had occupied Smithfield, the great open space behind the Hospital of St Bartholomew. The few trees that stood there were quickly stripped of branches and the smaller ones cut down to provide fuel for the fires the men lit as darkness fell. Sparks rose into the sky and the shadows of the men moving around in the orange glow of the flames made it seem as if a ghostly army was camped with them.

Meanwhile more and more men were pouring into Smithfield. What provisions they'd managed to carry from home or seize on the road they shared among their friends. Raiding parties, each of a hundred or more men, had been sent to the complex of buildings that lay around the field. The grounds of the priories of St Bartholomew, St John of Jerusalem and St Mary Clerkenwell had been stormed and the raiding parties had seized as many chickens, ducks, pigs and milk cows as they could find. Now the creatures were spit-roasting over the blazing fires, made hotter with the wood from the shattered byres and barns that had once housed them.

The smell of roasting meat and woodsmoke filled the air, making Hankin's stomach growl and his mouth water. He hugged himself with delight at the thought that those who lived in the vast buildings now knew what it was like to have their goods seized. The thought of eating *their* meat made the prospect even sweeter.

Farringdon began to speak. All those who were close enough to see him at once fell silent. 'I've had word from the men of London who support our cause and from Wat Tyler who leads the men from Kent. Sixty thousand Kentish men are camped south of the river.'

A great cheer went up. Hankin was breathless with excitement. Sixty thousand! He had never imagined there were so many people in the whole of England, never mind here, and all ready to storm London.

'The Kentish men have already broken into the prison of Marshalsea with the help of men of London and liberated the prisoners held there.'

Another cheer rang out. Hankin thought that only murderers and thieves were confined in prisons, but surely they would not have freed those. 'Who were held in there?' he whispered.

Giles shrugged. 'Poor men, men unjustly accused, no doubt, but whoever they are they'll be certain to swell our ranks.'

Farringdon was still speaking. 'They have also entered the palace of the Archbishop of Canterbury, Simon Sudbury, the Chancellor of England, the very man who imposed this vile poll tax upon us and all the other hardships used to beat the honest working man to his knees. Archbishop Sudbury is a traitor to the common people!'

'Is the traitor taken?' several men in the crowd shouted, among the hissing and cries of hatred.

Farringdon held up his hand for silence. 'Sudbury was not there. They say he's fled into the Tower with King Richard. But his palace was ransacked, his vestments torn, every record and document burned on a great fire. Everything he owned has been utterly destroyed. You who've had your homes invaded by his men, you who have had your goods seized, you who have seen all you have worked for destroyed, know that you have been avenged!'

A roar went up that brought men to their feet, stamping and clapping one another on the back. 'Death to the traitors! Death to the traitors!'

But Farringdon clearly had not finished, though it was some time before he could quieten the crowd again.

'I have saved the best news until last.' He paused, looking round at the vast ocean of faces. 'King Richard himself has agreed to meet in person with the leaders of the uprising tomorrow morning, on the south bank of the Thames.'

There were gasps of amazement.

'God's arse, I never thought the King himself would come to bargain with the likes of us,' Giles said. 'And him barely fourteen, not much older than you are, lad. Think of that.'

Giles said something else, but Hankin's attention had turned back to Farringdon. In the guttering torchlight, his features continually dissolved and re-formed, so that he seemed to wear the faces of a thousand different men.

'Wat Tyler will present our demands to the King himself. He will demand death for all the traitors of the common people! Death to John of Gaunt, to Archbishop Sudbury, to Bishop Courtney of London, to Bishop Fordham of Durham, to Robert Hale and all those men who tried to rob us with their taxes. Death to every one of those vipers who surround our brave young king and drip their foul poison into his ears!'

'Wat Tyler will place our petition directly in the King's hands and he will demand that every man named on that petition shall be surrendered to us, the True Commons. Every man named on that list shall be beheaded in a public execution before us all, and their heads placed on the Great Bridge, as are the heads of all traitors!'

Hankin's heart thudded in excitement. They were going to execute the Archbishop of Canterbury and John of Gaunt, the most powerful men in all England! And he was going to watch them do it. For the first time since those men had threatened his sister and ransacked his home, the impotent rage that had been burning inside him gave way to wild elation. It was as if all these weeks he had been pinned to the ground, unable to protect himself. But today he had thrown off his assailant and was pounding him to a pulp instead.

Farringdon raised his hands, like a priest at mass. 'Tonight begins the feast of Corpus Christi. The Body of Christ made flesh. Christ was a carpenter, a working man, a craftsman like many of you. He was forced by the priests and the tax-collectors to labour under the weight of His own cross as He carried it to the place of His execution. Could there be a more fitting day for the common man of England to free himself from his oppressors, to turn upon the tax-gatherers, the bishops and the lords and trample them under his feet? On this day, we will finally overturn the tyranny of serfdom for ever. And in generations to come, the freemen of England will look back and remember that on the feast of Corpus Christi a new parliament was born, the parliament of the True Commons! And each of you will return to your shires and villages with your heads held higher than any lord's, knowing that you were part of the greatest army in history, the army that set the people of England free for ever!'

If Farringdon intended to say more, he never had the chance. The field of men erupted into roars and cheers that Hankin thought must have been heard in the Tower of London itself, though he had little idea of where that might be. Farringdon was swept down from the wagon and carried shoulder high through the crowd, till Hankin lost sight of him.

Giles grabbed Hankin's arm. 'Come on, lad, let's get ourselves a share of that meat before it all disappears. My belly's rumbling so loudly I could eat the devil's arse if it was well roasted.'

But in spite of the best endeavours of the raiding parties, the beasts and fowls they had stolen did not stretch far among the thousands of men who sat around the fires that night. The few slices of meat and morsels of looted bread they received did little to blunt the sharpened appetites of men who'd been several days on the march, but not even hunger could dampen their high spirits. When the food ran out, the singing and dancing began. The men were not dainty maidens and they pounded in circles till the ground shook as if a herd of cattle was stampeding across it.

Hankin looked back towards the dark blur in the distance that was the great city wall. He grinned as he thought of the archers in the bastilles, peering out into the darkness, seeing the hundreds of fires and listening to the great roar of singing and shouting. He bet they were afraid of the rebels, afraid of him, for he was one of this great army and their fear thrilled him more than anything had before in his short life.

But as the camp finally grew quiet and men huddled down on the hard ground to snatch a few hours' sleep before dawn, Hankin lay awake. They had been talking about going back to their villages when this was over, marching home as victors from the fight. Discussing how they would farm *their* new land, for King Richard would force the manors and abbeys to divide their lands between the villagers. Craftsmen would be able to set their own prices. Bondsmen would be free to find work wherever they pleased and charge as much as they wanted for their labour.

But where would he find work? After the terrible row he'd had with his mother, after sneaking away in the middle of the night, leaving his father alone to work the river, Hankin knew he would hardly be welcomed back. Where could he go after their victory tomorrow? He had never in his life been among so many people and he'd never felt so alone.

Chapter 46

Children who fall into fits at the sight of a witch will recover if allowed to scratch or cut her and in doing so draw blood from above her breath.

Lincoln

The warehouse on the Braytheforde was quiet. A few cargoes had been dispatched in the cool of the early morning, before the sun's heat grew too fierce for men and beasts. Only one incoming wagon stood outside the great doors, half unloaded. Two paggers, the sweat running down their bare backs, were rolling barrels down the planks propped against the wagon and into the warehouse. They were taking their time, pausing between each barrel to take long swigs of ale from skins, much to the annoyance of the driver, who evidently wanted to get unloaded and slake his own thirst in the nearest tavern.

Fulk was sitting just inside the warehouse in the shade, where the cool breeze from the river would reach him. Leonia and Adam stood watching on the far side of the quay.

'There's another way in, isn't there?' Leonia asked. 'Another door? Catlin took me there once.'

Adam shook his head. 'Not into the warehouse. There's a door at the top of those stairs, at the side of the building, but that leads only to the tally room above the warehouse floor. It's just a loft where they store the records and things that would spoil when the river floods. But you can't get to the warehouse floor that way. Only way into the warehouse is past Fulk.'

'I want to see the tally room,' Leonia said.

'You can't. Fulk'll be furious if he finds strangers up there.'

'But I'm not a stranger. I'm Robert of Bassingham's daughter now. The warehouse belongs to him, so I've a perfect right to go wherever I like. Fulk daren't stop me. You wait here and count to . . .' Her smooth brow furrowed. 'Count to five hundred. Start when you see

316

me at the top of the stairs. Then you come over. You'll have to think of a way to make Fulk go back inside the warehouse with you.'

'No!' Adam backed away in alarm. 'I told you what he does. I don't want to go anywhere near him.'

'I won't let him hurt you. I promise. Trust me. You do trust me, don't you, Adam?'

Leonia gripped his arm, gazing earnestly at him with her huge brown eyes. The gold flecks in them glittered in the bright sunlight. He'd never seen a lion, except the painted ones on shields and emblems, but he imagined that if he ever did, their eyes would look exactly like hers.

'Just do as I say and all will be well, you'll see.'

She smiled and he found himself wondering what it would be like to kiss that soft mouth, not that he would ever dare.

He watched her picking her way around the wharf, stepping daintily over mooring ropes and ducking as men carrying planks and bales swung them perilously close to her head. Finally, she reached the warehouse. He walked a few paces to the side until he had a clear view of the staircase. She ran lightly up the steps, then disappeared through the door at the top. He began counting – *One, two, three . . . one hundred and sixty-five, one hundred and sixty-six . . . four hundred and ninety-eight, four hundred and ninety-nine, five hundred.* He started walking.

His legs were shaking as he approached the warehouse, and he thought he was going to vomit. He inched up to the open door. Fulk's eyes were closed and he was dozing, his fat backside spilling over a stool and his feet propped on a box. A bundle of tally sticks lay in his lap.

For a few agonising moments, Adam stood watching him, everything inside him telling him to run before Fulk woke. But just as he was about to turn and flee, Fulk grunted and opened his eyes. He blinked blearily at the boy, squinting to focus in the glare of the sun. Then he lumbered to his feet. Adam had not a single idea in his head about how he might coax Fulk deeper inside the warehouse but, as it turned out, he didn't need to.

Fulk grabbed him by the back of the neck and dragged him inside, shaking him, like a dog shakes a rat. 'You lazy little lump of pig shit. Where have you been? You're supposed to come here to help me. Wait till your father hears about this. You think I haven't enough to do with that milksop brother of yours getting himself drowned? You know what they do with boys at sea who are work-shy? They tie a rope to them and drag them under the keel of the ship, that's what. Maybe I ought to tie a rope to your feet and drag you across the Braytheforde.'

Fulk's fingers were squeezing so hard round his neck that Adam thought he was going to die. He was gasping for breath and struggling so frantically in the overseer's grip that he'd forgotten about Leonia, until Fulk gave a startled cry and stared upwards. Adam felt something whoosh past his head. Fulk screamed and almost in the same instant Adam heard a sickening crunch. The overseer released his neck and flew through the air. He landed with a crash on the floor.

Adam staggered sideways in horror. Fulk was lying on his back, his face pouring blood. White splinters of bone poked through the mangled flesh that had once been his nose. The two paggers came running in and skidded to a halt, staring in open-mouthed shock.

'The hook – how the hell— Why's it moving?' one gabbled in fear. 'It can't move all by itself, it can't!'

Adam felt something like raindrops falling on his hair. He touched his head and stared at his fingers. They were red. He stumbled backwards, staring up. A massive iron hook was swinging from a ship's rope in ever decreasing arcs above where Fulk had been standing moments before, scattering drops of blood in a shower onto the floor below.

Aghast, Adam stared up at the open platform above, but no one was there. No one at all.

Chapter 47

To cure a headache, tie a strand of a rope that has been used to hang a man round the head of the sufferer.

Smithfield, London

'Betrayed! We've been betrayed!'

Hankin, along with the other men, scrambled to his feet as a rider galloped straight through the middle of the camp, scattering the Essex men to right and left. He reined in his horse near the walls of the Charterhouse and wheeled round. Men began to run towards the rider, but there were so many that Hankin and Giles found themselves at the back of a vast crowd, with no hope of hearing anything the rider might be saying.

Soon after dawn that morning, as the bells for the Corpus Christi feast had begun pealing in the churches and chapels all over the city, the Essex men marched on Aldersgate once more and hammered on the thick wood with spears, ancient swords and staves, demanding that they be opened. But although the city gates should have been open at Prime, they remained firmly barred. With the knowledge that the King would shortly receive Wat Tyler and accede to his demands, the men did not attempt to storm them. They could wait. Soon, they told each other, King Richard himself would order them to be flung open and would even appear on the battlements above to welcome the Essex men as his loyal subjects.

Those who had ridden to London, or had seized horses from the abbeys they'd raided, set off at once to ride around the city walls to the other side of the Tower to watch the moment of their victory from the riverbank. It was rumoured that the King would sail from the Tower down to where the Kentish men waited on the opposite bank and would there walk ashore and sit with them.

For the first time in his life, Hankin wished he could ride. It wasn't so much the King he was longing to see, for they'd all see him soon enough, but the river: Giles had said it was so broad that a dozen boats could line up end to end and still not span it. That was beyond anything Hankin could imagine.

Now he couldn't understand what had gone wrong, though plainly something had, for an angry roar shot up from the front of the crowd. Men were shouting and jeering. Then some were elbowing their way back through the crowd, jostling and shoving those still trying to go the other way. Giles grabbed the arm of one as he pushed past. 'What's happening? What does he mean *betrayed*?'

The man scowled. 'The King wasn't allowed to talk to us. The rider saw it all. The King's barge, with its pennants, and all the attendant boats were rowing towards the bank where Tyler and the Kentish men were waiting. But that traitor Archbishop Sudbury was sitting next to the King, whispering in his ear. He persuaded him to turn back before they even touched the bank. The King never even landed!'

'The bastard!' Giles yelled. 'If I ever get to within spitting distance of Sudbury, we'll not need an axe 'cause I'll rip his head off with my bare hands.'

The howls of outrage redoubled as the news spread among the crowd. Most of the men were running back towards Aldersgate, brandishing whatever they had in the way of weapons. It seemed they would batter their way in by force of rage, but just as they reached the gates they swung open. Those in front stopped in their tracks, fearing that armed knights were about to charge out and attack them, but instead a stream of ordinary men like themselves poured out.

'With whom holds you?' the Londoners roared.

Thousands of Essex men bellowed back, 'With King Richard and the True Commons.'

'The watch have fled,' the Londoners shouted. 'Gone running home to hide behind their sisters' skirts.'

They turned and lumbered back inside. The Essex men, with whoops of delight, raced after them. Hankin found himself in the middle of a crowd running through the streets. He hardly had time to take in what he was passing. High walls hid the buildings behind them. Here and there, he glimpsed priests and others running down alleys to escape from the mob surging towards them. One man, plainly terrified, was hammering on a gate set into a wall begging to be let in, but Hankin never discovered if the gate was opened for he was swept past on a human tide and lost sight of it.

Soon the streets became narrower, and the houses and shops on either side had no protective walls round them. The pace slowed as the men were funnelled through smaller gaps. Hankin was breathing hard and glad to slow to a walking pace. He looked around for Giles and thought he glimpsed him ahead in the distance, but there were too many people between them to reach him.

The men were splintering off, smashing their way into lawyers' offices and running out with armfuls of documents, which they burned in the street. Others were carrying out silver goblets and richly embroidered clothes and throwing those on the fires. Some of the owners were fighting back. Others were cowering and pleading, trying to cover their heads. Wailing women fled with children howling in their arms. The Corpus Christi roses, which had decorated every door, lay trampled underfoot, as if their petals had been strewn on the ground for a king to walk upon.

One old woman was leaping and dancing round the flames of a bonfire, cackling, 'Away with the learning of clerks. Away with the learning of clerks.'

She laughed delightedly as the parchments crackled and blazed. A man staggered towards her under the weight of a chest of scrolls, but she ran and snatched it from his arms as if it weighed no more than a baby, tipping the whole lot onto the blaze. The wax seals bubbled, sending black smoke into the sky.

Hankin was too bemused to do anything except follow the men in front. He'd no idea where they were going or what they were going to do when they got there. He was sure that any minute someone was going to rush out and stop them. But no one did. Instead, as the men tried to kick down the door of a wine merchant, the watchman inside opened it and thrust his keys into their hands. He even helped them to roll the barrels into the street, where they used spears and rusty swords to broach them. As the dark red wine splashed out, they pushed their open mouths into the streams or slurped the wine from their cupped hands before hastening on. Hankin cupped a handful of the wine himself, but spat the sour liquid out at once. He'd never tasted wine before, and if that was what it was like, he'd no wish to do so again.

Then he caught the smell of Heaven itself. Hot meat pies! His stomach growled with hunger. He followed his nose to a little side alley ahead of him. The shutter over the open window, which could be lowered to form the counter of the tiny shop, had been hastily raised, but the fragrant steam of rich gravy, hot goose meat and freshly baked pastry wafted out of the crack.

Hankin tried to pull the shutter down, but it was bolted from the inside. He ran back to the street and stared around, searching for anything he could use to prise it loose. The door to a nearby house lay open, hanging from its broken hinges. The room immediately behind it had been ransacked, but a fire iron still lay on the floor. Hankin snatched it up and ran back to the shop.

He wriggled the end into the small gap between the ill-fitting shutter and the wall and pushed with all his strength. The wood splintered and fell away. He threw the iron aside, reached in and gathered up as many of the warm pies as he could.

He was about to make off with his prize when he heard a little cry and, peering through the hole he'd made, saw a man staring out at him, his arms tightly wrapped around a woman, shielding her head with his hand. For a moment man and boy stared at each other, the man's eyes wide with fear. A giddy exhilaration bubbled up inside Hankin and he laughed. This man was afraid of him. A man twice his size was terrified he was going to hurt him. Hankin stuck out his tongue at the man, then stuffed a pie into his mouth and ran off.

He ambled along, guzzling the pies, until he had almost made himself sick. And he still had two left. He was about to thrust them into his scrip when he saw a priest standing in front of the door of a tiny chapel, begging the rebels not to enter. Without thinking, Hankin took aim. The first pie landed on the priest's chest, but the second caught him squarely in the face. The men rocked with laughter as the gravy dripped from the cleric's chin and the broken pastry slid down his long nose. They came over to Hankin, grinning and slapping him on the back. 'Come with us, lad. They say the Great Bridge of London has fallen to the Kentish men. They're in the city. Rumour has it they've taken John of Gaunt's palace. Let's see what the thieving rat's been hiding in there, shall we? I reckon that must be it burning yonder.' He pointed.

'That's the houses of the lawyers, that is,' said another.

They ran on down the street, smashing in those doors that hadn't already been broken down, jeering and thumbing their noses at those who stood huddled at upper casements peering fearfully into the destruction below. Hankin joined in their laughter. He could do anything he pleased and no one dared stop him.

He felt the sudden gust of a damp breeze on his face, like the wind at home that came off the Braytheforde. They must be getting close to the big river of London. He was straining for a glimpse of it when he saw in front of him a great crowd of men pouring through the gates in a wall. The men he was with quickened their pace.

'That's it.' One nudged his fellows. 'That must be the Savoy Palace. John of Gaunt's own house. We shall have some rare sport this day.'

They ran forward through the gap in the wall. Hankin followed them. Then he stopped and stared. He'd helped his father deliver goods to a monastery before, and thought that huge, but this was vast. A gigantic sprawling building stretched out before him, bigger even than Lincoln Cathedral. And clustered round it was an array of smaller, thatched buildings, like mice around a great sack of grain. Was all this for just one man? Not even a king would need such a vast palace.

The roses and knot gardens in front of it had been trampled into the earth as if a herd of wild boar had been driven through them. The huge doors stood wide open and smoke was rising into the molten blue sky. Men were running in and out or lumbering down the stair-cases on the outside of the walls, their arms full of mirrors, robes, pots and urns, which they hurled into the fish ponds. Some had clambered onto the roof and were stripping off the tiles and hurling them into the courtyard below. A group of women were rolling barrels of silver plates and goblets out into the road, where men waited with hammers and stones to smash the precious objects to pieces.

Hankin dodged across the garden and in through the door. The vast hall, which stretched away in front of him, was the biggest room he'd ever been in. Long battle swords and hunting trophies hung from walls painted with gardens and forests, beasts and flowers, knights and maidens. But Hankin caught only the glitter of gold leaf between the billows of thick black smoke that rose up into the rafters, for a great fire had been lit in the centre of the hall. Men were stoking it with heavy tapestries, bed-hangings, rolls of parchment and leather-bound books. Others were beating plates and jewels, gilded goblets and ornate boxes with axes and hammers, before tossing them onto the blaze.

One man thrust a black fur robe into Hankin's arms. 'When we've done, Gaunt'll not even have a piss-pot to call his own. Burn it, boy, burn every single thing that that devil has stolen from us.'

Hankin heard his mother's sobs. *They took the lantern. They even*

323

took the lantern. Rage boiled in him. He tossed the fur robe into the leaping flames and galloped up the stairs, looking for anything else he could destroy.

But the first chamber he entered was almost bare save for a table too big to get down the stairs. He pushed open the door of another and found a carved footstool, which had been kicked into the corner. It wasn't valuable, but it would help the fire to burn. He stumbled back down the stairs with it, coughing against the thick smoke that was beginning to fill the upper rooms.

But the people below had stopped hammering and smashing. They'd all turned towards the open door, staring at someone struggling in the grip of three men. Hankin, whose eyes were watering in the stinging smoke, could only make out the dark outlines of the men framed against the dazzling sunlight streaming through the door.

'We caught him running off with a plate,' one of the men was shouting. 'Tyler's orders. "No looting," he said.'

'No one's to take anything from the devil's house,' another shouted. 'It's tainted with the blood of honest Englishmen. Everything must be destroyed.'

'And any man who dishonours our cause must be destroyed along with it.'

'Burn him! Burn him!'

They were pulling their prisoner towards the fire. He was fighting for his life, shouting at the top of his voice, 'I wasn't going to keep it! I swear on the Holy Virgin – taking it to be smashed in the street with the other silver! Listen to me! I beg you.'

But they ignored him. Several men darted forward to help drag the prisoner towards the blazing fire. As they passed the foot of the stairs, Hankin, rubbing the smoke from his eyes, found himself staring up into the terrified face of Giles as he struggled to break free.

For a moment he was paralysed with horror, then raced forward, kicking and tugging at the men who were holding Giles. 'No! He's one of us! Stop! Please stop! Let him go!'

Giles was still howling, 'With King Richard . . . and the True Commons,' as they hoisted him into the air by his arms and legs. As if he was a battering ram, they swung him forwards, backwards and forwards again, then let go. Giles landed in the middle of the bonfire. It collapsed under him, sending flames shooting out at the sides and roaring up around him.

Hankin had never in his life heard a man scream in such agony. The boy found himself running out of the door and was halfway across the courtyard before his legs gave way beneath him. He collapsed onto the ground and vomited every mouthful of the pies he had stolen. He knelt there among the trampled roses, too weak to move, stuffing his fingers into his ears to try to block out the terrible shrieks that split his whole being in two.

Suddenly there was a huge bang. He felt an agonising blow on his back as if he'd been tossed on the horns of a charging bull. He was thrown forwards into the dirt and all turned black.

Chapter 48

A houseleek grown on thatch or roof tiles will protect the house from lightning and catching fire.

London

Gunter stared at the muddy-grey river they called the Thames. He'd thought the Witham broad where it splayed out into the great port at Boston but had never imagined that any river, bounded on both sides by land, could be so wide. It was crammed with boats. Brown cargo wherries and little rowing boats buzzed in and out of the moorings, like flies on a midden heap, dodging between elegant longboats propelled by banks of oarsmen. Those craft were not made of plain brown wood and blackened with tar, like the ones on the Witham, but were richly carved and painted in shining red, blue, green and gold and hung with coloured pennants that streamed out behind them, like smoke from blazing torches.

Most of these ornate boats were heading out of the city, many piled high with chests, beds and other furnishings, as well as terrified families, who clung to one another. The helmsmen fought the swift-moving currents and tried to guide their masters' vessels out of range of the people on the bank who were hurling threats, dung, stones and rubbish at them. But that wasn't the only hazard the helmsmen had to cope with. Barrels, tables, books and objects smashed beyond all recognition bobbed in the water. It took Gunter a few moments to realise that the pale things drifting between the flotsam were corpses, some with their heads smashed to a pulp, others headless or naked with their bellies slashed open. A few, even in death, still clung to a wooden chest or a sodden bundle.

A little way beyond where Gunter stood was the vast span of London Bridge, with two great watchtowers, nineteen archways and even waterwheels to power the mills that jostled alongside the shops and houses that had once lined the span. But now the buildings lay in ruins, smoke still drifting up from them.

Gunter wrenched his gaze back from the river to scan the crowd. He'd guessed where the boy had gone as soon as he'd woken that morning to find his own stave and scrip missing. His only thought had been to bring Hankin safely home. Nonie, tearful, had urged him to hurry. The boy could have been gone only a few hours. Gunter could soon catch up with him. But it had not proved as easy as that.

Gunter had been lucky at first. A river-man who knew the boy had spotted him and had remembered in which direction he was heading. Carters had given Gunter lifts in exchange for him helping to load or unload their wagons. But between rides, he was forced to walk and, with his wooden leg, he couldn't match the lad's pace. Having to stop and ask in the villages if anyone remembered seeing the boy had slowed him still further.

Then he'd heard rumours that the rebels were marching on London. He could see for himself they were true for the villages were empty of men and of the fitter women too. Anyone who was able to walk, he was told, was on their way to see the King.

Gunter was as certain as any father could be of where his son was bound. What lad wouldn't have wanted to join that army? So he'd walked through the night, snatching an hour or two of sleep whenever he could stumble no further, then forcing himself awake to carry on.

He'd finally reached the gates of London early that morning. They lay open, unguarded. The stench of burning hung like a conqueror's flag over the city, while red kites and ravens shambled through the streets, picking over its bones.

All day he'd wandered through its alleyways, passing the smoking ruins of great buildings, peering in through the splintered doors of houses and smashed shutters of shops, stumbling over piles of broken furniture, pots, books and ledgers thrown into the streets. He'd only ever seen such devastation once before and that was when the Witham had flooded, bringing the Great Drowning to Lincoln.

Gunter had set off with no plan other than to find his son. It wasn't the first time that the lad had wandered off. He'd often gone missing at the Lincoln fair or in the streets of Boston, but sooner or later Gunter had always spotted him, even in a dense crowd. Several times that morning Gunter had hurried after what looked like a familiar head in the distance only to find that the boy did not in the least resemble his son. He'd begun to fear that he couldn't remember what his son looked like, or even how tall he was. As he stared at the vast river and the hordes swarming around it, he realised, with a chill, that a boy in this great city might simply vanish for ever, never to be found.

In desperation he barred the way of a woman hurrying towards him, dragging a little girl by the hand. 'Have you seen my son?'

She pulled the child to her, covering the girl's head with her arms. 'For King Richard! King – King Richard and the True Commons!' the woman gabbled.

Gunter was shocked by the fear in her face. He reached out a hand, meaning to calm her, but she backed away, dragging the child with her.

Both Gunter and the woman glanced round as they heard a great roar.

'Away with all learning! King Richard! King Richard!'

A great stream of men and women was marching towards them, heading in the direction of the bridge. They were filthy, their faces blackened with soot, their clothes and hands smeared with grime and dried blood. But from the way they swaggered and pranced, Gunter knew it was not their own.

The woman with the little girl stared upwards and moaned in despair. Gunter, following her gaze, saw what the marchers were carrying high on the pikes above their heads. Nine severed heads had been impaled on spikes, the eyes fixed wide open in a look of agony and horror. The splintered white bones of their necks poked out from the gore and drops of scarlet blood sprayed the heads of those below.

The people who had been jeering at the fleeing boats rushed up towards the procession, blocking their way. The man leading it threw up a hand, calling a halt.

'We bring the heads of the traitors to stand on the southern gate of the bridge where all traitors go.'

Two of the men who carried the pikes turned them so that the heads faced each other. The neck of one was so mangled it looked as if it had taken half a dozen blows with a blunt axe to sever it from the body. It had an archbishop's mitre secured to the top of the skull with a long iron nail.

The pike-bearers jiggled the heads up and down and spoke in high-pitched voices, making it appear that the two heads were talking to each other, like puppets at a fair.

'Hales, my faithful treasurer, what think you of this poll tax?' the head with the mitre appeared to say.

'It's a very fair tax indeed, Archbishop Sudbury,' the other replied. 'Let the poor pay to keep the rich. What could be fairer than that?'

The pike-bearer who carried the head of the Archbishop of Canterbury spun it around so that drops of blood from the neck fell on the crowd, like holy water sprinkled with hyssop. 'Bless you, bless you, my children.'

'Are we to lie together, Hales?' the archbishop's head asked.

'Don't we always, Sudbury?'

The voice of the pike-bearer shrieked in imitation of an outraged maiden. 'I will not lie with a man who has not kissed me first.'

The crowd howled with laughter as the open mouths of the two heads were pushed together. Finally, the procession moved off again towards the bridge, with the gleeful crowd bringing up the rear.

Gunter felt so sick he would have vomited but his stomach was empty.

The woman, still clutching the little girl, stared after them. A single spot of blood glistened like a ruby in the child's hair.

'If God can't protect the archbishop,' she murmured, 'then what's the use of prayers, or lighting candles? What's the use of any of it? If the whole world is mad, why should I stay sane?'

Chapter 49

Newgate is haunted by a black dog, which rears up as tall as a man. Snakes writhe from its head, and its body is open, exposing its beating heart.

London

'If you'll take my advice, Robert, you'll return home to Lincoln today. At least get on the road out of London before dark. Wait! Secure that chest properly before you put the next one on. If it shifts it'll bring the whole lot off the wagon.'

The merchant left Robert's side and hurried across his courtyard to where two manservants were loading his valuables onto a long wagon. Robert trailed after him.

'But I must get word to John of Gaunt. If the rebellion should spread to Lincoln there aren't enough of his men to defend his castle, never mind protect the city.'

The merchant worked his way round the wagon, testing straps and pulling at knots, ignoring the mutinous glares of his servants, who had just fastened them.

'Your faith in Gaunt is touching, Robert. But with the Savoy burned to the ground and Scotland threatening to attack, he won't send so much as a one-legged man to defend Lincoln. He's got far more to lose at his other properties round England.'

'But what if they should break into Lincoln Castle and seize the weapons stored there, never mind let loose the thieves and murderers as they did at the Fleet prison?'

The merchant glared at him impatiently. 'All the more reason for you to get back to Lincoln and employ what men you can find to defend your own property. If you're looking for help from the King, forget it. Half of his advisers have been butchered and if the mob get their hands on Gaunt, his head will decorate London Bridge with the rest.'

Robert found himself pushed unceremoniously aside by a stout maidservant, waddling beneath the weight of a travelling chest, which she pushed into the back of a smaller cart.

'Mistress'll be ready to leave within the hour,' she said gruffly, and disappeared back into the house.

Robert knew he was delaying them. Every minute counted. Who knew where the rabble would turn their attention next? He'd been grateful when a fellow merchant had offered his hospitality, though Robert knew he was thinking that an extra man could help defend the house if the rebels should attack. So far they had been left in peace. But having destroyed the houses and offices of lawyers, their clerks, the bishops and any nobility they could find, the rebels were fast running out of targets. A neighbour had come to warn them only that morning that a band of men and women had demanded money *not* to set fire to his house.

Robert was as frightened as the other merchant, but Catlin's words pounded in his head. She had told Leonia that the safety of the family, indeed the whole of Lincoln, depended on him. He couldn't return and say he'd made no attempt to summon help. No one who hadn't witnessed the destruction would believe the half of what he had seen. They wouldn't begin to understand the chaos here, and if he told them of the death of such powerful men at the hands of the blood-crazed mob, it would only increase their fear for their own city.

The merchant laid a hand on Robert's shoulder. 'Robert, I wish you'd reconsider. Come with us, just till we're clear of the city, then you can ride north.'

'Not till I've sent a message to Gaunt. I swore on my honour I'd do so.'

The merchant sighed, wiping his sweating brow on the back of his sleeve.

'There's a Flemish merchant by the name of Jacob der Weyden who lives close by the church of St Martin Vintry, the place we passed through on the way to the wine wharf last time you came to London. John of Gaunt sold this Fleming and some of his countrymen papers of exemption so they could trade without having to pay export duty.'

He held up his hands in sympathy at the outrage on Robert's face. 'I know! I know! And you wonder why they burned Gaunt's palace down. I tell you, it won't be Tyler and the Kentish men that Gaunt will need to fear if he ever shows his face here again. If the English merchants of London ever get their hands on him, they'll tie him to a spit and roast him alive, like the hog he is. But the point is, the Flemish merchants and Gaunt feed off one another. If anyone can get word to Gaunt and bend his sight towards Lincoln, they can. Mind you, those swine won't do any man a favour unless he can pay for it.'

'I will pay whatever they demand.' Robert patted his chest where he'd strapped the silver ingots under his clothes.

The merchant nodded grimly, then plucked at Robert's robe. 'And for goodness' sake, man, see if you can't find something plainer to wear if you're going to wander the streets. You stand out like a peacock among sparrows. What possessed you to pack your most sumptuous clothes to wear at a time like this?'

Robert grimaced. 'My new wife . . .'

The merchant rolled his eyes sympathetically. 'Wives! They'll be the death of us.'

The two men embraced as they said goodbye, each wishing the other the protection of the Holy Virgin and all the saints. The merchant promised to take Robert's horse and pack with him and leave them at an inn beyond the city gate, to be waiting for him when he left London. It was safer to walk the streets than ride: any man who looked wealthy enough to be mounted on a fine mare like Robert's might easily find himself a target.

Robert grasped the hilt of his sword tightly beneath his half-cloak. His friend was right, his clothes were too fine, but they were the plainest Catlin had packed. He took a deep breath and ventured out into the street beyond the courtyard. He was used to striding the streets of his own city boldly, meeting the eye of everyone he passed and nodding at those of rank, but for the first time in his life he felt like someone with no more standing than a villein. Men and women were roaming the streets, like marauding tribes of hunters, clutching cudgels, bows, even old swords. He watched them seize men, hurling them up against the walls of the houses and demanding they should join the rebels. He found himself scuttling between piles of half-burned debris, diving down alleys and keeping his eyes lowered so as not to attract the attention of anyone by meeting their gaze.

Dazed women crouched in the open doors of their burned-out houses. Dogs growled, defending shops that lay empty, their counters smashed. He felt himself walking through something sticky and saw he was stepping through pools of drying blood.

It took him a while to reach the Vintry: he had tried to avoid the main streets where most of the gangs prowled. *Behind the warehouses on the wine wharf, keep the bridge on your left*, his friend had told him. Robert vaguely remembered the wine wharf: he'd been there a couple of times before, but couldn't see any landmarks he recognised and was beginning to fear he had blundered into entirely the wrong part of the city.

Then, as he emerged from between two buildings, he saw St Martin's Church. The white marble pillars and pavement glittered in the afternoon sun. There was no mistaking the opulent houses that surrounded it. They brazenly proclaimed the wealth of their foreign owners in the gold gilding on the plaster carvings over the doors.

The houses in that area had been built years ago by the wine merchants who traded from the wine wharf, as the six-pointed stars set over the windows proclaimed, for that was their emblem. Now they were occupied by the Flemish cloth merchants. Robert knew that behind the tightly fastened shutters hung the finest and costliest glass windows in England, imported all the way from France.

He was about to step out of the alleyway when he heard a roar as if a great wave was rolling towards him. Sick with fear, he glanced in the direction of the sound. A huge crowd was swarming up the street. Those on the edge of the human tide paused to hurl stones and any other missiles they could find at the houses as they passed, but most could not have stopped had they wanted to, for fear of being trampled by those pressing from behind.

Robert flattened himself into a doorway, afraid to move in case they saw him. He prayed they would charge past him. But as they reached the church, they split into two groups, running round each side to surround it. They tore up stones and cobbles, hurling them at the windows and the stout doors. Robert cringed as he heard glass smashing and shrieks from inside. The mob was pounding on the doors with swords and axes. The thick wood splintered, but still it held.

Then, from the back of the crowd, six men staggered up, carrying between them a great tar-covered beam, which they had evidently taken from one of the wharfs. The crowd parted as they positioned themselves in front of the door and ran at it with the beam. The doors buckled inwards a little under the blow, but they did not yield. Other willing hands squeezed themselves between those already holding the beam to lend their strength. They retreated, then ran again at the doors. It took three or four attempts before, with a great splintering crash, they burst open. The men wielding the battering ram were almost trampled underfoot as the crowd surged in.

Screams and shouts came from inside and the rebels re-emerged, dragging the Flemish merchants out by their hair or heels. Those rebels still outside pounced on the prisoners and hauled them away from the church, holding them with their arms pinioned. Other Flemish men were herded out behind them, swords and spears pressing into their backs.

Three of the rebels rolled the battering ram into the centre of the crowd, yelling at them to stand back and clear a space around it. One of the Flemish merchants was selected, seemingly at random, pulled forward and thrown face down onto the ground.

A man grabbed his hair, dragging his head over the beam, so that his neck rested on the wood. Then another stepped forward with an axe. Screams of fear rose from the huddled merchants as they realised what was about to happen. The man on the ground began pleading and kicking, trying desperately to escape. Two laughing women flopped down on his thrashing legs to hold him still.

Robert turned his face away, but that did not prevent him hearing the piercing shrieks as the axe sliced into the man's neck. It took another blow to silence him, two more until, with a crunch of bone, the head was severed. Robert glanced back to see it being brandished aloft, blood pouring from the neck, the crowd cheering their approval.

As if the sight of the head was the signal, the rebels holding the terrified Flemish merchants began dragging them forward and forcing them to their knees. Some were thrown over the wooden beam, others simply had their heads hacked from their shoulders where they knelt, with swords, axes or knives.

Those who tried to fight or run were stabbed or hamstrung, until they fell to the ground, unable to defend themselves. Their heads were sawn off without resistance. None of the rebels was a trained executioner. Those who died or were at least rendered insensible by the first blow were the fortunate ones. How many bodies were tossed onto the pile? How many heads were kicked around that crowd – twenty, thirty? Robert lost count. Splashes of blood ran down the white marble columns of the church and spread around the feet of the crowd, a pool of ever-widening scarlet that seemed to seep into every corner of that street.

In the meantime, others were breaking down the doors of the nearest houses, dragging out boys scarcely older than Adam and men so old they couldn't walk without a stick. All were hauled into the space in front of the church. They shrieked in fear as they saw the pile of headless corpses.

'Not Flemish,' one old man wailed. 'Not Flemish. Servant, servant!'

'Say bread and cheese,' his captors demanded.

The old man stared at them bewildered.

'Say it, say bread and cheese,' they insisted, yanking his beard.

'B-brote und—'

The rabble laughed, and forced him to his knees.

Then a cry of crazed delight rang out as a huge blond man dressed in a long damask robe was dragged up the street towards the church.

'It's him. It's the merchant Richard Lyons! They've got the bastard!'

Robert stared in horror. He knew him only by sight, but he was one of the richest merchants in London. He'd once been a favourite at Court. Surely they wouldn't dare to harm him. But they did. Richard was a burly man and fought his captors hard, but there is only so long that an unarmed man may hold out against so many. When he finally fell to his knees in the lake of blood, his fine damask robe was already slashed in half a dozen places. Men jostled for the privilege of delivering the *coup de grâce*, as huntsmen vied for the honour of bringing down the stag.

Robert didn't wait to see the rusty axe blade fall; he turned and staggered back up the alley, trying desperately to fight down the nausea that was threatening to choke him. He stumbled on, scarcely knowing where he was going except that he had to go north, away from the river, north to a gate, any gate. He was vaguely aware that he must be in the cordwainers' district. He gazed around, trying to get his bearings. North . . . north . . . It had to be that way. If he could reach the wall he could follow it round.

'There's another one,' a woman shrieked. 'I seen him! He came from the Vintry.'

Dazed, Robert turned his head. An old woman, her skirts soaked with crimson, was leaping up and down in a strange jig, waving and gesturing. He blinked at her and turned to hurry on. Then he felt himself grabbed from behind.

'That's him. Saw him there myself. He's another of those Flemings, trying to escape the justice of the True Commons he is.'

They spun him round and Robert found himself surrounded by half a dozen men and women, all armed. His hand reached for his sword hilt, but he'd seldom in his life ever had cause to draw a weapon in defence and the movement was clumsy. His arms were pinned behind his back before he had touched the hilt.

'Shall we take him back to Vintry?'

'Take him to Cheapside. They've a block set up there.'

'Wait!' Robert protested. 'I swear I am no Flemish merchant.'

Filthy blood-stained hands stroked the fur trim on his tunic. 'Ah, another servant, is it?' a man said, grinning. 'Don't know many servants who dress in fur, do you, Peter?'

''Gainst the law for a servant to wear fur. Their masters wouldn't want them dressing like them, would they?'

'I am a merchant. I don't deny it,' Robert said desperately. 'But I'm English just like you . . . from Lincoln, in the north. I swear to you by the Blessed Virgin. I hate the foreign merchants as much as you do.'

'That's so, is it? What were you doing with them in the Vintry? Some deal was it, to put good honest Englishmen out of work?'

Robert tried to think of an explanation. Telling them he was trying to send word to John of Gaunt would see him run through on the spot.

'I was lost. I don't know this city.' Even to Robert that sounded feeble.

The man gave a mocking bow. 'Lost, is it, Master? Well, there's a shame. Let's show this fine gentleman the way, shall we? All the way to the block.'

Hands clutched at Robert, pushing him forward. He fought them with every inch of his strength, knowing he was fighting for his life. He managed to wrest one arm free and used it to smash back hard against one of those standing behind him. Robert cried out as something struck him savagely across his back and felled him to the ground. White flashes of light burst in his eyeballs and he fought back the pain. A boot thudded into his ribs.

'Cut his head off here. Not worth the effort to carry him to Cheapside. We could have half a dozen or more of the bastards' heads off in the time it'll take to drag him there.'

Terror and pride made Robert struggle to rise in spite of the throbbing pain in his back. He was not going to make it easy for them.

He was not going to lie with his face in the mud while they hacked at his neck.

But feet pressed him down again. Someone grabbed his hair, stretching his neck.

'I'm Robert – Robert of Bassingham from Lincoln. I've done no . . .'

He felt the whistle of a blade above his head, and his heart seemed to freeze in his chest.

'Stop! Stop! I know this man. He's English.'

The hand pulling his hair relaxed a little.

'So he says. But he's still in league with the foreign merchants. He was seen in the Flemish quarter.'

'His eldest son was murdered by the Florentine merchants in Lincoln for speaking out against them. If he was in the Flemish quarter it was to kill foreigners, not trade with them.'

There was a moment's pause, then a gale of laughter. The feet pinning Robert down released him. He was bruised and gasping for breath, and it took several attempts for the rebels to haul him to his feet. His legs trembled beneath him. He wiped the mud from his face and closed his eyes, swaying, as the ground tipped under him.

'You're sure you recognise this man?'

'Known him since I were a bairn.'

The voice was vaguely familiar, but Robert couldn't name its owner. His eyes were watering from the grit. He blinked several times and tried to focus. The blurred face he saw he seemed to know, but he couldn't grasp why.

Hands were brushing him down and patting him on the back. 'Be off with you. Go that way, if you don't want to run into more trouble. Go west to Ludgate. Wouldn't do to be seen in Cheapside with that costly tunic.'

'And if anyone challenges you, say, "With King Richard and the True Commons". Then they'll let you pass.'

The rebels hurried off in the opposite direction. Robert staggered to a wall and leaned against it, no longer sure his legs would hold him up. He had a throbbing pain in his back and his ribs hurt like the devil each time he tried to suck in a breath, but the pain was almost a blessing. At least it meant he was alive. God's blood, if that man hadn't come along and spoken up for him . . . He shivered. He raised his head, searching for his rescuer, but the street was deserted.

Chapter 50

As a heretic was lifted onto the pile of wood on which she was to be burned, she blew in the face of the executioner and said, 'Here is payment for your work.' A hot wind passed over him. His face swelled and sores broke out upon his hands. The heretic was burned to ashes, but within days leprosy had infested the body of her executioner and he was dead.

London

Gunter sat with his head in his hands staring out over the vast river. It was drawing towards evening. The heat still hung heavy in the narrow streets, but at least over the Thames a breeze had sprung up, blowing the pall of smoke and the stench of blood back into the city, as if proclaiming the river wanted no part of it.

For two days, Gunter had hunted through every street and alley he could find, but he knew that even as he searched one street, his son could easily be walking away from him down another and he'd never know it. He'd been mad even to imagine he had a hope of finding one boy among so many.

What if his son was dead? He saw again Master Robert pinned down in the street, the rusty blade raised high above his head. The shock of hearing him shout the familiar name had made Gunter act without thinking. But he'd seen other men, just like Robert, pleading for their lives and he had done nothing, said nothing. He'd been too afraid that the mob would turn on him. Suppose men had walked past Hankin when the crowd had him pinned to the ground, and suppose they, like him, had been too afraid to save the boy.

He shook himself impatiently. He didn't even know for certain Hankin was here. The boy might never have come to London with the rebels. Maybe he'd turned for home somewhere along the road and was back safe in the cottage in Greetwell. Perhaps Hankin had never had any intention of joining the rebellion. He might have run away from home to seek his fortune at sea. He'd always been fascinated by the huge ships that docked at Boston.

And all the time Gunter was in London, Nonie, Royse and little Col were at home, unprotected, with him not earning a single penny to feed them. He had to return to Greetwell. He could do nothing more here.

As Gunter scrambled to his feet, he slowly became aware that the streets had grown eerily silent. They'd been filled with shouts and screams, the splintering of furniture, smashing glass and crashing masonry. But now the loudest noise was the screeching of gulls overhead. A sense of foreboding made his blood turn cold. He hurried along the bank.

A beggar on crutches limped towards him. Something bulged under his ragged tunic. He stopped as soon as he caught sight of Gunter, bending over to try to disguise what he was carrying.

'With whom holds you?' he whined. 'With King Richard and the True Commons,' he answered himself, before Gunter had a chance to say a word.

Gunter continued walking towards him.

'With King Richard and the True Commons,' the beggar repeated, as if it was a charm to ward off evil. He cringed away, fearing attack.

Gunter held up his hands to show he carried no weapons. 'Where is everyone? What's happening, do you know?'

The man cocked his head on one side and peered suspiciously at him, as if the question was a test to which no one had told him the answer.

Gunter tried again. 'Have the rebels gone?'

'Gone. Gone to Smithfield.' The beggar jerked his head to the north. 'Gone to meet the King. He's going to give them everything they want. Going to make Wat Tyler chancellor of England, so they say, and give him a great palace. Going to make John Ball archbishop of all England, they say that 'n' all. But if you was to ask me . . .' he gave a leery wink '. . . *I'd say* it's a trick to get them out of the city. You'd not catch me going there. King said he'd meet them last time, but he didn't even land. It's a trap, that's what it is, and they're the little mice all scurrying into it.' The beggar chuckled, and was still laughing as he limped away.

Gunter hesitated, trying to think. If all of the rebels had gone to this field then if Hankin was with them that was where he'd go too.

Were the rebels really being led into an ambush? He had to find his son and get him out before it was too late. Yet if Hankin was not even in London, he himself would be walking into that trap. But he couldn't abandon his son, not if there was any chance of finding him, any chance at all.

The beggar had pointed directly away from the river. The field must lie in that direction, though he hadn't said how far. Gunter gazed around. His path along the bank was blocked by the rubble of a great building, from which smoke still trickled in several places. One of the walls, which had evidently stood on the water's edge, had fallen into the river, and the roof had tumbled inwards, bringing down several storeys on top of one another.

Gunter clambered up on a heap of fallen masonry, which seemed to be the remains of a tower, hoping that if he got high enough he might glimpse the field the beggar had talked about. But he could see only buildings, some still standing, some in ruins or burned out. In front of the mound of rubble on which he stood there was what must once have been a garden, though now it was filled with all manner of rubbish. Beyond that a gate lay open to the street on the other side. If he cut through the garden to that gate, it would be far quicker than trying to find a way round.

He scrambled, slipping and sliding, over the fallen masonry. Here and there wisps of smoke rose from fires still burning deep below. Some stones still glittered with fragments of gold leaf or scarlet paint. Caught between them were pieces of cloth, bits of wood, a glimmer of silver. It was like a river in flood, where you saw things bobbing in the water that vanished before you had time to recognise them, except that this water had been turned to stone. It took him some time to cross the petrified river. He was afraid to move too quickly in case the stones shifted and snapped his wooden leg, or broke his good one.

Eventually he clambered down the other side and began to pick his way through the ravaged garden. Several pigs had found their way in and were rootling through the dirt, and a dog was cocking his leg against a great heap of charred barrels and smashed chairs.

A movement near the high wall caught his attention. A woman was crouching, helping a man to drink from a beaker. The man caught sight of Gunter and must have said something to the woman for she turned and called to him. 'Have you bread? For pity's sake! Can you spare anything?'

Gunter hesitated. He had a little cheese in his scrip. It was all he had left, and even that he'd been driven to snatch from a looted shop. He wanted to keep it, for God alone knew when he'd next find something to eat, but guilt pricked him. The cheese was stolen. He had no right to it. He limped towards her, trying not to trip over the smashed furniture and broken pots. As he came closer, he saw that half a dozen people were lying in the shelter of the wall, bloodied and mangled. He couldn't tell if they were alive or dead. He lowered his eyes. He couldn't bear to see any more corpses. He pulled the cheese from his bag and handed it to the woman.

'Bless you, Master, bless you.'

'Is he your kin?'

She nodded. 'I can't move him and I'll not leave him.'

'The rebels hurt him?'

She snorted. 'He was with the rebels, doing his duty, tearing down this cursed palace. But some cod-wit threw kegs on the fire. Thought they were full of silver but they weren't. Full of gunpowder. Brought half the building down on their heads. My man, he was near the blaze and a piece of metal shot out of the fire and went straight through his thigh. Did for these others too. Can't do nothing for 'em, save give 'em water. No bugger'll help me.'

She savagely dashed away the tears that had sprung into her bloodshot eyes.

'Mind you, I reckon it's worse for them.' She pointed to the ruins. 'There's men trapped somewhere under that lot. I can hear 'em yelling sometimes. I tried to get some men in the street to help them, but they were too drunk to listen.' She shrugged. 'I don't suppose they could have done much anyway. It'd take an army to dig them out from under that.'

'The rebels have all gone to Smithfield,' Gunter said. 'I'm bound there myself. I'll send men back to help. They'll want to rescue their own.'

The woman gave him a scathing look. 'No bugger'll help,' she repeated.

Gunter was walking away when he heard the cry. The voice was so cracked and broken that only he could have recognised it.

'Faayther! Faayther . . .'

He whipped round. At the far end of the line of bodies, a little figure was struggling desperately to lift his head.

Chapter 51

To make a girl dance naked you must write on virgin parchment the name 'Fruitimiere' with the blood of a bat. Cut the parchment on an altar stone over which mass has been said, then place it under a doorstep over which the girl will pass. When she steps over it she will be forced to come to you, strip naked and dance without ceasing, even to her death, unless you remove the parchment.

Mistress Catlin

Ever since I'd started climbing the steep hill to the top of the city I'd had an uneasy feeling someone was following me. But dozens of men, women and children were travelling the same route as I was, good-wives, beggars, pedlars and goose-girls from the city all mingling with the steady stream of pilgrims who were plodding up to visit the shrines in the cathedral. Why should I imagine any were interested in me? I drew to the side, glancing behind me several times, but I could see no one I recognised.

When I reached the top of the hill, I turned away from the cathedral and went through the castle gate, across its bustling green and towards the far gate that led out of the city to the west. It was late in the afternoon and few traders came in to Lincoln by that route – most made their way into the city via the north or south gates – but I couldn't help glancing behind me once more.

The watchmen barely looked up as I passed, too engrossed in a game of dice and too hot or lazy to stir themselves. I hastened through the small copse on the other side of the road towards the high meadow. The ground was baked hard, showing brown between the short, wiry strands of grass, like the pate of balding man.

Across the far side of the meadow, a small grove of elms surrounded a spring that bubbled out from between the rocks forming a small pool, before it trickled away into a stony brook and vanished into the earth. A fairy spring, some called it, while others knew it as St Margaret's well. When the trees were no bigger than saplings someone must have placed iron horseshoes around them and now, centuries later, they had grown through and around them so that horseshoes stuck out from the trunks like tiny steps.

On Midsummer's Day, girls came here at dawn to discover whom they would marry. Others bathed here when they were with child, or carried flasks of the water back to the homes of women giving birth so that they might be safely delivered of their infants, for the water was said to be holy. Mostly the place was deserted: there was no shortage of wells and springs within the city walls from which good-wives could draw water closer to their homes.

At first I thought the grove was empty and felt the hollow ache of disappointment. But as I drew closer, I smiled. He was waiting for me, lying stretched out on the ground, dozing in the sun. He'd set a flagon of wine to cool in the trickling water. I stood and watched the slow rise and fall of his chest with the same shiver of delight I'd felt the first time I had laid eyes on him.

We had abandoned the tower in the lower part of the city for our trysts. The stench of Butwerk middens and the festering river mud below was enough to quell even my desire. This spot was far sweeter, but it was too exposed and I feared someone might stumble upon us.

My beloved's eyes were still closed beneath the dappled gold and apple-green light, but he whisked his elegant hand across his face, driving a gnat from his cheek. I pulled off my shoes and hose, luxuriating in the feel of sun-warmed earth beneath my feet. The grass by the stream grew cool and soft. I tiptoed through it and, taking care that my shadow didn't fall upon him, I knelt behind him and pressed my mouth to his, feeling at once the hungry grasping of his lips. But still he didn't open his eyes.

Without warning, his hands shot up to my shoulders and he jerked me forward so sharply that I rolled over on top of him. Fiercely kissing my face, he pulled down the front of my gown so that he could nuzzle my breasts. I resisted, pulling away from him.

'Who were you dreaming of?' I demanded. 'Who did you think was kissing you?'

'A pretty little milkmaid. Jealous?' He laughed, as I punched his shoulder.

'You wouldn't dare,' I told him.

Turning away from me, he lifted the flagon of wine from the pool and poured it into the two goblets he drew from his leather scrip. He dipped twin red cherries into the wine and touched them to my lips. I licked the drops from them and pulled them into my mouth, gnawing the sweet, juicy flesh.

He dangled another. But I pushed it away and sat up abruptly, glancing over my shoulder towards the castle. Though we were hidden from the gate, I could see the walls rising above the line of trees. A small dark splinter of a figure moved across the top of them.

'What's wrong?' he asked, following my gaze.

I shivered. 'I kept thinking I was being followed here and thought I saw someone just now watching us.'

My lover shaded his eyes with his hands. 'It's only the watchman on the castle wall, doing his rounds. If he can see us so far away he must have the eyes of a hawk.'

'No, over there.' I pointed towards the bushes a little way across the meadow. 'I thought I saw movement.'

'If someone is there, it'll be one of the goat-boys looking for a place to nap out of sight of his master.'

He tried to pull me down into the grass again, but I pushed him away. 'Not here. It's too open. We have to find somewhere else to meet next time. I can't risk tales being carried back to my husband.'

'What are you worried about, my sweet one? Even if every priest in Lincoln swore on Christ's foreskin they'd seen us naked together, you could still convince Robert it was a lie. He's infatuated with you. He'd more readily believe the Virgin Mary herself was a whore than that you were anything less than a saint.'

He dipped his finger into the wine and drew it over my lips, then reached up to lick away the droplets.

I turned my face aside. 'You're wrong. A man in love could discover his wife with a half-eaten babe in her hands, blood smeared on her lips, and he'd swear she'd been trying to save the child's life. But let so much as a whisper of an illicit kiss reach him and, true or not, he'd fly into a jealous rage and never trust her again. We have to be careful, my beloved.'

He sat up and began savagely to shred a blade of grass. 'And don't you think I'm jealous knowing you share Robert's bed night after night and he can take you any time the mood seizes him? You won't let me fuck you one afternoon when he's miles away. Is that the thanks I get after all I've done for you?'

'How do you know I still have a husband?' I said. 'The gossip in the marketplace is that the streets of London are piled with corpses. That was why you and I sent him to London, wasn't it? If he's killed there, no one will blame me for that and you will be able to have me in any place you choose, whenever it pleases you.'

'And if he isn't?' he said, tearing up another grass blade.

'If he returns alive, having contacted Gaunt, Robert's reputation will grow in the city and so will his wealth. I cannot lose. I will find a way to dispose of him. But the precise manner of his death will take a good deal of thought. Another in the family so soon after Edith's and Jan's, and even old Father Remigius might start to wonder. I will have to find someone who will be blamed for Robert's death without question so that it never occurs to anyone to look for another hand in this.'

I plucked a buttercup and held it to his cheek, so that the gold reflected on his skin.

He pushed it away impatiently. 'I begin to think you've no intention of getting rid of him. You're in love with Robert and it's me you're playing with.'

I laughed. 'I said I never intended to fall in love with Robert and I always speak the truth. Do you think that a butcher looks at a goat grazing in the field and thinks how lovely its coat, how sweet its face? No. He sees it skinned, chopped and being sold for a good profit. Do you really imagine I could fall in love with a corpse? From the moment I selected Robert out of all the men in Lincoln, that was what he was – a rotting cadaver. Dear Robert's grave was dug on the first day I went looking for him at the guildhall. The only question you need to ask is how I will push him into it.'

Chapter 52

Hay ricks and thatched roofs must be finished with a green branch or straw cock to prevent witches from landing on them and to ward off fire and storms.

Lincoln

Adam heard the bell ring outside the high gate that led to the stable-yard. He peered out of the casement. Tenney, a stout stave in his hand and a wicked-looking knife tucked into his belt, strode across the yard and opened the shutter over the grille. At once, he laid aside the stave and, yelling for the stable-boy, slid back the bracing beam and flung open the gate. There was a clatter of iron horseshoes on the cobbles as Robert's mount trotted in, and Tenney hurried to close and brace the gate.

Robert leaned forward over his horse's neck, trying to swing himself onto the mounting block. He was visibly wincing and his movements were stiff and clumsy, as if he were injured. Adam remained standing at the casement. He was in no hurry to greet his father. If he was in pain, his temper would be worse than usual. As if he were watching a wild pigeon dragging a broken wing, he was curious, but he felt strangely unconcerned. He couldn't even be bothered to go down to the great hall and tell Catlin her husband was home, and he knew Leonia wouldn't.

Turning his head he said softly, 'Robert's here.'

Leonia smiled. 'Told you he'd come today,' she whispered. But she hadn't told anyone else.

She was sitting on a chair, combing her long black curls. She had already put on the blue gown with the gold trim Robert had bought for her. Not the necklace, though. It had gone. Leonia said her mother had taken it, and Adam was sure she was right – she always was. She'd been furious, but she'd said not a word to Catlin.

'I'll punish her for that, but not yet. I want to make her wait.'

346

Adam shivered with excitement, thinking of Fulk lying on the warehouse floor, his face a mass of blood. He wanted to ask how she would punish Catlin, but he knew she wouldn't tell him till she was ready.

'What about them?' Adam pointed to the floor below.

Leonia smiled. 'Wait . . . Wait till he comes in.'

Adam glanced back out of the casement. Tenney had taken the reins from Robert's hand and thrust them at the stable-boy. 'Hold the beast steady, lad. Here, Master Robert, put your weight on my shoulder.'

It took several minutes for Robert to ease himself to the ground. He stood there, bent over like an old man. Then, with obvious effort, he pulled himself upright and limped towards the door.

Leonia crossed the solar and ran down the stairs, closely followed by Adam. She flung herself at Robert, seizing one of his hands and kissing it. 'I've been so worried, Père. I feared something terrible had happened.'

Robert hugged her, though his eyes closed briefly as if the movement caused him pain. He fingered her soft, glossy curls, but as he glanced up, Adam saw his expression harden at the sight of Edward and Catlin sitting side by side, murmuring to one another, when he entered.

Catlin rose gracefully to her feet, but the smile on her lips did not reach her eyes. 'What a delightful surprise, Robert. We weren't expecting you. The news is so grave from London, I thought you might have been detained there longer. Were you received well at John of Gaunt's palace? You must tell us about its splendours. I hear it is magnificent.'

'I saw no splendours in London,' Robert said dully. 'Only ashes.'

His gaze wandered back to the young man, who had not even had the courtesy to rise from the chair in which he was lounging. 'Master Edward – still here? I'd thought you would be out searching for employment. You must be sorely in need of some means of supporting yourself, though perhaps you have already found work. You've bought some fine new clothes, I see.'

'I've indeed been fortunate enough to secure a position,' Edward said, with a grin. 'My mother has engaged me as your new steward.'

Robert's face flushed with anger and he rounded on Catlin. 'Since when does a wife engage a steward for her husband's business? When

I'm ready to replace my son I'll find my own steward. I told you I would not employ Edward. He knows nothing of the business.'

'But you did not find a steward, did you, Robert?' Catlin said tartly. 'And while you were away being entertained in London, there was an accident at the warehouse. Your overseer, Fulk, a lifting hook hit him in the face. By some miracle he lives, but his jaw and nose were smashed. The bone-setter and physician have done what they can, but he cannot speak, and even if he mends, they say the blow to the head has driven his wits from him. Who knows if they will return?'

'Fulk? God's blood!' Robert lowered himself stiffly into a chair. 'Was it the Florentines who did this?'

Adam's gaze flicked to Leonia, but her expression gave nothing away.

'It was an accident, wasn't it, Adam?' Catlin said. 'Your son saw it happen.'

Adam felt his face grow hot as his father turned to him.

'Carelessness by one of the men?'

Adam's eyes darted back to Leonia. She held his gaze steadily, giving just the tiniest nod.

Adam lifted his head. 'The rope hadn't been tied off properly. The knot must have worked loose and it swung down and hit him. No one can remember who tied it.'

'But *you* should have checked it. You must always check up on the men! Haven't I told you that a hundred times?'

'But, Père, Fulk was the overseer,' Leonia said, her eyes brimming with innocence. 'Shouldn't he have checked?'

Robert's tired eyes softened. 'Yes, my dear. I suppose the man has only himself to blame, when all is said and done.'

'So you see, Robert,' Catlin said, 'with the men so careless even when they are closely supervised, I was in despair, fearing for what might happen to your business with no one to direct them. I had to engage someone until you returned, and who better than my own son? At least we know we can trust him. I don't have your experience in employing men, Robert. I daren't risk hiring a stranger for fear he might turn out to be a thief or a rogue.'

'My poor mother couldn't possibly be expected to run the business with neither steward nor overseer to guide her and to direct the men. I felt compelled to offer my services, at least until you returned.'

Catlin gazed earnestly at Robert, her expression now as soft and gentle as her daughter's. 'Please tell me I have done right, my sweeting. I couldn't bear it if you were angry with me.'

Robert still looked far from happy, but he said grudgingly, 'I suppose I could hardly expect a woman . . . But now that I've returned I will take control.'

'But you still need a steward,' Catlin reminded him. 'And since Edward has so gallantly stepped in to help me, it would be ungrateful and churlish to dispense with his services. Besides, what would be the point? You'd only have to put yourself to the great trouble of finding another.'

Adam had never seen his father so exhausted. There was a bruise on his cheek, and the way he kept his arm wrapped about his ribcage made him wonder if he'd been thrown from the horse.

Diot waddled in with a jug of wine, which she set before Robert. ''Tis a mercy you returned home safe, Master Robert. Mistress has been fretting something fierce for you, pining away she has. She's such a faithful, tender heart, just like her poor mother.'

She darted a sly grin at Catlin, whose eyes flashed menace. Diot's grin instantly fell from her face and she busied herself pouring a goblet of wine for Robert.

'Pining' was not the word Robert would have used to describe his wife's demeanour when he'd entered the hall, but he was too sore and weary to pursue the thought. He took several deep gulps from the goblet Diot handed to him.

'Apart from the accident at the warehouse, has all been peaceful here? Tenney came armed to the gate. Has someone tried to break into the house again?'

Diot and Catlin both started to speak at once, but Catlin silenced Diot with a look.

'We received word that rebels from London are marching up to York, and they plan to come through Lincoln. I ordered Tenney to make the house as safe as he could and—'

'They say Norwich's been sacked,' Diot interrupted. 'Houses burned, and the justice of the peace dragged from his own bed, set in the pillory and beheaded there, like a common felon. That can't be true, can it, Master Robert? What'll we do if they come here?'

Robert closed his eyes, pressing his hand across his mouth, trying to stop himself vomiting. His fingers were trembling. He took a deep breath. 'Lincoln's safe for now. The rebels were turned back at

Huntingdon yesterday. The townspeople came out and barred the bridge, so they couldn't cross the Ouse. It's a bridge that's easily defended and the only crossing place for miles.'

'But what of your mission, Robert?' Catlin asked. 'Shall John of Gaunt send men to defend us?'

Robert heaved himself to his feet, with a grunt of pain. 'Gaunt's still in Scotland, but the rebellion's crushed in London. Wat Tyler, one of their leaders, was killed when he went to make his demands of the King, who led the rebels into a trap. He accounted himself well, I'm told.'

'Then it's over,' Catlin said. 'Thanks be to the Blessed Virgin, we're safe.'

'How can it be over,' Diot whined, 'if they burned down Norwich and Ipswich, and Cambridge too, so they say? We'll be butchered in our beds, I know it.'

'Stop screeching, you old baggage,' Edward said, rising from his chair. 'You're worse than the market alewives. *Saints preserve us, the sky's falling in!*' he wailed, hunching his back and pressing his face into Diot's, waggling his finger in a cruel imitation.

She jerked away. 'One of these days, Master Edward . . .' she spat. 'I'll not be mocked. You'll be—'

'Edward's only teasing, Diot,' Catlin said soothingly. 'You know how fond he is of you. You're as dear to us as if you were our own family. And we will take care of you. You don't need to fear the rebels, Diot, not *them.*'

The old woman frowned, gnawing her lip. Edward, grinning maliciously, snatched up a goblet and thrust it towards her, waiting for her to fill it with wine. Diot pushed past him and waddled towards the kitchen, muttering that she didn't care what anyone said, she'd be sleeping with a knife in her hand from now on.

Edward poured wine into his goblet. 'Little Maman's right. None of us needs worry about a few ragged labourers armed with pitchforks. Robert's only a merchant, not a justice of the peace. What reason would they have to kill him or us?'

'They don't need a reason,' Robert said, staring at the wooden table.

He was silent for a few moments. Then, with a great effort, he seemed to pull himself out of his reverie. 'If you're acting as my steward, Edward, we'd best go to the warehouse and you can show me what precautions you've taken.'

Edward waved a hand dismissively. 'You don't need to trouble yourself with that today. Such a journey at your age . . .' He faltered under Robert's furious glare. 'Besides, there's little to see at the warehouse. I've set men to keep watch, and I've moved some of the more valuable goods into the castle, in case they should set fires at the quay.'

'What?' Robert cried, and clutched at his ribs. 'You've put them in the one place the rebels are bound to attack!'

'Several merchants have done the same,' Catlin said. 'They won't storm the castle. They wouldn't dare attack Gaunt's property.'

But Robert was already halfway out of the door, yelling at Edward to follow. Edward's eyes flashed wide at Catlin in silent appeal for her to intervene, but she merely shrugged indifferently and he had no choice but to follow Robert.

As soon as the two men had left the hall, Leonia looked up at Catlin, with disarming innocence. 'You didn't think Père was coming back, did you, Mother? You thought he was going to die in London.'

Adam stared at Leonia, but she merely continued to gaze, wide-eyed, at her mother.

'Naturally, I was terrified your stepfather might come to harm. I prayed daily for his safe return.'

'Is that where you go every afternoon? Do you go to *pray*, Mother?'

Chapter 53

A family will only prosper if an animal be buried alive in the walls or floors of the house, so that its spirit will lend the house strength and it will not fall or burn.

Greetwell

'Set us down here,' Gunter told the carter.

The man reined in the horse and swivelled round. 'You're sure you don't want me to take you to the Gilbertine priory? It's only a little further and I hear they've a good infirmary.'

'His mam'll tend him. He'll mend.'

Gunter slipped an arm under his son and tried to lift him, but the boy yelped.

'Let me help you.' The carter slid down from his perch and came round to the back of the cart. He helped Gunter pull the boy forward so that Gunter could sling his son over his shoulder.

'He doesn't look too good,' the carter said doubtfully.

Hankin's face was pale and beaded with sweat. His eyes were screwed up against the pain. The back of his tunic was shredded to ribbons, and pale, watery blood was once again seeping through the bandages beneath.

'He'll be better when he's in his bed,' Gunter said firmly.

'You're not planning to carry him home?'

'It's not far by the track.'

The carter shrugged and climbed up to the seat, slapping the reins on the back of the horse. Gunter shouted his thanks and the man lifted a hand in acknowledgement, but did not turn again.

Gunter waited until the cart had disappeared round the bend, then made for the river. It was difficult to scramble down the steep bank with the boy across his shoulder. Several times he slipped and Hankin cried out as the movement jerked him but Gunter reached the bottom safely and laid him gently on the grass next to the water. He hunkered down beside his son to wait, massaging his aching stump. The end was rubbed raw and bleeding inside the wooden leg, but he daren't take it off to examine the wound, fearing that if he did, he wouldn't be able to cram it back into the hollow. Time enough to see to it when he'd got the boy safely home.

He prayed that one of the boatmen he knew would come along soon, and would agree to take them to Greetwell. Boats passed, but he didn't know the men aboard. He let them go. He'd no money to pay a stranger.

He'd not dared to let the carter know he was a boatman or allow him to carry them to the cottage, though it would have spared both himself and Hankin more pain. They were hunting the rebels down right across the country. Henry Despenser, the Bishop of Norwich, was leading a company of men-at-arms through the fenlands, trying and hanging rebels on the spot wherever he found them. It would take only a casual remark from the carter that he had given a lift to a wounded boy to bring soldiers thundering to their door. Safer if the man didn't know where Gunter lived or his occupation. That way they couldn't be traced.

Gunter had watched the men returning from Smithfield. A long, shabby procession, wearily dragging their feet, flanked by the King's men on horseback escorting them over the ruins of London Bridge and out of the city. People said one of the rebel leaders, a man called Tyler, had been stabbed as he presented his demands to the young King. Richard had assumed command, urging the rebels to follow him away from the town to Clerkenwell fields, but once there they'd found themselves surrounded. When they saw Tyler's head on a pike, they'd surrendered and the King had allowed most of them to return in peace to their homes, but not for long. Now he was seeking vengeance. Gunter looked at his son. He was only a few months younger than King Richard. His youth would not protect him.

Gunter had carried Hankin out of the city on his back, but had straightway taken a different track from the Essex men. He'd guessed what was coming. He'd begged lifts on carts, wagons and boats, and one old woman had taken pity on him and let the boy ride on her donkey. An accident, Gunter had told them all. The horse pulling their cart had been startled and bolted. The boy had fallen under the wheel. The cart and horse were lost.

The carters had nodded sympathetically. 'It happens. Why, there was this one time when . . .'

Everyone had a story of tragedy or near disaster to tell. That was life. Misfortune always struck when you least expected it.

Hankin moaned. The sun beat down on him. Gunter went to the river, wetted the edge of his tunic, came back and dabbed his son's sweating face with it, squeezing a few filthy drops between the boy's cracked lips.

He rose and shielded his eyes with his hand, scanning the river for any face he knew. He'd have to invent a new story for the boatmen. They'd know he'd never owned a cart. He only hoped he could make the boy understand. His wits were wandering in his fever. If he should let slip the wrong word, they might both hang or worse.

There was something else, something he'd tried hard to push beneath the surface of his mind, but it kept floating back. Had Master Robert recognised him on that London street? The man had seemed so dazed and terrified it was hard to tell if he'd even seen him. But suppose Robert had remembered. Suppose he came looking for Gunter. How would he explain what he was doing in London?

Gunter cursed himself. He'd been a fool to interfere. Why hadn't he let the man die? What had Master Robert ever done for him? If only he had turned the other way, or passed along that street just a few moments later, it would all have been over. Yet he knew that if it happened again, he would try to save him. It would have been different if Robert had been a stranger, but a man can't just stand by and watch someone they know be slaughtered, can he?

July

A swarm of bees in July is not worth a butterfly.

Chapter 54

To discover a thief, take a cock from the hen house and place him under a pail. Let each of those suspected touch the pail and the cock will crow when the thief touches it.

Lincoln

'What do you mean *stolen*?' Edward shouted. 'You had a dozen bales of Lincoln Green cloth in that load.'

The wagoner looked sullen. 'Not my fault, so it's not. You want to be complaining to the bishop, you do. That stretch of road is his responsibility. Goes through his lands. Bushes and trees so thick with leaves alongside that track, a dozen warhorses could be keeping pace with you and you'd never know. He's supposed to see to it the branches are cut back so footpads can't lie in wait behind them. Half a dozen of them, there was. Leaped out at me, they did, and threw this stinking sack over my head, tied me up and left me. Took me an age to free myself.'

'Six?' Edward said. 'So you had time enough to count them before they trussed you up.'

The wagoner glowered at him. 'There was a swarm of them, at any rate. It's a miracle I'm not lying dead in ditch.' The man fingered a swollen black eye.

Edward groaned. 'When Robert finds out I didn't use one of our regular men, he'll have a fit of apoplexy. Though, knowing my luck, it won't be fatal, more's the pity. I don't know why I let myself be talked into trusting you.'

''Cause I charge half what your regulars do,' the wagoner said. 'They're robbing you blind. You got a good bargain from me.'

'Not when you lost me my goods, I didn't!'

The wagoner was a squat, well-muscled man, who could easily have got the better of Edward in a fist fight, but Edward had the advantage of height. He took a step closer to the man, so that he was looking

357

down at him. 'How do I know you're not in league with them? You could have arranged the whole thing.' He poked a finger at the wagoner's bruised eye. 'You could have asked one to give you this, just to back up your story. Worth suffering a bruise or two for your share of a heavy purse.'

The man took a step or two back from the jabbing finger. 'Now, you look here. I'm not in league with outlaws. Honest Jack, that's me, ask anyone.'

'Then you'll be eager to tell me who these thieves are and where they took my cloth,' Edward said, closing the distance between himself and the wagoner again, driving the man perilously close to the wharf's edge.

'Had their faces half covered so I wouldn't recognise them even they was to pass me in the street. But if you was to ask me—'

He broke off, as he caught sight of Master Robert emerging from the side of the warehouse. He came limping towards them, his arm wrapped around his ribs and brow creased in pain. Edward swore softly but so foully that even the hardened wagoner looked startled.

Robert's gaze darted suspiciously from Edward to the wagoner and back again. 'Trouble?' he demanded. 'What's happened?'

'Everything's fine,' Edward said soothingly, as if he were placating a child. 'You should be at home resting, as Hugo Bayus advised. You mustn't neglect your new bride, you know.'

'Your mother's out riding,' Robert said coldly. 'And I can hardly rest knowing my business is in the hands of a squab.' He jerked his chin towards the wagoner. 'Has this man been fighting with our paggers?'

'I have not, Master!' the wagoner broke in indignantly before Edward could answer. 'I was defending your cloth from the ruffians who ambushed my wagon.' He pointed to his black eye. 'Got this for my pains, so I did.'

Now that he'd started, the wagoner was determined to pour out the whole story and Edward could do nothing except watch Robert's face turn from pink to purple, like a rapidly ripening plum.

Robert, breathing hard, turned on Edward. 'And what happened to the man you sent to ride with him to keep a look-out?'

'Only trying to save you money,' Edward muttered sulkily. 'You're always complaining about how much you have to pay out in wages. Why pay two men?'

358

'*Why pay two men?*' Robert repeated incredulously. 'I'm surprised you didn't just load my cloth onto an ox cart and send the beasts to find their own way to York. That way you wouldn't need to pay any man at all.'

Edward opened his mouth, but Robert had already started talking to the wagoner.

'You said you were attacked not far from Burton? They won't risk carrying the bales far in daylight. They'll have hidden them somewhere close by and they'll retrieve them after dark. Probably try to move them by river – that would be the safest for them. Foss Dyke's the nearest and from there they could get them out onto the Trent and go north or south. So they're bound to have a boat waiting north of Burton fens – the water's too low south of that. Right, then, you'll come with me now to Sheriff Thomas. Lead his men back to the spot where you were ambushed, so that they can hide and wait.

'And as for you, you numbskull,' Robert said, glaring at Edward, 'you can go with them. A night lying in the fens among the midges might teach you to think in future. And you'd better pray to every saint you can name that Thomas's men recover my cloth, or you'll find yourself walking out of Lincoln in beggars' rags, because I will be taking everything you own to pay for it.'

He turned to walk away, but Edward leaped forward, grabbed Robert's arm and spun him round, taking immense satisfaction at hearing the gasp of pain as his ribs were jolted.

'I'll be going nowhere in rags. Have you forgotten the money you lost for us with that stupid investment on *St Jude*? My mother may have kept silent about it, but that doesn't mean I will.'

Robert jerked his sleeve from the young man's grasp. He was shaking with rage. 'How dare you threaten me? It was your mother's money that was invested, not yours, and I have more than made up for it now. As my wife, she shares everything I own. But you are entitled to nothing and that is exactly what you will get from me!'

Chapter 55

When a woman has been overlooked by the evil eye and has the falling sickness, she may be cured if nine bachelors each give her a scrap of silver and a coin. The silver is to be made into a ring, which she must wear ever more, and the coins given in payment to the ring-maker. If a man is so afflicted, then the silver and coins must be given to him by nine virgin maids.

Lincoln

That hag Eadhild has found me again. I felt her scabby hand creeping round my thigh as we gathered in the churchyard in the dark of night, standing silent among the yew trees, watching, waiting.

A girl had been newly buried there on the north side among the felons, the mad and the unbaptised babies. She had committed self-murder, hanged herself from the beam in her mother's byre, so the compassionate and merciful priests refused her a Christian burial. They laid her face down in the earth and sprinkled her with salt to try to keep her in her grave, but we knew she would not stay. It was Eadhild who called her forth.

'Killed herself for love,' the old hag said, 'like me, and like me she'll take her vengeance on the faithless one who betrayed her.'

The old hag stood at the foot of the grave, beneath the blind windows of the church and stretched out her scabby hand. There came a shrieking deep within the earth, as if a mandrake were being wrenched from the ground. The girl rose, pale as bone, from the mound, the rope still about her neck. The tears in her eyes now burned as flames and the lips he'd kissed had turned black with his treachery. From that hour, her faithless lover would sleep no more.

But not all men are faithless. There was one man in Lincoln who had discovered too late that he loved a woman, but now that he had, he was determined not to abandon her.

*

360

'I have told you repeatedly, you cannot see her,' the nun said wearily. 'It disturbs the women to have strangers about.'

'But I'm no stranger,' Tenney said. 'Known Beata for years, I have, ever since she were a young lass come to work for Master Robert.' He peered anxiously through the grille in the gate, but could see little more than the top of a wimple and a pair of eyes surrounded by wrinkles.

'I'm sorry,' the nun said, in a tone that made it plain she wasn't at all.

The shutter that covered the grille was slammed across. But it wasn't until Tenney turned away from the gate of St Magdalene's that he remembered he was still clutching the basket. He raised his hand to ring the bell again, but let it fall. He'd called there nearly every day since he'd been forced to deliver Beata to the nuns. Each time he went, he pleaded with them to let him see her, if only for a minute. But they refused. He would hand over the little gift he'd brought for her – sweet-smelling roses or a bunch of ribbons, a roasted sheep's-foot or a basket of ripe pears – and they assured him they would give them to her. But Beata had sent no word to him in return.

He wondered if she had told them not to admit him. He wouldn't blame her if she had. He'd lied to her. Told her she would stay there only a week or two so she could get some rest. Then he'd come and fetch her again. She'd been so tormented from lack of sleep that she couldn't seem to take in what he was saying. But the moment the gate had closed on her terrified face, he knew he'd done the wrong thing. Not an hour had passed since when he hadn't cursed himself for it. He should have ignored Master Robert's orders and taken her instead to his cousin's cottage, hidden her there until she was well. He prayed the nuns were treating her kindly.

'I take it you haven't told him.' The deep, rasping voice came from just behind Tenney. 'I've been watching the house and the women are still there.'

Godwin was squatting against the wall of St Magdalene's, but he hauled himself slowly to his feet, his hand pressed to the rough stone. The man seemed, if anything, more gaunt and hag-ridden than when Tenney had last seen him. He stood for a moment, bent double, catching his breath, and in his mind Tenney saw again the ghastly image of the scarred skin beneath the man's shirt, drawn tight across the bony ribs.

361

'You don't care if your master lives or dies, is that it? Or is it that you didn't believe me?'

'They'll not let me alone with him,' Tenney said. 'Those women put the evil eye on my Beata, I'd swear it. It was as if there were hands about her throat, choking her, when she tried to speak out against them. Master Robert had her put in here as if she were a stranger to him instead of a woman who's cared for him and his own for years.'

Godwin came closer, his dark eyes bright as black flames. 'So you do believe me. You've seen their sorcery for yourself.'

'Aye, and I've seen what happened to a poor innocent woman who tried to stop them.' He gazed up at the grim high walls of St Magdalene's. 'I tried to ride with Master Robert to London, thinking I'd be able to tell him all then, for if I was far enough away, their curses couldn't reach me. But she put a stop to me going, as if she knew what I meant to do.'

'Then I must try to speak to your master again,' Godwin said. 'What more can she do to me that she's not already done?'

Tenney plucked at his thick beard. 'You can try, but I don't reckon you'll get near him, never mind make him tarry long enough to listen to your tale. I don't rightly know what happened in London, but he's been as wary as a whipped hound ever since, shies from his own shadow. Seems to think every man is out to do him harm, everyone except her, of course, and that brat of hers. They're the only ones he trusts now.'

Godwin reached into his shirt. He stumbled closer to Tenney, holding out a blackened object, about the size of a walnut. Tenney bent over and peered at it. Then jerked his head back.

'Looks like the hand of an imp! Wherever did you get it?'

The thing resembled a tiny human hand with five curled fingers, but the back of the hand was covered with dense hair as black as the wrinkled skin on the palm.

'A monkey's paw,' Godwin said. 'A sailor aboard the ship I came home on gave it to me. Saw the wounds on my chest and my arm and said I could do with a change of luck. It is a powerful amulet. It was only through its help I tracked the witch Catlin down. It will protect you. Throw it on the ground between yourself and the witch when she is casting any spell and it will break the enchantment.' Godwin again held it out to him. 'Take it.'

'What am I supposed to do with it? Wander around behind the master, day and night, flinging this down every time I fear mischief?'

'Fool,' Godwin said impatiently. 'Use it to protect yourself while you warn him.' He thrust it into Tenney's hand.

Tenney recoiled. The fingers were cold, leathery, but the palm was unexpectedly soft. It was like holding the hand of a dead baby. He hesitated. It looked more evil than the witchcraft it was supposed to guard against. But that was often the way, for Father Remigius said the Almighty had fashioned each herb to resemble the sicknesses it had been created to cure so that man would know which to use. And God had certainly created monkeys, or Tenney supposed He had.

Tenney hastily thrust the monkey's paw into the leather scrip that dangled from his belt. It could do no harm, and he was sorely in need of any help he could get, no matter where it came from. He slid his arm from the basket and held it out to Godwin. 'A pie in there.' Then, seeing the wary expression on Godwin's face, he added, 'Don't fret, I bought it myself in the market. It's not been near the house.'

Godwin impatiently thrust it away. 'Don't want your charity,' he said gruffly.

'I brought it for Beata, but the nuns'll not let me give it her. Not taking it home for that gannet, Diot, to thieve.'

Seeing that Godwin still would not take it, Tenney set the basket on the ground and walked away.

'The girl . . . Beware of the girl more than any of them,' came the gruff voice behind him. 'Her powers grow stronger by the day and with them grows her hunger.'

Chapter 56

The hand of a man hanged on the gallows has healing powers.
If it be stroked across a sore, tumour or goitre, the evil shall pass
to the dead man and the sick will be cured. If a woman be barren
she should go to a gibbet at night, climb up and reach through
the bars and draw the corpse's hand across her womb three or
seven times and her curse will leave her.

Lincoln

Tenney heard the two horses in the stable whinny as they sensed Master Robert's horse approaching down the street. He'd been listening all morning for his master's return. His horse always gave a distinctive snort as it came close to the gate, as if it knew it would soon be relieved of its burden and be able to bury its nose in a bucket of oats.

Tenney snatched up the monkey's paw and hurried out. He still hated the feel of the thing, but it gave him courage to have it in his hand. If he could get the gate open before the master had a chance to ring the bell, then with luck the three women would be so busy yammering to the sheriff in the house that they wouldn't realise he had returned. Tenney was determined he would tell him today, right now, even if he had to drag him into the kitchen and bar his way until he'd heard all.

Robert looked mildly surprised to see Tenney rushing out to open the gate while he was still a yard from it, but he made no comment as his manservant caught the reins he handed to him.

'Master Robert, there's summit I must tell you in private. You're not going to like it, but you have to know. I've done you good service over the years and I reckon I've earned the right to ask you to hear me out.'

'Whatever it is, I'm not discussing it in the street.' Robert looked anxiously around as if he feared any passer-by might be holding an assassin's knife. 'It can surely wait until I'm off this damned horse. Lead us inside, man.'

Tenney hesitated, clutching the monkey's paw tighter in his great fist. But the horse could smell its own stable just feet away and would not be prevented from reaching it now. Before Tenney could make up his mind, it barged through the gate.

'Thing is, Master Robert . . .' Tenney began, as Robert pressed down heavily on his shoulder to dismount.

'Père,' Leonia's voice called cheerfully. Both men looked up as she came running across the yard. 'Thomas Thimbleby of Poolham has come to see you.'

'The sheriff? God's bones, why didn't you tell me he was waiting, Tenney? The sheriff wouldn't come in person to my house at this hour unless it was important. Maybe Jan's murderer's been discovered.'

Tenney tried to step in front of him. 'But, Master Robert, I must speak—'

'Later, man, later,' Robert said impatiently.

Leonia flattened herself against the wall as Robert hastened past her and into the hall. She looked back at Tenney, standing helplessly in the courtyard, and tossed him one of her most innocent smiles. 'People always say I'll listen *later*, don't they, Tenney? But when they finally do, it's always *too* late.' She vanished into the dark shadow of the house.

Sheriff Thomas was seated at the table, mopping up the juices and last fragments of flesh from some herrings with a morsel of bread, which he stuffed into his mouth with the eager appetite of a man who'd missed his breakfast. His well-fleshed face had grown increasingly haggard over the last few weeks. What had been a post of honour had suddenly become one of immense responsibility and the burden was evidently taking its toll.

Catlin was standing close to him, so close that for a moment Robert wondered if Thomas and Catlin were . . . He dismissed the thought with a shake of his head. Catlin was his new bride and Thomas was his friend. They'd never dream of cuckolding him.

'Is there trouble? Has there been another uprising?' he asked, too anxious to bother with any of the usual pleasantries.

The sheriff drained his mug of ale and looked hopefully about for more, which Catlin was quick to supply. 'It's to prevent more trouble that I'm here,' he answered, taking another swig. 'A royal messenger arrived last night. King Richard's declared that all the charters granting manumission to the villeins that he was forced to sign while the rebels were attacking London are to be cancelled. He's met with the envoys from Essex and told them that the villeins will not be freed from their obligations. They'll remain as bondsmen for ever and so will all their descendants. Not only that: because of the murder and destruction they carried out, he told them their servitude will be harsher than it's ever been before under a King of England.'

'As they richly deserve!' Robert said firmly. 'What I witnessed in London . . .' He shut his eyes at the memory. 'Granting freedom to them would be like allowing a pack of wolves to roam about our cities.'

'But won't that inflame them the more?' Catlin asked.

The sheriff pursed his lips. 'I don't doubt that it will, but the young King is determined to rule with a fist of steel. Gibbet cages are being erected in every village and town, even where there's never been one before, and plenty of men are being executed to fill them. Bishop Despenser has hanged, drawn and quartered some of the ringleaders himself. Others have been cut to pieces wherever they've been caught. Apparently the rebels slaughtered some Flemish merchants in London. I don't know if you heard of it when you were there, Robert?'

Robert swallowed hard. There were nights when he woke himself with a cry almost as loud as Beata's. He dreamed about those heaps of corpses, feet pinning him as the vast crimson lake crept towards him.

Thomas did not appear to notice the effect his words were having. 'The King's messenger said that instead of handing the guilty men over to the executioners they delivered them to the widows, mothers and daughters of the Flemish merchants and told the women to hack the heads off those who'd killed their menfolk. Old ladies wielding axes – have you heard of such a thing? But Richard is determined to round up every last man or boy who took part in the rebellion and there's to be no mercy shown any of them.'

He leaned forward. 'That's what brings me here, Robert. He's ordered every county to set up a Commission of Array at once to draw up plans to put down any new rebellion at the first whiff of trouble but also to seek out the names of any men or boys who took part in the rebellion. They're to be arrested, questioned and the details of their crimes sent to London. I don't think we'll find many from these parts, but we must try to produce some names, to show our

366

loyalty to the throne. This is certainly not a good time for any man or, indeed, city to have their allegiance questioned.'

Thomas's expression was as grave as Robert had ever seen it, and with good reason.

'On the King's orders I must appoint ten commissioners and, of course, knowing how faithfully you represented our merchants in London, you'll be eager to do your duty as one of them.'

'No! I . . . I can't do it!' Robert rose abruptly from his chair and crossed to the casement, standing with his hands behind his back, staring out at the street. 'I've neglected my business for too long . . . I haven't the time.'

'I haven't made myself clear,' Thomas said. 'It wouldn't be a question of you having to seek out these rebels yourself. I have informers to do that. If people are questioned directly, we will learn nothing. This has to be done subtly. Men drinking quietly in taverns listening to the gossip, women encouraged to report anything suspicious among their neighbours, in exchange for a few pennies. No, the commissioners are simply there to order the arrests of any reported to them and question them about their crimes. A few meetings are all that's required.'

'I'm not the man for this,' Robert said, turning to face him. 'There are many others who'd be far more capable.'

'But most have only heard the stories of destruction and murder. Few others in Lincoln have witnessed it in person, as you've done. You know, first-hand, what these rebels did, Robert. You know what questions to ask of them. We need your counsel.'

The sheriff rose and swung his cloak about his shoulders. 'It would do your business no harm if you came to King Richard's attention as a man who'd worked to bring his enemies to the gallows. When he needs merchants to provision the army, and indeed his own court, he'll be looking for loyal men.'

Thomas crossed to the door, pausing to take Catlin's hand and raise it to his lips. Still holding her hand, his gaze darted to Robert, who was standing with his back to him at the window. 'See if you can persuade your husband, Mistress Catlin. I sorely need his services,' he said. Then he bent his head so that his mouth was almost touching Catlin's ear, his fingers briefly caressed the trembling pulse at her throat. 'A neck as pretty as this deserves to be hung with only the finest gold and jewels,' he whispered. 'And I have it on good authority, there will be a deal of money to be made from this, perhaps in time even an invitation to the King's court. And you would surely outshine any other woman there. Try your best, Mistress Catlin. You could coax a man to anything.'

Almost as soon as the door had closed, Robert felt Catlin snuggle up beside him, her hand slipping into his and her fingers entwining themselves about his own. 'You're too modest, Robert. You'd do a splendid job as a commissioner. You deserve this honour.'

Robert snatched his hand from hers. 'It's not an honour. It's a death sentence. As soon as the rebels discover who the commissioners are they'll target them and their property to ensure they're silenced. Do you think I want to see my warehouse burned to the ground, or feel a knife in my back, or have poor little Leonia kidnapped or threatened?'

'No rebel would dare to harm an important man like you, Robert,' Catlin said.

'They cut off the head of the Archbishop of Canterbury, so they certainly wouldn't hesitate to murder me.'

He hadn't told her how they'd forced him down in the filth of the street, how he had been moments from having his own head added to those being kicked like balls about the streets. He couldn't bear to think of it, never mind speak of it. He cringed at the humiliation, made worse by the knowledge that he would have died pleading for his life.

'But the archbishop was killed by a great mob in London,' Catlin said. 'This is Lincoln. Who would hurt you here? You heard the regard the sheriff has for you. I think he plans to make you head of the Commission. Think of it, Robert, think of the business you would gain – royal business, he said. You're always complaining about the Florentines and foreign merchants undercutting you and stealing your trade. With the money you'd make from royal patronage you could open a dozen new warehouses, employ a score of men to buy wool and cloth for you. You could drive every foreign merchant in Lincolnshire out of business and out of this city, just like that.' She snapped her fingers.

He rounded on her, fury and fear in his eyes. 'And what good would a dozen warehouses be to me if I am lying in a grave next to my son?'

'You said you wanted justice for what the Florentines did to Jan.

This would be your chance to destroy them. I can't believe you'd let a few miserable villeins intimidate you. Have I mistaken you, Robert? I thought you were a man of strength, a man who was afraid of no one, a man who could protect his family. Have I married a coward?'

Chapter 57

A witch cannot die until her familiars or imps are dead. If a witch desires to put an end to her suffering she must call each familiar by name and order it to die. Then, when the last is dead, she too will die.

Greetwell

Edward's horse tossed her head irritably in the heat, trying to rid herself of the cloud of flies crawling round her eyes. Edward flapped them away from his own face with as much irritation. Strictly speaking, of course, it was not *his* horse. If it had been, it would have been meat for the hounds and hide for the tanner's yard long ago. The nag was well past her prime, broken-winded, her belly distended, her flanks shuddering as she heaved. But that old tight-purse, Robert, reckoned the horse still had another year of work left in her, provided she was walked, not galloped. What more did Edward need to carry him around the environs of the city? *A bloody sight more*, he thought sourly.

The afternoon sun burned hot on his back and head. He tried to turn the horse sideways so that he could get some relief from the miserly shade of the spindly birch tree, but the stubborn mare was having none of it. She had her own head in the shade and refused to move. He glanced back up the track towards the city. God's arse, where was the woman? Catlin always thought the entire world would wait on her pleasure. She was always disappearing on some mysterious errand or other. A more suspicious man, he thought, might wonder if she had a lover.

He'd almost decided to turn for home when he spotted her trotting towards him along the riverbank astride her perky little palfrey, whose chestnut hide gleamed red in the hot sun. Her mount seemed deliberately to lift its head as they approached, flaunting its youth and vigour in the face of the swollen-kneed old mare. The sight did nothing to lighten Edward's mood.

'I've been waiting for hours,' he snapped.

Catlin pursed her lips in annoyance, and the sunlight mercilessly exposed the deep wrinkles that were forming at her mouth. Catlin, Edward thought, was beginning to look her age.

'Leonia delayed me. She's becoming tiresome. She flirts with Robert like some marketplace whore.'

Edward chuckled. 'Jealous, are we? Young Leonia knows exactly what she does to men and how to get them to pour everything she wants into her lap. And you of all people can hardly blame her for that. She's been taught by a mistress of the art. '

Catlin glowered at him. 'She certainly has Robert by the nose.'

'That's a good thing, surely. It distracts her. Let her play with him for now. She's headstrong and you can only force her hand so far. This whole affair will be far easier to manage if she consents to it willingly.'

'You're a fool if you think she'll walk blindly into this with a sweet smile,' Catlin snapped. She shook her head as if a thought was buzzing around it. 'The way she looks at me, the questions she asks, with that wide-eyed innocent expression, it's as if she knows everything I do and is laying some trap.'

'She's a child and knows nothing. How can she? You're her mother, you can keep her under control. Harsh discipline, little Maman, that's what she needs. Break her. Make her as afraid of you as that brat Adam is, and she'll do as she's told.'

Catlin gnawed at her lip. 'If anyone's afraid, it's me not her. You saw what she did to Beata.'

Edward stared at her. 'I thought you'd had a hand . . .'

'We both know Beata had to go, but I'd almost succeeded in persuading Robert to dismiss her. After she dashed the wine from his hand, he was already on the verge of it. It would only have taken one more incident and that was easily arranged. But Leonia . . . Beata was terrified of her in the end, and I'm starting to believe she had good reason.'

'Beata was mad,' Edward said. 'The mad howl at the moon and scream at the sight of water.' He leaned over and kissed Catlin. 'I can handle Leonia, little Maman, don't you worry. All that matters is that she stays safe and well until Robert is dead. And the point is, little Maman, when will that be? My dear stepfather looks as healthy as any man of his age, far too healthy. I warn you, I will not wait for my inheritance until that lecher's in his dotage.'

371

'This cannot be rushed, Edward. If he should fall sick so soon after his wife, then people will begin to remember what Jan said. If he'd met his death in London, no one would have questioned it, but now that he's back, I must work softly. But there's something far more urgent we must attend to first. Robert was on the verge of having you thrown out of this city after your stupidity in allowing that cloth to be stolen. He was even convinced you were in the pay of the gang of thieves. You know how he's been ever since the uprising. If he sees two birds sitting together on the thatch he's convinced they're plotting against him. Your threat to spread abroad that tale of *St Jude* didn't help. When will you learn that challenging men like Robert only makes them more intransigent? It took all my powers of persuasion, which are not inconsiderable, to stop him dragging you straight to Sheriff Thomas. If so much as a bent nail goes missing from another cargo, which it is bound to unless the thieves are caught, you will find yourself banished from Lincoln or, worse, on trial for your life.'

Edward scowled. 'Those bastards made me look like a fool. And thanks to them I was forced to spend half the night with Thomas's men on those hellish marshes, almost getting myself drowned, not to mention being eaten to death by midges the size of kestrels.' The mere memory of it made him scratch vigorously at his arms and neck. 'And after all that, the thieves didn't appear. Never mind conspiring with them, if I could lay my hands on them, I'd rip off their arms and shove them up their arses.'

Catlin gave an exasperated sigh. 'As it stands, Robert is bound to leave the bulk of his estate to Adam, not least to prevent you inheriting it if it should come to me. Naturally I could milk the business dry before Adam comes of age, but that would be tedious and it would leave the business in ruins, which means we'd get no more out of it. It would be much simpler if Robert were to make you his heir.'

'He's hardly likely to do that. You just said he'd gladly have me whipped out of town or better still hanged by the heels.' Edward plucked at his clothes, screwing up his face as if he was picking up a used arse-rag. 'Look at me! I'm dressed like a scabby serf and see what he gives me to ride! A nag that can barely stand upright on its own legs. The wages he pays barely leave me enough to place a single bet on a fighting cock at the pits. I won't stomach this for much longer. I insist you get rid of him now!'

Catlin turned her face fully towards him and met his gaze steadily.

The words she spoke next were uttered so quietly that afterwards Edward wondered if he had misheard them.

'Take care, Edward, take very great care. I am mistress of more than just Robert's house. We both know what I can command. Don't presume too much, or you will lose all.' Catlin's palfrey moved restlessly in the heat and she tugged at the reins, so sharply the mare whinnied in protest. The expression in Catlin's eyes was so chilling that Edward felt a shudder of fear. She had never spoken like that to him before. Something had changed.

But the next moment she was smiling sweetly, as if the conversation had never taken place. 'Edward, can you not see? If you were to deliver the thieves to Robert, not only would it clear you of any suspicion of involvement, but it would make him trust you like a son.'

Edward, still reeling, gaped at her. 'What? . . . And just how am I to do that? I told you, the thieves never came back that night. I have no idea who they are.'

'No, but the boatmen do or, at least, they have their suspicions. Diot heard something interesting yesterday when she went to Butwerk, concerning a certain boatman and his son. She told me she'd learned it in the marketplace, of course. One of these days I'll make her regret trying to deceive me, but I let her think her secret is safe for now. The snippets she brings me are useful.'

Catlin pointed with her riding whip. 'I believe the cottage we seek lies just round that bend.'

'The thief lives there?' Edward's eyes were bright with excitement.

'Not there, but in that cottage we'll learn what we need to know.' She glanced up at the sun. 'The menfolk will not be returning home for some hours yet.' She flicked her whip lightly across Edward's hand. 'Let me lead the conversation when we're in there. If you go in threatening in your usual fashion, we'll learn nothing. It takes sweet honey to draw out a splinter, not a knife.'

Catlin squeezed her palfrey's flanks. Her skirts brushed Edward's leg as she trotted past, leading the way down the track. The sweat was crawling down his face. His shirt was sticking unpleasantly to his back. He was overdressed for the heat. The high collar of his cotehardie chafed unpleasantly against his chin, and he was sure he was getting the first itchings of a heat-rash.

He watched Catlin's trim figure swaying gracefully in front of him, as her palfrey trotted along the path ahead. She looked as cool as if she had just emerged from the river, clad in a dark moss-green gown with a russet surcoat over it. Her long dark hair nestled on the back of her neck, caught up in the gold net caul beneath a round hat embroidered with unicorns. It was said that unicorns would lay their heads in a virgin's lap. Catlin was certainly no virgin, but she could persuade any man she pleased to lay his head in her lap. The thought of that lard-lump, Robert, doing so made him want to kill them both.

Catlin treated him as a child and expected him meekly to take whatever humiliations Robert handed out, as if he were a servant. *Be patient. Be quiet.* Well, his patience was fast running out. If she didn't act soon, he would act for her, and Robert would be lying in that graveyard alongside his wife and both his idiot sons before the month was out. It was high time, thought Edward, that he showed Catlin he could be just as ruthless as she was. Perhaps that would make her treat him with respect.

Edward brought down his whip sharply on his horse's flank. She leaped forward, but almost at once slowed to a leisurely amble. Edward cursed. It seemed to him the nag was walking even more slowly than usual to prove that she had no intention of behaving as frivolously as the young palfrey in front. He kicked her viciously, but only succeeded in making her skip sideways, coming perilously close to plunging them both into the river. He daren't risk the whip again and was forced to let her walk at her own pace, which did nothing to improve his mood.

When he finally caught up with Catlin, she was sitting astride her mount in the shade a little way from a cottage on the riverbank. As soon as he approached, she swung her leg gracefully over its back and dismounted. She handed him her reins and walked down the track towards the cottage. Edward was left to tether both horses in the cool of the trees, then hasten after her.

The cottage door was shut, an unusual sight at most times, but especially so in this heat. A small boy was squatting in front of it, firing stones from a sling at some invisible target in the reeds. As soon as he caught sight of them, the child scrambled up and fled. Catlin rapped on the door and stood back. A woman opened it a crack, peering out. Her face was flushed and her lank hair was escaping in greasy strands from beneath a linen cap.

'A fine day to you, goodwife. I'm Mistress Catlin, wife to Robert of Bassingham who owns this cottage. Your husband is Master Gunter, is he not? And you must be his wife, Nonie?'

374

The woman gave a clumsy bob behind the door. Her expression was one of undisguised fear. 'My man isn't here. He's out on the punt . . . won't be back for hours yet.'

'No matter. It's the cottage we've come to see. This is my son and Master Robert's new steward, Master Edward. He must make an inspection of the cottage.'

'Are we to be evicted?' Nonie's fear had evidently turned to sheer panic. 'Please, I've bairns to take care of! We've paid the rent. I know it was late. Gunter couldn't find the work and what with the poll tax . . . but next time, I swear—'

'Calm yourself, Goodwife Nonie.' Catlin smiled reassuringly. 'There's been no talk of eviction. But Master Edward must ensure that you're keeping the cottage in good order as you are required to and not letting it fall into disrepair.'

Nonie appeared far from reassured. 'But Master Jan inspected it only a few months ago.'

'Master Jan is dead and the new steward must see it for himself. Otherwise how will he know if its condition has got worse next year?'

'My bairn's sick,' Nonie said desperately. 'A fever . . . a contagion . . . you might catch it.'

'I heard talk in the marketplace of an *accident* that had befallen your boy,' Catlin said. 'That cannot be catching, surely.'

With obvious reluctance, Nonie opened the door, stepping aside to let Edward and Catlin enter. She made to close it again, but the heat and stench of the room were suffocating and Edward shot out his hand to stop her. 'Leave it open,' he said, flinging it wide. 'I need the light to make my inspection.'

In truth, there was so little to inspect in the cottage that a single glance might have been considered over-diligent. The furnishings consisted of nothing more than two narrow beds crammed against either wall and a rickety table newly cobbled together from assorted pieces of old wood fished from the river. Besides the woman, the only other occupants of the cottage were a thin, pale girl in the corner, about Leonia's age. At the sight of them she shrank onto her haunches on the beaten-earth floor, wrapping her arms tightly about herself and buried her face in her knees.

A second child, a boy, lay on his stomach on one of the beds. His face was scarlet from the heat and beaded with sweat. A cloth covered his back, through which a greenish-brown stain oozed. Much of the foul stench in the room seemed to be coming from him. Nonie's eyes darted frantically from one to the other of her children, as if she did not know which to protect.

This is a complete waste of time, Edward thought irritably. It was as plain as a priest's tonsure that this woman's husband wasn't receiving a share of any stolen cargoes. By the look of it, he was not even being paid a few coins to turn his face to the wall. But Catlin didn't seem in the least discouraged.

'How did your son come to be hurt?' she asked, in a tone of seeming genuine concern.

'Boat . . . cargo when he was loading,' Nonie said, without looking at her. 'Fell . . . caught his back.'

'Poor mite.' Catlin's brow furrowed in motherly sympathy. 'I hear there've been a number of accidents with cargoes. Many lost overboard or damaged.'

'My Gunter never loses any cargoes,' Nonie said indignantly, 'and he's never damaged one, not in the whole time he's been punting, ever since he was a lad.'

'Except the one that hit your son,' Catlin said.

Nonie looked flustered. 'Cargo wasn't damaged . . . just my Hankin.'

'Then he was a brave lad to try to save the cargo,' Catlin said. 'Master Robert will be most impressed to hear that. But I hear other boatmen are not so careful, are they? I expect Gunter has a few things to say about them.'

Nonie bit her lip. 'He doesn't like carelessness, but he wouldn't speak ill of any, Gunter wouldn't.'

'A good, honest man, I'm sure.'

Hankin moaned as he shifted his leg, trying to get more comfortable.

'His wound looks bad,' Catlin said. 'Let me look. If I tell my apothecary what the wound needs, I can have him prepare something to help.'

She took a pace to the bed, but Nonie sprang between them. 'Don't trouble yourself, mistress. It's no sight for a gentlewoman. There's a woman lives in Butwerk is good with herbs. Everyone in these parts goes to her. She's giving him what he needs.'

'I insist. The boy's in pain and the apothecary will have physic far more powerful than any cunning woman can brew from a few leaves.

My husband would never forgive me if he learned I had left one of his tenants to suffer, especially one who risked his life to save his cargo.'

Thrusting Nonie firmly aside, Catlin peeled the cloth from the boy's skin. A deep gash ran across the small of his back, the wound gaping wide as a mouth. Its blackened lips had not been pulled together with stitches to help it heal and she could at once see why. The raw flesh inside was charred and all around the wound were a hundred tiny burns.

Hankin cried out in pain as the wound was exposed to the air. Catlin quickly laid the ointment-soaked cloth back in place.

'The cargo seems to have been remarkably hot,' she said quietly. 'Was it burning when it fell?'

Nonie cast a look of despair at her daughter, but the child did not look up. 'Gunter burned the wound . . . with a hot knife . . . so it wouldn't fester.'

'Then I must certainly get the boy something that will soothe the pain of it and help it heal. We'll soon have him back on his feet. I imagine your husband will be glad of that. He must find it harder than ever to find work without the boy to help, and with rent being due soon. . .'

Tears sprang into Nonie's eyes and she began to sob. Catlin caught her arm and gently guided her to the other bed, sitting down next to her.

'While Master Edward inspects the roof and the outside of the cottage, why don't we have a little talk, woman to woman? So much easier when there are no men around, with all their high-minded principles. They haven't the least idea what it takes to keep children clothed and fed, do they? My poor husband died the very hour my little daughter was born and I was left to raise her . . .'

Edward took the hint and walked out into the hot sunshine. Behind him he could still hear Catlin talking gently. '. . . honest men like Gunter, while other boatmen cheat him by bribing and stealing, getting work that should be putting food in your own children's bellies . . .'

For the first time that afternoon, he found himself grinning. So that was what Catlin was up to. She was good, he had to admit. His mother could have coaxed the devil himself into giving her the keys of Hell and he would never realise that he'd been played.

Chapter 58

Faggots of wood brought for the fire must contain at least thirteen sticks or more to burn Judas, else good fortune will leave the house with the smoke and bad luck will enter through the door with the wood.

Greetwell

'Why did you let that woman near him?'

Gunter tossed his mutton-bone spoon back into the pottage. He'd barely swallowed more than two mouthfuls. He'd come home ravenous, but his appetite had soured as soon as Col had blurted out the news that a lady and a man on horses had come to the cottage. Nonie hadn't mentioned the visit, which in itself both alarmed and angered him. She'd always shared every scrap of news with him when he returned each evening, usually before he'd a chance to get through the door.

Nonie snatched the abandoned bowl from his hand, tipping the pottage back into the pot. 'If you're not hungry . . .'

'Why did you even let them in? I told you to keep the door closed. I warned you not to let people come prying.'

Nonie glowered at him. 'I'd no choice. The new steward said he had to inspect the cottage, and as soon as they came in Mistress Catlin saw Hankin was in pain. She was kind. Said she'd send us some physic to heal him quicker, so he could go back to work. We have to let her try, else it could be months before he's right, if he ever is.'

'Women like her don't do things to be kind,' Gunter said. 'She must have wanted something. What did you tell her? What did she ask you?'

'How he got hurt, that's what. And I said what you told me to say, except she's not stupid, Gunter, no more am I. It's as plain as a hen's egg that boy wasn't hit by a cargo. His back is burned, even I can see that, and so could she.'

Gunter felt what little pottage he had eaten turn into a hard lump in his craw. 'Did she say as much?'

Nonie shrugged. 'Asked if the cargo was on fire. I said you'd seared the wound with a hot knife to stop it turning bad.'

'And she believed that?' he asked urgently.

'I think she did, which is more than I do,' Nonie snapped. She glanced at Hankin, who was sleeping, with little Col curled up like a dog at his feet. 'He says things when the fever takes him, wild things about a man screaming. Keeps begging me to make him stop. Then he says they'll burn him for the pies. I can't make head nor tail of it, Gunter. What happened? Why won't you tell me?'

Gunter shook his head wearily, massaging his aching stump. 'Just nightmares is all. Everyone gets them when they're sick, you know that. When you were taken with milk fever after our Royse was born, you thought the house was sailing off down the river and you were drowning. Remember?'

'Aye,' Nonie said darkly. 'But I wasn't soaked in river water. That lad's raving about burning and he's the burns to go with it.'

She rose and pulled the pot from the fire, wiping the sweat from her face. It was as hot as a baker's oven inside the cottage. She dipped a cloth in a pail of water, and as gently as she could, so as not to wake him, she laid the cool cloth across the back of Hankin's neck.

'I've heard him talking to the two drowned bairns today, Gunter. Said they were calling to him from the river to come and play with them. I had to hold him down to stop him trying to crawl out to them.' Nonie lowered her voice to a whisper. 'This fever's taking hold and the dead know it.' She glanced fearfully at the closed door. 'They're out there, waiting for him. I tell you this, Gunter, I don't care what you say, I'll talk to a hundred Mistress Catlins if one of them can heal my son. I'll not stand idly by and let the river ghosts take him.'

Gunter rested his head in his hands and closed his eyes. Every muscle in his body was screaming with tiredness. All he wanted to do was sleep, but he knew he wouldn't be able to. Three men had been seized at Boston. A neighbour had denounced them, said they'd helped the Norfolk rebels. Their families swore it was not so, but all it had taken was one word from a man who bore a grudge. Old scores were being settled up and down the land. The King's men were sidling up to people on the quiet, offering money to any who'd give them a name in secret. They said they wouldn't even have to come to the trial. Their neighbours would never know who'd whispered the poison.

The old woman in Butwerk, who'd been making ointment for Hankin, she'd surely not make the connection herself, but what if she mentioned the burns to one of her other customers, someone who realised he and Hankin had been missing from the wharf when the riots were at their height? But the justices would need no informers if Master Robert had recognised him that day in London. Was that why he'd sent his wife and steward? To discover if Hankin was also involved?

Should he take Hankin and go before it was too late? He could lay him in the boat and be far downstream long before dawn. And what then? Where could he go with the boy in that state? They couldn't live on the river, not without being seen, and he knew from the struggle he'd had to bring the lad home that he couldn't tramp the countryside with Hankin in his arms, looking for somewhere to hide. A few nights out in the open without proper food or physic would surely kill the boy. But what was he supposed to do? Sit here and wait for the soldiers to come and drag them at the horse's tail to the castle? After that, the execution: being hacked to pieces, or the slow strangulation of the rope, if they were lucky?

For the thousandth time, he cursed his own stupidity in speaking out. He should have let Robert die. If it had been the other way round, the merchant wouldn't have lifted a finger to save him. Robert would see Gunter hanged as a rebel. For what other cause would a lowly boatman have to be in London?

Gunter struck his forehead with his fists. Why was he such a fool? If he'd bribed Fulk, if he'd stolen like Martin. What did a few thefts matter to a man like Robert? He was so wealthy he'd never even notice a few bales and barrels going missing. He deserved to lose them, raising the rents when he knew men were struggling to feed their families. If Gunter had only done as the other men had and taken enough to pay the tax, Hankin would never have run off. He'd brought his whole family to ruin for the sake of his pointless honesty. It was men who robbed and lied, bribed and cheated who were rewarded, not the honest men, the stupid, gullible fools like him.

He'd watch his son hang beside him. His wife and children would be forced into a life of beggary, for as an executed felon all he possessed would be forfeit to the Crown, even the boat. For the first time in his life, Gunter understood why men threw themselves into the river. Maybe that was the only way to help his family. Kill Hankin, then himself. His wife would at least be able to sell the punt. And Hankin would be spared the misery of prison, then the pain and terror of a public execution. No father could watch his son suffer that.

Gunter wandered out of the cottage, staring up at the vast arch of stars, stretching from the tiny lights in the cottages high above him on the Edge to the dark fenlands, and beneath them the glint of the twisting river, gurgling in the darkness.

Ever since he was a boy, the river and the stars had been the only constants in his life. When the world had fallen into chaos and the Great Pestilence had swept away everything he knew and all those he loved, the river and the stars had remained. He stared down at the black ribbon of water. He shuddered as he remembered Jan's corpse in his hands. Could he do it? Would he have the strength to kill himself when the time came? He didn't know. The only thing he was sure of was that he must protect his son.

Chapter 59

*If cut hair is thrown on to a fire and burns brightly it is a sign
that the person will have a long life, but if it shrivels or smoulders
it is an omen of impending death.*

Lincoln

There were times when I was sorely tempted to send my ferret Mavet
in to bite Robert's backside, but even that wouldn't have made him
listen, for fear had eaten into the metal of his spirit. Fear makes a
man barricade his mind as well as his house, and Robert was starting
to believe that everyone he saw was out to kill him. It's when a man
feels under siege that he clings most stubbornly to what he thinks he
knows: to break faith with himself, when all around are attacking,
would be more than he could bear.

Wherever he went, Robert was certain he was being watched or
followed. And, of course, he was right. Godwin was behind him like
his own shadow, constantly changing his garb to disguise himself,
dressing in whatever he could steal, but there is something about the
way a man stands and walks, the way his sleeve hangs empty that
cannot be disguised, and though Robert hastened through the streets,
meeting the gaze of no man, he would catch sight of the still figure
from the corner of his eye and veer away, like a startled horse.
Eventually, though he'd sworn he would never do it, he had even
taken to hiring an armed linkman to accompany him whenever he
left the house, to ensure that no stranger could get within a yard of
him.

Robert's nights were no better than his days for the demon horse
invariably carried him back to the streets of London, to the blood
that flowed in an ever-widening scarlet lake and the feet that pressed
sharp as an axe-blade on his neck. He woke sweating and exhausted.
And there is nothing more likely to make a man feel hard-done-by
than lack of sleep.

In his misery he concluded that there was only one person who had any thought for his welfare: his sweet and adoring stepdaughter. No one else, especially his new wife, seemed to be in the least concerned about him or his safety. But Leonia could always bring a smile to his face, and she did so now as she entered the solar bearing a jug of wine.

'You shouldn't be fetching my wine, child. Where are Tenney and Diot?'

Leonia carefully positioned the jug on the table. 'Diot's so slow, and Tenney said he was busy, but he wasn't. He's lazy.'

He'd have to have words with the man. Tenney was growing increasingly moody. It was hard to get two words out of him, and where once he had looked everyone straight in the eye, now he shuffled around with his head bent, like an old beggar in search of lost coins or scraps. Robert supposed that Tenney was still aggrieved because Beata had been sent to the infirmary of St Magdalene, but he wouldn't tolerate a servant sulking. When hired men were allowed to think they could dictate . . . His hand began to tremble again as he took the goblet of blood-red wine Leonia held out to him. He tried to put it to the back of his mind. He didn't want the child to see he was unnerved.

'Where's your mother, Leonia?'

The girl busied herself straightening the jug on the table, as if she were ashamed to answer. 'She rode out to meet Edward. He was visiting the cottagers. She's always going out with Edward, since she made him steward.'

She made him steward. Robert felt more than a twinge of annoyance. Even an innocent child had observed that Edward's allegiance was to Catlin, not him. And what reason would Catlin have to visit the cottagers, with or without Edward, leaving little Leonia to perform the duties his wife should have been at home to carry out?

He forced a smile to his face and drew a stool close to his chair. 'Come, child, sit down here and tell me all you've been doing. Have you spent the gold piece I gave you to make up for not bringing you something pretty from London?'

She ignored the stool he'd made ready for her and instead slid onto his lap. Putting an arm round his neck, she wriggled her buttocks over his thighs to get herself into a comfortable position. She kicked her legs out straight in front of her.

'I bought new shoes. Do you like them, Père?'

Her slender feet were clad in soft leather that cradled the ankles. The slit down the front was closed by three horn buttons. The toes were pointed, the points not nearly as long as those worn by Robert, but the height of fashion for a woman. Each shoe was decorated with piercing in the form of an ouroboros, a snake devouring its own tail.

'Charming . . . but did not the cordwainer have something more . . .' Robert hesitated, unwilling to hurt her feelings. 'Flowers, perhaps.'

Leonia gazed down, flexing her toes so that the snakes seemed to undulate over her feet. 'I asked him to make the snakes. I like them, don't you, Père? I didn't want to look like all the other women.' She turned a beaming smile on him.

'Trust me, my dear, you will always stand out from them.'

She tilted her head to one side, her eyes filled with anxiety. 'Is it because I'm ugly? Mother says I am very plain.'

Robert frowned. 'That's nonsense. You're the prettiest child I've ever known and you are surely going to flower into a most beautiful woman, one day.'

Robert was not given to praising children. His own parents had never done so and he, like them, believed it spoiled a child's character to be petted or told they were clever or handsome. He probably would not have complimented Leonia on this occasion, however pretty he thought her, had he not been so annoyed with Catlin that he would have said anything to contradict her.

He reached up and rubbed a lock of Leonia's hair between his finger and thumb, bringing it to his nose to smell the sweet perfume of damask roses that clung to it. 'For one thing, you have these glossy black curls, just like satin.'

A radiant smile lit Leonia's face. She kissed his cheek, snuggling into him. He was glad he'd made her smile again.

'Then,' he said, running a finger lightly over the back of her hand, 'there is your golden skin, the colour of the sweetest honey.'

She giggled. 'And what about my lips? What are my lips like?'

He chuckled indulgently, entering into her game and, for the first time in weeks, found himself relaxing a little. 'Let me see, your lips, what do they remind me of?'

She parted them slightly, lifted her face and pressed her soft mouth to his own, squirming her round little bottom against his crotch.

Afterwards, Robert told himself a hundred times it was not his fault. Before he realised what she intended, she'd seized his hand and was pushing it inside her gown, rubbing it against her soft nipple. He felt the silky mound of her little breast in his hand. Her mouth was hot against his. Her kitten tongue fluttered over his lips. He felt his member rising between his legs, the heat rushing up his spine till he couldn't even think what—

'Leonia!' Catlin was standing in the doorway, Edward just behind her.

Leonia turned her head and in a flash her mother had caught her by the wrist and dragged her from Robert's lap.

'What are you doing with my daughter?'

Robert struggled up from the chair. 'Nothing . . . The little slut flung herself on me. Is this how you bring her up to behave?'

Catlin rounded on her daughter. 'Is this true? Of course it is. Don't try to deny it. I've seen you flirting with my husband, sitting on his lap like some stew-house whore. I won't tolerate it, do you hear? This time I shall teach you a lesson you won't forget!'

Catlin strode over to a small box that stood on the chest and opened it. Robert saw a flash of silver in her hand. She pushed Leonia onto a chair. Then, before anyone realised what she intended, she grabbed a handful of Leonia's long black curls. There was a rasping sound and the hank of hair fell to the floor. Leonia shrieked and clapped her hand to the patch of shorn scalp.

'God's blood, what are you doing?' Robert tried to catch his wife's hand, intending to take the scissors from her. 'There's no need for that.'

She spun round, the sharp points of the twin blades just an inch from his chest. He'd never seen such dark fury in her face. 'It would seem there is every need, Robert,' she said grimly. 'It's what they do to whores, isn't it?'

Leonia sprang from the chair and ran across the room, but her mother caught her by the hair and dragged her back, flinging her into the chair again.

'Let me go, you old hag! You'll be sorry. I'll make you sorry.' Leonia struggled to free herself, but Catlin was stronger.

'Not as sorry as I will make you. Edward! Hold her.'

He hesitated, then hurried over and pinned Leonia's arms to the chair. He looked down at her, grinning, as if he were enjoying every moment. She stopped struggling and stared up at him, unblinking.

His smile abruptly vanished, as if a bucket of water had been thrown over him, and he hastily turned his face away, though his fingers tightened round her arms.

Catlin set to work with grim determination, shearing as close to the scalp as she could. There seemed to be far more hair on the floor than there had ever been on the child's head. The locks kept slithering down until Robert felt he was suffocating under the rising mounds of hair. He knew he should stop his wife, but to do so would make it seem that he was admitting it was his fault. But it wasn't. The girl had seduced him, deliberately tried to arouse him. She'd taken him entirely unawares. But she was a child, just a child. She couldn't have understood what she was doing, could she?

All the time her mother was cutting, Leonia neither moved nor uttered a sound. She kept her furious gaze fixed on Edward, as Catlin roughly pushed her head this way and that, as if she were plucking a dead bird. When only an uneven stubble covered her daughter's scalp, Catlin straightened. 'Let her go.'

Edward sprang away from Leonia as if she were a dog that might savage him as soon as its muzzle was removed, but she rose and walked stiffly to the door. Only once did her hands jerk up as if to touch her head, but she clamped them at her sides before they could. Robert thought she must be weeping and trying to conceal it, but when she reached the door, she turned and there was no trace of a tear in her tawny eyes. The golden flecks were more prominent than Robert remembered. For a moment he thought he was staring into the eyes of a great cat, filled with savage rage and hatred. Then, before he could blink, she was gone.

Chapter 60

It is written that King John of England was murdered by a wicked friar who squeezed the secretions of a toad into his drinking cup.

Lincoln

As soon as the door closed behind Leonia, Robert staggered to the table and poured himself a goblet of wine, which he drained without setting it down, then choked as he remembered who'd brought it for him. He tried to avoid looking at the mound of black curls encircling the chair.

'That was harsh, my dear. Surely there was a better way . . .'

'I think it will serve as a salient reminder, Robert.' Catlin calmly returned the scissors to her box, as if she had used them to snip a loose thread. 'Nuns cut their hair to remove temptation from men, don't they?'

Robert flushed, and caught the smirk on Edward's face. Anger blazed in him. 'And if you'd been here this afternoon, wife, as was your duty, this would never have happened. Why exactly was it necessary for you to visit the cottages with your son?'

Catlin's eyes were as cold as the grave. 'Edward is not yet acquainted with the area or the tenants. And it's as well that I did ride out, for I'd the good fortune to meet Sheriff Thomas on the road. He was asking again, Robert, if you had yet made up your mind to sit on the Commission of Array.'

'I made plain when he asked me the first time that I have guild matters to attend to and, with business as poor as it is, I need to be out buying and selling, not wasting my time compiling lists and listening to testimonies. Every hour spent doing that is throwing money into the Braytheforde.' He flinched as the image of Jan's bloated white face floated again before his eyes.

Edward crossed the room and poured two goblets of wine, one of which he handed to Catlin. The other he took back to one of the chairs and sat down with it. The insolence of this gesture made Robert's jaw clench. His stepson was treating the house as if it were his own.

'But, Father, I'm here to relieve you of that burden so that you can take your place where you should, in the service of the King and Lincoln.'

Edward had never dared to use such a familiar term as 'father' before. Robert had given him no such leave, and only his guilt over Leonia prevented him from seizing his wife's son by the scruff of his neck and hurling him out of the house.

'If I am any relation to you at all it is as *step*father and I will decide how I shall employ my time, *Master* Edward,' Robert said coldly. 'May I remind you that, thanks to your incompetence, if that indeed was what it was, I lost a cartload of the best cloth. And, thanks to your idiocy, the thieves got clean away. Only the intervention of your mother prevented me having you arrested as an accomplice. She convinced me you really are that stupid.'

Edward jerked as if he were about to leap from his chair and punch Robert, but Catlin shot out a hand and pushed him down, shaking her head at him. 'Until such time as my son has proved himself worthy of your trust, naturally he'll take no more decisions without consulting you. But if business is poor, Robert, that's all the more reason we shouldn't risk offending the sheriff by churlishly rejecting this honour. Thomas is an influential man. And, as he said, the King rewards loyalty. With armies on the verge of war in France and Scotland, wool and cloth will be sorely needed for gambesons to protect the soldiers, as well as for tunics. One royal contract would be worth a thousand times more than any other and you wouldn't need to wear yourself out riding round the country, begging to sell a few bales of cloth here and there.'

Robert slammed his goblet onto the table. 'And what use would a royal contract be if my warehouse is burned to the ground? It's the work of minutes to destroy a fortune, as I saw in London. You have no idea what these men are capable of, Catlin. Great buildings brought crashing down. Men dragged from their own hearths and slaughtered, wealthy men, noblemen. If you had seen it . . .'

'But that is the point, Robert. None of the council did see it and some are beginning to ask why John of Gaunt has not yet sent reinforcements here. If you refuse to serve on the Commission, some may begin to question if the message was delivered at all, and indeed where exactly your loyalties lie. Thomas says that your close friend Hugh de Garwell is already suspected of being a rebel. He was a Member of Parliament and a mayor of Lincoln.'

'Hugh? Have they arrested him?'

Catlin lowered her eyes, fingering her goblet. 'Naturally, Sheriff Thomas would not confide such matters to a woman, but the very fact he mentioned it must surely be a warning that if you do not accept . . .'

Edward tipped the last of the wine down his throat. 'It's all round the wharf that men are being tried and executed within the hour. Not just hanged either, but dragged by horses till they're dead or having their noses, ears, pricks and limbs hacked off and being left to bleed to death. I give thanks I can prove I was quietly going about my business in Lincoln during the riots. I pity those who can't.'

Robert crossed to the casement, staring sightlessly into the street. Not for the first time since he'd returned from London did he wonder if Catlin had any care at all for his safety. The tender, affectionate woman he'd married had vanished, leaving in her place a woman who seemed as hard as the devil's hoof. The ruthlessness with which she'd punished Leonia had shocked him. Yet perhaps it was him who was being unreasonable. The girl had behaved like a harlot. It was a mother's duty to correct her. And surely Catlin's anger was proof she loved her husband and was jealous of any woman, even her own daughter, who might steal his affections. Jealousy sprang from love, didn't it? He winced, remembering poor Edith's rages.

Catlin was right about something else too. He had failed in London. He couldn't risk any suspicion of disloyalty, not with treason being whispered behind every keyhole. However much he feared the rebels, the fear of being accused of treason was worse. The killings he'd witnessed by the rebels, though brutal, were positively merciful compared to how King Richard and his minions were punishing traitors. Catlin was trying to protect him, as any loving wife would.

The gibe she had made about him being a coward still burned into him, not least because he had accused himself of the same fault. Were his fellow merchants whispering it behind his back? He could not bear to have anyone, especially his own wife, despise him.

'My sweeting,' Catlin said softly, as if she could hear his thoughts, 'Sheriff Thomas has assured you that the names of the commissioners will be kept secret, known only to him and King Richard. No one

389

in Lincoln will have any idea that you are a commissioner. They won't be lying in wait for you. Why would they? Besides, as Edward says, with the summary executions taking place, even the most hardened rebel will not dare show his hand now. They'll all be lying low in their cottages or slinking off into the fens and praying they're not found.'

'I suppose I have no choice.' Robert sighed. 'Very well . . . I'll send word to Thomas.'

He was still gazing out of the window so he didn't see Catlin pick up one of the shining black curls and slide it into the hollow behind one of the bloodstones in her necklace. Neither did he witness the knowing smile his wife and her son exchanged. If he had, he might have been even more terrified than he already was.

Chapter 61

Peg O'Nell is a water sprite who haunts the river Ribble. She was a maid at Waddow Hall and her mistress drowned her, using witchcraft. Every seven years since then the water sprite has taken a human life in revenge.

Beata

I was sitting in the cool of the cloister, with three of the older patients. The afternoon was hot and stifling as a baker's oven so we'd been allowed to take our mending outside – linen ties that had snapped from caps, sleeves torn from habits, patches to be added to the shifts of the sick, which had been scrubbed so often they'd worn into holes. The work in the infirmary didn't stop for the lay sisters or for us.

After those nights I'd spent locked inside freezing baths I'd learned quickly. I'd learned to walk like the nuns, my hands clenched together inside my sleeves so their agitation did not betray me. I kept my eyes cast down and lips pressed together, like the young novices. That way you didn't draw attention to yourself. That way they thought you were well. The nuns approved. The lay sisters didn't care, so long as you did what you were bade and didn't cause them trouble.

But I knew fine rightly that they'd never let me out, even if I never had another fit. Some poor creatures had been walled up in the infirmary for years. They'd been brought to St Magdalene's as young lasses, sick with a fever, or a pox of the skin, or their belly swollen with a bairn that should never have been conceived. But even when they were well again, their families didn't want them back, so they stayed, cleaning and baking, washing and digging. And I'd be caged with them till the day I died.

Then they'd dump me in the cold earth without coffin, candles or mourners, and when the mound had settled, grass and weeds covering it, the nuns and lay sisters, the sick and the mad would walk over me as if I'd never been born. Sometimes I fell into such misery at the prospect of the long, lonely years that lay ahead I thought it would be a blessing if I really did run mad. At least then I'd not mark the passing of the days.

Sister Ursula came bustling into the cloister, fanning herself with her hand, her face scarlet as a strawberry beneath the tight coif. She glanced up at the black clouds massing behind the cathedral and clicked her fingers impatiently at us. 'Rain's coming. Are there still clothes out drying?'

'Some of the lay sisters' robes,' a woman answered. 'They always take so long to dry. We fetched the linens in ages ago.'

Sister Ursula clapped her hands, as if we were small children. 'Fetch them, fetch them quickly, or they will need washing again . . . Not you, Joan,' she added hastily, as a wheezing woman struggled to stand on her swollen legs. 'By the time you get outside, we'll all be another year older.'

The rest of us hurried out to the small garden where the heavy robes were stretched over lavender and rosemary bushes so that the oils from the plants scented them as they dried to keep away fleas and moths. The first drops of rain were already spattering us as we ran round, gathering up the garments. It had to be done with care. Snatch them from the bushes and they might snag or tear. The rain was falling hard by the time we had reached the far side and the wind was gusting up the hill.

'Go on in!' I shouted. 'I'll bring these last ones.'

The others didn't need to be told twice. Clutching their bundles, they scuttled for shelter. Hugging the washing to me, I ran to take shelter under an overhanging roof. The rain cascaded down. I mopped my wet face on one of the robes.

The grounds were deserted. Everyone had rushed to take cover from the sudden downpour. Inside, I could hear the lay sisters slamming shutters and doors to prevent them banging in the strengthening wind.

I'd not planned it, but suddenly I saw my chance. Dropping the bundle of clothes, I struggled out of my wet gown and pulled on one of the coarse brown robes. Without giving myself time to think, I ran towards the gate. At any moment, I expected to hear someone yelling at me to come back inside, but no one did. Even when I drew the bolt, I thought the sister who kept watch in the hut nearby would rush out. But the noise of the wind and rain must have covered the sound, and if she noticed someone slipping away, she wasn't going to suffer a wetting to investigate. Lay sisters came and went freely on all kinds of errands, and the nuns treated them as if they were cod-wits, so I reckon she thought me a lay sister who hadn't sense enough to wait for the rain to ease.

As soon as I'd closed the gate behind me, I put my head down into the wind and ran till I was out of sight of the infirmary. The parish of St Mary Magdalene is inside the city walls, but they had built the infirmary outside, north of the walls, so that the patients wouldn't suffer the bad humours of the city's stinking ditches – leastways that's what the nuns said. But the lay sisters had told me it was because the people in Lincoln were afeared we might give them a contagion or infest their dreams with our madness.

I reached the shelter of some trees and stopped, trying to decide where to go. I had to reach Master Robert's to warn him about Leonia. But if the girl was there, she'd cast the evil eye on me again and curse me into a fit so they'd take me straight back to the infirmary. I wiped the icy rain from my face, as I thought of those nights spent locked in darkness and water, the eels swimming towards me out of my dreams. I'd die rather than go back. Although Lincoln was the only home I'd ever known, I had no choice but to leave it.

But where could I go without money? Sister Ursula was right: without a position or family, I'd find myself begging on the streets. Tenney – he would surely help me. He'd not been to visit me or sent word since I'd been in the infirmary, but if he saw me, he'd not turn his back on me. I'd have to wait for him to leave the house and speak to him alone, convince him he had to warn Master Robert. He'd not listened in the past, but he must now.

I couldn't risk entering the city by any of the northern gates. If the nuns had discovered I was missing, those were the first they'd have watched. Better make my way around the side of the city and enter from the south. They'd not be expecting me to come that way.

The rain stopped as suddenly as it had started and the sun came blazing out, turning the drops on the leaves into rainbows. The baked earth and wet vegetation steamed, smelling like a fresh-baked pie. Now that the rain had stopped, the nuns would venture out again and someone would trip over the robes I'd dropped. Sister Ursula would send the lay sisters to search the infirmary for me, even if only to make me wash them again. I cursed myself for not hiding them. With a frightened glance over my shoulder, I hurried on as if the devil were snarling at my heels.

No one so much as glanced at me when I sidled in through the Stonebow gate. At least the guard there had not yet been alerted, but perhaps the nuns had gone straight to Master Robert's house and were already waiting there to drag me back.

When I finally reached the familiar street, I hid in a neighbouring doorway and watched, but all seemed quiet. The windows and shutters of Master Robert's house were closed against the rain, but the courtyard door was open and the yard brush bobbed in and out, as someone pushed mud, dung and waves of water through the gate into the open gutters of the street outside. I edged a little closer and saw that Tenney was wielding the broom, trying to clear the courtyard after the downpour.

I called to him softly, not knowing if Diot might be lurking in my kitchen. He peered round the gate, a puzzled expression on his face, looking even more bewildered when he saw a lay sister in brown robes beckoning to him. But he abandoned the broom and came hurrying over. 'Sister, is there news of . . .' His jaw fell as slack as that of a dead fish when he recognised me. 'Beata! I'm right glad to see you.'

His face broke into a beaming smile, and he came closer, his arms wide as if he was going to hug me. Then he let them drop, staring awkwardly at my robe. 'Are you one of them now?'

'Muttonhead! Can you imagine me on my knees in church every day? I dressed up like this to get away from them.'

He glanced anxiously up and down the street as he drew me into the shadow of an archway. 'I came as often as I could, but they said you were too ill to see anyone. I thought maybe it was me you didn't want to see.'

I felt sick with anger and relief. So Tenney had come and I never knew. He was outside all those days when I thought he'd forgotten me and they'd never told me.

'I'd have given my right arm to see your daft face,' I said, gripping his great hand and felt an answering squeeze. 'But I've not much time. Soon as I'm missed, they'll come looking for me. I have to get away, leave Lincoln. But I'd never rest easy knowing Master Robert's in danger. I promised Mistress Edith I'd look out for him and Adam. I know you didn't believe me afore, but you must believe me now, Tenney. That woman's pure evil and that brat of hers is worse. They mean to harm Master Robert, Adam too. Please, Tenney, I can't risk speaking to the master. He'll send me straight back to the Magdalenes. It's you who'll have to warn him.'

'She's right,' a voice rasped behind me.

I spun round. A man was standing at my elbow, his dark eyes burning into mine. I almost fled, but Tenney grasped my arm. 'That's Godwin, the man hunting Widow Catlin.'

The man's gaze darted to Tenney, then back to me. 'Tenney told me what they did to you and, believe me, you were fortunate to escape so lightly. Your master and his son will not be so lucky. Those fiends will act soon and there is little time left to stop them. Mother and daughter are building their traps, and when they're set, neither father nor son will escape them. I've tried to warn your master and the boy, but I can't get near either of them. Beata, try to convince this husband of yours he must speak out, now, today.'

Godwin's voice was as harsh as the raven's cry and made me shudder to hear it, but when he spoke the word 'husband', it gave me a strange warm glow. I expected Tenney to set him straight, but he didn't.

'There's neither of you needs to waste breath convincing me,' Tenney said. 'A family of demons is what they are. And it's not for want of trying—'

He broke off as we heard footsteps in the street. Two men-at-arms were splashing towards us through the puddles. Before I could blink, Godwin was scuttling down the street and had vanished from sight. I would have run too, had Tenney not gripped my wrist, holding me still. The two men stared at us curiously, as they passed by.

'Now then,' one said cheerfully, 'you keep your hands off her. I heard those nuns took a knife to a man's prick for messing with one of their own. Wilder than a pack of mad dogs those sisters are when they're riled.' The men laughed and strolled on.

My guts twisted. 'If those men learn I'm missing they'll remember seeing me and come straight here.'

Tenney nodded grimly. 'I've a cousin – you've heard me speak of her, lives t'other side of Torksey. She's a good soul, heart as large as her brood of bairns, and that's saying something. I reckon she'd be glad of another woman around the place to help, though she'd not be able to pay you, save for meats and roof over your head. But I'll give what coins I've saved to tide you over. I'll find you a change of clothes too, case they've put a watch on the gate. We'll have to take the cart, for you can't get even partway up the Foss Way with the river being so low.'

'But you will speak to the master,' I urged. 'I'm so afeared for him and the boy.'

'I swear it. I'll tell him all I know, even if I have to knock the stubborn old goat on the head and tie him up to make him listen. But it must wait until I've got you safe out of the city, where those nuns can't find you.'

Drawing me behind him, he peered into the courtyard. 'There's no one around. Hide yourself in the kitchen. I'll be as quick as I can.'

Afore I knew it, he'd crushed me to him and pressed his lips against mine in a loving kiss, half smothering me with his thick black beard. 'I'll be back, Beata.'

I stood there, stunned, for a moment, still feeling the heat of his lips tingling on my mouth, the tickling of his beard against my cheek. Tenney had kissed me! After all these years he had finally kissed me. I think I'd be standing there still had he not shoved me inside the kitchen. The banging of the door as it shut jerked me out of my daze.

It was hot and dark in there. Only the dim ghost of daylight drifted in through the smoke vent behind the oven, and a hell-red glow flickered across the walls from the flames of the cooking-fire. But I knew my own kitchen well enough to find the lantern that always hung from a nail near the door. I lit the candle from the fire. Fortunately, Diot could not move that, though it was more than I could say for the rest of my kitchen.

Nothing was where it should have been. Jars and boxes were on the wrong shelves. Spoons, ladles and knives lay scattered about, as if Diot had merely dropped them, unwiped, where she'd last used them. Two live carp were gasping in a barrel of stagnant water, and feathers were spilling out of the overstuffed sack in which I collected the pluckings of the birds, for the lazy cat had not troubled to fetch a fresh one.

Afore I knew it, I was starting to tidy and rearrange my shelves. It was a foolish thing to do for Diot would see at once someone had been into the kitchen, but I couldn't help myself. I tried to stop, but I couldn't bear to sit still. Fear of discovery and elation at Tenney's kiss made me so agitated that if Sister Ursula had seen me then she might have been right to call me mad.

I heard a noise outside, the clatter of hoofs on the stones, the grinding of metal, something rasping across the wooden door. My heart was thudding. Had they come for me from Magdalene's? Were they searching for me? I crept back to the lantern, snuffed out the flame and crouched in the corner behind the table. I heard sounds at the back of the kitchen, a grating against the bricks behind the oven. I kept as still as I could, though my heart was thumping so loudly I was sure it was echoing right across the courtyard. I tried to convince myself it was only a cat scrambling down from the roof. Strays often huddled up there to get the warmth on a cold day. Not that they needed it now. It was hot enough in that kitchen to roast a pig in ice.

The air was growing thicker and sweat was pouring off me. Tenney must come soon. Were they still searching? Was he trying to lead them away? My eyes were watering and my throat was tickling and burning. I tried not to cough, but I couldn't help it. I pressed the skirts of my robe to my face, trying to stifle the noise, but I was hacking my lungs out. All thoughts of keeping silent were forgotten as I blundered forward in a desperate search for something to drink. I found only a flask of vinegar, but still I sipped it, hoping it would stop the cough. But it only made me gasp for breath.

Then I realised why I was choking. The small kitchen was filling with smoke. I stumbled across to the oven. I could see no light from the vents, nothing except black smoke rolling under the hood from the oven. Diot must have neglected to brush the vents clean of soot. I pulled the oven door open desperate for the light from the flames. But even more smoke poured out into the room.

Blinded, my eyes streaming, I fell to my knees, crawling back across the floor. It could only have been a few paces, but I couldn't find the door. My head hit wood and, for a moment, I thought I'd reached it, but it was only the leg of the table. I dragged myself round it, groping wildly. Suddenly I felt the stone of the wall. Then my fingers were touching the rough boards of the door. I reached up, hauling myself to my feet, until I grasped the iron latch. Hanging on to it, I flung my weight against the door, but though the latch gave, the door opened no more than a crack. My lungs felt as if they'd been torn out. Smoke was in my head whirling round and round, obliterating every thought, except one. *Don't let me die! Tenney! Tenney! Help me! Help me!*

Then I heard a child's voice singing, high and clear like an angel: *See little song-bird baked in the pie.*

Chapter 62

Cats bring the Great Pestilence, especially those that belong to witches. If a cat is suspected, it must be caught, killed and dried, then placed up a chimney to protect the house.

Lincoln

Tenney had harnessed the horse to the cart, then laid sacks and a few empty barrels in the back between which he could conceal Beata, should anyone come looking for her before they got clear of Lincoln. It had not taken him long to retrieve the precious stash of coins he'd hidden beneath a loose flag behind the stables. Finding clothes for her was more difficult. After she'd been taken to the infirmary, the few garments she had left behind had been torn into rags by Diot, and nothing of Diot's would have fitted Beata, for she'd always been half the woman's girth and, since her stay in Magdalene's, was now even thinner.

He'd dared not steal anything of Catlin's. In the end, he had found some old clothes of Jan's in a chest. It was not uncommon for women who had to toil alongside men in workshops and tanners' yards to dress in breeches, instead of cumbersome skirts. With luck the city guards would not look twice at her.

For all that he was desperate to get Beata away as quickly as possible, he couldn't stop a stupid grin breaking out on his face each time he recalled the stolen kiss. She'd not pulled away from him, far from it. It had gratified him to feel the kiss returned and her body melting into his before he'd had to rush her into the kitchen.

Why shouldn't he leave Lincoln too? He no longer felt any loyalty to Master Robert, not after the way he had banished Beata just because she had fallen ill. It proved the master wouldn't hesitate to turn him out in favour of a younger man, no matter how many years of faithful service he'd given. Ever since Master Robert had returned from London, he had seemed mistrustful of everyone, including his own manservant. Tenney was hurt and bewildered.

If he could just spirit Beata away, then, in a week or two, he could follow, once he had ensured they'd given up searching for her. He would have time to make one last attempt to warn Master Robert, for he knew Beata and Godwin would never stop mithering him if he didn't. He'd go to the warehouse and tackle the master there. Then, if he still refused to listen, Tenney could leave with a clear conscience, knowing he had done all that a man could do. Beata was all that mattered to him now. They could move on together. He'd find work. He could turn his hand to most things, and why shouldn't he? Other men were leaving their masters to seek a better life.

He ducked through the doorway and was about to step into the yard when he saw that the horse and cart were standing right in front of the kitchen, the side of the cart hard against the door. He frowned. He was certain he had tethered the horse securely near the courtyard gate. What was it doing across there?

Tenney was about to hurry out, when he caught sight of someone coming towards him. He groaned. Leonia was skipping across the courtyard. He prayed that Beata had already hidden herself in the cart, for he didn't know how he would smuggle her into it with the girl watching. Rolling the stolen clothes he was carrying into a bundle, he tried to step around Leonia, but she barred his way.

'Where are you going?' she asked.

'Who says I'm going anywhere?' Tenney avoided her gaze, though he could feel her great owl-eyes searching his face.

'So why did you harness the horse, if you're not going somewhere?'

'A few errands, is all. Wood and other things want fetching.'

'Can I come?' she said brightly.

Startled, he looked at her. Her eyes were shining with excitement, as if she'd been promised a rare treat.

'Master Robert'd not take kindly to his daughter riding about with—'

He broke off. The horse was neighing and rolling its eyes. It stamped and half reared in the shafts, straining against them. Then Tenney saw the reason. Smoke was curling from under the kitchen door and billowing out from beneath the cart. But though the horse was evidently panicked by it, for some reason Tenney couldn't fathom, it wasn't pulling away from the door.

He stared at it stupidly. Then, dropping the bundle, he shoved Leonia aside and sprinted across the courtyard. He tried to drag the horse forward, but the creature wouldn't budge. It twisted its head as if someone far stronger had hold of the bridle and was pulling it back. He caught sight of Leonia, standing in the doorway watching, her eyes fixed on something by the horse's head. She was witching the horse! Briefly, Tenney felt himself bewitched too. He was frozen to the spot, unable to move or think. Then Godwin's words flashed into his head. Desperately, he scrabbled in his scrip for the monkey's paw and flung it on the ground between himself and the girl.

He expected a flash of light, a cry of fear or rage from the girl, but nothing happened. Leonia began to laugh, her eyes flashing with mockery. The horse was neighing shrilly in fear and trying to kick out. But it was held fast.

Tenney snatched up the whip that lay ready in the cart and brought it down as hard as he could on the horse's flank. It reared and shot forward as though suddenly released. It was all he could do to grab the terrified beast before it bolted to smash itself and the cart to pieces against the wall. It took him several long minutes to bring the terrified creature under control.

Tenney tore back to the kitchen and wrenched open the door. A billow of dense smoke sent him staggering backwards. He scrubbed his eyes with his knuckles, frantically trying to clear them. Then he saw Beata, lying on the threshold, her arm outstretched and limp, her head curled onto her chest. With a cry of anguish, he dragged her out into the courtyard.

She lay unmoving, her face white, dark smudges of smoke around her nostrils and mouth. He hauled her into a sitting position, supporting her chest against his forearm as he thumped her back, willing her to live. 'Come on now, lass. Don't leave me, not now. Where would I be without you to mither me? I need you, lass, I need you!'

Frantically he pummelled her back again, trying to make her draw breath. But she didn't stir. She flopped forward across his arm, like an old pillow. Kneeling on the flags of the courtyard, still wet from the rain, Tenney rocked her lifeless body back and forth, howling like a child.

But then came the sweetest sound in all the world: Beata gasped.

Master Robert was adamant that birds must have stuffed the wet straw into the vent to build a nest. He'd never paid any heed to the habits of creatures that did not make him a profit and, in consequence, he had little notion of when birds nested. The only thing that puzzled him was why Beata had remained in the kitchen when it was filling with smoke, but he concluded that it was further proof of her madness.

Sister Ursula, who had arrived with a lay sister to report Beata's escape, told him the mad were cunning and sly. It was, she said, a blessing that Beata had been rendered insensible. In her jealousy of poor Mistress Catlin, God alone knew what she might have done. She'd doubtless gone into the kitchen to find a knife or an axe to butcher the entire family. The good nun crossed herself fervently. They'd had a lucky escape. The Blessed Virgin had surely been watching over them.

Sister Ursula declared she would take the crazed woman straight back to St Mary Magdalene's and she assured Robert that Beata would henceforth be kept chained in fetters from which not even the devil himself could escape. Master Robert and his family could sleep soundly in their beds, for the tormented soul would never again leave the room in which she would be kept, much less the infirmary.

Tenney uttered not one word. He listened, head bowed, to all that they said. Then, without looking at any of them, he gathered the wheezing Beata into his arms and slid her gently into the back of the cart, tenderly propping her against a bale of hay to make it easier for her to breathe and covering her with his own cloak. He fetched a water-skin and held it to her lips. She drank gratefully, giving him a frightened smile.

Sister Ursula nodded her approval. 'I shall ride with you.'

She walked round and stood expectantly by the front of the cart, beckoning to the lay sister to come and help her up. But Tenney clambered into the driver's seat, flicked the reins across the horse's back and turned the cart so sharply that Master Robert was forced to do the unthinkable and lay hands on a consecrated nun to drag her away from the wheel before it struck her. As the tail of the cart disappeared through the gate, Master Robert found himself shouting into thin air, demanding that Tenney stop at once. For the first time in more than thirty years, his manservant ignored him.

Tears running down his ugly face, Tenney kept driving, on and on through the streets and lanes of Lincoln, out through the city gate, down the long road until he was far beyond the sight of castle and cathedral. He was, if he had paused to think about it, a wanted man, a thief who had stolen a valuable horse and cart. That was a hanging offence. But Tenney had gone beyond thinking. He had to get the woman he loved away from that house of death. He would keep her safe, even if he had to cross all England to do it.

August

A rainy August makes a hard breadcrust.

Chapter 63

Sailors bought knotted thread from witches in case they were becalmed at sea. As each knot was undone so the strength of the wind was increased, but they took care never to undo the last knot for that would call up a violent storm.

Lincoln

Robert, closely followed by an armed linkman, strode along the quay-side towards the warehouse, tearing open the heavy, ankle-length robe that was suffocating him in the afternoon heat. The houppelande was the height of fashion, with its high collar and voluminous folds, and as a cloth merchant Robert felt he should set an example by wearing it. But even he was forced to admit that it was the most damnably uncomfortable garment on a day like this.

The indolent breeze from the Braytheforde brought no relief. It merely carried the stench of the sewers and middens into every part of the lower town, for in this heat every green, slime-filled ditch was fermenting, sending out bubbles of noxious air. His foot slid on some rotting fish guts, sending up a great buzzing cloud of flies. The linkman caught his arm and managed to stop him crashing to the ground. Robert, embarrassed to be steadied as if he was an old man, shook off the supporting hand and hastened on until they reached the door of the warehouse, where he dismissed his guard with a small coin.

Wiping his sweating brow, he stepped inside. It was scarcely any cooler in the building, but at least he was out of the sun's glare. He removed his turbaned hood and tossed it onto a stack of kegs, glancing around. To his great annoyance the warehouse seemed deserted.

'Adam!'

His son did not appear, but his shout brought the watchman hurrying from somewhere in the back recesses. He bobbed up and down in little bows as he scurried towards Robert, like a bird pecking for worms.

407

'Master Robert . . .' he panted, scarlet in the face from the heat. 'I didn't expect to see you, not so late in the afternoon. Last load's been brought in. I was about to brace the doors.'

'My so-called steward sent word to meet him here.'

The watchman looked around as if he wanted to be quite certain of Edward's absence before he replied, 'He's not here, Master Robert.'

'I can see that,' Robert snapped. 'And my son?'

The watchman shuffled uneasily. 'He was here.'

'When did he leave? He hadn't come home when I left.'

The watchman looked increasingly uncomfortable. 'I – I don't rightly know. I didn't see him leave. But the girl was here earlier. I saw her round the back near the stairs. I thought she'd come to fetch Adam. She's been here before looking for him.'

'A girl?' Robert asked sharply. 'What girl?'

'Your stepdaughter, Master Robert. They go off together sometimes. I thought maybe . . . she'd come to tell him he was wanted at home.'

Robert frowned. 'Are you sure it was Leonia?'

He'd been convinced Leonia had not set foot out of the house since her mother had cut her hair. No girl would venture out in public looking like that. Catlin had given her a voluminous cap to wear, but Leonia had stubbornly refused it. She'd come to the table with her head bare and her chin raised defiantly, as if she wanted her mother to be constantly reminded of what she'd done. Not that she had spoken a single word to either Robert or Catlin since that night.

The watchman considered the matter for a long time before he said, 'Aye, I'm certain it was her. Though with her hair shorn and wearing those breeches, I thought at first she was a boy. She had such lovely hair . . . Physician cut it, did he, Master Robert, to keep her strength up?'

'Yes . . . she had the summer fever,' Robert said, grateful to be handed an excuse. 'The physician thought it might lead to a fever of the brain if her hair wasn't cut.'

'Holy Virgin be praised that she's well again, Master Robert.'

The sound of footsteps behind them made them turn. Edward sauntered through the door, and behind him four of the bailiff's men escorting two sullen-looking captives.

When he saw Robert, Edward grinned. 'I have a gift for you, Father.'

Robert's hand clenched into a fist, which he might well have used had the watchman not been present. He struggled to control himself. He did not care to have his family business bandied around the city, which it would be if he told the young cur exactly what he considered their relationship to be.

'You,' Edward said to the watchman. 'Shut the doors and admit no one.' Turning to the bailiff's men, he said, 'Bring this pair up to the counting office. Then you can wait down here till we decide what's to be done with them. There's a cask of small ale in the corner. You can quench your thirst with that. This way, *Father*.'

Robert glared at his back, sure he was deliberately using the word to provoke him into losing his temper. Edward swaggered out into the bright sunshine again, up the wooden staircase outside and through the door to the open platform above the warehouse floor. He dragged two stools behind the table, seating himself on one and offering the other to Robert, with a wave. Robert felt his temper rising with every passing moment. The bailiff's men pushed their two prisoners in front of the table, then clattered back down the stairs, desperate to ease their parched throats with the ale they'd been promised.

Robert, ignoring the proffered stool, studied the pair, who slouched before the table. Both men appeared to have been dragged there without warning. They were clad only in short, filthy breeches, their chests bare and greasy with grime and sweat. The older man had a crooked nose, probably once broken in a fight, for he had the muscles to indicate he might be handy with his fists. The younger one was evidently his son, for he had the same mud-brown eyes and hound-like face. Robert recognised them as boatmen who often delivered cargoes for the warehouse, but he'd never said more than a few words to them in passing.

'What's this about?' he demanded impatiently.

'Don't ask me,' the older man said. 'We were just mooring up, same as usual, to wet our whistles in the inn, when *he* comes up and wants to know if I'm Martin of Washingborough. I says I am, and the next thing I know, we're being dragged along here.'

'And I haven't had my dinner,' the lad complained. 'M' stomach's falling out of my arse and my throat's that dry I could light a fire with it.'

'Not dry enough that you can't talk,' Robert said, reminded of just how thirsty he was. 'Well, Master Edward, I assume you must have some reason for dragging these men from their labours.'

409

'Indeed I have, Father.' Edward pressed his fingers together and rested his elbows on the table. 'As you know, a good number of accidents have befallen our cargoes over the last months – bales falling off boats or being snatched, barrels being breached, not to mention a wagon being robbed on the road to York. I don't take kindly to having my own kin cheated. I'd already guessed your overseer Fulk was behind it. He had to be in collusion with some of the boatmen. He was probably arranging for the cargoes to be transported elsewhere and sold on. He would've had contacts through his work here. But he's hardly in a position to give us names now. So I've been making a few enquiries of my own among your tenants, Father, and found a woman who was only too willing to give us the name of one of the boatmen who was cheating us.'

Martin and his son had been listening without any reaction. Then it seemed to dawn on Martin what he was accused of. 'I hope you're not meaning me!'

'Of course I mean you,' Edward said. 'Why else would I have had you brought here?'

Martin's hand darted to the knife in his belt, but Edward had seen the movement, seized one of the measuring rods on the table and brought it down so hard across Martin's wrist that the wooden rod snapped in two. Martin gave a yelp as the knife fell from his hand, spinning across the floor and coming to rest against Robert's feet. Robert crouched and picked it up, wincing at the pain in his back, as he did so. He rammed the knife into his own belt.

'If you're going to question a man, at least have the sense to see he's disarmed first, you imbecile,' Robert snarled. 'Get the boy's knife too.'

Rubbing his bruised wrist, Martin glared balefully at Edward. 'Whoever gave you my name was trying to cover their own tracks. I've lost a few cargoes, I grant you, but I can't help it if those Florentines deliberately ram my punt and grab a bale. It's them that's the thieves. Master Jan, he was a proper steward, he was. He knew it was down to the Florentines. That's why they pitched him into the Braytheforde, 'cause they knew he was going to lay charges.'

Robert grunted. 'The quarrel my son had with the Florentines concerned the theft of a large sum of money and the confiscation of goods from their warehouse. I hardly think those men would bother with the price of a few barrels and bales when they've stolen thousands.'

'Men'll stoop to anything when they've a grudge just to annoy the other bastard. My neighbour, he let the pigs into our vegetable patch 'cause he swore I'd taken his hammer. And another time he—'

'But as I understand it,' Edward interrupted, 'the thefts started long before Jan had any quarrel with the Florentines. Isn't that right, Father?'

Robert, though still irked, was forced to agree.

'So that brings us back to the deal you made with Fulk,' Edward said triumphantly. 'Was it you who stove his head in? Falling out among thieves, was it? Did he not give you your share of the plunder?'

Martin's son, it seemed, had only just caught up with the conversation. He took a step forward, raising his fists. 'Who are you calling a thief? My faayther's no river-rat. Like he told you, bales just got filched, that's all.'

Despite the meaty fist waving dangerously close to his face, Edward didn't flinch. 'Do you expect us to believe that a lad of your size, not to mention your father's, simply stood by and let thieves lift the cargoes from your punt without putting up a fight?'

The lad opened his mouth, but his father seized his shoulder and hauled him back. 'Way they work is, they ram your punt, push you into another boat. Then, when everyone's distracted, arguing and trying to push away from each other, they swipe what they can while your back's turned. If they're on the outside of the tangle, they can get clean away, while you're still trying to find a gap wide enough to push your quant into the water. They even work two boats sometimes, one to jam you in while the boat with the thieved goods on it gets far downriver.'

'And I suppose this is all the work of the wicked Florentines, is it?' Edward asked, his tone heavy with sarcasm.

'Them and others,' Martin said sullenly.

'What others?'

'How should I know? I don't go drinking with river-rats.' He shot a furious warning glance at his son, who seemed on the verge of jumping in again. 'Anyhow, who gave you my name?'

'That's not your concern,' Edward said.

'I've a right to know. Law says if there's witnesses testifying against you, you've a right to know who they are.'

'Only if they bear witness in a trial,' Edward said.

Robert's eyes narrowed in suspicion. He was certain that Martin and his son wouldn't hesitate to steal the bark from a dog when its

411

back was turned. But believing and proving were two different things and he wasn't about to have these men arrested on the say-so of Edward and be made to look a fool when the charges were dismissed.

Martin's expression suddenly changed. 'You said it was a woman, one of your tenants. It was that stupid mare Nonie, wasn't it? She's always hated me, and her Gunter's had it in for me ever since my lad here threw his boy into the Braytheforde for attacking me without cause. His boy's got a vicious temper, just like his faayther. If it hadn't been for my lad, Gunter's brat would have knocked me off the jetty and I'd have cracked m' head open on the punt. Gunter, and that woman of his, would accuse me of anything to get back at us. He's always been jealous of me and my lad 'cause we get more work than him. But I could tell you something about him, something that's far more valuable than a few bales o' wool.'

'What is it you have to say?' Robert demanded.

Martin glanced below at the bailiff's men who were sprawled on bales and kegs, swigging from their leather beakers and laughing at some tale of the watchman's.

'What I have to tell, I could get a deal of money for. There's men going round the inns offering a month's wages and more for the kind of information I have.'

'Have you got the effrontery to ask me for money when you stand accused of theft?' Robert thundered. 'I've a good mind to have you thrown into the castle prison this very hour.'

The men below stared up at the sound of the raised voice and one sprang to his feet in readiness.

Martin glanced nervously down at them. He held up his hands as if he was appalled by the very idea of being paid. 'Master Robert, I was only saying just so you'd know what I'd got to tell you is important. Word is that you're a commissioner for the King and it's my duty to tell you what I know.'

In spite of the heat of the day, the sweat on Robert's body turned to ice. How the devil had he found that out? If a common boatman knew, the word must have spread all over the city. But the swearing-in had been carried out in secret and Thomas had assured him that he alone kept the list of names in his records to which no one, but his own clerk, had access. Whoever had spread his name abroad might as well have painted a cross on his back. Was that a smile he glimpsed on Edward's lips?

'Master Robert?'

He turned irritably. Martin was waiting for a response. 'Out with it, man. What is this *important* information?'

'I'd tell you in an instant, Master Robert, if I wasn't afeared to speak. If word got back to him that it were me told you, it doesn't bear thinking what he might do . . .' Martin stared pointedly at the bailiff's men waiting below.

Robert sighed. He'd half a mind to have the man arrested at once, but he turned and shouted down, 'You can go. We won't be needing you any more today. Thank you for your pains. Has my steward paid you?'

They nodded.

'Then leave us. You too, watchman. Take your ale outside and guard the door. I'll tell you when we're done here.'

They waited in silence as the watchman opened the door and the men trailed out, though not before refilling their leather beakers from the cask of ale.

Robert mopped his dripping face. The heat was more intense up here in the eaves of the warehouse than it was on the ground. A couple of flies buzzing round their heads alighted on the beads of sweat that ran down Martin's naked chest.

'I had some cider sent down from the house, Father,' Edward said. 'Will you take some?'

He lifted a dripping flagon from a large clay jar full of water where it had been left to keep cool. Two beakers stood ready on a nearby shelf and he poured some into each, taking a mouthful from one and handing the other to Robert, who gulped it gratefully.

Martin and his son licked their dried lips, watching them with covetous eyes.

'Speak,' Robert said, setting the beaker down, 'and I warn you, this information of yours had better be good. I can always send the watchman to fetch the bailiff's men again.'

Martin dragged his gaze from the beaker of cider Edward was still grasping. 'When the riots was on in London, the boatman, Gunter, wasn't in Lincoln, nor that brat of his. No one saw them on the wharf or along the river.'

Robert felt as if a door had been flung open in his head. Gunter! Yes! He was the man who'd spoken up for him on the London street. He'd tried so hard to block out the events of that terrible day that,

413

until this moment, his mind had refused to put a name to the face he saw nightly in his dreams.

He understood where this was leading and was desperate not to hear it, but he knew he must. If it came out later that a king's commissioner had refused to listen to information about the rebels, his reputation would be in ruins or, worse, he might be accused of colluding with them.

He took another swig of cider to give himself time to think. 'This Gunter and his son were probably working further down the river or among the ships at Boston.'

'That's the thing, though,' Martin said, with a sly grin. 'They weren't working at all 'cause their punt was moored up next to the house. They keep it covered at night, same as the rest of us, but in daylight you can see there's a boat under the reed mats. And they weren't sick neither, 'cause one of the neighbours called in on that wife of his a couple of times and she says there weren't no sign of Gunter or his son in the cottage. Nigh on three weeks they were gone. That family hasn't got a pot to piss in. They can't afford to spend their days like lords, idling away their time.'

Robert winced, gripped by a sudden cramp in the belly. He grasped the edge of the table and lowered himself to a stool. He knew better than to gulp cold cider when he was as hot as this. Wasn't he always telling that stable-boy not to let the horses drink cold water when they were in a sweat for fear of the colic? He should have heeded his own advice.

He took a deep breath and tried to ignore the pain. 'They might have found work elsewhere . . . pagging . . . work on a farm . . . if they couldn't get cargoes. That doesn't prove—'

'But I know something that does,' Edward interrupted. 'When we went to call on the tenants, Gunter's son was sick in bed. His mother said he'd been hurt when a box or some such fell on him, but Catlin insisted on looking at the wound. The boy's back was burned, and not the kind of burn you'd get from falling into a hearth fire. It looked as if something had been fired into it, like a burning arrow only wider, bigger. It was plain his mother was lying about how he'd been injured. It can't be a coincidence that Gunter and his son were missing at the very time of the rebellion, and for them to turn up with one wounded as if he'd been in a battle. I'm certain . . .' He trailed off and stared at Robert. 'What is it? Are you sick, Father?'

414

Robert doubled up in agony. He fell from the stool onto his knees, moaning and clutching his belly as violent pains tore through it. He clutched weakly at his gown, trying to pull it away from his chest so that he could breathe. His heart was thumping in his chest so hard that he was certain it would explode.

He clutched at Edward's leg. 'Bayus . . . fetch Hugo Bayus. Hurry!'

Chapter 64

The dust in a house must be swept inwards before it is collected and taken out, for if a woman should sweep the dust outwards through the door, she will sweep away all the wealth and good fortune of the family.

Greetwell

Gunter looked down at the sleeping figure of his son. He lay on his side, his face turned towards him, sweat glistening on his flushed cheeks. Robert's wife had sent no ointment from the apothecary, not that Gunter had expected her to, though Nonie stubbornly refused to believe she would not keep her promise. Gunter knew his suspicions had been right. Mistress Catlin had only come to discover if Hankin had been part of the rebellion.

The boy's dark lashes fluttered against his cheek. Lashes, as Nonie often said, that would be the envy of any lass, but were wasted on a lad. Beneath the closed lids the boy's eyes rolled restlessly. *Giles, Giles! . . . Pies . . . I didn't . . . Please no . . .*

If you died, did your nightmares stop, or did they go on for ever with no hope of you waking from them? They would for Gunter. If he killed himself, he knew there could never be any end to his torment. There was no forgiveness for self-murder. How could there be? You could not confess it.

But for the boy, if he were to die in innocence, if he had confessed his sins, his nightmare would be over. But Gunter dared not take the boy to a priest. In Norfolk, they said, Bishop Despenser was hearing confessions, then sending men straight to the gallows for what they confessed. No priest could be trusted now. Too many abbeys and churches had been attacked. They would show no mercy to the rebels, respect no secrets. He couldn't let the boy be taken alive. He couldn't watch his child's face and limbs be mutilated, see his terror, listen to his screams. He had to do it, do it now before it was too late.

He went to the window and glanced out. The light glinting off the river was blinding in the afternoon sun. Nonie was outside tending their little patch of vegetables and Col was firing his sling at any bird foolish enough to perch in the nearby trees, though he hit none. Royse was in the byre. He might not find another chance to be alone with the lad and they could come for him at any hour.

Gunter knelt by his son's bed. Taking the boy's hot little hand in his, he whispered, 'Hankin, you must listen to me.'

The boy grunted and his eyes fluttered open, then closed again.

Gunter squeezed his hand. 'You must confess, Bor. You must tell all that you've done wrong, just like you do to the priest. I'll not be angry and I swear I'll tell no one, but we can't go to the church. You're too sick. So you must confess to me . . . in case . . .'

Without opening his eyes the boy murmured, 'Am I dying? I don't . . . want to die.'

'No, son, but we never know when death may strike. We must always be ready.'

'Don't . . . let me die, Faayther.'

A hard lump rose in Gunter's chest. 'Try to think, Hankin.'

The boy muttered something, but Gunter could make little sense of it. He'd no idea if he was confessing or simply crying out in his dreams.

He knelt by Hankin's bed. 'Blessed Virgin, take him straight to Heaven. He's innocent. He's not a bad bone in his body. Whatever he's done, I'll pay the price for it. Whatever he was forced to do, it was my fault. I should have protected him. I should have protected them all. Blessed Mary, don't hold it against the boy, punish me for his sins. I'll take them, take them all on me. He's only a bairn.'

The boy's breathing had fallen into the shallow but steady rhythm of sleep. His lips parted as he sucked in the stifling air.

Sweat ran down Gunter's face. He slid the sheepskin from the bottom of the bed and paused, looking down at the smooth red cheek. Then, as gently as he could, with trembling hands, he pressed the fleece over the boy's face.

Gunter had thought his breathing would quietly stop. But at once Hankin tried to push the skin away, thrashing his arms and legs. He was as weak as a nestling, but still he fought desperately for his life. Gunter felt Hankin's hands grasping at his own arms, trying to push him away. Tears streamed down his face as he pressed harder, willing the boy to surrender and die.

'I'm sorry. I'm so sorry. Forgive me.'

Nonie, crouching down, tugged at the bindweed that had wrapped itself around her beans. It grew so much faster than any crop, snaking out in the night to choke the plants. Why did weeds grow so vigorously and food so slowly when the same rain and sun touched them both? She rocked back on her heels, wiping her hand across her dripping forehead. As she raised her head, she caught sight of someone standing on the riverbank in front of the cottage, but against the sun's glare, and the dancing glints from the river, she couldn't make out who it was.

Grasping her weeding stick, she struggled to her feet, wiping her grimy hand on her sacking apron. She shielded her eyes. Two children stood hand in hand close to the water's edge, a girl and a boy. They were looking at the little cottage.

Nonie was still unable to see them clearly because of the glare. She guessed the children had been sent with a message. Maybe someone needed goods transporting or wanted to be taken downriver. She hoped so: they needed every penny Gunter could earn. She took a step forward.

'Your faayther wanting to hire the boat, is it?'

The children didn't turn their heads, or make any sign that they'd heard her.

'Come here,' Nonie called, a little irritated now.

Hankin! Hankin, come and play. The words were so faint, so high-pitched they might have been the breeze in the tree-tops or the piping of a lark, except there was no breeze, no lark.

'What do you . . .'

The words turned to stone in Nonie's mouth, for she suddenly knew why the sun was shimmering so brightly around them. Water was streaming from their clothes and hair, as if they had just risen from a lake, or a river – water that did not stop flowing. Nonie's head slowly followed the direction of the children's gaze. She stared at the closed door of the cottage. Then, with a single shriek, she flung down her stick and ran.

The door opened behind Gunter. Nonie flew across the room, clawing at him, with all the fury of a she-wolf. 'Holy Virgin, what are you doing to the bairn? Get away, get away from him!'

418

Shoving Gunter violently aside, she grabbed Hankin, tore the sheepskin from his face and hauled him into her arms. She rocked back and forth, as the boy clung to her sobbing and gasping for breath.

Gunter reached out a hand to soothe the lad, but Nonie slapped it away. 'Don't touch him! Don't you dare touch him!'

'I had to, Nonie. If they arrest him . . . I couldn't let them take him alive.'

'Why should anyone arrest my son?' Nonie clutched Hankin to her. 'They should arrest you, that's what they should do. Trying to smother your own bairn. You've run mad. You want locking up, you do.'

'But, Nonie, you don't understand the danger.'

'What danger? The only danger he's in is from his mad father, that's what. Get out! Get out!' she screamed.

Gunter, his eyes blinded by tears, stumbled to the door and out into the blazing sunshine. He sank against the wall, shaking violently, his chest heaving as he sobbed. He was so distraught he didn't even notice the men dismounting from the horses at the side of the cottage. Only when they were almost upon him did he realise he was not alone.

'Gunter of Greetwell. I am here on the orders of the King's Commissioners to arrest you and your son for high treason.'

Chapter 65

*Witches can turn themselves into foxes. The hunt will often see
them run into a cave or cottage and think they have trapped
them, only to find nothing inside except an old woman.*

Lincoln

Hugo Bayus descended the stairs slowly, muttering to himself. Adam
stood by the casement of the hall below, staring out into the street.
He didn't turn, not even when the physician ruffled his hair.

'No need for you to mope around indoors, young man. Your father
is recovering well. He'll soon be up and about again.'

'I said as much to you this morning, didn't I, Mistress Catlin?'
Diot said triumphantly. 'I said he was on the mend.'

'That is good news, isn't it, Adam?' Catlin said. 'We were all so
worried.'

Adam wasn't. He'd felt not the slightest concern when they'd brought
his father home on a cart two days ago, groaning in pain and raving
like one of the mad beggars who accosted people on their way to and
from the cathedral. Edward and the carter had hauled him up the stairs
and the physician had hurried round soon after. The pains had lasted
for two days and nights, but today he lay still and quiet. Adam was
disappointed. He'd hoped the sickness would last longer, much longer.

'Will he make a full recovery?' Catlin asked.

'He's weak, of course. He should rest in bed for several days more,
but knowing your husband, Mistress Catlin, I doubt he will. But he
should have only a beef bonet for the next two days, nothing richer
than that. See that the beef is well ground and seethe it in a good
measure of blood and water. Beata will know. She's skilled at preparing
such dishes.'

Adam turned to stare pointedly at his stepmother. She was seated
at the table next to Edward, in front of a stack of parchments and
ledgers. Mother and son exchanged glances before Catlin spoke.

'I'm afraid Beata no longer works here.'

The physician's bald pate gleamed in the sunlight from the casement. 'A pity, but I'm sure you will manage.'

'Course, we will.' Diot bridled. 'I'm twice the cook that mad trollop ever was, and you don't have to fear waking up with your throat slit when I'm in charge of the kitchen.'

'Will the sickness recur, Master Bayus?' Catlin asked.

'I am not certain it was a sickness,' the physician said cautiously.

Diot glanced swiftly at Catlin, alarm and fear on her plump face, but Catlin's expression didn't change.

'Course the master was sick,' Diot said hastily, her face flushing so red, she herself might have had a fever. 'Half the city's been taken bad. Stench from the ditches, that's what caused the sickness and no mistake.' She plucked agitatedly at her skirts, her eyes repeatedly darting towards Catlin.

'Certainly in this infernal heat many in the city have fallen ill with the summer flux,' the physician said, 'but Master Robert had none of the usual symptoms. His only complaint was the severe pains and the madness . . . that is to say, the delirium that often accompanies fever of the brain, yet he appears to have no fever. I've enquired of the other physicians of my acquaintance and none of them has had a patient with such an illness. It seems to me, Mistress Catlin . . .'

He hesitated and looked at Adam. 'Why don't you run outside and play, young man? I'm sure you must be itching to be out on such a day. I'm not so old that I don't remember such things from my own boyhood.' The old man gave the chuckle of one who fondly recalls a childhood that only ever existed in their dreams.

'He's my father,' Adam said. 'I've a right to know what's wrong. More right than anyone else in this house. It's them you should be sending out.'

Edward half rose from the table. 'You little brat!'

But Catlin grasped his arm. 'He's just a child, Edward, and naturally he's concerned for his father.' She smiled icily. 'Adam, do as Master Bayus says. Go outside. I'll discuss this matter with you later.'

Adam was on the point of refusing, but he saw her fingers turn white as she gripped the table and sensed she was becoming dangerously angry. His nerve failed him and, as slowly as he dared, he walked from the room. When he opened the door, he almost collided with Leonia, who was standing immediately behind it. She shrank into the shadows. But as soon as he had closed the door, she tiptoed back, a finger to her lips, and leaned her shorn head against the wood. Adam joined her. He could hear Hugo Bayus talking.

'As I say, Mistress Catlin, I do not believe this to have been a summer fever. It bears all the hallmarks of poison.'

'I've not poisoned anyone!' Diot shrieked. 'I'd swear on every holy saint that ever was.'

'Don't be foolish, Diot dear.' Catlin gave her tinkling laugh. 'Master Bayus is certainly not accusing you, are you?'

'I wouldn't dream of suggesting that anyone in this household . . .' Bayus said hastily, as if he feared Diot might start crying.

'Quite,' Catlin said softly. 'But who on earth would want to poison my dear husband, Master Bayus?'

Leonia twisted her head round to look at Adam. She was smiling gleefully. He opened his mouth to speak, but she pressed her cool little fingertips to it, flicking her eyes warningly towards the room.

'Any man in your husband's position will have enemies, and I understand he has been made a Commissioner of Array. There are many who would wish to harm those who render such loyal service to the Crown.'

'Have the others been attacked?' That was Edward's voice.

'I fear I cannot answer that,' Hugo Bayus said. 'It's not known who the other members are. Only Master Robert's name seems to be bandied abroad, though how that came to be, I'm at a loss to know.'

'But I gave my husband a ring with a serpent's tongue embedded in it to render any poison harmless. He's always careful to touch the ring to every dish when we dine away from home.'

The physician gave a nervous little cough. 'Master Robert tells me that shortly before he became ill he drank some cider. He says he was distracted and cannot recall if he took the precaution of touching the ring to the liquid.'

'There was certainly no poison in the cider,' Edward said emphatically. 'As Master Robert will tell you, I drank first from the same flagon. He saw me. It didn't taste mouldy or tainted and I suffered no ill-effects.'

'The poison may have been in the cup, not the drink. Was it left unattended at any time?'

'It was standing in the tally room a good hour or more before I returned,' Edward said. 'That room is reached by the staircase on the

422

outside of the warehouse. Anyone could have crept up there unobserved.'

Hugo Bayus grunted. 'Then I should take the utmost care, Mistress Catlin. If the poison was intended for Master Robert—'

'What do you mean, *if*?' Edward said. 'Who else could it have been intended for?'

'Without knowing who committed the crime, I really cannot tell,' Bayus said. 'But, of course, your stepfather was the most likely target. Let's just be thankful that it was not a lethal dose. Now I must take my leave.'

Leonia grabbed Adam's hand and they ran out into the courtyard. Moments later the door opened and the physician came out in search of his horse, jamming his hat on his head to keep the sun from his bald pate.

Leonia and Adam ducked out of sight behind the kitchen and as soon as he had ridden off they slipped out of the yard. Adam turned in the direction of the river, but Leonia tugged at his arm. 'No, this way.'

They climbed the steep hill and turned into one of the small alleyways whose steps led up to Pottergate and out through the city wall. They were panting after the climb in the heat and paused to draw breath and stare out over the valley below. They were standing on the edge of the escarpment; above them and just visible over the city walls was the great cathedral. To the right lay the Bishop's Palace, vineyards sprawling down the slope below, but where they were standing the hill ended in a sharp cliff.

Opposite, on the other side of the valley, another huge cliff curved away to the left, and to the right lay the flat basin of Braytheforde harbour, crammed with boats which, from that height, looked like tadpoles swarming in a puddle. Between the scarp and the distant cliff, the glittering river wound through flat fields and hamlets towards the fens. A dense, shimmering heat rose from the land below, mingled with the smoke of cooking fires, so that the little cottages seemed like midges dancing in a haze.

Leonia dived between two trees and scrambled over the edge of the cliff. Adam hesitated, peering down. He couldn't see any sign of her and for a moment was terrified she'd fallen to the bottom. Then he heard her voice calling from somewhere close below him. Clinging to the bushes, he picked his way down the rocks, until he saw a broad grassy ledge. There didn't seem to be any way of reaching it.

'Jump,' Leonia urged.

He was afraid, but he couldn't refuse. He jumped, wincing as his knee jarred when he hit the ground. The brief rainstorm of a few days ago had done little to soften the baked earth. There was no sign of Leonia.

'Where are you?'

'In here . . . behind you.'

He saw only a few scrubby bushes clinging to the rock. Then he glimpsed her hand waving from behind one. He edged forward, and parted the bushes. What he had taken to be merely a dark shadow, he saw was the entrance to a cave, long and low, like a grin on the cliff face. Leonia was squatting inside on the rough ground. Adam crawled in and sat beside her. It was blissfully cool, though it smelt of fox and cat. Suddenly he felt very safe, as if no other person in the world could ever find this place.

As his eyes adjusted to the dimness he saw that the cave contained the remains of what looked like large pots. One had a great serpent cut into the clay, curving right around to bite its own tail. Some of the pots were whole, but others smashed, the shards lying in what seemed to be piles of ashes and charred fragments. He picked up something, thinking it to be a stone, but it was too light for that. He realised it was a piece of bone.

'What is this place?'

Leonia touched the wall as if it was a shrine. 'I found it a long time ago. There are more like this, but mostly further round, where there's no ledge and I can't get into them. It's a special place. Only I know about it, but I'm going to trust you with all my secrets now, because I know you'll never tell, will you, Adam? We keep each other's secrets. We share everything. We take care of each other.' Fleetingly, she touched his cheek. 'We'll always take care of each other, won't we, Adam?'

He felt his face grow hot. His skin tingled where her fingers had stroked him. He wanted to hold his cheek, so he could keep feeling the touch of her hand, but he was afraid she would laugh at him. He hugged himself in delight. She had brought him to her secret place. A place no one else in the whole world knew about. It was theirs now, hers and his together. She did trust him, she really did. He was desperate to do something – anything – in return, but he could think of nothing to give her. He knew that whatever he said or did would not be good enough to match this.

Leonia reached behind her, and lifted a flat piece of stone. Reaching

424

for his hand, she tipped some amber beads into it, with some long bear's claws and a piece of gold. After dutifully examining them, Adam dropped the beads and claws back into her lap and held the gold up to the sunlight in the entrance. It was the head of an animal, with red garnet eyes and twin bands of garnets running down over its head from neck to snout.

'There are people here, dead people,' Leonia said. 'I hear them whispering. That golden boar belonged to one of them.'

Adam dropped it, as if it had burned his hand. It bounced a couple of times before coming to rest, quivering, in front of Leonia. She scooped it up and replaced all her treasures under the stone.

'Aren't you going to ask me?'

One question had been throbbing in his head ever since Robert had been brought home sick, but he hadn't dared to ask.

He took a deep breath, holding himself stiff against the anger he felt sure would explode from her. 'Did you make a poppet to punish Fath— Robert?'

She didn't answer. He glanced sideways at her. He couldn't see her expression clearly, only the glitter of her eyes in the shadows.

'I don't mind if you did,' he added quickly. 'In fact I'd be glad. I wanted to hurt him after what he did to you. He deserves to be punished. He should have stopped Catlin. It was him . . . he touched you. She should have cut him, not you.'

His eyes stung with tears and his chest felt crushed beneath the weight of his hatred. His father was old, disgusting. When Leonia had told him what he done to her he'd almost vomited. His rage was due in no small part to the fact that he had lain awake night after night dreaming of kissing Leonia himself, but he hadn't done it because she was his sister. Robert kept telling him Leonia was his sister. Adam felt dirty and ashamed for even thinking of touching her.

And then Robert, who was supposed to be her father, had laid his hands on her. That was worse, far worse, than a brother doing it. Adam wanted to smash his face to a pulp, like they had smashed Fulk's face. He cursed himself for not being there to protect Leonia. If he had, he would have fought Robert for her. But then for Catlin to cut her hair, her beautiful hair . . .

'Did you, Leonia? If you hurt him, I'm glad.'

'If I had, he wouldn't be getting better.' She turned to face Adam. 'If I'd punished Robert, he'd be dead.'

425

Adam was startled. He'd been so sure she'd done it and he'd been pleased she'd had her revenge. But he believed her when she said she hadn't. Leonia had never lied to him. If she had made a poppet, she would have told him.

'Do you think Hugo Bayus was right, then? It was poison? But who did it? Was it . . .' Adam hesitated. Should he tell Leonia that he'd seen Catlin putting the drops into his mother's posset? He'd never dared before because Catlin was her mother, but Leonia hated her. Maybe she'd believe him, even if his own father didn't.

'It was Edward who poisoned the cup,' Leonia said. 'He's not very good at it, though. He wants Robert dead so he can have his money.'

'But if my father's dies, his money'll be mine,' Adam said indignantly. 'I'm his son.'

'But they won't let you have it till you're of age and, because you're a boy, that won't be until you're twenty-one. They'll let Catlin look after it till then, 'cept she won't. She'll give it to Edward – at least that's what he thinks.'

'Your mother can't do that!' Adam shouted. 'I won't let her. I'll warn my father. I'll tell him everything!'

'He won't believe you. He never listens to you.'

Picking up a fragment of the bone, she traced a pattern in the ash that had spilled out from one of the jars. Adam leaned closer. It was a serpent swallowing its tail, like the one on the jar and on the shoes Leonia wore. Although he knew his eyes must be playing tricks in the dim light, it seemed to him that the snake was undulating across the floor of the cave towards Leonia and wriggling up beneath her skirts.

Without lifting her head, she said quietly, 'Catlin killed your mother, Adam. You know that, don't you?'

A rush of relief and anger flooded through him. 'I told them – I told them she had, but no one would listen, except Beata and Jan, and Robert locked Beata up and Jan's dead.'

Leonia laid a cool hand on Adam's arm. 'That's why they have to die, Adam. Robert and Catlin have to be punished. You want that, don't you? You want to help me punish them? You want to kill them, don't you, like she killed your mother?'

Adam nodded, his fists clenched over his face. He wanted that more than anything in the world at this moment. He wanted them both to die, and when they were dead, he would laugh and laugh and never stop laughing.

'We needed them to marry so we could find each other,' Leonia whispered. 'But we don't need them any more. And when they're dead we'll have everything we want from them.'

He felt her soft arm round his shoulders and her hand on his, pulling his fingers away from his face. She turned his head towards her, brushing away his tears of rage. He smelt her violet-sweet breath, watching in a trance as her mouth came slowly towards him. He felt her soft, warm lips press on his. As he closed his eyes, she took his hand and cupped it gently around her little breast.

Chapter 66

If the fire in the hearth burns in a hollow, like a grave, someone present in the house will shortly die.

Mistress Catlin

I couldn't sleep. Robert had fallen into a near drunken stupor, which he had seemed compelled to do every night since he'd returned from London in order to sleep at all. The beast lay on his back in our great bed and his rumbling snores were so loud they made the bed shake. Every time I began to doze from sheer exhaustion, I'd be startled awake by his sudden snorts and gasps before the snoring resumed, heavier than before. The night air was sticky and oppressive. Robert's sweating carcass radiated heat, like a baker's oven. I felt as if I were being smothered.

I slid out of bed, slipping on the new fur wrap Robert had bought me to cover my naked body. Opening the casement, I leaned out, trying to catch whatever breeze might be blowing up from the river, but it brought no blessed coolness, only the stench of rotting fish and mud. Far off, a dog was howling and its cries were soon caught up by others, baying across the city, like watchmen calling news to one another. I paddled through the pool of silver moonlight on the floor, quietly opened the door and made my way past the sleeping children down the stairs to the great hall.

Diot was sleeping in the courtyard. She'd melt into a puddle of lard indoors in the sweltering heat. Besides, she knew I was furious with her and was keeping well out of my way. The fear on her face when Bayus mentioned poison would have been enough to convince anyone she'd done it. I could have strangled her. How could anyone so foolish be my . . . I shuddered and thrust away the thought.

Tenney, of course, had not returned. I told Robert to declare the manservant and his whore both thieves and have them hunted down and hanged. I would enjoy watching that. But Robert was still insisting that Tenney would never simply abandon his employ, much less steal anything so valuable as a horse and cart. He was convinced that, as soon as he had delivered Beata to her people, assuming she had any, he'd be back to resume his duties as before. It was a mystery to me how a man so gullible had ever held onto his business.

Still, there would be time enough later to deal with Beata and Tenney and see that they paid dearly for their theft. For now, it was as well that they were out of the way. Robert was quite alone and unprotected. I could take my time disposing of him and savour every moment.

Edward lay on his straw pallet in the great hall. He was awake. I could see his eyes glittering in the moonlight, which seeped through the cracks in the shutters. He was staring malevolently at the ceiling, for even down in the hall, Robert's snores rumbled through the floorboards.

A single candle burned at the far end of the hall and I poured a goblet of wine for myself and Edward, and knelt beside him on the floor. He sat up, taking a great gulp. 'The old hog's in fine voice tonight,' he said. 'I take it he's recovering.'

'No thanks to you,' I snapped. 'What did you think you were doing with that cider?'

'What makes you think I—'

'Don't try to deny it,' I said. 'You're lucky Bayus is so blinded by Robert's wealth and position that it never occurred to him anyone in this *respectable* family would attempt such a thing. You're a fool, Edward. Putting poison in a drink is the work of a child and about as subtle as cleaving someone in two with an axe. Even an apprentice physician would have seen that Robert didn't have the summer fever. At the very least you might have ensured you weren't there when he was taken ill.'

'It's not my fault,' Edward muttered sulkily. 'I hadn't intended to be there. By the time it took effect, I should have been laying charges against Martin before the sheriff. Robert would have been alone in the warehouse and would have died alone, too, by the time anyone found him. Given his great bulk, I thought it'd be at least an hour before anything happened.'

'But you didn't think, did you?' I said. 'And now Martin's gone straight to the sheriff and tried to ingratiate himself by not only reporting Gunter and his son for treason but also saying that you and

I saw the burns on the boy's back. Suppose we're called as witnesses. Who else might be in the court? The justices travel on a wide circuit.'

'And I suppose Sheriff Thomas told you all about Martin, while you flattered him and flirted till he didn't know which way round his head was stuck on. I feel sorry for him. It's like watching a partridge wander blithely towards a fox. You do realise, don't you, that Thomas is only sheriff for a year? Though, I grant you, he'll still be a plump capon to pluck. He's a wealthy enough lover even for you, little Maman.'

I ignored his childish petulance. He was only lashing out because he knew how stupid he'd been. He was at heart no more than a little boy. I smoothed the white flash in his dark hair.

'You would do well to follow my example and make a friend of the sheriff. We are going to need him when Robert is dead. But I told you to wait, Edward. I said I would deal with Robert.'

'I can't afford to wait!' Edward drained his goblet. 'Leonia's thirteen, old enough to marry, so if the claim isn't made before her next birthday, I'll never get my hands on my land . . . *our* land. Besides, I won't stand for the old bastard giving me orders and treating me like some scullion while he's slobbering over you. I'll not put up with it much longer. Get rid of him now or I'll do it for you. Next time I won't make any mistakes.'

I stroked his hair until I felt him relax beneath my fingers. Then I slapped his face so hard that he fell back against the pillow with a cry. 'You think to threaten me? Don't make me choose, Edward. You might not like my choice.' Shaking with anger, I turned and climbed the stairs back up to the bedchamber and my sleeping husband.

It seemed I was losing control of both Edward and Leonia and I couldn't afford to do that. They thought they could challenge me and I wouldn't tolerate it. Leonia would not try anything more with my husband, not after last time, I was sure of that. Perhaps Edward, too, needed shearing, just to remind him of whom he was dealing with.

He was right about one thing, though. Time was running out for both Edward and Leonia. Robert was no closer to regarding Edward as a future heir. In fact, the more time they spent in each other's company, the greater became their mutual loathing. My sweet boy did not have the disposition for crude commerce, for which I was eternally grateful, but Robert was continually measuring him against that bumpkin Jan and finding him lacking. It was only a matter of

430

time before Robert's shredded nerves snapped and he had Edward thrown out of Lincoln, or worse.

I pulled my wrap closer, feeling the soft fur caress my bare buttocks and thighs, like my lover's fingers. A shiver of pleasure tingled down my spine. Why wait any longer? The sooner Robert was dead, the sooner my lover would be lying in that bed. We wouldn't need to hide in some filthy tower or the corner of a field. We could be in each other's arms, day and night, whenever we chose.

The great mound of flesh gave another whistling gasp and the bed groaned in protest as he turned over to resume his relentless snoring. My fingers itched to press a pillow over his face and hold it down until I had smothered the very breath from his sweaty carcass. But I restrained myself. Believe me, it's not as easy to kill a man in that way as one might imagine, however satisfying.

Besides, the most delicious idea had just occurred to me, one that would throw no suspicion on me at all. In fact, if I played the grieving widow well enough, the King himself might press a handsome settlement upon me for the sake of his loyal, but tragically deceased servant.

I looked down at the dark hump beneath the covers. Before the next full moon that body would be stretched out cold on the table below in the great hall, like a slab of the roast beef to which he was so partial. And I would indeed be mistress of all.

Chapter 67

Night after night, a man was tormented by human voices chattering beneath his window and saw several cats, mice and toads gathered there. Thinking them to be witches' familiars, one night he attacked them with an axe. The next day three old women in the village were found dead from axe wounds.

Lincoln Castle

A shaft of grey light drifted sluggishly through the tiny grille in the door. Gunter woke and, for a few precious moments, thought he was at home in his own cottage, until, with a rush, all his senses kicked in at once – the prickling of straw on his skin, the sour taste of vomit in his mouth, the groans and snores, the stench of sweat, piss and shit of men. He leaned forward, trying to ease the cramp in his leg, weighed down by the heavy iron fetter around his ankle. When they'd dragged him into the cell, they'd taken his wooden leg from him, claiming he might use it as a weapon. Besides, they chuckled, he wasn't likely to need it where he was going. The loss had made him feel more vulnerable and helpless than the fetter around his good leg.

There were six men in the tiny cell in the castle. It was where Gaunt's men-at-arms were usually held if they had offended their superiors. Each man was attached by chains from his legs to a central pillar. More chains hung from the walls behind them, so that, if necessary, prisoners could be stretched backwards, over sharp pieces of wood, their wrists fastened to the wall behind, unable to move at all. Gunter prayed this torture would not be used on them. Hankin would be in agony.

Hankin! A sudden panic drenched him and he tried to wriggle closer to the boy. He was lying on his side, his face turned away from his father, and in the dim light, Gunter couldn't see if he was breathing. He reached out and touched him. Hankin jerked backwards, startled out of sleep.

432

Gunter patted his shoulder. 'Easy, Bor. How're you faring?'

With a groan, Hankin shuffled as far away from his father's hand as the chains on his leg would permit. Gunter felt a stab of pain. His own son was frightened of him, more frightened even than of the men-at-arms who had come for them. He didn't blame him. How could he explain that he'd only wanted to spare him the horrors that lay ahead of them? How could you tell your own son you'd knelt at his bedside and prayed for him to die?

At least from the brief touch Gunter knew his fever had not returned. The men-at-arms had been merciful to the lad. Seeing that he could not walk, one rider had carried the boy in front of him, slung face down over the horse. The jolting and bumping must have been painful, but at least he had not been made to walk as Gunter had.

Gunter's wrists had been bound to a long rope and he had been forced to limp all the way to the city, then up the steep hill to the castle. The deep lacerations and bruises to his wrists and the grazes to his leg and arms bore witness to the two occasions he had slipped and fallen from sheer exhaustion, but the rider had paused long enough to allow him to pull himself to his feet again. He knew many would not have done that.

They heard a jangling of keys and the heavy door creaked open.

'Keep your heads down and put your hands on your knees, where I can see them,' the soldier called. 'One wrong move from any of you and I'll have you all in full chains.'

Hankin struggled to sit, groaning as he did so. Gunter glanced at him, but the boy wouldn't look at him. The soldier dropped bread and pieces of salt pork into the lap of one of the men, shaking his head at the man sitting next to him. 'You'll be going hungry again, Mack. Your daughter's not brought anything today. Maybe she'll bring you some supper, if she thinks on it. Mind you, from what I seen of her and young Hob at back of castle last night, I reckon she's got other things on her mind. You want me to remind her, if she comes to help him polish his pike tonight?'

Mack snarled a mouthful of threats, but the soldier only grinned. 'Watch what you say, 'less you want your back stretching.'

The soldier walked round to stand behind Hankin. 'Your mam sent this for you and your father.'

He dropped a package wrapped in sacking into the boy's lap. Bread, a piece of dried eel and two onions rolled out.

'She's here? Can I . . . see her?' Hankin asked.

The soldier laughed. 'You'll see her – at the gallows. The justices'll make sure she has a place right at the front so she can watch you dancing on the rope. Wouldn't want to miss that performance, she wouldn't. We always make sure we keep the best spot for the wives and mothers. Only fair.'

One of the other prisoners looked up. His face was swollen down one side and his eye blackened and closed. 'He's not been tried yet. None of us have. They have to give us a trial. It's the law.'

'Don't you fret, you'll get your trial. Tried and executed within the hour, that's the way of it. What I mean is, they'll start the execution as soon as sentence is passed and you've been shrived, but I can't promise how quickly you'll die. Depends on how they do it.' The soldier grinned.

Gunter glanced at his son, but Hankin was staring straight ahead at the pillar, his jaw clenched as if he was trying hard not to cry. Gunter could see he was terrified.

'But I've done nothing,' the man protested. 'I swear by all the saints. I was helping my brother. He lives up Grimsby way. Send word to him. He'll tell you. A dozen honest men saw me there and they'll swear to it.'

The soldier shrugged. 'Nowt to do with me. There's a list. If your name's been put on the list, that's it. Commissioners send names to London. Then, when there's a judge free, he'll come here and try you, 'less they send you to London. You'll have to argue your case then. Now it's my job to keep you locked up safe here, till they decide what's to be done with you.'

Gunter raised his head, taking care to keep his hands on his knees. He didn't want to give the soldier any cause to make conditions worse. 'Robert of Bassingham. Was he the one who named me?'

The soldier kicked him lightly, but without malice. 'You know you can't be asking me that. They don't want your families taking revenge on those who inform. Mind you, I reckon they already have. They say someone tried to poison Master Robert. Wasn't you, was it? There again, doesn't much matter if it was. Can't execute a man twice over, can they?'

Chapter 68

*You may protect a cow or a child from the evil eye, if you hang
a wreath of rowan about their neck and recite, 'From witches and
wizards and long-tailed buzzards, and creeping things that run
in hedge-bottoms, Good Lord, deliver us.'*

Lincoln

The sun was sinking, ripening to blood-red in the sky. It had rained
earlier, a sudden deluge that had turned the dust and dried dung on
the paths instantly to cloying mud, as slippery as slush. Godwin had
taken shelter outside the city walls at the top of the hill. The rain
had stopped as quickly as it had begun, and as the earth began to
steam, he picked his way down towards the gate that led into the
lower city, following the line of the high cliff edge and trying not to
slip on the steep slope.

He was so intent on watching where he placed his sandals that he
barely noticed the two small figures climbing up the track towards
him. When he heard a voice that sounded familiar, he glanced up
and, recognising the pair, swiftly pressed himself behind the angle of
the city wall.

The boy he'd come to know as Adam was climbing the steep track
towards him, in the company of the witch's spawn, Leonia. Her close-
cropped hair shone like polished ebony in the sunset. The boy smiled
at her, trotting alongside, as trusting as a puppy, and Godwin was
seized with the desire to run and snatch him away from her, but he
forced himself to remain hidden. Just before they reached the place
where he was concealed, Leonia squeezed between two trees and
disappeared. Adam followed. Cautiously, Godwin crossed the track
and peered over the edge, just in time to see Adam vanish into the
bushes on a wide ledge below.

He knew even before he approached the edge that Leonia was
leading Adam into a snare. One from which he would never emerge

alive. She would use him, as her mother had used all the men she had entrapped, then taken a cruel delight in watching them die. Godwin was sure that the power to make men suffer, the power to kill, meant more to Pavia than even the money she bled from them and that the same venom coursed through her daughter's veins, exciting her, making her stronger with every conquest she devoured.

As quietly as he could, Godwin clambered awkwardly over the edge of the cliff, grasping the wiry bushes and tree roots to stop himself falling. His foot dislodged a small shower of stones. He froze, looking down, but the children did not appear. He breathed again and eased himself onwards, until his foot touched the ledge. He crouched on the wet grass, but could see no sign of them. Had they climbed further down? He was about to creep to the edge of the ledge when he heard low voices coming from behind him. He crawled towards the cliff face. The voices were coming from behind a bush, but sounded strangely muffled.

'I don't want him to touch you again.' The boy was speaking.

'As soon as you bring Catlin in he'll stop. Besides, after that he won't be able to do anything. They'll both be punished. They must be.'

'But I can't . . .'

'You can. I know it. I showed you this place because I trust you, Adam. We take care of each other, remember. See? I've made a cord for you to hang a bear's claw round your neck. That will make you stronger than any of them. Hold out your hand.'

Adam gave a little gasp of pain.

'Squeeze three drops of your blood into the water.'

Godwin shuffled closer, peering through the bushes, and only then did he see the slit in the rock. It was dark inside the little cave, but a narrow shaft of light fell on Leonia's hands. She and the boy were sitting cross-legged, facing each other. Leonia was holding a curved piece of bone that looked like a fragment of a skull. She was using it to scoop cloudy grey water from a big clay pot, drizzling it onto Adam's bare head, once, twice, three times. A mixture of water and wet ash slid down his forehead, in blasphemy of baptism.

Each time Godwin saw Adam, he saw himself staring out of the boy's eyes. He'd been much the same age when Pavia had come into his life and not a day had passed since he had returned from France, a broken travesty of a man, that he'd not cursed himself as a fool for the easy trust he'd put in that witch. She'd taken everything from him, his father, his sisters, his home, his inheritance, his name, and had left him to suffer and die at the hands of the French. The cruellest betrayal of all was that she had first made a little boy love her as his mother. He would not allow her daughter to destroy another innocent boy, the boy he'd once been.

It was all he could do to stop himself shouting a warning to Adam, but he knew it would be useless. Even if he could make the boy tarry long enough to listen to his tale, Adam would not believe him. Would he have believed it himself at his age? Adam was in thrall to the girl, bewitched by her. He'd defend her, fight for her to his own death, if she told him to.

Godwin cautiously backed away and retreated up the cliff, waiting impatiently in the shadow of the wall until the children emerged over the edge and sauntered back down the path that circled the city wall. When they reached the corner, Leonia stopped and turned her head, looking back up the path to where Godwin was hiding, a triumphant expression on her face. For a moment, Godwin felt a throb of fear, as if she was warning him she'd known all along he was there. But then he realised she was not looking at him. Her gaze was fastened on something further up the track behind him. Drawing tighter into the shelter beneath the stone wall, he turned to see what she was watching but the path was empty, save for something black and furry that shot across into the bushes. She must have been watching a cat. When he peered out again, the children were gone.

As swiftly as he could, Godwin climbed back over the cliff edge and this time he crawled right inside the cave. He supposed it must be a burial chamber of some ancient tribe, long gone from the earth. The clay urns were decorated with all manner of strange beasts – boars, bears, snakes and wolves. Many had been smashed, spilling ash and fragments of bone over the floor.

Godwin, crawling on all fours, searched carefully. His chest grew tight as he struggled to breathe in the dust and ash. The great rock above him seemed to be slowly sinking towards him, trapping him, crushing him, as if he was once more back in the dark hole of that French oubliette. His arms were trembling and sweat ran down his face, but he forced himself to remain inside. He needed something the girl would recognise that would bring her back here alone. But it was hard to make out any object in the dim light. What would she understand as a message? A fragment of pot? No, that wasn't enough.

His foot slipped in the dirt and he heard a grating sound as his sandal knocked against something behind him. Turning awkwardly he saw that he had dislodged a small slab of stone and beneath it, in the twilight, he caught a glint. He crawled towards the little hollow. There, lying in a nest of ash, encircled by amber beads and bears' claws, was an amulet in the form of a golden boar's head studded with garnets. Godwin's mouth was as dry as the charred bones around him, but his parched lips cracked into a smile as he snatched up the golden boar, kissing his fist in triumph. *You shall not suffer a witch to live!*

Chapter 69

*If a man who has been baptised touches a witch with a branch
of rowan, the devil will carry her off when he next comes seeking
a victim.*

Mistress Catlin

I waited for him in the tower. I swore I wouldn't go back to that
filthy place, but trying to slip out of the city at night without the
watchmen asking questions had become impossible since the uprising.

Behind me in the city, the blazing torches set pools of orange and
mustard light flickering down the darkened streets. In front of the
tower, the dark red fires of Butwerk glowed, illuminating nothing save
the distorted shadows of creatures that slid between them, like
monstrous bats. Raucous laughter, yells and occasionally a scream of
pain rose up with the stinking smoke of the fires, but who laughed
and who cried out in darkness, only the inhabitants of that desolation
knew.

Now that the sun had gone down, a chill wind from the river
whined through the window. I shivered. We would not be naked
tonight, but soon, soon we would be together in Robert's own bed,
if all went to plan.

I heard his footsteps on the wooden stairs and hastened to the
trapdoor, holding out a hand to help him as he climbed through it.
He kissed me briefly, then drew away, staring at the filthy bare boards,
his face wrinkled in disgust.

'At least you might have had Diot bring the sheepskins. I've made
love to you in some piss-poor places, but I draw the line at hard
boards.'

'You'd prefer my husband's bed.'

'You know I would.'

'Then, in a few days, you shall have it.' I reached up and stroked
his face. 'Haven't I always given you what you wanted?'

439

Laughing, he caught me round the waist and, lifting me, whirled me round, like an excited child. 'You've thought of a way?' He set me down, and held me by the shoulders. 'Tell me how you'll do it.'

'How *we* will do it,' I corrected him. 'Thanks to my diligently spreading the word, every man in Lincoln knows he's a king's commissioner, so it will come as no surprise to anyone if he is found with a dagger in his chest.'

He giggled. 'It'll come as no surprise to Robert either. He's convinced every man in England is out to assassinate him. But who's actually going to . . .' His expression suddenly turned serious. 'Not you, surely.'

It was my turn to laugh. 'The whole point is to induce someone else to do it, someone who's certain to be caught and hanged for it. That way no possible suspicion can fall on me. And as a poor woman tragically widowed after only a few months of blissful wedlock, I can beg the King for a sizeable purse, maybe even lands, in recompense, since my husband was cruelly murdered by one of the King's enemies while doing his duty for the Crown.'

He flicked his finger across my lips. 'Your powers of persuasion, my angel, are matchless, but even you will have a hard time *inducing* a man to stab Robert if he's certain to be executed for it. Anyone murdering a king's commissioner will be tried as a traitor, and his death'll be drawn out and agonising as a warning to the rabble. No, my sweet, you go to any of the taverns down by the wharf and you'll find a dozen men in each who wouldn't hesitate to cut the throat of a holy abbess for a fat purse, but even they wouldn't be stupid enough to do it unless they could make good their escape afterwards. And, besides, assassins for hire have a dangerous habit of returning later and asking for more money not to turn king's approver and spill all to the justices in exchange for a pardon. We'd never be free of them.'

'Ah, but if a man doesn't know he's to be the assassin . . .' I said, sliding my hand up the inside of his thigh and feeling him squirm. 'The only place Robert feels safe is in his own hall. That is where he lets down his guard. He always was a creature of habit but now he clings to it, like a babe to the breast. Every day when he returns home, he pours himself a goblet of spiced hippocras and flops into his chair near the tapestry to gulp it. It will be simplicity itself to drug the wine.'

'Poison? Again?' He shook his head. 'You're losing your touch, my angel. If it happened in Robert's own hall, even Hugo Bayus would suspect someone in the household. And you wouldn't be able to shift the blame to Tenney or Beata, unless you were thinking of letting Diot burn for it.'

'A tempting thought,' I said, 'save that the old hag would blurt out all she knows long before the flames reached her. But you should listen to me more carefully. I made no mention of poison. *Drugged*, I said. What I shall put in his wine will only befuddle him, dull his senses, make him slow to react. It'll seem to him nothing more than the effects of drunkenness. It won't kill him. You will.'

'Me!' He drew back, eyes wide in alarm, holding up his hands, as if he were pushing away the very idea.

'Yes, you, my beloved. You will hide behind the tapestry, and when you see he can no longer defend himself, you'll slip out and stab him. If he's still alive when the knife goes in, his blood will pour out naturally and no one will think to look any further into the cause of his death than the blood-stained dagger they'll find dropped in the corner of the room.'

'You're right, because they'll be too busy looking for the man who plunged the dagger into him – me!'

'Not if you use this.' I held out a knife.

It was a vicious blade set in a plain mutton-bone handle, but its owner had cut his own mark on the handle to distinguish it from the hundreds of other almost identical boatmen's knives.

My lover stared blankly at the knife. Much as I adored him, at times even I had to admit his wits were not the sharpest.

I patiently explained: 'When Robert was brought home ill from the warehouse, this was stuck in his belt. I removed it as I undressed him. I checked the mark on the handle against the marks in the payment ledgers. This is Martin's sign, as the justices will clearly see when the two are compared. It'll be all the proof they need of his guilt, for everyone knows he had motive enough to kill Robert.'

'But all Martin has to do is to show he was elsewhere at the time of the murder and, knife or not, he'll be proved innocent. '

'But he will not be elsewhere,' I assured him. 'Martin will receive a message that he is to be rewarded with a fat purse for having identified Gunter and his son as rebels. The message will ask him to come to the house to collect his payment in the early evening, soon after Robert returns home. The boatman will think there is nothing odd in that. After all, Robert would hardly want to be seen handing over money in so public a place as the warehouse. Neither would Martin wish to be identified as an informer. It would make perfect sense to him that it should take place privately in Robert's hall. And Martin is greedy. He won't hesitate to come.

'When he arrives, he'll find the courtyard empty and the door to the house open. He'll walk into the hall and discover the body. I'll come in behind him and, in horror, beg him to check if my dear husband still lives. Then, when he has blood on his hands, I'll rush out into the street and scream for help. He'll be trapped inside the house. Even if he runs for it, he's bound to be seen by someone at that time of day, and I will swear on every shrine and relic in Lincoln Cathedral that I came in and saw Martin plunge the knife into my husband, who was threatening to have him arrested for theft. The men-at-arms who brought Martin and his son to the warehouse will testify that he had already been seized once. No one will doubt his guilt.'

I stepped closer, and ran my hand over my lover's groin, feeling his prick swelling under my touch. 'And then, then my dearest Edward, no more towers or fields for us. You will be unwrapping me in the comfort of Robert's own bed.'

He bent down and kissed my mouth passionately. 'And that is why I adore you, little Maman.'

September 1381

If dry be the buck's thorn on Holyrood morn,
'tis worth a kist of gold.
But if wet it be seen ere Holyrood e'en,
bad harvest is foretold.

Chapter 70

If a storm is raging, it may be stilled if a woman strips herself naked and presents her body to the storm. For this reason figureheads of bare-breasted women are often set on the prow of a ship to still the waves and abate the tempest.

Lincoln Castle

Keys jangled outside the heavy wooden door as the gaoler sorted through the bunch dangling from the massive ring to find the right one. The men heaved themselves into a sitting position, placing their hands on their bent knees, their heads bowed.

Gunter touched his son's shoulder. 'Wake up, Bor.'

The lad stirred sleepily, then realised who had woken him and flinched away, dragging himself upright. Every time he did it, Gunter felt another piece of his heart die inside him. He'd never thought to see a child of his draw away from him in fear or hatred, and he knew from the expression in Hankin's eyes that the boy felt both whenever he looked at his father.

The men eyed each other anxiously as the door opened. Was this it? Was this where the trial would begin and their lives end?

'Maybe my feckless wife has finally stirred her arse to bake me a pie,' Mack said hopefully. 'About bloody time.'

Gunter felt sorry for him. After the first day, no one had brought food for him. He suspected Mack's wife had sent food, but it probably went straight into the belly of Hob, one of the soldiers on duty at the castle for, according to the guards, his daughter was always hanging round the gates waiting for him. The other men shared a little of what their families sent in, and occasionally the gaoler would take pity and bring him a crust from a burned loaf, or a bone with a shred or two of ham still clinging to it. But it must be hard to think your family didn't care if you starved.

At least Nonie, however much she despised her husband, still

445

faithfully sent food for him and Hankin, making the exhausting walk into Lincoln and up to the castle each day. But he couldn't imagine how much longer she could afford to feed them, as well as Col and Royse, when there was no money coming in.

Had she sold the punt? It would be better than waiting for the King's men to take it from her as soon as sentence was passed, for money could be more easily hidden. If she took Royse and Col and left Greetwell before the trial, the money from the punt would be enough to keep the three of them fed and warmed through the coming winter, with a chance to start again somewhere new. He wished he could tell her to do just that. He should have warned her of what was going to happen, told her what she must do. Yet again, he had failed them.

The door groaned open. Mack's face fell as he saw there was nothing in the gaoler's hands except his ring of keys and Gunter's wooden leg thrust under his arm. A second guard stepped into the room, menacingly thumping a stout stick against his palm to make plain what would happen to any prisoner who caused trouble.

The gaoler pushed himself between Gunter and Hankin. He dropped the leg into Gunter's lap. 'It's your lucky day, Bor. You're going for a little stroll.'

A look of alarm flashed across all the prisoners' faces. Much as every man prayed to be delivered from that place, the fear of being taken to a worse fate was writ clear in all their eyes.

Mack leaned forward. 'Where are you taking him? The justices – have they come?'

'One of the commissioners wants to question him,' the gaoler said indifferently. 'I dare say there are more charges to be added to his list of crimes.'

As Gunter wrestled his stump into the wooden peg, he felt the man fumbling at the lock that fastened the iron on his good leg to the pillar. He pulled the fetter from Gunter's cut and bruised ankle. Blood began to flow painfully back into his numb foot. Gunter leaned forward to massage it, but the gaoler hauled him to his feet. 'Hurry, Bor. You don't want to put the old bastard in an even worse humour by keeping him waiting.'

Gunter hobbled towards the door. His ankle kept buckling beneath him and the gaoler was forced to support him to keep him upright. Gunter twisted round, staring at Hankin's back.

'What about my son? Is he not wanted too?'

'Nothing was said about the lad. My orders are to fetch you, that's all.'

Gunter wanted desperately to say something to the boy. Suppose they didn't bring him back here. Suppose this was the last time he ever saw him. 'Hankin? Hankin, forgive me, son, for everything.'

But the boy didn't turn his head or show by the smallest sign that he'd heard.

Gunter's shoulders sank, and he allowed himself to be dragged out of the cell into the narrow passage beyond. There they paused, while the guard locked the door behind them. Just as it closed, Gunter heard a faint cry: 'Don't hurt my faayther. Please don't hurt him!'

With one guard leading and the other shoving him from behind, Gunter was hurried along the passage and up a narrow spiral staircase. He was so unsteady that several times he slipped, banging his good knee hard against the stone steps above. His weakness unnerved and angered him. Ever since he was a lad he'd had to fend for himself, and his strength was something he'd prided himself on. He'd always been able to depend on his own body, but he felt the shadow of old age creeping up on him. Soon would come a time when he wouldn't be able to walk for miles, or move a laden punt or even defend himself. Then a worse thought crossed his mind. Suppose he never reached old age. What if his life was to end today?

They entered a large rectangular hall and from there he was herded up another staircase. From the slit windows he glimpsed snatches of colour from the streets beyond the walls, like the stray notes of a song, familiar yet not named. But he was not allowed to linger.

Finally the gaoler knocked on a heavy wooden door and, hearing some faint reply from within, pushed Gunter into a long room. At the far end was a dais, on which stood a table and high-backed chair, while in front of it were ranged many seats, from highly carved and ornate chairs to crudely cobbled benches. The crest of King Richard and that of his uncle, John of Gaunt, Constable of Lincoln Castle, hung as twins above the dais, as if to show the two were equals, but beyond that there was little decoration in the room. Gaunt had not lavished any of his huge fortune on Lincoln.

A man stood with his back to them, peering out of one of the slits, a man of some wealth, judging by his long gown and turbaned hood. The belt around his hips was wide, and fashioned from the finest red leather studded with silver stars. He turned at the sound of the door

447

opening. Gunter blinked. It was hard to reconcile the gravitas of the man with the last time he had seen him, lying in filth, his face splattered with blood and dirt, an expression of abject terror in his eyes.

For a long time the two men stared at one another, then Robert tore away his gaze and addressed the guards. 'Leave us. Wait at the bottom of the stairs. I'll call for you when I've done.'

The two guards exchanged uneasy glances.

'Master Robert, we can't leave you alone with – with a rebel. Suppose he should escape.'

'If you wait at the bottom of the stairs, as I instructed, you will be able to ensure he doesn't,' Robert said curtly. 'Can you see another way out of this chamber? A cat would be hard put to squeeze through the window and even then he'd have to sprout wings on the other side.'

'But suppose he attacks you. They've murdered—'

'I assume you searched him before you locked him up, unless you're in the habit of allowing your prisoners to run around armed. Well? Then go!'

Robert waited by the window until he heard the clatter of the men's footsteps retreating down the stairs, then took a few paces towards Gunter, turned one of the chairs to face the prisoner and sat down. He was breathing hard and looked pale, sick even.

'You saved my life in London.' He spoke softly, in contrast to the way he'd addressed the guards.

Gunter said nothing, afraid that any admission would only incriminate him.

'You're one of my tenants. You've carried cargoes for me.'

He paused, but Gunter didn't reply. He knew a question was coming, one he still did not know how to answer.

'Why did you defend me? If you'd said nothing, they'd have carried out their execution and there would have been no witness to testify that you had taken part in the rebellion. Did that not occur to you?'

Gunter stared down at his grimy hands. 'I was shocked to see you there, Master Robert, and . . . what they were going to do . . . They said you were one of the Flemish merchants. I had to put them right. You didn't deserve to die.'

'Neither did the Flemish merchants,' Robert said sharply.

'I know nowt about that.'

'Meaning you didn't attack them or you don't know if they deserved to be butchered?'

448

Gunter was again silent. He couldn't tell what was going on in the man's head. Why was he questioning him? What was he trying to find out? Was he going to trick him into betraying Hankin?

Robert rose from the chair and began to pace up and down in front of the dais. 'Why did you join the rebels in the first place, Gunter? That's what I can't understand. Why would a man like you, with a wife and children, risk everything? You're freeborn, not a villein. Did you think to become rich, was that it? To steal gold or to overthrow the nobility and live like a lord of the manor? Was that what they promised you? What did you think you could change? There will always be men who rule others, and those who do, whoever they are, will always be wealthy because of it. Would you have us ungoverned, every man taking what he wanted, the strong stealing from the weak and our shores left unprotected, so that any foreign king who looks on this island with greedy eyes may simply walk in and conquer us?'

Robert stopped pacing and turned to face Gunter. 'And your son. From what I recall he's about the same age as my own, just a boy. Why drag him into this madness? Did you have no care that at best he might be killed and at worst mutilated and hanged?'

'My son wasn't there,' Gunter said fiercely. 'Only I went. Let him go and I'll confess to anything you put to me.'

Robert sank down weakly into the chair. 'You're a fool! Your son is the certain proof you were both there. That's what they will say in court, even if I don't testify. Neither of you was seen in Lincoln for the best part of three weeks, and when you returned you brought back the boy injured. Any man who was there knows about the fires and explosions. Any half-competent physician or even a humble soldier can recognise the marks of burning gunpowder when they see them. They'll examine him, Gunter, and his wounds will seal the guilt of both of you, not merely as ones who marched to London, but as ones who fought and destroyed it. That is high treason and it merits the worst of deaths.'

Gunter felt all hope draining out of him. He had nothing left to lose. He took a pace forward, though his good leg could barely hold him upright. 'My lad never . . . He marched to London, it's true. He ran away from home after we'd quarrelled, meaning to join the rebels. But you said it yourself, he's just a boy, too young to understand what he was doing. It was all an adventure to him . . . But when he saw what happened, he was sick to his stomach. He took no part in it, I swear. Someone threw some gunpowder onto a fire afore the killings even started. He was wounded. He could do nowt save crawl into the shelter of a wall.

'I went to London to search for him. When I found him, he was in that much pain, he couldn't stand. I'd to carry him home. He didn't harm anyone, I swear on his mam's life. Don't let them hang him. I spoke out for you that day, Master Robert. You speak out for him – a life for a life. You can do what you want to me. I'll say I'm guilty to whatever charges you bring against me. But let him go home to his mam, his sister and little brother. They need him. Without a man to work for them, they'll starve. Whatever trouble the boy's in, I'm to blame, for I'm his faayther. I should have kept him from it. I deserve to hang for that, but not Hankin, not my son.'

For a long time Robert stared at him. Gunter's leg almost buckled beneath him and it was all he could do to keep himself from sinking to the floor. But he would not give in to it. He would not have any man think he was grovelling to him, begging like a coward.

At last Robert rose and climbed onto the dais, seating himself at the table. He smoothed out a parchment and ran his finger down it. Then he picked up a pointed stick that lay ready beside it and scratched at a spot on the document. He blew the dried ink away and, dipping a quill pen into a pot, he wrote two names on the parchment. Without a word, Robert crossed the room and called for the guards. He didn't once look at Gunter.

Gunter felt cold and numb to the very marrow of his bones. How could he walk back into the cell and tell his son that, once again, he had failed to protect him? He felt no bitterness towards Master Robert. You couldn't ask a wolf to spare a lamb. It was in their nature to kill, just as it was in the nature of the wealthy to show no mercy to the poor. Life had taught him to expect nothing more. His only anger was against himself for being honest, for being a fool, for not learning that you had to grab whatever you could in this life before others snatched it for themselves.

As the guards marched in and seized him, he turned once more to Robert. 'Just the boy, spare the boy!'

Robert ignored him and addressed the guards: 'When you've released this man and his son, send the bailiff to me. There are two men I wish to have arrested.'

The guards stopped dead as if they'd been struck a sharp blow.

'Release them, Master Robert? But their names are on the list of rebels.'

'It would appear the wrong men have been arrested. The names of this man and his son were never on the list. Can't you read?'

The two guards looked at each other and shook their heads. Of course they couldn't. Why would they need to do that?

'The men who should have been arrested were Martin of Washingborough and his son. Arrest them. Let this man and his boy go free.'

Chapter 71

The seven whistlers are the souls of the damned that range the earth as birds. Whenever their cries are heard, death or disaster shall follow as surely as night follows day.

Lincoln

Godwin hid outside the city gates at the top of the hill and waited until the moon rose. The road outside the wall was deserted, save for a couple of scavenging dogs. They snarled as they caught his scent. He hurled stones at them until they slunk away into the shadows. He crossed the track and peered over the edge of the cliff down onto the grassy ledge, now washed grey in the starlight. Far below, in the deep darkness of the valley, the cottagers' fires glowed red as dragons' eyes.

It took several attempts before Godwin could summon the courage to lower himself into the darkness. He dropped the last foot or so. The grass was slippery after the rain and he slid to the edge of the ledge before he was able to stop. He lay there, his limbs trembling at the thought of how close he had come to falling. The friar's robes were cumbersome, but he'd returned to wearing them tonight. They sanctified the execution he was about to carry out. It would be Divine Justice.

Afraid to stand up in case he slipped again, Godwin crawled to the bushes and, forcing his way behind them, burrowed into the cave. He could see nothing inside, as if an invisible curtain were shutting out the moonlight, but he groped around until his fingers encountered one of the urns. He traced the pattern on it – a great serpent encircling the jar, devouring its own tail – the ouroboros. He smiled to himself. That his hand had been guided to this particular symbol was a good omen, for it was the same design as the ring the witch had used to trick his father into believing his only son was dead. It was fitting that her daughter should die here, among the burial urns. Pavia would have her child ripped from her as his own father had. He wanted her to feel all the pain of a parent's grief, before he dragged her from this world into the sulphurous fires of Hell. For her, there would be no release from that torment, no ransom paid, just as she had plotted for him.

Godwin had planned exactly what he would do. He'd contemplated using a dagger, but he knew that, in the dark, he could not be certain of striking a fatal blow. Besides, he couldn't risk being seen with blood on him in case he ran into the watchmen or someone else who might remember. But, most of all, he was afraid of the girl's blood: a person's spirit lives in their blood and hers was an evil one that might leave her body and possess anyone her blood touched.

He would have to strangle her. But a man cannot easily throttle anyone with just one hand, not even a child. Godwin drew the cord from his friar's scrip. It had taken time to fashion it into a wide noose, but he had grown accustomed to using teeth and a single hand to do deftly what most men did with two good hands. He was relying on the darkness to conceal his movements from the girl, attack before she realised what he intended.

Fling the noose over the child's head. Pull the end down with his good hand, until it fastened about her slender throat. Keep pulling until he'd dragged her to the ground. Pin her down with his knees and, using the stump of his right hand as a lever, push against her body, pulling the cord tighter and tighter with his good hand until she was dead.

He'd practised many times until he could pull the cord tight so quickly she wouldn't have a chance to throw it off. When she was no longer moving, he would take his time. Make quite sure she was dead. Then fling her body off the cliff to crash down onto the roofs of the houses far below, her bones shattering, like clay jars. They'd carry the broken remains to Pavia and he would be watching from the shadows, waiting to hear her scream.

Godwin started as he heard the rattle of loose stones that meant someone was scrambling over the edge of the cliff and suddenly there she was, standing on the silvered grassy ledge, silhouetted against the moon. He could see the glint of starlight in her eyes, but nothing of her expression.

'You received . . . my message.' In his excitement, Godwin was struggling to breathe.

By way of an answer, Leonia held up the golden boar's head between her thumb and forefinger. It glittered in the bone-white light that haloed her shorn head.

Godwin beckoned to her to come closer. 'I knew your mother long ago . . . We are kin, you and I . . . I wanted to meet you, after all these years. I have a gift for you, little sister. Your mother might not want you to have it. But I know you can keep a secret.'

He was relying on Leonia's curiosity and greed. But if she grew suspicious, her only way out was to scramble back up the cliff face, and the moment she tried, he would be behind her with the noose.

But Leonia did not attempt to run. Instead she slowly paced towards him, parting the bushes until she stood right in front of the cave. It was as if she was inviting him to kill her, daring him to do it. Another step and she was within his reach. But even as Godwin raised his hand to fling the noose about her slender white neck, he caught sight of something moving above him on the lip of the cave.

At first he thought a bat was hanging there. The bulging eyes were bluish-white in the moonlight, opaque, dead. But the wet black snout wriggled as if it was trying to smell what it could not see. A thick purple tongue protruded between sharp white teeth, tasting the air. The creature was small, its head no broader than Godwin's hand, but even as he watched, it began to swell, as if it were engorging with blood. Its claws were as sharp as death.

It hung above Godwin for a moment, suspended, then sprang at him, striking him in the stomach and knocking him to the ground. He screamed and threw himself sideways. Its talons raked his back, tearing the skin. Its four long fangs bit into his flesh. He tried to crawl out, but the twigs of the bushes had turned into vipers, twisting and slithering up in a great swarm towards him. He scuttled backwards into the cave, trying to wedge himself into the rock, but there was no rock. There was nothing but emptiness, a void that went deeper and deeper into the black heart of the world.

The demon bounded across the floor after him, its claws rasping on the stone. Its sinuous body flattened itself, and as Godwin shrieked and fought to push it away, it crawled on top of him. Its oily black fur brushed over his skin. It pressed its ever-increasing weight down on his chest until he was fighting for breath. It fastened itself on his face, the wet snout pressing against his nose, as its four long canine teeth flashed like daggers. Its hot, purple tongue flicked over Godwin's lips, pushing between them, filling his mouth. Its foul breath seared his lungs. He tried to scream one last time, but the only sound that emerged was the strangled gurgle of his final breath.

Leonia slipped the little golden boar's head back into her purse and, turning her head, gazed out over the valley below. One by one the tiny ruby and gold lights of cottage fires and candles were going out and darkness was flowing in like the drowning tide.

It would be three days before an urchin, hiding from his tormenters, found Godwin's body in the cave. The discovery of a corpse, he knew, would transform his position in the gang from runt to hero. Gleefully he called them to come and look. They scrambled over the edge, threatening to throw him off the cliff if this was another of his hoaxes. But their sneers and jeers died away as they caught sight of the man lying on the floor of the cave. Four neat holes had been punched through the coarse cloth of his robe, from which four streams of blackened blood had run to pool beneath him, staining red the fragments of bone on which he lay. The man's twisted mouth was wide open, as if his life had been severed in a scream and in his staring eyes was an expression of pure terror. That look so unnerved the boys that not even a double-dare would induce any of the little gang to touch the corpse, in case the stump of his arm should come to life and strike them dead.

For the adults, however, the death of a nameless vagabond in a stinking cave was hardly worth investigating. The deputy sheriff, to whom the matter was reported, summoned the coroner, as he was legally obliged to do. A dozen sullen citizens were rounded up and coerced into acting as jury, but all were anxious to get the whole matter over as quickly as possible and cursed the corpse for putting them to such trouble.

The four puncture wounds in the chest of the cadaver stirred a vague memory in the coroner's mind. He was sure he'd seen something like it on another corpse, but since he was forced to examine bodies all over the county, he couldn't remember where he'd seen that pattern before.

The deputy sheriff was absolutely certain where he'd seen similar marks.

'Remember that merchant's son,' he murmured, sidling up to the coroner, 'the one they fished out of the Braytheforde? You reckoned his wounds to have been made by a quant or an anchor. But it looks like you was wrong about that, wasn't you, Master Coroner?' he added, with malicious glee. 'This couldn't be a ship's anchor, could it, not on dry land and way up here?'

The coroner swore under his breath. He did recall the other corpse now, but the deaths of a merchant's drunken son and a begging friar could hardly be connected, especially after all these months, and he had no intention of being made to look an incompetent fool. Discreetly he opened the purse hanging from his belt. Gold has many great attributes, not least the power to miraculously erase a man's memory.

'It would appear,' the coroner said loudly, addressing the jury men, 'that someone repeatedly stabbed this unfortunate man or he stabbed himself in a frenzy and flung the weapon over the edge of the cliff.'

The deputy-sheriff gave him a conspiratorial wink and fingered the coins in his palm.

But there was still the mystery of the noose found lying beside the corpse. Had someone tried to throttle him, or had he come to the cliff-face with every intention of hanging himself and failed to find a suitable tree? Either way, there was little point in anyone wasting any more time or money pursuing the matter. The most pressing problem now was what to do with the body, for if there was any chance it was self-murder, it could not be accorded a burial on consecrated ground. They debated the matter earnestly and concluded that since the deceased was found, hermit-like, in a cave, dressed as a Friar of the Sack, whom everyone knew took religious zeal to the point of madness, the safest course was simply to wall him up in the cave in which he'd died and leave God and the devil to fight it out over his soul.

Chapter 72

If a skull be removed from the place where it rests, death and disaster shall follow till it be restored.

Lincoln

Welcome to the kingdom of the dead, Godwin, welcome to my kingdom.

They say the spirit of the last man to be buried in a patch of ground is doomed to guard it until another can be found to take his place, so if I were you, my darlings, I wouldn't open any caves on that cliff in Lincoln, unless you want to stay there until the great wolf Fenris breaks the chain that fetters it and the stars fall from the sky. Godwin is going to have a long, lonely wait all alone in the dark, but before you start feeling sorry for him, my darlings, remember he would have murdered an innocent little girl. And surely child-murderers deserve the worst of fates, don't they?

But we must return to the living. We're not quite finished with them yet.

It was late in the afternoon when Robert finally left the castle. The heat was unremitting, and every inch of his body felt wet and sticky. The high collar of his woollen houppelande chafed his neck. Flies crawled everywhere, generated from the slime-green mud that suppurated in the ditches and streams. Even the water in the Witham was unusually low and choked with weed. The flat-bottomed punts could still make the journey between Boston and Lincoln, but keeled craft lay beached along the banks, unable to move until the next rains.

The latest news from London was that so many rebels' bodies hung in gibbet cages about the town, or had been quartered and nailed to doors, that the stench was making people ill. Markets had had to be abandoned, for stallholders and customers alike were vomiting and fainting, not just from the sight of the bloated green corpses, but from the smell, which even tainted the bread and meat. Townspeople had started tearing the bodies down and burying them, but the boy-king was having none of that. He'd ordered them dug up and gibbeted again. He was determined this was a lesson no one would forget.

Robert felt no pang of guilt for adding Martin and his son to the list of rebels. He owed Gunter his life and prided himself on always paying his debts. He believed that neither Gunter nor his son had had any hand in the killings. But two names were needed to fill the gap in the list. Martin and his son would have hanged anyway, if it could have been proved that they'd stolen from the merchants. So justice would be served. Besides, if witnesses could be found to prove their innocence, no harm would come to them, except for a few weeks spent chained up in the castle, which they richly deserved.

Robert pushed his way through the throng in the castle courtyard towards the great doors that opened out into the city at the top of the hill. He was in two minds whether to go to the warehouse or make straight for home and a large goblet of hippocras. His back was aching and he couldn't even summon enough energy to worry about the latest folly Edward might have committed at the warehouse.

Yet he found himself reluctant to return home. Catlin's tongue was growing more savage by the day and she always found some reason to push him away if he attempted to touch her. He tried to tell himself that the relentless heat was to blame. All the men were complaining it made their wives irritable. But often when he woke in the night, her part of the bed would be empty. Edith may have endured rather than enjoyed love-making, but she had never forsaken his bed, even in anger. She'd been brought up to be a dutiful wife.

Something caught the edge of Robert's vision and he turned his head. On the far side of the thronged courtyard, a familiar figure was urging her palfrey forward in the direction of the gate that led to the road and fields beyond the city. For a moment, Robert felt relieved. At least he would have some peace at home for an hour or two. He was just about to walk on, when he saw another figure he knew enter through the city gate. The man was looking ahead of him as if he were searching for someone. Then he saw the man's gaze fix on Catlin. As if she knew he was behind her, she turned in the saddle. It was only a small gesture, a beckon of the fingers, answered by the briefest of nods from the man, but it was enough. In that instant, the suspicions that had been hovering unformed, like a dark miasma, at the

458

back of Robert's mind suddenly gathered into a solid, menacing shape.

Catlin, with a nod to the guards, trotted through the gate out of the city. Minutes later, the man followed. Robert forced himself to wait for them to get well clear of the castle wall before he limped through the gate. He walked down the rise and edged along the bottom of the castle mound, until he had a clear view of the track beyond, prepared at any moment to step behind the trees if either of them should turn. But they did not, which only added to his fury, that both should be so arrogant as to feel themselves safe from discovery.

He watched them enter the small grove of trees around St Margaret's pool. Catlin waited on her palfrey for the man to take the bridle and tether the beast. She swung her leg across the horse's back and he grasped her slender waist to lift her down. Robert saw the fierce embrace, the lingering kiss, watched Catlin pulling him down onto the tinder-dry grass.

Swiping furiously at the flies that buzzed around his face, Robert limped as fast as his sore back would allow down the track and across the sun-scorched meadow. Catlin was lying on top of the man, her skirts raised, her mouth working hungrily on his. He was running his hands over her bare thighs. But as Robert stumbled towards them it was the man who saw him first. His eyes widened in alarm, and he struggled up, tipping Catlin onto the hard ground. She screeched in annoyance as she was flung aside. The man scrambled to his feet as Robert advanced towards them. He stumbled backwards, the white streak of hair falling across his face.

Robert ignored him and, seizing his wife's arm, dragged her to her feet. 'You filthy whore! You could be put to death for this – both of you. This is a crime against God and nature. Edward is your son, your own son! How could you fornicate with him?

'As for you,' he spat at Edward, almost purple in the face with rage and disgust, 'to lust after your own mother – the woman who gave birth to you! They will cut off your balls and that will only be the start!'

Edward had turned very pale and had backed so far away from Robert's fist that he was teetering on the edge of the stream.

'She's not my mother, you slug-wit! Do you honestly think I would bed my own mother?'

Robert's jaw hung slack. 'Then I don't . . .' He stared at them in bewilderment.

Catlin gave a mirthless laugh. 'He's my lover, not my son, you fool.'

Edward slid to her side and took her hand. They stood facing him.

'I don't believe . . . Not your son? But you said . . .' Robert was struggling to take it in. Then the full implication hit him like a fist in his belly. 'You brought your lover to live in *my* house! You gave him my wine to drink, my food to eat, installed him as my steward?'

Catlin shrugged. 'I hardly think you can complain. You brought me into your house while your wife was still alive and you'd have eagerly climbed into my bed then, if I'd let you. Why should it be different for a woman?'

Robert's face had turned dangerously pale. 'How long . . . how long have you been *lovers*?'

'Since Leonia was an infant. She believes Edward to be her brother. The world thinks nothing of a mother and son living together, but a woman and her lover . . . And you certainly wouldn't have married me, if you'd known who he was, would you?'

Robert felt as if the ground had fallen away beneath him. 'I treated you with respect, devotion, even. I loved you. You made me fall in love with you. And you . . . all that time . . . all the time we were together . . . you were betraying me!'

Catlin's lips curled in a faint smile, as if she was the tutor of a particularly stupid child who had just managed to solve a simple sum. 'Women have only two means of making their way in this world. You can make men lust after you, but what kind of life is that, spreading your legs for them, letting them wither your face and your heart until no man desires you? Better by far to make men fall in love with you so that they spread all they own at your feet. If my weakness is that I was born a woman, you cannot blame me for using it to trap men, for men are quick enough to use their strength against us. It is a game of chess and it amuses me to watch the pieces fall, knowing I control the board.'

Robert's hands clenched into fists at his sides. 'I hope you still enjoy that game, mistress, when I have you charged with adultery and—'

'But you won't, Robert. You were a fool, a vain, self-important donkey. I only used the weapons you fashioned yourself and placed in my hands. And it's that same self-importance that will stop you bringing a charge of adultery against me, for you will not want the whole of Lincoln to learn that the master of the Merchants Guild

460

was such a fool that he could be duped into taking his new bride's lover into his house and employing him as his steward.'

Robert stared at the muscles rippling in her slender white throat as she taunted him. He saw his hands circling it, squeezing it, throttling the lying breath from her body. Every fibre of his being wanted to kill her, wanted to see the fear bulging in her eyes, to see her lying lifeless on the burned grass. He stepped towards her, reaching for her neck. But Catlin didn't flinch. As he met her triumphant gaze, he knew that even to slap her would allow her to win.

Before either of them could move, Robert drew his sword and thrust the point of the blade to within an inch of Edward's throat.

'You – drop your purse and knife on the ground, and you, mistress, I'll have yours too and your wedding ring.'

He was gratified to see the shock on their faces. They hesitated. Robert raised the blade and slashed it across Edward's cheek. A thin curtain of blood ran down his face. Edward yelped and pressed his hand to the wound, staring in disbelief at the smear of scarlet on his finger.

'Your purses!' Robert repeated.

They hastened to unfasten them from their belts. Catlin tugged at her ring and dropped it on the grass, eyeing him warily. Robert scooped them up with his free hand, rage numbing the pain in his back. He walked across to where Catlin's palfrey was tearing up tufts of grass and, sheathing the sword, he stuffed the purses, knives and ring into the saddlebag. Then he unfastened the reins.

'I'll give you both until curfew tonight to leave this city. You will take nothing with you, not even your own daughter. She will stay with me. I would not have that sweet, innocent child corrupted by your filth. You'll walk out of here and be thankful I am not having you whipped out at a cart's tail. At daybreak I will go to Sheriff Thomas and tell him it was you who poisoned my poor wife and attempted to poison me. I will have you both declared outlaws, wolf-heads, and I'll see to it that every man's hand in England is raised against you. I suggest you put as much distance as you can between yourselves and Lincoln tonight or you will be dragged back here in chains.'

461

Chapter 73

To prove if someone be a witch or not, drive an iron nail into their footprint in secret. If they are guilty they will be compelled to return to that spot and pull it out, but if innocent they will continue on their journey without knowing.

Mistress Catlin

'He means it!' Edward said, not taking his eyes from the distant figure of Robert as he led the palfrey through the castle gate. 'What are we going to do?'

'You heard him,' I said. 'He won't go to Thomas until the morning. He means to punish us, yes, but mostly to frighten us into staying away. He doesn't want us brought back to Lincoln in chains. Even now, he's thinking of his precious reputation if this should come to trial. He won't want the whole city to know he's a cuckold and a fool.'

Edward's fists were clenched so hard, his knuckles had turned white. 'I won't be driven out to beg on the road. And we need Leonia. Without her, we won't have a hope of getting hold of Warrick's money or lands. It is all entrusted to her. But if he really does go to the sheriff and have us declared outlaws, we'll lose it anyway.' He slammed his fist into the nearest tree-trunk in fury. 'I'd like to boil that sanctimonious bastard in one of his own piss-vats.'

I pressed my fingers to Edward's mouth. 'The only place Robert will be going is into the graveyard to lie alongside that wretched wife of his. It is all arranged, my beloved. That's what I came to tell you. Robert is even now on his way home, hot and tired. He's had a shock. The first thing he'll do when he reaches his house is pour himself a soothing goblet of hippocras, hippocras laced with dwale. And he won't stop at one cup, given the mood he's in, he'll gulp a full flagon.

'I've hidden Martin's knife for you and sent the stable-boy to tell Martin to come to the house at the striking of the Vespers' bell. All we have to do is wander slowly back to the house, by which time Robert will probably have fallen asleep, and even if he hasn't, he'll be so drugged he won't be able to protest, much less defend himself. After you've done the deed, go up to the solar, change your clothes and wash yourself with the water I've put ready and stay there. I'll hide in the kitchen until I see Martin cross the courtyard and go into the hall. It can't fail. By the Compline bell tonight, Robert will be laid out cold on his own table and the only person the sheriff will be hunting is Martin.'

'I'll enjoy sticking a knife into his fat carcass,' Edward said, through clenched teeth. 'Seeing the fear in his eyes as he watches his blood spurt out. I only hope I can resist the temptation to hack him into tiny pieces.'

Two red spots appeared on Edward's cheeks and I could see the excitement burning in his eyes. He bent and kissed me hard on the lips, squeezing my breast in his fist. Then he gave a shout of laughter, and a raven pecking at the guts of a dead squirrel flapped into the nearby tree with a disgruntled squawk.

'Before the year is out, I shall be master of all Warrick's lands and Robert's business too. You shall be my queen.'

'I told you I'd take care of you, my beloved,' I whispered. 'Don't I always?'

Chapter 74

If a man is dying, his death will be prolonged if his head rests on a pillow stuffed with the feathers of pigeon or game-birds. To help the man to die, the pillow must be drawn sharply away from under him, so that he may pass into the next life. But if you would delay death, place a bag of feathers beneath him and he will linger.

Lincoln

Robert hitched the palfrey in the shade of the stables, but had neither the will nor the strength to heave the saddle from the poor beast. He hobbled through the yard and into the house.

'Tenney . . . Beata!' he bellowed, from habit.

But only a flood of silence washed back at him. He cursed himself for forgetting they no longer worked for him. It was high time he reconciled himself to the fact that Tenney would never return, with or without the cart. Every person he had ever trusted had betrayed him. He supposed that was another crime he should report to Sheriff Thomas in the morning, for all the good it would do now. But, hurt and enraged as he was, part of him knew he would not mention Tenney to the sheriff. He couldn't see the man hanged. There were worse crimes, far worse, as he'd learned to his cost that day. He tried to calm himself, but it wasn't easy. He could hear his own blood pounding in his ears and such a tight band was gripping his chest that he felt as if he were suffocating.

To think that only a few days ago he'd wondered if Sheriff Thomas and Catlin had grown too close. He almost wished it had been Thomas with whom she'd betrayed him. He still couldn't stop thinking of Edward as Catlin's son, and the image of them lying together in the grass made him feel sick.

He crossed to the chest where the jug of hippocras stood ready, with his favourite goblet, and poured himself a larger than usual measure, but he didn't sink into his chair to drink it. His back was aching, with violent twinges, as if the devil himself were thrusting his pitchfork into the bone. He was sure that if he sat down he'd never be able to rise again. Still grasping the goblet, he heaved himself painfully up the stairs to the solar. He wanted nothing more than to lie down in the cool of his bedchamber and sleep.

The solar, too, was deserted. Catlin's scissors lay in the centre of the table, as if she had dropped them there in haste. The sight made him wince and he averted his eyes as he pushed open the flimsy door in the wooden partition at the far end of the room, which screened off his bedchamber.

A sweet, dizzying perfume assailed him, so strong that it almost sent him reeling backwards. He stood in the doorway and stared. The shutters were closed to keep out the heat and the room was lit by a single candle on the table beside the door. It was blessedly shady and cool, but that wasn't what had halted him in his tracks. The small chamber had been transformed. The bed was festooned with garlands of flowers. They hung in loops from the heavy drapes, and were twined round the four posts. Rose petals, lavender, bergamot and fresh leaves lay strewn on the wooden floor. The scent was stifling in the closed room.

'Do you like it, Père?'

Leonia stepped from behind the screen in the corner. She was dressed in a simple white shift, her shorn head bare, save for a garland of rosebuds.

Robert gave her a bewildered smile. 'What is all this?'

'It's the feast of John Barleycorn, Père. Had you forgotten? Everyone decorates the house with flowers. I wanted to make the bed pretty for you and Mother. You do like it, don't you?'

Leonia moved gracefully towards him and dropped a demure curtsy. He took a great gulp from the goblet he was holding and stroked her cheek. 'Your mother is . . . Your mother won't be returning to this house.'

He'd not planned to say it. Indeed, he'd not even given a thought to how he would explain Catlin's absence to the child. But now that the words were out, he expected her to look surprised, tearful, and he braced himself for the onslaught of questions he was sure would follow, but none came. The expression on her face was as serene and unperturbed as it had been on the day her poor little dog had been slaughtered.

465

'Then I'll take care of you, Père. Don't I always?'

Thank God, she was nothing like her mother. One day soon she'd make some man a loving wife. 'You're an angel, my dear.'

Indeed she truly looked like one, except for her hair. Not that it made her ugly, far from it: it showed off the colt-like curve of the slender neck and the high cheekbones to perfection, but still when he thought of what Catlin had done to her . . . He found himself pathetically grateful that Leonia had finally forgiven him, as if he were a callow youth who'd been returned to favour by a mistress who had spurned him. At least there was one person in this world who loved him and would never betray him.

Leonia took the goblet from his hand and placed it on a side table. Then she began to unfasten the silver buckle of his belt.

'You look so weary, Père. Is your back paining you again?'

He was touched that she was even aware of it. He couldn't recall making any mention of it in front of her, but she had evidently noticed. She had such a tender heart. She pulled the heavy belt from his hips and laid it aside. Her slim little fingers deftly worked up the row of buttons on his robe.

'Why don't you lie down? That will ease it. I had Diot put fresh linen on the bed so it's cool for you.'

He looked down at the rosebuds on Leonia's head. 'Why do you never wear the golden rosebud I gave you? Don't you like it?'

Leonia's white teeth tugged at her lower lip. 'I loved it, Père, more than anything else I ever had . . . but Mother took it away from me. She gave it to Edward.'

'What?' Robert's anger blazed again. 'I will see that woman pay . . .'

Leonia glanced up, looking fearful. Robert tried to calm himself. He stroked her delicate hand. 'I'm not angry with you, child. You cannot help who your mother is.' A sour bile rose in Robert's gullet and he snatched up the wine again, taking a huge thirsty gulp. 'I'll buy you another necklace . . . a dozen necklaces.'

Leonia undid the last button and tugged at the heavy folds of the robe, helping Robert to ease it from his shoulders. He stood there in his shirt and hose. Leonia clasped his great paw in hers, tugging him towards the bed. 'Please, Père, lie down and rest.'

The soporific perfume was having a soothing effect on Robert. Angry though he was, he was also incredibly weary. Pacing the floor in a fury would not help his back. Better to rest and plan what he would say to the sheriff in the morning and to his fellow merchants. Thomas would be discreet. He knew better than most the value of a man's reputation in business. But Robert would have to concoct some tale to explain his wife's disappearance to his guild brothers. Otherwise the townsfolk would invent their own tale, which, knowing them, would be worse even than the truth.

He eased himself onto the bed and watched Leonia unbuttoning his shoes. He couldn't begin to think why he hadn't waited and married her when she came of age. Plenty of widowers took brides younger than her.

Leonia handed him his goblet. He struggled to sit up.

'No, Père, you'll hurt your back. Let me!'

She climbed up on the bed beside him, slipping her little arm about his shoulders to support him as he leaned forward to take another gulp of wine. Then she tenderly rearranged the pillows beneath his head.

Adam crouched in the stables until he heard Diot returning from the market. He scurried out, taking the two heavy baskets from her and hefting them in through the kitchen door. She looked surprised, as well she might, for Adam was not normally so obliging.

'Mistress Catlin not back?' she asked, dabbing at her deep cleavage where sweat flowed, like a river between two hills.

Adam said nothing. He helped Diot to unpack her purchases – eggs wrapped in straw, a root of dried ginger, a crock of butter already half melted in the heat, leeks and a live chicken, its legs bound tightly and its blackcurrant eyes watching them.

'Fetch me the small axe from the stable, will you, lad? I'd best get this bird killed and plucked. Master'll be home soon.'

'He's already home,' Adam said.

Diot wiped her hands on her grubby kirtle. 'Why didn't you say? He'll be wanting his wine or some cool cider in this weather.'

She started across the courtyard, but Adam stepped quickly in front of her. 'Leonia's already fetched the wine. She said he was sleeping, didn't want to be disturbed.'

'Aye, well, a nap'll do him good. He's fair dauled, what with his business and all these meetings. Wish I had time to take a nap myself.'

They glanced up as the gate to the stableyard opened. Catlin edged in, looking warily at the house. She tucked her riding whip under her arm as she peeled off her white kid gloves.

Adam raced over to her, his heart thumping with excitement, but he was struggling not to let it show. *She didn't know what was going to happen. She didn't know!* He hugged their secret to himself.

Catlin looked startled at seeing him and frowned. Her face was pale and damp. She plainly found the heat trying. In the cruelly bright sunlight, the wrinkles seemed etched even deeper around her mouth and eyes. 'I thought you'd be at the warehouse, Adam. Your father will be vexed if you aren't there. Has . . . has he returned?'

Adam tried hard not to smile. This was easier than he had imagined. 'He came back ages ago. He's up in the bedchamber.'

Catlin stiffened. 'The bedchamber? Didn't he want his wine?'

'Oh, he took it with him. I saw him through the doorway. He's probably asleep by now.'

'Asleep?' Catlin's gaze darted upwards to the casement and her mouth curved into a smile. 'And where is Leonia?'

'Still up in the chamber with Father. I haven't seen her come out.'

Catlin's mouth tightened. 'What's she doing up there?' Without waiting for an answer, she gripped Adam's shoulder. 'Go straight to the warehouse. You don't want to make your father angry, do you? I think you should stay late to make up for not being there this afternoon. It's what your father would expect. It sets a good example to the men. If they see you shirking, they'll become resentful and start to do likewise. Off you go at once and see you stay there this time!'

She gave Adam a little push towards the courtyard gate. He ran across as if he had every intention of doing as he was told, but outside he flattened himself against the wall and waited, peering through the tiny gap between the wood and the wall, until he saw Catlin disappear inside. Slowly, he opened the gate just wide enough to slide through and slipped into the relative cool of the stables.

Moments later the gate opened quietly again and Edward, casting furtive glances around, picked his way across the courtyard and into the house. Adam followed, pausing in the doorway. He could hear Catlin and Edward arguing in low voices.

'. . . I've just seen Martin,' Edward was saying. 'He was being dragged through the city by the sheriff's men. He's not coming . . . and you said the hall . . . you said Robert would be in the hall. This isn't what we planned.'

The stairs creaked. Adam knew it was Catlin's footsteps. She was going straight to the bedchamber. He hugged himself in anticipation. He'd worried that somehow he would fail Leonia, that he would not say the right things to make Catlin go upstairs or that he'd fumble his words and she would grow suspicious. But everything was perfect and Leonia would be so pleased with him.

When Catlin opened the door that separated the solar from the bedchamber Robert was lying stretched out on the bed sunk in a deep sleep. Leonia was lying beside him, propped up on her elbow, her head resting on her hand. Her shift was pulled up and Robert's hand lay between her bare thighs.

Catlin shrieked and flew to the bed, the riding crop raised in her hand. Leonia was already scrambling off the bed, but she was not quick enough. She raised her arm to shield her face as Catlin struck. The whip caught her across the forearm and at once beads of blood blossomed along the angry welt. She slid off the bed and ran behind a wooden screen.

'You little bitch!' Catlin screamed.

With a groan Robert pulled himself upright. He was struggling to focus. His voice was slurred. His tongue seemed to have become too big for his mouth.

'Dare you . . . come back here! Warned you . . . told you to get out . . .' He tried to swing his legs off the bed, but couldn't seem to make them obey him. 'Sheriff . . . sending for Thomas right now.'

He glimpsed a movement in the solar and his face contorted as he saw Edward hovering in the doorway. 'Get him out of my house!'

Catlin lunged at Robert. 'You dare to accuse me of adultery when you've taken your own stepdaughter as your whore. You vile lecher!'

She raised the whip as if she meant to strike him. But he grabbed her wrist, trying to wrest it from her hands.

'He's a lecher, but he isn't a murderer too, like you, is he, Mother?'

Leonia had moved towards the door and Adam, coming up behind Edward, had slipped round him to stand beside her.

'You do know that Catlin murdered Edith, don't you, Robert?' Leonia said calmly. 'Just like she killed my father. You helped her, didn't you, Edward?'

'If I was going to murder anyone, it would be you, you ungrateful brat,' Edward said savagely.

'But you can't, not yet, because my father left all his estates to me, not Catlin. If I die all my father's money will go to my uncle. You need me to stay alive until I'm old enough to marry you, don't you, Edward? That's the plan, isn't it? Once I marry you all my inheritance becomes yours and you'll murder me then, won't you, you and my mother together?'

Catlin took a step back from the bed. 'Do it, Edward! Don't just stand there. Use the knife. Kill him! He's drugged. You're stronger than him. Strike now!'

'But you said Martin would be blamed . . . you swore . . .' Edward gestured with the blade towards Adam and Leonia. 'And what about them? I can't do it in front of them. It's too dangerous.'

'They're just children,' Catlin shrieked at him. 'We can deal with them later. You have to do it now! If you don't, you'll hang. We both will. Kill him. Just do it, you fool. Strike!'

Leonia lifted her chin. 'He won't do it, Mother. He's too scared. But I will, because I am your daughter, and you and that filthy old man have to be punished for what you've done.'

Leonia, watching the dumbfounded expression on Catlin's face, threw back her head and laughed. She reached down under the top of her shift and pulled out something hanging around her neck. It was Catlin's bloodstone necklace. One by one, she slid open the little compartments at the back of each stone, shaking out the locks of hair so they fell to the floor – brown, blond, black, grey and a strand dyed saffron yellow.

'Look at them, Robert. Look at all the people she killed, all the people who are coming for her. They're all here, Catlin. Their ghosts are waiting for you.'

Robert saw Leonia reach for the candle on the table, but he still didn't comprehend the danger. His mind seemed to be enveloped in a fog. He watched, as if from far off, as she flung the lighted candle onto the flowers on the floor. He saw one of the rose petals smoulder and shrivel. Then, suddenly, a circle of flame flashed around the bed and leaped up the hangings. But it was only when the hem of Catlin's skirts caught light, only when she began to shriek, that Robert understood what Leonia had done. The flowers and the bed-hangings had been soaked in perfumed oil. In the same instant, he saw to his horror that he was completely surrounded by flames.

His first instinct was to shrink back into the centre of the bed as

470

the fire leaped up around him. He caught sight of the terrified expression on Edward's face in the solar, and the children standing, hand in hand, in the doorway, smiling. Flames shot along the canopy over his head. Robert threw himself off the bed.

Catlin reeled into the corner of the room, trying to beat out her skirts and tear her gown from her. Robert made a lunge for the door, but the two children were standing there, unmoving. Then, hand in hand, they raised their arms. Robert could make no sense of what his drugged mind saw: snakes seemed to writhe in front of him and a creature with a black-furred face and sightless eyes bounded towards him, snarling, its sharp white fangs bared to strike. Robert screamed, and threw himself to the floor in the doorway just as the blazing drapes came crashing down, engulfing Catlin in flames.

By the time Diot had come lumbering up the stairs, the whole bedchamber was ablaze, floor to ceiling in a rolling mass of flame. The heat was so fierce and the smoke so dense that no one could get inside. Nothing could be done to help Catlin trapped in there, burning alive. Diot could only grab the children and hurry the poor little mites out to the safety of the street.

Neighbours came rushing with ladders and buckets of water, grappling hooks and brooms to beat out the blaze. They managed to contain it. The bedchamber was gutted and the fire had burned through the floorboards, scorching the ceiling below, but it could have been worse, everyone said. The house, being made of stone, was still standing. And the tapestry, of which Robert had been so proud, remained miraculously undamaged. The crown in the maiden's hair and the gold of the boar's collar gleamed more brightly than ever.

Diot hugged her two charges to her massive breasts, rocking to and fro, the tears streaming down her sooty cheeks.

'My poor, poor sweet babe . . . such a terrible way to die . . . If I'd thought for a moment 'twould end like this . . . Thank the saints that you lambs was both saved.'

Across her broad back, the children smiled triumphantly at one another.

Then, as Diot led them away, Leonia turned around and gazed back down the street to where I stood with Mavet. She opened her clenched fist and blew a single rose petal towards us. It drifted in the wind, higher, higher over the great city.

471

We watched it disappear. She walked away and we followed her. Mavet and I will always follow her. She has always known we've been there, protecting her, teaching her . . . *killing* for her. After all, I am her father. Isn't that what fathers do? And Mavet has discovered humans are more fun to terrorise than rabbits, much tastier too. A single bite from those four sharp canines is all it takes, doesn't it, my little demon of death? You might say we three are the most unholy trinity – father, daughter and our own little incubus.

Epilogue

*At the darkest hour of the longest night, the hell-wain drawn by
the headless black horses trundles through the streets of the town,
gathering up the shrieking souls of the dead.*

Poor old Godwin, he understood a little, but there is much he did
not. Pavia, Margaret, Catlin, and those were but a few of her names,
did murder three husbands and a few others along the way, but it
was not with witchcraft, as Godwin believed, though you can hardly
blame him for thinking that. She didn't need spirits or spells to aid
her. She was more than skilled enough to manage things on her own.

It was Christmastide, that season of goodwill towards men. Our
little daughter, our Leonia, was but three years old, and as delicate
and beautiful as a Christmas rose. I was deeply in love with her mother
and never tired of thinking up new ways to please her. So when
Catlin's long-lost son, Edward, arrived, recently returned from sea and
overjoyed to be reunited with his dear mother, like Robert I was a
fool and indulged my wife by taking in her son. After all, no man
could be so cold-hearted as to turn away his stepson at Christmas,
for even a beggar is welcomed to the fire at that season.

On St Stephen's Day, Catlin gave me one of her most charming
smiles. 'Warrick, my sweeting, it's such a bright day and we've been
sitting far too long around the fire. We should go hunting. I've been
telling my son what a fine rider you are and he is longing for some
sport.'

I was surprised and a little annoyed, for Catlin had shown no
interest in hunting before, preferring dancing and mummery. But
now that her son wanted to hunt, she had decided she enjoyed it.
But it would have been foolish to allow my churlishness to prevent
me doing what I'd been itching to do since the Christmas feasting
had begun. Hunting was my passion, riding out with my hawk on
my fist and the hounds following one of my greatest joys.

So I was on my feet before the words had even left her lips, pulling on the new pair of gauntlets she had offered as a Christmas gift, whistling up the hounds and sending stable-boys scurrying as I called for the horses to be saddled. I kissed my little daughter, Leonia, goodbye, promising her the prize from the finest beast we brought down.

We were riding over the heath, with some of the men and stable-boys following on foot to retrieve the hawks and carry any kills that might be made. There'd been a frost, which lingered, sparkling on the bare branches of the trees. The ground was as hard as burnished steel. Edward and I were both riding with goshawks, using the hounds to put up the game, and vying with each other over how many hares, rabbits and game birds our hawks could kill.

Catlin was carrying a peregrine falcon, though, of course, only sending it out when the hawks were safely on the glove. Several times I noticed her turning her head to look at me instead of watching the spectacle of the hunt, even when her own bird was flying. At the time, I foolishly thought it was pride in my prowess for, though I say it myself, I was a far more daring and expert horseman than Edward. But now I know she was watching for the first signs. And she did not have long to wait.

I started to feel unnaturally chilled. Then, the next moment, I was roasting. Sweat was running down my face. The latter was hardly to be wondered at for I was riding hard. But I was dizzy and couldn't control my movements. My arms and legs started jerking, so much so that the goshawk on my fist was bating and repeatedly throwing herself upside down, swinging by the leather jesses around her legs, the ends of which were clamped tightly in my gloved hand. Dimly I knew that I should stop and dismount, but I was seized by terror. The baying of the hounds behind me was growing louder and louder, but I knew they were not mine. I turned in the saddle and saw, to my horror, a pack of monstrous hell-black hounds running straight towards me, each one encased in a ball of scarlet and blue flames that streamed out behind them as they came.

Some of the servants came running up, trying to grab the reins of my horse, but the hounds were closing in and I knew it was me that they hunted. I spurred my horse away from them.

'The hounds, the hounds of fire,' I shrieked. 'Draw your bows and kill them!' But the men didn't seem to understand what I was saying.

I must have flung my hawk away from me, for I could see it

wheeling overhead, shrieking, like a monstrous griffin. Its talons had grown as long as swords and it was diving at me. I covered my head with my arm and spurred my mount mercilessly on until the poor beast was foaming at the mouth.

It was only a matter of time before the horse slipped on the frosty grass and threw me. I fell against the trunk of the tree, striking my head against the broken stump of a branch. My wife and Edward came galloping up, the servants running behind. I thought it was the hounds of fire that had surrounded me. I lashed out wildly, screaming and shouting in my terror.

One of the servants pulled off my gauntlets and began to rub my hands and head with ice from a pond to bring me to my senses. And my wits returned just long enough for me to see the smile of triumph that passed between my wife and her so-called son. I knew in that instant that they were lovers and I knew, too, that they had murdered me. That was my last thought as life ebbed from me, and the very last thing I saw as a living man was my wife and her lover, standing hand in hand. And so I found myself dead. Strangely I was as aware that I was dead as I had once known I was alive, which, trust me, my darlings, is a curious sensation until you grow accustomed to it.

At the funeral Catlin sobbed piteously on her son's shoulder. It was a tragedy everyone said, a terrible accident. Although that didn't stop the whole manor, indeed the whole village, speculating as to the cause of my sudden reckless flight and why I had been babbling about the hounds of fire. Some said the hare my goshawk had caught was a witch in disguise or my horse had trodden upon a patch of St John's wort and become hag-ridden; others said the devil's hounds had come to drag me to everlasting torment.

Many believed the latter, and rumours began to circulate in the village that I, Warrick, had been a debauched and evil man, who had raped innocent girls, then cast them aside. I'm surprised they didn't add that I had eaten their babies too, for I had, it seemed, treated my poor long-suffering wife with such cruelty that she had been nothing short of a saint for suffering me so long.

The villagers would have been sadly disappointed to learn that the devil didn't rise up and drag me screaming to the fires of Hell, but neither did any angel reach down and haul me up to Heaven. Since the thief crucified beside Christ was the only one to speak up for Him as He hung dying, you'd have thought that Jesus would have assigned a corner of Heaven's kitchen for the not-quite-saintly of this world. You'd think, wouldn't you, that a man who'd ended his days on a cross might have some fellow feeling for the unjustly condemned? But all kings who come at last to their thrones are quick to forget that once they had wiped their own backsides, as any beggar, so there were no angels for me. And I'm glad of it, for how else could I be here to protect my beautiful daughter? Besides, I'm not sure they let ferrets into Heaven and I'd miss old Mavet.

Oh, that bitch of a wife killed my poor little Mavet too, all because he came running to my coffin. He knew something was wrong, could smell the poison. Ferrets have more love and loyalty in a single claw than most men do in their whole bodies. So she locked him in a box and threw it on a fire, just to be sure the imp wouldn't draw attention to the glove.

And that, as you will have realised, is how she did it. No witchcraft, no spells, just an unguent of her own devising, smeared inside that thoughtful gift. It works as well on nightcaps and bed linen. Her ointments made her victims grow sick. Sometimes they went mad, but always they died. As I told you, my dear wife had a rare talent.

But now you want to know what happened after the fire. Well, of course, you do, my darlings, and I shall tell you. When the smoke cleared, Robert was found by his neighbours lying unconscious in the corner of the solar where he'd crawled. Miraculously he lived, if you could call his existence living. Badly burned, he was taken to the infirmary of St Mary Magdalene where the lay sisters tended him throughout his few remaining years. He did not leave their walls again, save for that last journey to the church to be buried by his guild brothers between his two loving and faithful wives. Whether he was happy confined to the nuns' tender care, no one ever knew, for the only sounds to escape from his mouth were grunts.

'Eat your swill, like a good little piglet,' the lay sisters would say, as they spooned the grey gruel down his throat.

And they'd laugh at their own merry wit, when Sister Ursula was not within hearing, of course, for they'd precious little else in life to offer them amusement, save the pleasure of tormenting those whose lives were even more miserable than their own. There was no hippocras in St Magdalene's, at least not for the likes of them or poor Robert.

As for dearest Edward, he was arrested as soon as those two orphaned children tearfully explained to the sheriff how that wicked man had lit the fire. He was charged first with the murder of his mother, but a charge of treason was swiftly added. For he was Robert's steward and to attempt to kill your master is, as we all know, treason. And after the summer of rebellion, the justices were not disposed to take a lenient view of such matters. Where would we be if any Tom, Dick or Harry thought he could rise up and overthrow his masters?

Sheriff Thomas went so far as to suggest that Edward had been trying to start another rebellion, right there in Lincoln. Thomas was commended for his vigilance in arresting the ringleader before anyone else could be hurt. And when his term as sheriff thankfully came to an end, he prospered very nicely under his new royal patronage.

Naturally, Edward tried to blame my sweet, innocent daughter, but that only compounded his guilt. Diot, slow-witted but ever loyal, fearfully confessed that she thought Edward had already tried to poison his master, which the good physician, Hugo Bayus, claimed he had suspected from the start. Gossip is a powerful weapon. It's been known to send men to the gallows.

But at least Master Edward had the comfort of not being alone in his final agony for, rest assured, I was there, waiting for him, when his spirit finally left his tortured body. As I told him, it's never wise to make enemies of the dead, for you have to spend the whole of eternity with them. And, believe me, his torments were only just beginning, for that old hag, Eadhild, took quite a fancy to young Edward, so much so that she forgot about me.

As for my beloved daughter, I'll say only this – remember, if you ever take your gaze from a witch, even for a moment, she will vanish.

Historical Notes

The weather-lore, anti-witchcraft charms and spells that head each month and chapter are taken from medieval ecclesiastical writings, recorded British folklore, and from medieval spell books, known as grimoires.

Poison – Throughout history there have been many alleged incidents of people being murdered by means of clothing impregnated with poison. King John of Castile was said to have been killed by a Turk who put poison in his boots and Henry VI was rumoured to have been murdered through the wearing of poisoned gloves. A certain Madame de Poulaillon confessed to having dipped the tail of her husband's shirt in a solution of arsenic to bring about his death, though he got wind of the plot and had her arrested before harm was done.

To find out if she really could have killed her husband in this way, Dr Lucian Nass shaved the rump of a guinea-pig and gently rubbed it with an arsenic preparation; it died two days later, showing symptoms of arsenic poisoning. This suggests that a combination of the friction of impregnated clothes or bedding against skin, with body heat and sweat, might allow small quantities of certain poisons or hallucinogens to be absorbed, which would, over time, accumulate in the body to cause illness, delusions and eventually death.

Witchcraft – In England, during the reign of Saxon King Athelstan, murder by witchcraft, which included the use of spells and charms, was made punishable by death. As with all crimes, trial was often by ordeal. William the Conqueror reduced the sentence to banishment. The death penalty for practising witchcraft was not reintroduced until 1563, but even then the crime had to involve injury to people or their livestock before a sentence of death could be passed. But people accused of witchcraft in earlier centuries could find themselves accused of the far more serious crime of heresy, which carried the death penalty.

The inspiration for the character of Pavia/Catlin in this novel came from the trial records of a wealthy Irish woman, Alice Kyteler, who in 1324, with eleven members of her family, was accused of seven counts of witchcraft and sorcery. Bishop Ledrede claimed that Alice was the leader of a group of witches, who held nocturnal meetings at which they sacrificed to the devil and used spells to entrap and murder men. It is the first recorded instance of a woman being accused of gaining her supernatural powers through sexual intercourse with the devil.

Alice had had four husbands and the accusations of witchcraft were initially brought by the sons of the first three, who swore she had murdered their fathers for their money and was attempting to kill the fourth. This charge seems to have arisen because the sons of the first three marriages had been disinherited in favour of her favourite son William Outlaw. Petronilla, Alice's maid, was burned alive at the stake for heresy after confessing under torture, but Alice herself escaped and vanished without trace.

The last witchcraft trial to be held in England took place in 1944. Helen Duncan was arrested in Portsmouth on 19 January 1944 and prosecuted under the 1735 Witchcraft Act. It was alleged that she had used witchcraft to obtain military information, predict the sinking of a ship, and pretended to conjure the dead, using a parrot medium called Bronco. The prosecution claimed that she regularly produced ectoplasm and, though court witnesses offered to show how easy it was to fake this, the judge refused to allow the demonstration and Helen was found guilty and sentenced to prison for nine months.

After her release she returned to conducting séances, but in 1956, the police raided the premises when she was in a trance. She collapsed and died. The official cause of death was diabetes, but her supporters claimed her death was caused by damage to her psychic energy from being suddenly brought out of a trance.

Friars of the Sack – The Friars of the Order of the Penitence of Jesus Christ, were commonly known as the Brothers of Penitence or Friars of the Sack because of the shapeless, sack-like robe, made of coarse cloth, they wore with wooden sandals. The order was founded in Italy and came to England in 1257, opening a house outside Aldersgate in London. They had friaries in France, Spain and

Germany, but lost them in 1274, when Pope Gregory X banned all begging friars, with the exception of the four mendicant orders of Dominicans, Franciscans, Austin Friars and Carmelites. But the English Friars of the Sack continued in defiance of the pope, surviving until the Reformation under Henry VIII. They lived an austere life, begging for all their needs, refusing to eat any meat and drinking only water.

In Lincoln there are records of a friary belonging to the Friars of the Sack in Thorngate, to the west of Stamp Causeway and south of St Hugh Croft. It must have been established some time before 1266 because, in that year, the friars were granted part of the common land of the city to enlarge their oratory. But they appear to have left this site by 1307 when the Abbot of Barlings tried to acquire it. It is not known if this was when they left Lincoln, but they seemed to have vanished from the city by the time of the Black Death in 1348.

Florentines – The incident of the theft of goods from Lincoln merchants actually took place, though it was in 1375. Members of the societies of Strossi and Albertini of Florence left Lincoln with £10,000 worth of goods (nearly half a million pounds today), which they had not paid for, almost ruining the local merchants. The mayor and bailiffs seized the goods of Florentine merchants living in the city who were members of the same society, among them Matthew Johan. The Florentines appealed to the King who ordered their goods restored, but the Lincoln and Florentine merchants eventually came to an agreement to enable the Lincoln merchants to recover the money owed to them.

Lincoln – Sheriff Thomas (1351–1398) is recorded variously as Thomas de Thimbleby of Poolham, Thomas Thimelby and Thomas Thimotby de Iruham. It is common to find great variations in the spellings of names of this period. He married Dorothy Swynford, and in the 1800s it was claimed she was one of the daughters of the infamous Katherine Swynford, John of Gaunt's mistress. But there is no evidence that Katherine had a daughter named Dorothy, so it is unlikely they were related.

In 1380, the old guildhall in Lincoln, where Robert first sees Catlin, was in a bad state of repair. The townspeople eventually took matters into their own hands and pulled it down around 1389, fearing it might collapse and crush people. In a letter to King Richard II in 1390, the mayor complained that certain of the townspeople were refusing to contribute to the cost of building a new one. The King commanded that everyone should be made to pay, but the money raised seemed to have been misappropriated: in 1393 Sir John Bassy, mayor of Lincoln, was ordered by the King to investigate what had become of the funds to build the new guildhall and pave more of the Lincoln streets.

The new guildhall was eventually built over the Stonebow gate, which was the southern gate to the city in both Roman and medieval times, but the complex of buildings was not finally completed until 1520. It is still in use today as the city's council chambers and occasional court room, while the dungeons of the adjoining prison house the city's treasury. Visitors can take guided tours around this fascinating ancient building.

The tower in the city wall, where Catlin and her lover meet, had ceased to be used as a defensive tower by the 1380s and, in 1383, was leased by the mayor and people to John Norman with a plot of adjoining land in Butwerk. He was allowed to use it 'without interference' unless *ryderwak* was invoked: if the city came under threat in time of war or civil conflict the tower could be commandeered for defence. Sadly, it is no longer standing.

But the Greestone Stairs, built before 1200, are still in daily use in Lincoln. Originally known as the Greesen from the Old English word for 'steps', it is a long flight of stone steps outside the city walls that linked the medieval dwellings of Butwerk, at the bottom of the city near the river, to Eastgate in the upper part. The steps led through the postern archway (the rear gate) into the cathedral grounds. For part of the way, a broad stone track still runs alongside the steps, once used by ox carts and for dragging goods up and down. The Greesen is today reputed to be the most haunted street in Lincoln and numerous locals and visitors have reported feeling someone grab their ankle as they ascend the steps, causing them to fall heavily. They have the bruises and cuts to prove it!

The two children who came between Jan and Godwin in Greetwell and were seen by Nonie are also well-known Lincoln ghosts. The pair are said to haunt the river Witham. When she is first seen, the little girl appears alone, staring frantically into the water. She vanishes but

481

reappears, further down the river, this time walking happily hand in hand with a younger boy. It is believed the girl jumped into the river in a desperate effort to rescue her little brother, who had fallen in, and both drowned.

Peasants' Revolt – A shortage of tenants and workers in the years after the Black Death led landowners to try to cut their costs and solve their massive debt problems by raising rents, taxes and tolls while keeping wages at pre-plague levels. They also tried to re-impose forced labour on men and women who were descended from serfs or villeins. This led to a series of violent uprisings by the poorer classes right across Europe, and violence against people and property erupted in one town after another as the fire of rebellion spread. Chief among the rebels in Lincoln were tenants of the estates of the Hospital of St John of Jerusalem. The imposition of a new poll tax proved to be the match that lit the flame of revolution in England. Many people initially tried to get out of paying by not recording members of their household or servants.

Sir Robert Hale, prior of the Hospital of St John of Jerusalem and owner of several wealthy estates, was appointed as overseer at the Exchequer; when examining the registration returns he discovered that between 20 and 50 per cent of the population who should have been paying the poll tax were not recorded. Realising the local bailiffs were massively under-recording, he appointed commissioners to go out with sergeants-at-arms to check. There was outrage that some of the commissioners subjected young girls to crude and violent physical examinations to find out if they were virgins. As these rumours spread, men who could do so were forced to pay the tax for their young daughters or sisters even though they were not fifteen, rather than subject them to this violation, which, of course, was exactly what the commissioners wanted. This added to the fury of the populace.

The massacre of the Flemish merchants and the sacking of the Savoy Palace, belonging to John of Gaunt, were among the most widely recorded incidents of the rebellion in London. At the Savoy, one of the rebels was thrown onto the fire by his own comrades and burned alive for suspected looting. By mistake, several barrels of gunpowder were also thrown onto the fire, causing an explosion that trapped thirty rebels in the wine cellar. Their cries for help could still be heard a week later. They finally died, still trapped beneath the rubble.

In order to impose order on the streets and to identify and punish the rebels, a Commission of Array was set up in Lincoln, consisting of wealthy landowners and nobility, all of whom were to remain anonymous for fear of reprisals.

Timeline of the Events of the Peasants' Revolt

1380 – November
- A poll tax was imposed of 12*d* for every man and woman over the age of fifteen. Two-thirds to be paid by the end of December, the rest by June.

January
- Only a fraction of the revenue anticipated had been collected. The records were checked and it was found there had been widespread evasion of the registration for the poll tax.

March
- Commissioners with sergeants-at-arms were sent out to inspect returns and check households; the date for final payment was brought forward from June to 21 April.

30 May
- Royal commissioners arrived in the town of Brentwood in Essex to enforce poll tax collection. But the citizens refused to pay the tax and chased the commissioners out when they tried to arrest ringleaders. Over the next few days disturbances broke out throughout Essex and Kent.

10 June
- Violence erupted in Essex and Kent. There were attacks on property, particularly abbeys and buildings belonging to anyone connected with the legal profession. Rebels from Kent occupied the city of Canterbury.

11 June

- Fourteen-year-old King Richard II arrived in London, having travelled by barge from Windsor, as Kent and Essex rebels marched on the city.

12 June

- The rebels and the city fathers met for discussions at Blackheath. King Richard and his household took refuge in the Tower of London.

13 June

- A meeting between King Richard and the rebels at Greenwich was aborted at the last moment, when Richard's advisers forced him to turn back, fearing for his safety.
- The Savoy Palace owned by John of Gaunt was destroyed.

14 June

- At Mile End Richard negotiated with the rebels and agreed to their demands, but inadvertently encouraged the hunting down of 'traitors to the people', which resulted in the rebels executing some of his closest advisers, including Archbishop Sudbury and Robert Hale, and the massacre of the Flemish merchants.
- Violent rebellion broke out in Norfolk.

15 June

- King Richard and Wat Tyler met at Smithfield, but Tyler was killed and the rebels were led into a trap. Law and order was restored in London and the rebels were escorted from the city.
- The prior of Bury St Edmunds was murdered and the archives of Cambridge University were destroyed.

16 June

- Violence increased in St Albans, and the Suffolk rebels took Ipswich.

17 June

- Judge Edmund Walsingham was murdered at Ely. Peterborough Abbey was attacked, and the Earl of Kent was sent to round up the rebels in Kent.

18 June

- Rebels attempted to march from London via Lincoln to attack York. They were stopped by townspeople when they tried to cross the river Ouse at Huntingdon. Norwich was attacked by the rebels.

20 June

- Commissioners were sent into East Anglia to rout the rebels.

22 June

- John of Gaunt took refuge in Scotland.

23 June

- Rebellion broke out in Scarborough.

26 June

- Bishop Despenser routed the rebels at North Walsham in Norfolk.

2 July

- Richard II cancelled all of the charters freeing the villeins, which he had granted on 14 June, and reinstated the rights of the lords and landowners.

5 July

- Orders were given for Commissions of Array to be established to organise the King's faithful subjects to resist the rebels.

15 July

- One of the rebel leaders, John Ball, was executed at St Albans. Between July and November, when the amnesty was finally signed, hundreds of Englishmen were arrested on the say-so of neighbours, chance remarks overheard in inns, or servants taking revenge on masters.

5 September
- A Commission of Array in Lincolnshire was ordered to send evidence of rebel crimes to Chancery. The ex-mayor and MP Hugh de Garwell was named but later pardoned on payment of a fine, on the grounds that he hadn't killed anyone.

9 December
- The appointments of existing commissioners in Lincolnshire were revoked as they couldn't be trusted. New ones were appointed.

Glossary

Ambry – In the context of a house or castle, this was a cupboard, which either hung on a wall or stood on the floor in the chamber or hall where the master of the house or his guests slept. Food, such as cold meats, pies and pastries, was placed in the ambry at night, so that the master, mistress or any guests could help themselves to a snack, known as a *reresoper*, without disturbing the household. This was often necessary to settle the stomach after a night of hard drinking. An ambry can be distinguished from other cupboards used for storage of vessels or linens because it was pierced or had bars at the front, originally covered by cloth, to allow the circulation of air. It was also known as a livery or dole cupboard, because in larger households it contained the amount of food deemed enough for the guest's retinue.

Attainder – means 'tainted'. A felon found guilty of a capital offence was subject to forfeiture, which meant that all their property and possessions were forfeit to their feudal lord, or to the Crown. But an Act of Attainder could additionally be brought against the felon, so that their descendants, in perpetuity, were never again allowed to enter contracts, bear a title or own land. In effect, they lost all rights as a free man or woman on the grounds that they had tainted blood. Attainder was usually used by kings to punish nobles found guilty of treason or of the murder of someone close to the King, but could be invoked by men of lower rank who were wealthy enough to pay for the legal procedure.

Beef bonet – A bonet was a broth thickened with breadcrumbs or other ingredients, such as ground almonds, cream, curds, honey or egg yolks. Dishes such as 'hens in bonet' or 'beef bonet' were simple broths of stewed meat, often cooked in blood, thickened with bread and flavoured with spices. They would have been considered nourishing and easily digestible food for invalids.

Bloodstone – Green jasper or chalcedony containing dark red spots of iron oxide. It was also known as heliotrope because it was symbolically linked to the sun. In the Middle Ages it was believed that it would instantly stop haemorrhages if the afflicted part was touched with the stone. It also prevented the wearer from being poisoned. The bloodstone was supposed to have the power to turn the sun red and to call down thunder and lightning. It gave the wearer the gift of second sight, while protecting them from the madness that frequently accompanied such a gift.

Boar – In Norse tradition the golden boar, associated with Freyr and Freyja, had a mane of fire that could illuminate the darkest night. In Valhalla, each night the gods killed and ate a boar, known as Saehrimnir, which was restored to life each morning. In Europe a ghostly boar was said to run with the Wild Hunt during storms. The boar was the most frequently sacrificed animal among the Saxons: because of its strength, bravery and fearlessness, it was seen as a fitting gift for the gods. Only the courageous would dare to hunt them. A number of golden boar heads used as amulets or to decorate warriors' helmets have been found in Saxon hoards in Lincolnshire. In Viking, Celtic and Saxon cultures the boar symbolised strength and resolution.

Bor – Dialect form of address used for boys and men by Fenlanders and river-men in some parts of Lincolnshire and East Anglia.

Broggers – In the wool trade these men bought fleeces and skins directly from the individual farmers and cottagers, then collected them together to sell on as loads to the merchants.

Civey, Civet or Cyve – A richly spiced stew made from the meat and blood of any game animal. It could be used to dress the meat of the game animal itself or as a stock or sauce in which to cook other meat, or fish such as haddock.

Consistory Court – The highest bishop's court and the busiest, for it oversaw the execution of wills and trusts, resolved tithe and debt disputes and accusations of defamation. It also dealt with marriage law, including broken contracts and runaway spouses. Mostly it heard the cases in which people were suing each other, rather than answering charges brought by the Church. The judge, known as the Bishop's Official or Commissarius, was usually a university graduate, tutored in law. Those called to testify were questioned in secret with no opportunity for advocates to cross-examine their opponent's witnesses, but they could submit a list of questions and arguments to the Bishop's Official, which he could put privately to the witnesses, plaintiffs and defendants.

Dauled – A dialect word meaning the person is tired, weary, or exhausted.

Dwale – *Atropa belladonna*, otherwise known as deadly nightshade. Dwale comes from the French, meaning 'mourning'. It was thought to be a key ingredient in witches' ointments, used to help them to fly or transform into animals, and the ointment might well have caused them to hallucinate that they were flying or transforming. Dwale was widely used in the Middle Ages in sleeping draughts. Chaucer refers to it when he says, 'There needeth him no dwale.'

In the Parthian Wars, Marcus Antonius's troops were said to have been killed by dwale being added to the drinking wells. According to legend, in AD1010, the Scots mixed the juice with food for the invading Danish army; the soldiers became so stupefied that the Scots were easily able to slaughter them.

Fog-head or Fog-breather – a derogatory name for the English used by people originating from better climates who considered the island to be permanently damp and foggy, which made the English dour and dull.

Gambeson – A padded quilted tunic, which was worn under or over armour by knights, or was worn instead of armour by the common foot soldiers. It was also known as the acketon, aketon, hacketon or hauketon. 'Gamboised' meant quilted or padded. They could be stuffed with wool, straw, grass or cloth. Such garments were hot and cumbersome, so soldiers usually donned them just before engaging the enemy in battle, which left them vulnerable if they were unexpectedly ambushed.

Green sickness – A medieval term for a wasting sickness that was probably severe anaemia. Symptoms might include pallor, dizziness, tiredness, breathlessness, pains, and brittle hair and nails. There are several different types of anaemia, but a common cause in the Middle Ages would have been dietary deficiency, particularly among the poor and certain religious orders that followed a strict ascetic diet. In the Middle Ages, green sickness was often associated with people who were melancholic, grief-stricken or lovesick.

Small but regular doses of some poisons, such as mercury, can produce similar symptoms and eventually death. However, it was only too easy to attribute any illness that caused the sufferer mysteriously to waste away to sorcery or the evil eye, especially if the victim had been previously healthy.

Hand-fasting – This started as a betrothal ceremony in Saxon times when the couple would swear to be faithful to each other for a year, after which the engagement was either annulled or a full wedding would take place. In the Middle Ages it became a lay wedding ceremony, performed by the couple and their families without a priest. The culmination of the ceremony was when the couple held hands and had a cloth, rope or garland wrapped round their hands. Other customs might include the couple leaping over a bonfire together hand in hand.

Formal weddings were often too costly for poor families. A priest would ask for a fee to perform the ceremony, and if the couple were not freeborn, the lord of the manor also required a payment to permit the marriage. If a man's wife had run away, or if a woman's husband had gone missing at sea or in war, the Church deemed they were still married unless they could prove their spouse was dead. If they could not, the abandoned partner could not legally remarry, so hand-fasting was a way round this.

Hippocras – Wines in the Middle Ages were often highly acidic so were mixed with other ingredients to improve the taste. Hippocras, which, according to medieval legend, was believed to have been invented by Hippocrates, was drunk by those of high status and was made from red or white wine flavoured with ginger, cinnamon, pomegranate, sugar and an ingredient known as *turesole*, which was possibly made from sunflower seeds. A cheaper version, drunk by those of lower status, was made from wine, ginger, cinnamon, long pepper and honey. Spiced wines were usually served after the cloth was taken off the table at the end of the meal.

Jetons – These were small, round, flat discs of brass or bronze, often stamped to look like coins or decorated with patterns, coats of arms or mottoes. They were used by merchants for adding and subtracting large sums of money, and calculating tolls and taxes. A board was divided into black and white squares, known as checks, each square representing a number or amount of money. (From this we get the term 'Exchequer'.) By moving the jetons around the board, complex calculations could be made without the use of costly parchment and ink. Jetons are often excavated in archaeological sites or dug up in gardens.

John Barleycorn – is thought to be one of the oldest harvest festivals in England. The word 'barley' comes from the Anglo Saxon *Beow*, and the figure of John Barleycorn may have his distant origins in the mythical Anglo-Saxon hero Beowa. There are many pre-Christian rituals in which the king or spirit of the grain is slain, then rises again to bring about the return of spring and new crops. John Barleycorn is killed and ploughed into a field, but his head rises from the earth, covered with green spikes. He is gathered up, crushed and burned, and the blood containing his spirit is ceremoniously drunk to bring strength and new life to the drinkers. This myth was stylised in post-Christian centuries so that it eventually became a tale of the different processes involved in producing beer or whisky from grain. It has been immortalised in a number of ballads, the earliest surviving possibly dating to the reign of Elizabeth I.

Kempy – There are three types of fibre found in a fleece of many breeds of sheep – wool, which has different textures depending on the breed; hair, which is stiffer than wool, more like dog or horse hair, and kemp, which is white, bristly and coarse. Kemp, which is found mainly around the legs and head of the sheep, doesn't easily take a dye of the type used in the Middle Ages, so it could ruin a batch of yarn if a good even colour and texture were required.

Linkman – A link was a burning torch, usually in the form of a stout stick covered with a ball of rags at one end that had been soaked in a flammable substance, such as pitch. It was used to light the way through the streets. (The word 'link' probably comes from the Latin *lychnus* meaning lamp or candle.) At night, men or boys would hang around outside taverns and cockpits with these blazing torches and offer to light the way home through the dark streets in exchange for a small fee. But sometimes the linkmen were in the pay of thieves and would lead visitors who didn't know the town, or men who were the worse for drink, into some quiet alley or courtyard where thieves would be waiting to rob them.

Lich gate – The word 'lich' or 'lych' means corpse and this was a small roofed gate at the entrance to the church graveyard, where the bier could be set down and the corpse-bearers given refreshment before continuing up the path to the burial plot or the church door. Some bearers would have to carry the body many miles over marked corpse roads to reach the church and, when they arrived, might have to wait for the priest, churchwarden and sexton to be fetched, since word might not have reached them that a burial party was on its way.

Many churchyards had two gates, a lich gate and a bridal gate, because it was considered very unlucky for a bridal party to enter through the lich gate. If they did, either the marriage would die or, worse still, one of the couple would be a corpse before their first wedding anniversary.

Mavet – The name of the narrator's ferret means 'death' in Hebrew, but it is also used as a proper name to indicate the embodiment of death, as in biblical phrases such as a 'covenant with Death', or 'first-born of Death'. So Mavet also means the 'Demon of Death' or 'Angel of Death' (Malach Hamavet). Mavet also was the name of a Canaanite god of the underworld, mortal enemy to the god Baal.

Mortrews – The name of the recipe comes from the mortar in which the ingredients were pounded or ground. Chicken and pork livers were boiled together to make a broth. The livers were taken out, pounded to a paste and mixed with breadcrumbs, softened with some of the broth. They then added egg yolks and *powdour fort*, which was a mixture of ground spices such as pepper and cloves. The mixture was then boiled again, seasoned with salt, ginger, sugar and saffron. It was left to set until it resembled a modern pâté. Poorer households would not have been able to afford the costly spices to season it, so for them it would have been a simpler dish intended to make a little meat go further by mixing it with breadcrumbs.

Mutton or beef olives – Thin, beaten slices of meat, spread with egg yolks, spices, suet and onion, then rolled up and baked, making convenient finger-food. They were sprinkled with vinegar and spices before serving.

Nine Men's Morris – A game of strategy that dates back to Roman times and was often played in monasteries. The modern board has twenty-four points. One player has nine black pieces or 'men', the other nine white ones. The object is to place your men on the board to achieve a 'mill', a line of three balls. If you can do so, you are allowed to remove one of your opponent's balls until one player only has two remaining pieces on the board, and therefore loses the game. The number of holes and men varied and dice were sometimes used. Some board designs reflected the sacred mysteries of both Christian and pagan religions. Giant boards were often constructed in monasteries or in public places and there is a board carved into the base of a pillar in Chester Cathedral.

Pag – A Lincolnshire dialect word meaning 'to carry a load on your back'. Paggers were men who loaded and unloaded boats and wagons, or were paid to carry goods to someone's house. In estuaries and on the coast they would also carry men and women on their backs across the wet mud or sand at low tide, when the passengers were disembarking from boats or ferries. In later centuries, 14 May was known in Lincolnshire as Pag-Rag Day, when servants packed up their meagre possessions and left their old employees to find new masters.

Pattens – Shoes had very thin soles in this period and many city streets remained unpaved and were thick with mud and refuse, including rotting food, fish guts, animal dung and even human excrement thrown from night-pots out into the streets. Men and women often wore wooden pattens, tied over their shoes with a band of leather or cloth, to lift their feet above the dirt when walking in the street or to protect them from contact with cold flagstones in the house or church in winter.

The pattens of this period consisted of a thick wooden sole raised up on two wooden V-shaped wedges, one across the ball of the foot, the other at the heel, with the sharp points of wedges resting on the ground so that the patten made the least possible contact with the dirty street.

The V-shape of the wedge meant mud and dung would more easily slide off. These pattens could lift the wearer up by about four inches and, rather like walking on stilts, must have taken practice to walk in and probably caused some nasty sprains if you slipped or fell off.

Periwinkle – The Latin name for this flower is *Vinca* which means 'bind', because the plant twists. In medieval times it was used in funeral wreaths, and criminals on their way to executions were garlanded or crowned with periwinkle as a sign that they were about to die. Also known as sorcerer's violet, devil's eye or, as Chaucer called it, *parvenke*.

Pipkin – A small earthenware pot used for cooking. In poorer households it could be transferred straight from the fire to the table as a common dish from which all could help themselves.

Serpent's tongues – These were sharks' teeth, which were occasionally washed up on beaches, as they are today. People in the Middle Ages lived in constant fear of being poisoned, probably because many suffered stomach pains and vomiting after eating, due to poor food hygiene. Serpents' tongues and unicorn horns, which were probably the horns of narwhals, were considered infallible defences against every type of poison. Those who could afford to do so often wore rings embedded with serpents' tongues or other antidotes such as agate, serpentine or toadstones to counter the ill-effects of poison. By incorporating one of these stones into a ring, you could discreetly touch anything you suspected of being poisoned without offending your host.

Snails – Edible snails, believed to be introduced to Britain by the Romans, were often carried by medieval travellers as convenient, portable and nutritious snacks. Live snails encased in a parcel of damp moss or grass could be kept for many days until they were required. If you didn't have time to stop to cook during the day, the snails could be roasted in the fire at breakfast, then popped into a bag or scrip to be eaten later as you walked or rode along.

Steddle – A Lincolnshire dialect word for the base of a stack of grain, peat or wood. It was important to construct a good sturdy base or the whole stack might tumble down. By extension, a person who was

495

pear-shaped with a broad bottom and chunky legs was described as having a good steddle.

Sumptuary Law – There were many sumptuary laws passed from the Middle Ages through to Elizabethan times in an attempt to curb excess and maintain class differences. The Sumptuary Law passed in 1363, called the Statute of Diet and Apparel, was designed to limit what the lower classes were allowed to spend on clothes and food at a time when wages were rising because of a shortage of labour. The nobles were complaining that prices of luxury goods were rising because of new demand from the lower orders.

Under the 1363 law, agricultural workers, such as ploughmen and shepherds, could not wear cloth costing more than 12*d* per yard and were supposed to wear a simple blanket-like garment girdled with linen. Craftsmen could not wear clothes worth more than forty shillings, and neither they nor their families could wear silver fastenings, silk, velvet or sable fur. Only knights and those of higher rank could wear velvet, satin, imported wool, damask or sable fur. But there was huge variation in how strictly these laws were enforced.

Tally – Many ordinary men had poor literacy skills. Even if they could read and write, parchment was expensive and documents easily forged, so business was often conducted using a tally. This was a stick into which notches were cut down the length to record the number of bales, barrels or livestock being sold or transported. The stick was split in two vertically, or two sticks were laid side by side and notched simultaneously, and each man would keep one. When the two were put back together, it was immediately obvious if any of the notches had been altered to falsify the number of bales or boxes. Hence we still use the expression 'their stories don't tally' when people give conflicting accounts about an incident.

Viaticum – Meaning 'provisions for the journey'. This was the final element of the Last Sacraments. The dying person would first confess their sins and be absolved by the priest. The priest would then anoint them with chrism (holy oil) in a ritual known as Extreme Unction and finally offer them *viaticum* – the Eucharist, the consecrated bread and wine, which would be the last thing the dying person would eat or drink in this life.

Wool-walker – Otherwise known as the fuller or tucker, he was vital in the wool and cloth trade for two processes: scouring the woollen cloth to remove grease and dirt, and milling or thickening to make the fibres tangle together, which, if not done thoroughly, would cause holes to form in the garment as the fibres pulled apart in wear. The fuller or walker would first pound the cloth in a vat of stale urine to scour it, then trample on it in the urine, feet bare, to mill it.

This was highly unpleasant work as the ammonia fumes from the stale urine could cause the walkers to pass out and drown in the vat. The fumes also caused long-term respiratory and eye damage, and fullers could catch nasty infections. So by this period in the Middle Ages, fuller's earth (a soft clay) was beginning to replace urine in the cloth trade. But it was mainly found in the southern counties of England and had to be dug out, baked in the sun, formed into a powder and transported. So, particularly in the north, it was far more expensive than using local urine, and many cloth-makers were reluctant to switch to it, as long as there were fullers desperate enough for employment to scour and mill the cloth in the old way.